PORTLOCK

CAITEE COOPER

Acknowledgements

First off, if you've made it this far, thank you! Yes, *you*, holding this book in your hands right now. You matter, you're fabulous, and I wish I could give you a high-five (or handshake, or hug, or significant side-eyed look from waaay across the room—whatever you're comfortable with.) I'm honored that you let this story live and breathe in your mind for a few hours of your precious time. For artists of all stripes, that is a gift beyond compare.

There are many other people who deserve a shout-out for helping this series come to life. To my editors, beta readers, and proofreaders, thank you. (Special thanks to Chris C. for all your hard work and thorough comments. If this trilogy is halfway decent, it's because of your patient, supportive teaching.) Thanks again to Nikki B., Kate E., Karah S., Kayla J., Shelby C., and all my other betas, as well as my alpha team: Mom, Dad, Jaxon, Alice, Clara, Kari, Shay, Natalie, and anyone else who lent their sharp minds and eyes to the task of reading the messy, early copies of these novels. I'd also be remiss if I didn't thank Brandon Sanderson for teaching fiction writing so openly, accessibly, and brilliantly. This random stay-at-home mom from the middle of nowhere will forever be grateful that you put all your lectures on YouTube.

When bringing a book to life, there are a lot of moving parts to manage, so thank you to everyone who helped with the logistics of bringing this all together. Those of you who have backed Kickstarters, lifted me up when I was discouraged, watched kids so I could frantically type (I'm looking at you, Elinor!), stopped to chat with me at craft fairs and book signings—thank you. You may never know how precious you are to me, but you've touched my life. When the going gets tough, it's your faces I see. Also, special shoutout to the McLeods and the Jankes for all your help on the finer points of boating and Alaska's topography (Lucas, you're a life saver!), and for taking a chance on some random kids with a story to tell.

On an even more tender note, thank you to my family. Mom and Dad, I love you both so much! Steve and Kari, same to you! To my wonderful siblings (and in-laws on both sides), thank you. Another big shoutout goes to Evan and Levi for being patient with me, your crazy mother. I love you boys!

The second-biggest thank you, second only to God, goes to Dallin. Thanks for poking so many holes in my plot, for the brainstorming sessions, for talking me down when I just wanted to quit, and most of all, for believing a good version of me was still in there even when I had completely lost sight of her. Thanks for being patient with me when I get all existential and weird about things like time, and chocolate (and how I always seem to be running out of both.) I adore you. Here's to eternity!

And finally, thank you to the One who knows how all the stories end, who's walked through every possible dark night of the soul, and who still loves us beyond comprehension. Even if I can't quite reach, I'll always be trying to take your hand.

For Dallin

Contents

Chapter One

—————————————————————

"I can hear our baby."

Sam bolted upright, the sheets engulfing him and Darien falling in a heap around his waist. "You *what?*"

Darien's huge, dark eyes flicked to his. "I can *hear* it."

Sam's mouth fell open. He'd taken hits by defensive linemen that shocked him less than what his wife had just said. "What—*how*? What's it saying? What—?"

"Just a second. Give me a second."

Her chest rose and fell in a shallow breath, and she closed her eyes. Sam stared. Years of working with sick and hurting animals had made Darien all but bulletproof; she was one of the most emotionally stable people he knew. He took a deep breath, then lay down and pulled her close. Sniffling, she rolled onto her side and buried her face in his chest. Sam held her, caressing her shoulder with his fingertips.

"I'm *stunned*, Sam."

"I ... *yeah*!" He hesitated. "What are you hearing?"

Darien pulled back to look at him, a little smile playing at the corners of her lips. Sam's heart skipped. That *smile* ... he didn't think he'd ever get used to how beautiful she was.

"It's so happy. So content." Darien tipped her head back onto the pillow and stared up at the ceiling, her eyebrows drawn together. "It doesn't think like we do. All I'm getting is the most basic of emotions, but—"

"That makes sense. It barely has a nervous system at this point, let alone a brain."

"True, but it's just so ... it's so *pure*." Darien shook her head a fraction, her voice becoming a whisper. "This feeling is the most peaceful thing I've ever experienced."

Sam gazed at her, trying to find words that were adequate to convey what he felt. After a moment, he gave up and pulled her in again.

"I'm so glad you're her dad," Darien murmured.

"Hey, me too—" A jolt went through him. "It's a girl?"

A delighted chuckle burst out of Darien. "Obviously, I can't know for sure, but ... it *feels* like she's a girl. I don't know how to explain it." She went quiet for a moment. "That wouldn't be disappointing to you, would it?"

"No! Not even a little!" Sam let out a short laugh as a fresh wave of wonder coursed through him. It was all so real now; in a little over seven months, he'd be holding his newborn child in his arms.

My newborn ... daughter?

The thought made him feel both strong and infinitesimally small. But he still couldn't stop grinning.

Darien tucked her head under his chin, and Sam shifted into a more comfortable position, his gaze settling on the beautiful sight outside their luxury suite. The moon hung full and low and bright in the star-flecked Hawaiian sky, glinting off the metal balcony and washing the dull concrete patio in silver. A pang of regret hit him; if only they'd been able to relax here, to be normal honeymooners—

Darien stiffened. Sam pulled back in time to see her smile vanish, replaced with something uneasy, haunted. "Ankle Tickler's back."

"Like, you can *hear* him in your head again?"

"Yes." Darien pressed a hand to her eyes. "The same as it was a few minutes ago. I'm not sure he ever left, actually. I was just too distracted by our baby to notice."

"Is this ..." Sam suppressed a chill. "Is this another Wormwood scenario, or ...?"

"No. At least, I don't think so."

Darien started to push herself upright. Sam released her and followed her lead, scanning the dark hotel room. It was all gleaming hardwood, polished marble, and creamy white furniture—there was no sign of the freakish little demon that had haunted their entire trip.

But ...

A shimmer of movement caught Sam's eye. He glanced at the balcony, then did a double-take. A cloud of what looked like mist was forming out there, coalescing into something tall and humanoid even as he watched. Dread filled him; he glanced at Darien. She, too, was staring out over the balcony, but there was no sign she'd noticed the demon forming on it.

Another one only I can see, then. Sam rubbed his eyes. Eight hours with his new ... ability? power? curse? ... and he was already exhausted. But when Darien leaned forward and cupped her temples in her hands, Sam's heart clenched. What was worse: being bothered by monsters only he could see, or overhearing the thoughts of every single one of them in aggregate, whether he wanted to or—?

Every single one of them?

He glanced at the balcony again. "Darien?"

"Yeah?"

"Um ..." The thing was still there, but hadn't come in yet. Maybe they'd get lucky and it would go find someone else to feed on—though he felt bad for hoping it would.

"Yeah, Sam?"

Sam shook himself. "Sorry. Can you hear my thoughts, too? Or just Ankle Tickler's and the baby's?"

"Just his and the baby's. I think, anyway." She put her head down again. "Maybe those two are the most distinct because I had a hand in creating both of them."

"Right." Sam glanced again at the hovering, unnatural thing on the balcony. "Can you feel any others?"

"Well, *yeah.*" Darien let out a long sigh through her nose. "Sorry. I'm not frustrated at *you,* just—"

Sam put a hand on her shoulder. "It's fine, Dar. It's okay."

She didn't look up, but her hand moved to rest over his. "Thanks. Aside from Ankle Tickler and the baby, it's just a constant dull roar of mental background noise."

"Like it was last night?"

"Worse. I can't tell how many there are, let alone differentiate between them. But they're louder. It somehow feels like I've become *more sensitive.*"

Yikes. Sam glanced out the doorway, and his stomach leaped into his throat; the thing on the balcony was drifting through the glass door toward them. Little bits of it flaked off as it moved, like shriveled, dead skin from a sunburn. Sam's lip curled in disgust. He'd never seen one do *that* before.

"There's one in our room, isn't there?"

"Yeah. It just floated in off the balcony." Sam cocked his head, studying it. Up close, the demon's weird flaking looked even more grotesque. It reminded him of the burns he'd seen on the victims of the Luxembourg House fire, the way they'd—

Stop looking at it, you idiot, before you change it into something worse.

Sam tore his eyes away, then clambered over to Darien's side of the bed and settled cross-legged next to her. "It feels wrong to turn my back on it. You sure you can't see this one?"

Darien glanced behind her—right at the demon—then shook her head. "I'm trying to decide if I can feel it or not." She scowled. "Damn it, I can't tell, Sam. I can't tell them apart."

Sam gritted his teeth and shoved his fear down. Sure, none of the weird, incorporeal, invisible-to-everyone-else demons he'd seen in the last twelve hours had hurt anyone. But twelve hours wasn't exactly a reliable sample size.

The hairs on the back of his neck prickled. He started to turn, but Darien grabbed his shoulder.

"Don't do it."

"I can't not do—*what if it's grown razor blades for fingers and is about to—!*"

Darien clapped a hand over his mouth, her brown eyes boring into his. "Shut. Up. Now."

Sam turned his face away, her palm sliding over his mouth. *Do something! Or at least think of doing something!* "On the flip side, what if I could turn it into a kitten?"

Darien raised an eyebrow. "This probably isn't the best place to try, don't you think? The last thing we want is for that to backfire and end up with a messed-up mountain lion rampaging through the Four Seasons. Or whatever scares you."

"What if what scares me is *it*, exactly the way it is right now?"

Darien gave a helpless shrug. "I don't know, Sam. All I know is that I don't want to find out."

Sam gaped at his wife. Her eyes were fearful, her face flushed. Worry for her—which, honestly, had been there since the Lady had come screaming into Ellie's room a week ago—reared its ugly head again. Studying the demons had been Darien's idea in the first place. And while she made a good point about not influencing this one for the worse, part of him was still alarmed by her sudden swerve into avoidance.

Sam leaned forward. "Darien, are you sure—?"

His stomach clenched, the sensation so intense that it stopped him cold. For a moment, he wasn't sure why. Then he realized ...

He could see the demon.

It was there, in his peripheral vision.

Flaking.

Sam jerked backward, nearly falling off the bed.

"What is it?" Darien yelped.

"It's the balcony demon." Sam scooted, plunking himself down between Darien and the demon, willing himself not to stare at it. "It's right behind us. *Right* behind us."

Her breath shallowed, and she went still. Sam realized too late that despite his attempts *not* to stare at the thing, his position gave him a direct line of sight into the bathroom mirror, revealing that the demons *did* have reflections—at least to him. He fixed his eyes on the tile floor, on the cross where the deep brown grout intersected. The room was lightening, its details becoming visible. Sunrise wasn't far off.

"They're so sadistic, Sam."

Still staring at the floor, Sam grasped Darien's hand. "What you're dealing with would drive me insane."

"Maybe that's why I got this curse and you got yours."

Sam let out a humorless chuckle. "You think there's someone in charge of all of that? To *that* level of detail?"

Darien shrugged. "On my best days, yes. I assume that that 'someone' knows us, and knows what we can take."

"Well, this may come as a shock," Sam grumbled, "but I'm not as patient as you. If there really is someone up—" he pointed vaguely skyward "—*there* in charge of handing out curses, I'm going to find them and punch them in the mouth."

Darien's answering snort was devoid of humor. "I don't know if I'd go straight to punching, but I'll admit I have questions."

They were quiet for another moment as the room lightened around them.

"Do I dare risk a glance?" Sam asked.

"We have to at some point, don't we? We have to be able to function."

"Yeah." Sam inhaled one last breath of Darien's fruity scent. Then, he looked into the mirror.

Only his scared reflection looked back.

The tension went out of him so quickly that he felt weak. "It's gone."

"Thank goodness." Darien slumped back against him. "Where do you think they go when they do that?"

"I dunno. Back to their world?"

"Can they do that if they're not near a gate?"

"I don't know, Dar." Sam wrapped his arms around her, wishing they knew more about these creatures. *And the world they came from. And all the other worlds that are apparently out there—*

No. He couldn't follow that line of thinking, or the terror it brought on would attract every demon within fifty miles. Instead, he looked up at Darien's reflection. "You've got to feel a little better now that it's gone, right?"

She shook her head. "I can't tell the difference."

Sam swallowed. "Just to clarify. When you say you're 'feeling' the demons' emotions, you're not actually *feeling* them yourself, are you?"

She looked him square in the eye. "Oh, I'm feeling them. But only sort of. It's like they're being ... *projected* onto my mind. They aren't really mine; they're an invasion. And I think my brain can tell, which is why it's such a weird experience." She drew her knees up and wrapped her arms around them. "But even though they're not actually mine—and I *know* it—they're intense enough to be wildly uncomfortable. And Ankle Tickler ..."

Sam waited as Darien gathered her thoughts.

"He's very, very intelligent, Sam. But the way he processes things isn't like people do at all. It's more like how I imagine animals think, except his clarity of mind is razor-sharp. He's curious about us, but also vicious and completely self-serving."

Sam cocked his head, thinking about how Silverskin, the Lady, Wormwood, and Death had behaved. "Do you think all the demons think like that?"

"No idea." She shivered. "I need a larger sample size."

Sam's heart sank. She was right, but what would that do to her mentally? Could it even be avoided?

"Anyway," Darien said, "I think Ankle Tickler knew the balcony demon was there. He became more ... attuned to that area, at least. He just didn't seem to care. I didn't notice even a flicker of social inclination in him during the last few minutes."

"That does fit with what Oliver first told us. That they seem to prefer hunting alone." Sam paused. "But I don't know, Dar. The Lady and Wormwood teaming up to chase—"

"That teamwork just speaks to their intelligence as a species, though. They *aren't* human, not even a little, but they can adapt and plan on a human level. At least, some of them can."

Sam looked out the window, at the now-empty balcony and the pale sky beyond. "It almost seems like there's a bell curve."

"Of intelligence? That feels accurate to me, based on our experience."

"Which, admittedly, is limited," Sam murmured. "But it does seem like the worst of them—the Lady, Wormwood, my demon, whoever this Death character is—are rarer, and most just run around invisibly sowing despair."

"I wish that were more comforting."

They were quiet for a moment. Finally, Darien spoke, her voice soft. "After our experience with Ankle Tickler last night, when he came and all but hung out with us, I was really hoping we were dealing with a reasonable creature, maybe even something that had the capacity for empathy. I was thinking of him like an elephant, or maybe a dolphin."

"Intelligent, not naturally kind or social beyond its own species, but can learn to be?"

Darien nodded. "But he's not like that, Sam. He's more clever, more independent … and infinitely crueler."

The flesh between Sam's shoulder blades seemed to writhe; his eyes flicked to the space underneath the couch. "We really need to get away from here."

"Our flight leaves at noon."

Sam turned to her. "Let's not stay here. Let's just shower and pack up and get the hell out of this hotel. It's not like Ankle Tickler is going to follow us."

Darien snorted. "I don't know about that. I think he likes us. In whatever way he can, anyway." She frowned. "No, he likes me. You're just a food source."

"*What*?" Sam sat up straighter. "Tell him he's a jerk."

"I don't have to tell him. He can hear you perfectly fine."

Sam spluttered, but Darien interrupted. "If it makes you feel better, I get the impression he sees most people that way. We're cattle to him." An unnerved look flitted across her face. "And I'm his favorite cow."

Sam shoved down his first impulse, which was to dive off the bed and show that creature exactly what happened when someone called his wife a cow. "Is he talking *back* to you now?"

"Sort of. He can understand every word we say. But again, he doesn't *speak* back because that's not how his mind works."

"He thinks more … pictorally? Is that the right word?"

Darien shrugged. "Sure. I get impressions, feelings, and ... *images*." She shifted, her face going thoughtful. "There's a lot of darkness. Part of me wonders if that's memories of his world, but it could also be because he's been hiding in dark places the entire time he's been here."

"Well, we did make him an ankle grabber." Sam scrubbed a hand over his face. *And I thought our situation was complicated* yesterday.

"Oh. Oh, wow." Darien blinked. "I just got a flash of really strange images, but now they're gone." She paused. "I get the feeling Ankle Tickler didn't want me to see those."

"You should probably try and remember them, then."

"It'd be easier if I *understood* them at all. And if all this extra noise would just ... *quit* for a second!"

Sam opened his mouth, then closed it again. Could he even help? Or would he just add to her mental clutter? He looked back outside; the sky was light enough now that the fronds of the palm trees were distinct against it. They swayed in a gentle breeze, the turquoise ocean lapping behind them, and he was struck by the stark contrast between the idyllic view and the seething riot of his own emotions.

So do something about it.

Sam stood, trying to ignore the fact that Ankle Tickler was probably under the bed—probably even within snatching distance—and put his hands on his hips. "Darien—"

He glanced up, and stopped cold. Another shape was forming in the space between the bed and the bathroom, less than ten feet away. It was nothing like the last one. Instead, it was a perfect sphere, made up of what looked like tendrils of smoke that stretched around it like a dark, sinister, rubber band ball. It drifted toward them, its motion slow. Eerie. Inevitable.

Sam gasped, but any words he might have said were stolen from his mouth as another demon started to take shape in the still-darkened bathroom. It formed more quickly than any he'd seen before, consolidating into a grayish, semi-transparent outline that looked ...

Sam's stomach twisted into a knot. It looked distinctly human, down to its individual fingers and toes.

"More of them?" Darien's voice was high, nervous.

"Yeah." Sam fixed his eyes back on Darien. "There's—"

But the sphere-demon was between them now—it had sped up while he was distracted with the other one. "There's one right between us, Dar. Don't move."

Darien's eyes widened, and she opened her mouth, but Sam didn't hear what she said. Because on the balcony, a third shape was forming.

"There are three now," he breathed. "Not counting Ankle Tickler."

"Quick, don't look at any of them."

"I wouldn't if I couldn't, but I swear a new one shows up every time I turn around—"

"Close your eyes!"

Sam scowled at the sphere-demon, which still hovered between them. "I can't! What if you're attacked—?"

"And what if you *change* one somehow?" Darien demanded. "We've played this game before, Sam. They'll probably just go away."

"Dammit. *Dammit*! Fine." Sam forced his eyes shut and took a deep, slow breath, just like he would before a game. His fear, his anger, his helplessness—no wonder the demons were swarming them. He was live bait. *Get a grip, dude.*

"I can't feel any difference between them," Darien said.

It took all of Sam's willpower not to open his eyes. "But you can feel that they're here?"

" ... Maybe? Now that you've mentioned it, I think I felt the overall ... *tone* of the room shift a little. But that could just be because I'm human, and suggestible."

"Well—"

"Shhh. No offense, just ... let me just feel for a minute."

Sam folded his arms and went quiet. For a long moment, the only sound in the room was the gentle whir of the fan blade and the hum of the mini-fridge in the corner.

"I think they're gone," Darien finally whispered.

"How confident are you?"

"I'm ... actually fairly confident." She sounded like it, too—hopeful, excited, even. "I think I felt them go."

"Okay. I'm going to open my eyes." *Willing* the demons to be gone, Sam cracked an eye ... and leaped back. The sphere-thing still hovered in front of Darien's face, but it had changed. Instead of thin ribbons of smoke, its body had turned smooth and shiny, like dark, marbled glass. Two yellow points flickered in its depths, like twin candle flames, or headlights on a dark highway, or ...

Or a pair of eyes.

Understanding crashed over him; it really was a nightmare. *His* nightmare: a creature he'd seen as a boy in some throwaway Halloween ad that had haunted him for months afterward. It had been his first memorable experience with the unknown, with monsters, with irrational, inexpressible terror.

And this creature had somehow reached into his memories, dragged it out, and embodied it.

"Darien," Sam stammered. "The Sphere's still here; it's *right* in front of you. And it's, it's my creation, but I didn't mean to—"

The twin lights rotated toward Sam as if the demon had heard him. As if it knew he was looking at it. Darien scrambled off the other side of the bed, backing toward the TV stand. "Let's throw everything in our suitcase and get out of here."

"I'll get everything in the bathroom—" Sam stopped as the Sphere glided after her. Its edges were getting crisper, its detail more defined. Tendrils of dark vapor wisped off its surface. He couldn't see its eyes; they were turned toward his wife.

"Hey." Sam started toward her. Black tendrils of smoke, or steam, or *something* were snaking out from the Sphere, surrounding her. "Hey! Darien, get away from—!"

He knew the instant she'd seen the demon. Her eyes went huge, and she stumbled backward, clapping her hands over her mouth to cut off her scream. Sam caught her arm and pulled her toward the door. "None of our stuff matters! Leave it!"

"It's too close!" Darien released his hand. "We can't get out the door in time!"

Cursing, Sam whirled in time to see her snatch a heavy-looking vase filled with fake flowers off the room's small desk. Sam spun and grabbed a decorative wooden bowl off the coffee table, grateful that they were staying in a place boujee enough to have authentic wood decor. He hefted it as the Sphere revolved toward them. Its glowing yellow eyes—there was no mistaking what they were now—glowered at them in a soulless, hungry leer. "I should've made us get real weapons last night."

"How could we have seen *this* coming?" Darien raised the vase; the flowers in it tumbled to the floor. "Even Ankle Tickler wasn't this aggressive this quickly."

Sam swallowed. "Doesn't matter now."

Come on. Oliver's driven off the Lady three or four times. You can do the same to this thing. He lunged for the demon, swinging the bowl at it with all his strength. To his shock, it clanged off its marbled-glass shell, the force of the blow jarring clear into his shoulder joint. He stumbled but managed to hold onto the bowl as the demon reeled, spitting black jets of smoke that felt like freezing water vapor on his skin. The places they touched started to tingle like they'd fallen asleep, or like …

"Jeez!" Sam scrambled backward. "That smoke is made of acid or something—"

Darien gasped and put a hand to her head. An instant later, a dark, lithe shape shot across the floor, its mad orange eyes reflecting the rising sun, its ugly, six-fingered hands making no noise on the hardwood. Sam watched in disbelief as Ankle Tickler—hackles raised, the hair on his back standing straight up—planted himself squarely between them and the Sphere.

"What the—?" Sam grabbed Darien's arm. "Let's get out—!"

"Wait, wait, Sam! This could be important! Their behavior—"

"Or we could get *killed*—"

A strange, warped growl drowned out the rest of Sam's words. Ankle Tickler took a step forward.

The Sphere stopped.

Ankle Tickler growled again, and Sam shuddered; the sound enveloped him in a way that didn't feel natural, scraping over his skin, *through* his flesh. For a surreal moment, the two demons seemed locked in a tense, silent battle. Hardly daring to breathe, Sam pulled Darien closer.

The Sphere pulled back.

Ankle Tickler took another step, his eerie growl rasping through the air for the third time. For a long moment, the Sphere hovered in the center of the elegant room like a dour, black moon. Then it darted for the glass door, passed through, and hurtled itself into the sky. Within a few seconds, it was nothing more than a black speck on a backdrop of pale blue.

Sam and Darien stared, openmouthed, as Ankle Tickler turned to look at them. Cautiously, Sam lowered the wooden bowl. "So what, you're protecting us now?"

The demon stared back. Sam suppressed a shiver, telling himself he couldn't throw the bowl at it. Despite what it had just done for them, something still felt … off. Wrong.

Darien released him and took a small step forward. "Hey. Thank you for—"

Ankle Tickler hurled himself at her feet.

Darien shrieked, stumbling backward. Sam caught her around the waist and shoved her behind him as dark fur flashed in his peripheral vision. Stinging pain erupted in his leg. He yelled in shock and lashed out with a foot, but Ankle Tickler was already scrambling back under the bed. An instant later, Darien's vase crashed to the wooden floor where the demon had been, cracking in two.

"Wish I'd have thrown that sooner," she snarled.

Sam grabbed her hand, wincing; it felt like his whole shin was on fire. "Come on." He dropped down on the couch. "Sit down. Feet up."

Darien crossed her legs, shooting one more glare at the space under the bed as she did. "Some favor. Let's see the damage."

Sam extended his injured ankle, crossing his good foot underneath his thigh so no part of him was touching the floor, and pulled up the leg of his sweats. He grimaced; the demon had slashed right through the fabric, leaving a nearly foot-long gouge that ran from mid-shin to his ankle. It gaped up at them, oozing red.

"Yikes." Darien leaned down and examined the wound, and Sam closed his eyes. Truth be told, Ellie wasn't the only one in the family who had a weak stomach. He did fine when hunting, but when it came to human injuries? That unfortunate family trait had gotten to him, too, though he'd done his best to keep that under wraps. He cracked an eye open, studying Darien so he wouldn't have to look at the blood he could now feel trickling down his calf. There was a grim set to her mouth, a fury that seemed to light her eyes from behind and carve the usually gentle lines of her face into something rigid and formidable.

Sam stared. *Ankle Tickler's going to get it.*

Darien looked up. "Under normal circumstances, I'd say this needed stitches."

"But it's not a normal injury."

"No, it isn't." Darien glanced down at her own ankle, the skin there smooth, tan, and healthy. There was no sign of the slash Ankle Tickler had given her only a few nights ago. "With how big it is, I'm still worried about the next hour or two, though. Or until it closes for good."

Sam shook his head. "It doesn't matter. We can't stay here. We need to get somewhere public."

"How's your pain?"

"It stings, but I can handle it." Sam steeled himself, then peered more closely at the wound. It tingled, and he could swear the bleeding had already stopped. Woozy, hoping his face wasn't too pale, he pulled back.

Darien was frowning at him. "Are you sure?"

"Yes. My body just doesn't like being cut open."

"Well, that's reasonable." She nodded toward the bathroom. "I really want you to wash that, but I don't trust Ankle Tickler to even let us over there."

Sam snorted. "I never trusted him."

"I wanted to." Darien looked toward the bed again, her face pinching with what looked like resentment. "But I shouldn't have."

Sam watched as her expression changed, her lips parting. It was almost as if she were listening to something. "Is he talking to you?"

"Not really." Darien's frown deepened. "I'm getting flashes of stuff, but it's all fragmented, like he's trying to figure out how to hide it from me." She let out a deep sigh and sat back. "His emotions are crystal clear, though. He feels superior, and possessive. He has no remorse or regret, not for anything. He thinks of us as his. Literally like we're *his* cows."

Sam swallowed and looked back under the bed. "So it was territorial aggression. He was just protecting a food source."

"I guess so." Darien shrugged. "I guess he attacked you to make *sure* we know he's not our friend."

"Well, there was no need for it. I haven't exactly kept my distrust of him a secret." Sam peered under the bed again, dread seeping through him. "Remember when you asked him last night what he was feeding on if we weren't afraid of him anymore?"

Darien nodded.

"What if ..." Sam shifted, punctuating his words with his hands. "Darien, what if he's hungry. What if he slashed me to—"

"To make you afraid of him again?"

Holding Darien's gaze, Sam shook his head. "No. To make *you* afraid again."

Shock flitted across Darien's face.

"Are you more afraid of him now than you were yesterday?" Sam asked.

Darien swallowed. "Yes. And I'm even more afraid of him right now than I was two minutes ago." She stared at the dark gap under the bed. "That level of ... of *manipulativeness* ... That terrifies me."

Sam followed her gaze. Then, he stood and limped toward their suitcase. "Let's get to Alaska. We've got to finish this."

Chapter Two

Oliver's consciousness swam back to the surface. And that's how it felt, too: like his mind was dragging itself through a brackish swamp full of mud, suffering, and oxycodone. Something thrummed under his left ear—the truck's engine. Its tires whirred over the asphalt highway, and the haunting, melancholy sound of a violin drifted through its speakers.

The truck dipped into a trough in the asphalt, then rose out of it just as quickly. Queasiness washed over Oliver as he realized how much rougher the road had become than it was a few hours ago. The air smelled like burned meat and something else—something crisp and slightly flowery he associated with clean laundry. Probably the air freshener that Ellie had hung up right before they'd left the lonely little cabin where both he and the Dark Lady had died. Where he, miraculously, had returned to life afterward. Where he'd told Ellie he loved her, learned that she felt the same way, and had finally driven off Wormwood for good.

How long ago was that, anyway?

Oliver cracked an eye open and nearly dry-heaved. Stifling a groan, he closed it, hoping his nausea would steady before he vomited; with third-degree burns all over his back and chest, that would be hellish. He turned his head a fraction of an inch, pressing his cheek to a cooler section of the seat. It was a sharp contrast to how the skin of his arm and shoulder felt: like they'd been pasted to the luxury leather.

Oliver grimaced. He was lying in the same position he'd fallen asleep in, twisted so that he was on his side as much as possible. His neck and hips hurt, but his protesting joints were nothing compared to the tearing pain in his chest, or the deep, pulsing throb between his shoulder blades. Sweat trickled down his forehead; hot air wafted over him from the direction of the dash. Ellie must be trying to keep him warm like their medical guide suggested, but she was doing too good a job.

On the other hand, dealing with *cold* ...

Inwardly, he shuddered. The prospect of goosebumps blithely erupting underneath his burns as if the tissues supporting them hadn't just been incinerated like the Luxembourg House ... *that* would be much worse than this.

"Oliver? Are you awake?"

Despite his pain, Oliver felt a burst of happiness at the sound of Ellie's voice. "Yeah."

"How're you feeling?"

"Been better. Least there's no Wormwood. What time is it?"

"Almost ten."

Oliver's eyes almost flew open. "*P.M.?*"

"Yep."

Guilt pricked at him. That meant she'd been driving for almost ten hours—on a rough road, too—and he'd been sleeping for nearly six of those. "I'm sorry. I didn't mean to—"

Ellie's palm brushed over the back of his hand. "Hey. We have a *very* limited time for you to rest this uninterrupted, so it's good you're taking advantage of it." Her voice quieted. "Once we get to Homer, I'm not sure what to expect."

"Expect Helen."

Ellie burst out laughing. "I love your aunt so much."

"She's an amazing person. I can't wait to see her and Henry again."

"Me neither."

Ellie's hand left his. When she spoke again, the timbre of her voice had shifted—she wasn't smiling anymore. "We're about fifteen minutes from a town called Whitehorse. I'm planning on stopping for the night there, and then trying to make it to Anchorage tomorrow."

"Good call."

"We can even try for Homer, depending on how I'm feel—"

"How far's Anchorage?" Oliver rasped.

"Google says thirteen hours," Ellie said, and Oliver's stomach swooped as the truck took another dip. "But if this road stays this bad I think it's going to take longer."

"Frost heaves," Oliver managed to grunt. "They deform the road."

"We get those in Colorado too, but—" She cut off as the truck slipped into another one, then rose out of it so fast Oliver's stomach threatened to riot again. "But not like this."

"You don't have melting permafrost in Colorado." Oliver's heart sank—and not just because he still had to cram his burned body into a truck for that many hours. Ellie had sounded bracing, but underneath, he could sense her exhaustion, her dread at having to push through yet another day like this. And with Homer being an extra four and a half hours from Anchorage ...

"I'll be more useful tomorrow," he said. Lamely.

"Yeah." Ellie's hand brushed his again. "We're going to sleep great tonight, and you're going to heal incredibly quickly, and we're not going to get into any fights with demons, and tomorrow will be much better."

A pained grin crossed Oliver's face. "We can hope."

"I'm manifesting really hard. Though," Ellie let out a huff, or maybe it was a rueful laugh, "I'm not sure if I have much faith in it, honestly."

"Hey." Oliver turned his palm upward and squeezed her hand, stifling a gasp as that small movement made his back and chest twinge. "I'm already getting better. It already feels better."

He gritted his teeth as waves of pain rolled over him. *I think. I hope.*

Ellie's thumb stroked across the back of his hand. "I wish I knew more about literally anything medical. I have no idea what to expect."

"'S'fine."

"Do you need another painkiller? It's been since this morning that you took one."

"Yeah. But let's wait until we get somewhere to sleep. No point stopping if we're ... if we're this close."

"Okay. I'll stop at the first decent place I can find."

"And I'll manage to open my eyes without throwing up," Oliver mumbled.

"You're feeling sick?"

The concern in Ellie's voice cut at Oliver. "I think it's because of the drugs."

"Not infection?"

"No." Oliver took another shallow breath. "Though that's ... hard to tell."

Come on. You can do this. Tentatively, he slitted his eyes open. His queasiness intensified, but not to the extreme it had reached the last time. Breathing deeply—or as deeply as he dared when any and all movement hurt like the devil—he opened his eyes the rest of the way.

Ellie sat straight-backed in the driver's seat, her fingers tapping lightly with the music. There were dark circles around her eyes, a thin red welt across her cheek, a grisly necklace of yellow-green bruises around her throat, and her forearm was discolored a deep purple. Her hair had come half-loose from the messy bun at the nape of her neck, and wisps of it hung around her face.

She looked grim and exhausted. But still so beautiful.

Oliver let his gaze stray behind her, toward the pinkish sunset. There were mountains out there; he could see them on the horizon. Big mountains, northern ones. It was starting to look more and more like home.

A weird, shivering tingle spasmed between his shoulder blades. Without meaning to, he hissed out a breath. The pain was incredible—unlike anything he'd experienced before this injury, a deep and throbbing ache that still threatened to consume him.

"I think I see a sign," Ellie said. "About a quarter of a mile ahead—hopefully it's a lodge or something. Hang in there."

He looked back at her in time to see her return her eyes to the road. The fingers on her left hand continued to tap in time to the music; her brow was furrowed, and she bit her bottom lip—her personal trifecta of worry signs.

"You haven't missed a beat," Oliver said.

"When we get there, I—what?" She glanced over at him, eyebrow raised.

"Your fingers. You're playing the violin on the steering wheel, and you haven't missed a beat." When Ellie looked flummoxed, he almost smiled. "Did you even know you were doing that?"

"Oh! Yes. It's my lame attempt at practicing, so my professor doesn't rake me over the coals when I get back." She brushed a lock of hair out of her eyes. "Besides, it helps me keep the anxiety under control. It's remarkably effective."

"Well, music *was* on the demon-killing list ... you sent ... *aargh*—"

The truck slowed, shifting Oliver forward. He bit the inside of his cheek against the pain. Dimly, he became aware of Ellie's voice. "... because this one looks good and we need to get you inside."

"Yeah," he managed. Worry gnawed at him; he tried to remember how long it had taken his brand to heal. A few weeks? More than a month? It could have been. Cursing the oxycodone, he wished his head were clearer. And he wished ...

He wished he could talk to Dean, get more of his help and his knowledge.

Part of him still hated that.

A low moan escaped Oliver as Ellie pressed harder on the brakes. He could tell she was trying to be gentle, but in the state he was ... well, there wasn't much she could do. He forced his eyes open as the truck turned, gliding underneath a beautiful arch made of skinned logs. A sign dangled from its top that read *The Caribou Inn*. Ellie pulled up to the front doors and parked, and Oliver tried to focus his bleary eyes. Light blazed through the lodge's massive windows. From his awkwardly reclined position, he could make out the top half of what looked like a caribou-antler chandelier, but couldn't see much else.

"How sure are you that Wormwood's really gone?" Ellie asked.

"Very."

"Okay." She opened her door. "I'll be back soon. Don't start any fights without me."

The door slammed behind her, and Oliver finally gave full voice to the cry he'd been suppressing for the last ten minutes. It was deep, ragged, and tearing. If he'd heard another human make it, he would've been appalled. He hoped he didn't attract something *not* human because of it.

Ellie returned a few minutes later, hopping into the truck in a whoosh of cool night air. Oliver had just opened his mouth to welcome her back when goosebumps stabbed into his ruined flesh like hundreds of white-hot needles. He barely bit back his scream.

Ellie slammed the door, looking horrified. "I'm so sorry."

"'S'fine."

"I ..." She shook her head, clearly frustrated at herself, then put the truck in gear. "I got us a private cabin instead of a room in the lodge. That way we won't destroy the whole building if we have to light another demon on fire."

"And so no one can hear me scream," Oliver grumbled.

Ellie stared at him.

He tried to chuckle. "Joke."

For a moment, he thought she might throw something at him, even in his condition. But then she just shook her head, muttering, "Unbelievable."

Seconds later, she pressed on the brakes, trundling into what sounded like a little gravel parking spot. Oliver turned his head as she shut off the truck, unpleasantly amazed at how many muscles in his back and chest were involved in that one small movement. A small cabin nestled between the trees, its dark windows gaping like sightless eyes. Other than its roof—red instead of green—it was similar to the cabin where they'd ambushed the Lady.

Ellie stared at it for a moment. Then, she twisted and reached behind them, reappearing seconds later with a handful of wooden arrows and a lighter. The smell of alcohol made Oliver's nose wrinkle; the arrows were tipped with cotton balls they'd soaked in hand sanitizer during yesterday's drive. Looking at them now, Oliver was reminded absurdly of dandelions.

Big, deadly, demon-killing dandelions.

"Better to be safe," Ellie said, reaching for the door handle again.

Alarm shot through Oliver. "Wait, Ellie—"

"Oh, you're right. I'm forgetting ..." She turned and reached into the back seat one more time. Grunting, she hauled a heavy blanket over the center console and threw it awkwardly over Oliver. Then she shoved the door open and hopped out, leaving the headlights blazing.

The door clunked shut behind her.

Oliver reached for his seat adjuster and whined louder than it did as it heaved him upright, where he could watch Ellie as she crept up the front steps. She paused to unlock the door. Ignoring the crackling sensations across his back and chest as he moved—and the harsh sound hissing between his teeth—Oliver forced his hand toward his own door handle.

The blanket slid off his shoulders, falling around his waist.

Goosebumps erupted across his torso again, and he lost a few seconds. When he came back to himself, emotions flooded through him in a hazy mental cocktail: frustration, a little humiliation, fear for Ellie's safety ... and also admiration. Sheer, undiluted admiration.

Which didn't change the fact that she was still in there. Alone.

Oliver shook himself as black spots whizzed on the edges of his vision. How long had he just lost consciousness for? How big was the cabin? How long should it take to search? Curling his fingers around the door's handle, he *made* himself pull, biting back a yell of agony. But it worked; the door unlatched and gave. The goosebumps came again—and with them, the black spots in his vision—but he managed to push the door open with his leg. He straightened, his breath coming in shallow gasps, his head light. *How* had he managed to hold Ellie the way he had that morning *and* win a showdown with Wormwood in this condition?

Oxycodone, said a small voice in his head. *That's how.*

A light turned on inside the cabin, casting a bright yellow square onto the dim ground. Oliver breathed a sigh of relief; it was unlikely a demon would do that. A few seconds later, the cabin door creaked open to reveal Ellie.

"I gave you that blanket because you were supposed to stay in the truck," she said as she jogged down the stairs.

"Is it actually you?" Oliver croaked. As if he could do anything about it if it weren't.

"I hate horror movies, love peanut butter and jelly sandwiches, the first thing you said to me was that I smelled, and we just listened to Samuel Barber's only violin concerto—Opus 14, the second movement, specifically—played by Hilary Hahn on one of her Vuillaume violins." She hopped over a tree root and reached out a hand. "Good enough?"

"Sure. I'm convinced." Oliver winced as Ellie draped the blanket across his shoulders. She looped an arm around his waist, steadying him without touching his bandaged burns, and he leaned into her as they walked. The blanket dulled the worst of the cold, but the goosebumps that managed to break through anyway still felt like little flames, writhing and burrowing so deep he thought they might reach his organs. Still, he managed to make his feet obey him, and then they were stumbling over the threshold into the cabin.

A fluorescent light blazed over a kitchenette in the corner, washing every surface—the countertops, the hardwood floor, the couch, the king-sized bed along the far wall—in a film of too-bright light. They stumbled over to the couch. Ellie helped lower him onto it, then pulled a little orange bottle out of her jacket pocket and unscrewed the lid. "You need to take one of these so we can re-bandage your burns."

Oliver held out his hand, eyeing the little white pill Ellie shook into his palm with faint disgust. "Here's hoping this is the last one." He popped it into his mouth, then took Ellie's water bottle with a shaky hand and drank.

"I hope so, too." Ellie stood. "Let me go get our important stuff while your medicine kicks in. Then we need to ..." Her voice trembled a little. "We need to clean them. We can video call Darien and have her look—"

"Ellie, you don't have to ... when the drugs kick in, I think I can manage—"

Ellie turned and put a finger to his lips, her face inches from his. "I'll help you, Oliver. I would never let you do this alone." A tiny smile crossed her lips. "It's what you do when you love someone."

She let her hand fall, then headed for the door. "Be right back."

Oliver lowered his head into his hands. The drugs worked relatively fast, but he wasn't surprised when Ellie was faster. She squeezed back through the front door mere minutes later, carrying the medical kit they'd taken from the cabin where they'd killed the Lady and an armload of what looked like clothes. She dumped the latter on the other side of the couch and plopped the medical kit down next to him. "Are the drugs working yet?"

"Don't think so. It's only been a few minutes."

"How's your pain?"

He groaned.

Ellie took his hand. "We can wait to unwrap your bandages until they've—"

"No. Do it."

Her eyebrows rose. "No waiting?"

Oliver looked up at the bed on the opposite wall. Even after his extended car nap, it was taking everything he had not to just crawl into it, pull Ellie in with him, and succumb to whatever hazy doze he could manage. "The sooner we get this over with, the sooner we can sleep. And the more sleep we get, the ... the better."

Ellie let out a deep breath. "Okay. Let me know if you need to stop."

She leaned around him, and then her arms were working, unwrapping, the bandage around his chest loosening with every round she made. His breath started to come faster; the pain was intensifying again. When open air hit those burns ...

Ellie paused. "Once I unwrap this round, I'm pretty sure the whole thing is going to come loose, so be ready."

"It feels ... sticky. Like it's bled some."

Ellie paled but nodded, and he wondered if she was thinking the same thing he was: that serious injuries—burns especially—often did nastier things than bleed while healing, even without being infected. His stomach swooped as she started unwrapping again, and he wished for the hundredth time that he could just go to a doctor so she didn't have to do this.

The smell hit them before the bandages were fully gone, acrid and intense. Ellie yanked her shirt up over her nose and kept—

Something *tore* at the center of Oliver's back. He bit off a cry, and Ellie cursed. "It's stuck."

Oliver squeezed his eyes shut, feeling the couch cushions dip as Ellie clambered behind him. "It's stuck to the middle of your back, where the burns are the worst."

"Just yank it off," Oliver whispered. His head was starting to cloud; the drugs were kicking in, though not as fast as he wished they would.

"Yank it off— What if it starts bleeding and I can't stop it?"

"There's probably a hospital here."

"We're here illegally."

"It's this or infection."

For a moment, there was silence, and ... and Oliver's pain lessened. He breathed, letting his torso expand fully for what felt like the first time in hours. Maybe that little delay had been a good thing.

Ellie let out a shaky sigh. "I'm so sorry, Oliver. I should've stopped us way earlier—"

"When? Where?"

"I don't know, but ..."

"It's okay. Drugs are kicking in. Just pull it off." His head was going light; nausea pricked at him. Maybe heavy painkillers didn't actually dull pain at all. Maybe they just made everything else feel so miserable that people forgot about it.

"Okay." Ellie sounded scared.

"It'll be fine."

Her fingers brushed the tops of his shoulders; a second later, her lips touched the back of his neck. This time, the shiver that crept across his back had nothing to do with pain.

Then, Ellie ripped the bandage off.

Oliver felt like half his back tore off with it, and it was that sensation as much as the pain that made him scream. The skin on his back and chest crackled as he hunched forward, pain spearing between his shoulder blades, throbbing with every heartbeat. Lights flashed at the edge of his vision, then everything went dark.

Chapter Three

It was late when Darien and Sam trudged out of Ted Stevens International Airport—late enough that the sun had already set, which was saying something.

They'd left the Four Seasons within ten minutes of the demons' attack, leaving all their toiletries in the bathroom; walking that close to the bed hadn't been worth the risk. Hair uncombed, teeth unbrushed, wearing whatever they'd managed to pull on while throwing their reachable belongings in their suitcase, they'd headed straight for the airport, hoping the traffic and security there would dissuade Ankle Tickler from following. To Darien's relief, it seemed to have worked; there had been no sign of the little monster anywhere.

The problem—she'd quickly relearned—was that where there were people, there were demons. And where there were demons, there were huge problems for her personally.

"Our car's eight minutes away," Sam muttered as they approached the big, sliding glass doors that led out into the pickup area. Darien blinked at the sound of his voice, caught between relief that he'd broken through the dull roar in her head and annoyance that she now had to deal with more than she was *already* dealing with.

That's just you being tired, she told herself. *That's not how you really feel.*

Unless … it was?

Darien suppressed her desire to curl up in a ball in a corner, gross airport flooring be damned. Her sensitivity was getting stronger; there was no denying it now. Last night, over dinner, a murky sense of unease had slowly leached into her, like the fraught hours between eating not-quite-right food and the first wave of violent sickness. Now, though …

She rubbed her eyes. While she couldn't tell individual demons apart, she could tell when there were lots of them. The flight itself had been a wonderful, six-hour reprieve. But the times in the airport that had bookended it? Well, she shouldn't have been surprised that demons would crowd around anxious airport-goers and frustrated TSA agents and harried flight crews and, and, *and* in an endless loop of human frailty and demonic sadism—

On instinct, she reached for the baby's mind, for that oasis of clear, calm, glowing happiness ... but stopped herself. *No. You don't know what that might do to her. Quit it right now.*

The glass door slid open and a rush of air swept over them. Darien shivered and crossed her arms—the breeze was cool, almost cold, and slightly humid; her tank wasn't going to cut it. "Hey, at some point I need to stop somewhere and get clothes I won't freeze to death in."

"Yeah," Sam said slowly, eyes still on his phone. "Let's worry about that tomorrow, though."

Darien frowned. "Our ringtones are on, you know. We'd hear them if they called."

Sam sighed. "I know. I just—" He looked up at her, and his eyes widened. "Jeez, I'm sorry, Dar! You must be freezing." He reached for her, pulling her against him. "I don't even have a jacket or anything—we *can* go shopping tonight if you want, I'm sorry I—"

"No, I'll be okay tonight." She burrowed against Sam and felt her heart soften, even as a dull pain started behind her eyes. "Our car's close, and our hotel room will have a heater. I'm fine, really," she added when he started to protest.

"Okay." Still frowning, Sam glanced back down at his phone, then up at her again. "I'm sorry I didn't think about you. I mean, I *was* thinking about you, I'm just so worried—"

"Sam."

He looked down at her, eyes grim.

"I understand. But we *know* they've tried to call us since leaving this morning, which means they're not dead."

"They survived last night, at least." He pinched the bridge of his nose, and Darien's heart went out to him. They'd called Ellie again, then Oliver, right after getting off the plane, but had been sent straight to voicemail. From a practical standpoint, Darien wasn't surprised; there were plenty of places on that long, remote highway that wouldn't have cell service. But from the standpoint of someone worried about people she loved ...

Abruptly, Sam turned, putting his back to the small crowd of people waiting to be picked up. "They're everywhere, Darien. Everywhere. And one of them's very ..." Sam's agitation seemed to deepen. "It's very concrete. That's the best word I can think of to describe it."

Darien frowned. "What do you mean by 'concrete'?"

"More … deliberate? More controlled? Like the Sphere, or the one I saw last night that was haunting the hotel clerk."

"And they're *not* all like that."

Sam shook his head. "Most of them are just shadows. Don't get me wrong, they're all different from each other, even as shadows. But they're not really … formed. For example, the Sphere started out as a shadow of what it eventually turned into, but it was … fuzzy beforehand. Indistinct. The majority of the ones I see look similar, like hints of what they could be." His frown deepened, and he crossed his arms. "Darien … what if they're baby demons?"

Darien wrinkled her nose. "Let's not call them babies or I'll start feeling bad for them. Juveniles is a better word."

"Juveniles, then. They could be juvenile demons."

Darien considered for a moment. "That kind of fits. Really, it does. I just …"

She winced as the demons' emotions surged again, a seething ocean crashing against the crumbling cliff of her mind.

"Are you okay?" Sam asked softly.

Darien shook herself. "I *have* to be okay, Sam. I can't stop it, so I just have to live with it."

For a long moment, they looked helplessly at each other. Then, Darien swallowed and squared her shoulders. "Okay, so our new working theory is that the shadowy ones you can see are juveniles."

Sam returned his stare to the wall. "Yeah."

"I wish we knew what caused them to change. Like the Sphere this morning. So we could stop it from happening again."

Sam let out a weary chuckle. "Easy. Just stop thinking."

Darien raised an eyebrow at him.

"I made the Sphere, Darien. He's my monster."

"What do you mean?"

"I was keeping an eye on it because it wasn't fading away like the others. And as I watched, it sort of *defined* itself. The eyes got more distinct, the body became blacker and more glassy-looking. And I realized ... it looked just like a monster I'd seen as a kid in some Halloween ad, *years* ago. And when I say years, I mean I was probably five or six, so it was—"

"It was a formative memory?"

"Yeah. Seeing that ad was the first time I was out-of-my-mind scared of something. I got over it. Or so I thought, at least. I haven't actively thought about it in over a decade." He rubbed a hand over his jaw and the day's worth of fuzz there. "Maybe it's because I've been thinking of my childhood more recently, because of the baby. Traditions I want to continue, things I want to do differently ..." He shrugged.

"Reasonable." Darien closed her eyes as the mental onslaught faded a little. Still, it wasn't enough. She was dying to sleep, or maybe launch herself into the sky again—*anything* to escape this. But since she couldn't, she might as well keep picking at the threads of the problem in front of her. "So *you* made it what it was. Just like I made Ankle Tickler an aye-aye."

"Yeah—no?" Sam cocked his head. "It was dark and spherical from the second I saw it. And like I said, even the shadows all look different from each other, so I didn't think much about the Sphere until it wouldn't fade away."

Darien closed her eyes. "Ugh, this is awful. Are they predisposed to *become* a certain way? Do they have to just *stumble* across the right person with the right image in their heads so they can metamorphose into their scary adult state?"

"I don't know, Dar."

"If that's the case, if it's all just random, how are we supposed to stop it?"

"We don't *know* if that's the case—"

Darien's phone buzzed.

"Sam!" She plunged her hand into the pocket of her leggings and brought the phone to her face. "It's Ellie! She's video calling!"

"Pick up—!"

But Darien had already swiped "accept." "Ell—"

"Shut up!" Ellie roared. "I need your help *right now!*"

Darien reared back; she'd never heard that level of fury in Ellie's voice. But as she studied her sister-in-law, she realized the look on her face wasn't anger at all. It was terror.

"We'll do anything," Sam said. "What's going on?"

Ellie panned the camera down, and Darien gasped. Oliver was lying on his side on what looked like a leather couch, stripped to the waist. His back was to the camera, and it was nothing short of hideous. A huge burn stretched between his shoulder blades, the skin taut and shiny and deepening to a sickly purplish-red in the center. Blood—dried and fresh—streaked across his skin, and little globs of what might have been pus caught the dim light as Ellie's hand shook.

The hungry, sadistic revelry in Darien's mind roared to a fever pitch, raising her dinner in her throat. She'd grasped for the baby's mind before she even realized what she was doing.

"Holy ..." Sam's face paled, and he whipped out his phone. "Dar, I'm cancelling our car. Let's find a quiet spot—"

"There." Darien grabbed Sam's arm, steering him toward a little concrete alcove—and the bench inside it—as he typed. "What *happened,* Ellie?"

"The Lady," Ellie said curtly. "Do you think these burns—?"

"Are you safe?" Sam cut in. "Is she going to—?"

"Yes-she's-dead-we're-as-safe-as-we-can-be! Now help me with—Oliver!"

Darien gasped. Oliver was stirring. An instant later, his low groan crackled through the receiver.

"Oliver," Ellie said again. He mumbled something indistinct, and Ellie's pale hand appeared on the screen, rubbing his shoulder. "I've got Darien and Sam on the phone. Are the drugs kicking in?"

Drugs? Darien cast another look at Sam; he looked as baffled as she felt.

"Yeah," Oliver mumbled.

"Good." Ellie's voice became clearer, like she was talking into the microphone now. "Darien, I have no idea what I'm doing and ... and I just need you to tell me what to do. Sam, too. Either of you, I don't care."

A jolt of emotion hit Darien in the stomach. She *felt* the demons pounce.

"Okay, uh ..." *Task at hand. Come on, focus!* "First, we need to see if it's infected, because if it is, he'll have to go to the hospital. Like, right now. It doesn't matter that neither of you is supposed to be in Canada."

Ellie cursed, but Darien barely heard her. She'd just realized she'd reached for the baby again. *Stop, stop, stop—*

"Ellie, get us as close as you can without losing the camera's focus," Sam said. He seemed remarkably calm.

Darien seized that calm, clinging to it the same way a nervous herd animal would to the confidence of another. "And we'll need your eyes, too. Take a really close look and see if you can see any green or yellow discharge."

"I don't."

"Okay, good. Neither do I, and that's a good sign." Darien studied Oliver's burns more closely, feelings of inadequacy rising in her belly as she took in the damage. The more she looked, the worse it got. She was just a pre-vet student; she'd never studied what to do in situations like this. And now a human being, a *friend,* depended on her. The haze intensified, her emotions beginning to riot and roil; she could practically feel the horde surrounding them, tearing at her mind like wolves at a live moose—

Stop! You know what infection looks like. And what it smells *like. Focus!*

"Ellie, what's it smell like?"

"Um, not great."

A chill rolled through Darien. *But ...*

She squinted at Oliver's back again. Though there was plenty of discharge, none of it had the oozing, phlegmatic look she'd come to associate with infection. That purplish section in the middle of his back, though ...

"Elaborate. Tell me exactly what you smell, and be as specific as you can."

"Um—"

"I smmmell like burned pork chops." Oliver's voice was soft. Barely understandable. Darien and Sam exchanged a worried glance.

"Y-yes," Ellie said. "I agree with that assessment."

"Can you smell any hint of rot?" Darien asked. "You know, garbage, rotting meat—?"

"I don't think so," Ellie said.

"No," Oliver said at nearly the same time. "I knooow what rot smells like. I'm not rotting."

Darien sat back and pushed her hair out of her eyes. Her fingertips came away damp; despite the temperature, she'd broken out in a cold sweat. She threw the realization on her mental pile of things to ignore. "Okay, another good sign. Is he feverish, Ellie?"

Ellie placed a hand on Oliver's forehead. "No."

"Good. Thoughts, Sam?"

Sam blew out a breath. "I think your assessment's the best we've got, Dar. I feel like if he were infected, he'd be in a lot more pain. But I also don't have your expertise."

Darien fought the urge to close her eyes. *I don't actually have any expertise.*

As if he'd read her mind, Sam released her hand. A moment later, she felt his fingertips underneath her chin, bringing her eyes up to meet his.

"Trust yourself," he whispered. "Ignore the noise."

Darien gulped, then turned back to the camera, trying to muster her confidence. "I don't *think* you've got an infection, Oliver. You really need to keep an eye on that patch in the middle of his back, though. Of everything I've seen, that's what worries me the most."

Disgust spilled into Ellie's tone. "What *is* it?"

Darien threw up her hands. "A really nasty third-degree burn."

"Is it normal that it isn't healing as quickly as everything around it seems to be?" Ellie asked.

"I don't know, Ellie! I don't know!"

"But you *have* to know! There's no one else!"

"Ellie." Sam's voice was low and firm. "Darien's doing the best she can. We all are. Remember, we're a team."

Darien cast him a grateful glance.

"You're right, Sam," Ellie said. Now she just sounded exhausted. "I'm sorry, Darien. I'm ... I'm really freaked out."

"It's okay. Um ..." She grabbed the cold, rough arm of the bench as the feeding frenzy swelled again. Did that mean one had come closer? Was it actively feeding on them? She thought she could feel ... *something* different. One single presence that was more potent than the others—

"Given the Lady's involvement," Sam said, "I assume this is an electrical burn?"

Darien blinked up at Sam, pulled from her thoughts. Usually, she would ask him what he could see. But since he didn't seem overtly concerned, she decided now wasn't the time. *As long as no demons are actively attacking us, that is.*

"Yes," Ellie said.

"Is he burned anywhere else?" she managed to ask.

"On his chest."

"Show us."

The camera swooped away from Oliver's back. Darien saw flashes of Ellie's feet and the hem of an oversized gray hoodie as she dropped off the couch and knelt in front of him.

"Here," Ellie said. The camera zoomed shakily in on Oliver's chest. It, too, was burned, though the injury wasn't as livid or large as the one on his back, and there was no sign of that sickly purple-gray color anywhere. "Can you see that?"

"Yeah." Darien examined the burn for a moment. It looked scabbed and ugly, but in the way it was supposed to be. "This doesn't scare me nearly as much as his back does."

"It's shrunk, too." The relief in Ellie's voice was palpable. "This part's definitely healing, and fast."

Sam glanced around them, then lowered his voice. "What drugs are you on?"

"Oxycodone," Ellie said. "Fifteen milligrams."

"How did you find ...?" Sam shook his head. "Never mind. Question for later. How long ago did you take one?"

"Dunno," Oliver mumbled, and Darien thought his voice sounded stronger.

"I'd guess fifteen minutes," Ellie said.

Sam grunted. "So it's just starting to kick in. It usually takes a bit." He sat back, seeming to study Oliver's face. "I know you don't need me to tell you how addictive those drugs are—"

"Oh, I know," Oliver said. "Believe me, I know it."

Sam studied the screen, his face pensive, and for the first time, Darien wished she knew all the subtext here. Oliver's past and circumstances had never been her business—and probably still weren't—but not having all the information everyone else had was still difficult.

Finally, her husband nodded. "Okay."

"So ... what happened?" Darien asked, wrapping her arms around herself. She was starting to shiver—that cold sweat hadn't done her any favors.

"I'll find another ride while they tell us," Sam whispered to Darien, tapping his phone's screen. That done, he slipped his arm around Darien, and they listened as Ellie recounted the chilling story of the Lady's double-ambush.

"So Oliver stabbed her with the poker, but she grabbed it and used it to shock him, and it ... well ... it killed him."

Darien's jaw dropped. "*What*?"

"It *killed* him?" Sam yelped.

Oliver mumbled something, and both Darien and Sam leaned forward to hear. "It stopped my heart. Damaged my organs. 'S'what I was told, anyway."

Darien stared at him. "Told ... by who?"

"Dean. My dad."

Sam stiffened. Darien looked over at him; his eyes were wide and stunned, and their conversation of the night before—his existential crisis about no longer understanding the world they lived in—came flooding back to her. She ran her thumb across the back of his hand, and his grip tightened within hers. In her mind, something *loomed*. Suddenly, she could feel his confusion, his marrow-deep dread of a future he'd never feared before.

And she enjoyed it.

Darien rocked back, revolted at what had just happened in her mind. *You aren't those feelings,* she told herself; if they were going to keep coming, she *had* to stay above them. Deliberately avoiding the glowing little mote of peace and light that was her baby, she focused every particle of her mind on the conversation as Oliver spoke again.

"'S'okay. Dean told me ..." Oliver grimaced. "You tell 'em, El. My mouth's stupid."

"I got it. You relax." Ellie cleared her throat, then told them what Darien was sure was a condensed version of Oliver's experience. Darien's head spun; *Oliver had been to the afterlife!*

"So I patched him up using what we had in the cabin," Ellie said, "which was a lot, actually; it was surprisingly well-stocked."

"Obviously, if you found oxycodone in there," Sam muttered.

"Yeah. We slept for five or six hours. Then Wormwood showed up, but Oliver kicked him to the curb because he has no shame anymore. We left him standing in the cabin's living room in a rage because he couldn't follow us, and we haven't seen him since. And good riddance, too. It's been so much easier—"

Realization struck Darien. She bolted upright. "Was there a wood stove in the cabin? To the right of the door?"

"... Yes?" Ellie said.

"And behind it, was there a little alcove in the wall that had split wood stacked about three-quarters of the way up? It had a broom leaning against it?"

"I—yes, there was an alcove with wood. I don't remember a broom, though—"

"There was a broom," Oliver grunted.

Waves of shock rolled over Darien. She turned to see Sam staring at her. "How do you know all this?"

"Because I ..." Darien pressed a hand to her forehead; the cold sweat was coming back. "Because I saw it in my nightmare this morning."

Sam's jaw dropped. "Wait, are you saying you were in Worm—"

Headlights flashed across their bench, sliding over the concrete as a black sedan pulled into the pickup lane closest to them.

"I think that's our car," Sam said.

Guilt pricked at Darien. "We can get another. I'm not *that* cold—"

But Sam was already on his feet. "No. You're suffering enough without adding hypothermia. Let's—"

"Suffering?" Ellie's voice was alarmed. "Wait, why are you suffering? Did something happen—?"

"Yes," Sam said, casting a glance at their driver, who was clambering out. "But it's not something we can talk to you about in a car with a random stranger."

"I'll send you a text," Darien said. Their driver had popped the trunk and was looking at them, his posture expectant. "Go take care of yourselves. Oliver, wash that if you can. In the shower, preferably."

"And let us know when you get to Anchorage so you can pick us up," Sam added. "We'll need to coordinate—"

Ellie flipped the phone around. Darien gasped when she saw her friend's face; she was bruised and cut, and her eyes were so shadowed with exhaustion that they looked sunken. "You came to Anchorage? *Why would you do that?!*"

"Maybe it had something to do with all the demons and near-death experiences we've all had over the last few days," Sam said. He looked sick, and Darien suspected his shock at his sister's appearance had sharpened his tone. "And maybe it's because our consciences can't let you face this alone anymore."

"But you can't come! Darien—the baby—"

"The problem is everywhere," Darien said. "It's not like Colorado's going to be better."

"Yeah, but Alaska's ground *zero*—"

"Ellie," Sam said. "We're already here. You need us. We won't let you face this alone. That's what family does."

"Heez right," Oliver slurred.

A thin smile broke out across Darien's face. "Your man's smart. We're coming to help you whether you like it or not. If you don't pick us up, we'll just hitchhike to Seldovia."

Ellie sniffed. "Fine. We'll see you tomorrow." She sighed. "And thank you."

Chapter Four

Ellie woke before Oliver, which was such a rare occurrence that it scared her. She sat up, bending over him. He was on his side, his face half-nestled into the pillow, one arm extended as if to reach toward her even in his sleep. His torso from the waist up was free of blankets and sheets, his breathing slow, deep, and even.

Not a single speck of red marred his bandages.

Relief swept over Ellie, and with it, love. For a moment, she just looked at him, a half-smile on her lips. Then, she slipped out of bed and crept to the bathroom.

Fifteen minutes and a speed-shower later, Ellie was gathering her toiletries—still deep in thought about the texts she'd exchanged with Sam and Darien the night before—when a knock sounded on the bathroom door. Heart pounding, she opened it … and relaxed when she saw Oliver. He stood there in his sweatpants, one hand braced against the doorframe, the other holding a bundle of clothes, his bandages swathed around his lean torso in a way that was extremely visually appealing, despite the reason they were there. Ellie studied his face. Though he still looked worn, his glacier-blue eyes were clear, his complexion healthy instead of pallid.

"Good morning, sleeping beauty," she said.

A grin crossed his face. "Hey."

Ellie let herself gaze at him for a second. Then, she turned and reached for her bag. "I just finished packing. The bathroom's all yours."

"I'll be fast. Then we can change my bandages and go."

Ellie squeezed around him, smiling as he touched her cheek briefly, then piled what little she'd grabbed from the truck the night before into a heap on the couch. She had just snapped the clasp open on the medical kit when a low creak sounded behind her. She whirled, but once again, it was just Oliver coming through the door.

Relief hit Ellie then, strong enough to weaken her knees, and she frowned as she realized her hand had gone straight to the knife at her belt. Bemused, she let it fall. *Oh, if Ellie a month ago could see me now.*

Oliver dumped his lounging pants on the pile and came toward her. He was dressed in his usual work pants and nondescript tee—navy this time. Though his movements were still slower and less graceful than normal, they seemed to be regaining some fluidity. And his eyes ... those *eyes*. They were fixed on hers, with that singularly Oliver expression that made Ellie feel like the blood in her veins had turned into honey.

"You seem like you're feeling better," she said.

He settled onto the couch. "Mornings are the best, in my limited experience."

Ellie started to unwrap his bandages. "How's your pain?"

"It's there." He winced as the cloth stuck a little.

"It looks like that spot in the center of your back is still determined to be a problem." Ellie set her jaw, then pulled gently at the bandage. To her relief, it gave. She swallowed her disgust, even as Oliver sighed in relief.

"That went better than last night."

"And thank goodness," Ellie muttered. "Also, please tell me if you want more painkillers."

"I will." His expression tightened as the last of the bandages loosened and fell around his waist, his back arching a little. "I'd like to try and go without, though."

"Yeah, they suck pretty bad." Ellie wadded up the used bandages, tossed them onto the floor, then turned to survey the damage. The burns on Oliver's chest were crusted with normal-looking scabs, as if they'd been healing for days, maybe weeks. His back was still in rough shape, but there were no more open wounds, no more blood, no more ... oozing. The soft, flaky, purplish spot they'd all been worried about had faded to a dull red; it no longer seemed like a fleshy black hole trying to swallow all the healthy skin around it.

The breath went out of Ellie in a rush of relief. "It's so much better, Oliver."

"It *feels* better."

"I didn't say anything because I didn't want to get our hopes up," Ellie said, "but I thought you might have turned a corner last night, when I didn't even have to help you shower."

Mischief sparked in Oliver's eyes. "Is that disappointment I hear?"

A flush bloomed in her cheeks. "If there weren't all these demons flying around everywhere ..."

Oliver laughed as Ellie moved in front of him, then started to bandage him back up, her heart lighter than it had been in days. When she was finished, he took her hand, tracing his fingers over the back of it in a light caress. Ellie's breath caught as he met her eyes, his expression turning serious.

Slowly, he pulled her down to sit beside him. "When you kissed me for the first time, you said it was because you couldn't tell me how you felt with words."

"I remember."

Oliver leaned forward. Heat simmered deep in Ellie's chest; he was still holding her hand, his fingers lacing through hers as their bodies pressed them together, his other hand sliding up to cup her cheek. "Let me tell you that I'm so grateful for you, Ellie."

He kissed her, careful, soft, and lingering, and she sighed.

"Let me tell you," he whispered in her ear, "that I admire you."

He pressed his lips to the side of her neck, her cheek, her temple. Ellie swayed, feeling deliciously weak as he rested his forehead against hers.

"Last ..." His hands settled around her waist, guiding her into a careful, gentle embrace that was still somehow as seductive as anything he'd ever done. "Let me tell you that I love you."

This time, his kiss was deeper, with just a hint of the ferocity that had stolen all of Ellie's rationality the morning before.

"I love you," he whispered again.

Ellie kissed him one more time, savoring his strength, the softness of his lips, minty from his toothpaste. "I love you, Oliver."

They stayed there for a moment, wrapped in a cautious embrace, not caring about time or demons or pain or *anything*, really. Then, Oliver pulled back and brushed her still-damp hair out of her eyes. "We'd better go."

"Right." Letting out a deep, quiet breath, Ellie made herself stand. "When this is all over, Oliver, I vote we go have the rustic woodland cabin experience that we deserve."

A slow smile crossed Oliver's face as he snapped the medical kit shut.

"What?" Ellie asked.

"I just ... know a place." He met her eyes, his own twinkling. "When this is all over, I'll take you there. Deal?"

Ellie looked into his eyes, her heart soaring. "Deal."

***

Once again, Ellie was driving.

We should win some sort of prize for the world's most insane road trip, she thought as she navigated one of the highway's endless curves. On their right, a vast lake sprawled, its fathomless water rippling in the afternoon sun. To their left rose mountains, a silent, white-and-green legion of them, so tall their tops scraped the underbelly of the sky. Ellie glanced down at her phone, then sighed. They were almost to the border. *Then it's just nine-ish hours until Anchorage.*

"That was a big sigh."

Oliver's voice pulled her out of her thoughts. She gestured out the windshield. "This is just so beautiful. I wish I had *any* emotional capacity to enjoy it."

Oliver grunted. She glanced at him, trying to observe him as thoroughly as possible in the second she felt like she could spare from the bumpy, winding road. He was hunched against the center console, propped up on his elbow. Ellie turned forward, once again amazed at the number of positions he'd invented to keep his back from touching the seat behind him.

"Me, too," Oliver said. Then, "Do you feel like it's been too quiet?"

The dread that Ellie had been holding at bay since Wormwood's banishment—his death, if what Darien had seen in her dream was true—tingled to the forefront again. "Yes. I'm sure the demons are up to something. I just wish we knew what it was."

"Yeah." Oliver was quiet for a moment. "I don't miss having Wormwood in my head. But he gave us little clues sometimes that were helpful. I almost feel like I'm flying blind now. Never expected that."

"Are you nervous about the border?" Ellie asked.

He nodded. "It's the one place we *have* to stop. Unless Dean's whispering secrets in your ear again, I don't think we can avoid it."

"He's not." Ellie frowned. "Have you heard from him at all?"

"No."

Ellie opened her mouth to ask how he felt about that, but a glance at his face stopped her. She faced forward again, choosing her words deliberately. "Well, if the internet's right about the Border Agency having to let you back in since you can prove citizenship, then demons may not have time to attack us. Especially since there will be witnesses and cameras."

"Though that didn't stop Death last time." Oliver went quiet as a huge sign bearing the words *Welcome to Alaska* appeared through the trees. "I guess we'll know soon enough."

They rounded another bend, and a squat, utilitarian-looking building came into view. Ellie tapped the brakes and let the truck coast as she studied it. Nothing seemed out of place. Still ... she couldn't shake the dread building in her stomach.

Oliver braced one arm against the dashboard, his eyes bright and alert as he scanned the woods around the complex. His free hand curled around the hilt of his hunting knife, which he'd stuck, sheathed, in his cup holder when they'd left Whitehorse.

Ellie forced her gaze forward again. Her stomach felt like it was boiling; it was hard to focus when something could swoop out of the building at any second, hell-bent on killing them. For a wild moment, she considered running the barrier, but that was guaranteed to land them in jail, where they'd be easy targets. Especially since their truck was so distinctively battered.

Calm down, she told herself. *This will probably work.*

Ellie rolled down her window as the truck squeaked to a stop ... and stared. There should have been a stern-looking border patrol agent behind the sliding glass panel, asking for their identification. Instead, the window gaped halfway open, dark against the building's bone-white walls. Nothing stirred inside.

"What the ...?" Oliver muttered.

"This doesn't make sense." Ellie wriggled upward as far as the truck's ceiling would allow, trying to see into the building. "Is anyone there?"

Silence. A chill swept down Ellie's spine.

"I don't like this," Oliver muttered. "I feel like we're being ..."

"Watched?"

"Yeah." Oliver straightened, scanning the thick woods around them, his shoulders tense from what Ellie suspected was both pain and nerves. "I think we should go."

"I ..." Ellie glanced toward the half-open window again. "This doesn't feel right. But we also don't want to get chased down and detained if they're just on a bathroom break—"

Oliver bolted upright, pain apparently forgotten. "Ellie, drive! There's something in the woods!"

The hairs on the back of Ellie's neck stood straight up. She hit the gas, tires screeching as they tore away from the complex and back onto the highway. In the rearview mirror, a shadow loomed, big and dark. Yelping, Ellie stomped on the pedal and the truck shot forward, throwing them back in their seats. Oliver made a pained *oof* as his back hit the leather.

"I'm sorry!" Ellie's eyes flew to the rearview mirror. Something big and gray was slinking back into the trees. Maybe it was her imagination, but even the forest seemed to recoil from it.

"Are you okay?" she asked Oliver.

He groaned softly, pulling himself forward. "Yeah."

Ellie clenched her jaw. She'd have to take his word for it; it wasn't like they could stop. "Did you see what that was?"

"Not well. I thought it looked like a person, but with a deer skull for a head. And ..."

Ellie's heart sank. *And that's the tone of voice you use when you don't want to tell me something awful.* Unbidden, her eyes flicked back to the rearview mirror, but there was no chance of seeing the monster, not with how much distance they'd put between themselves and it.

Not that I want to see it again, anyway.

A slow shudder rolled the length of her spine as she caught sight of the complex again, thoughts too horrible for words gathering in her mind like storm clouds. "Do you think," she said, forcing her voice to be calm, "that there's any way to help the people in there?"

"No," Oliver said softly.

They swept around a corner, and the trees opened up to reveal more green-and-white mountains, dazzling in the afternoon sun. Light glinted off a little pond on the side of the road. It wasn't that much bigger than the one in the cave.

The one that was getting closer by the minute.

Ellie's lungs constricted.

"There was blood on its chest," Oliver said, so quietly that she almost didn't hear it.

Ellie fought the urge to close her eyes. *And that's why you* have *to go.*

An hour later, a state trooper whizzed by them. Then two more, lights blazing.

"Do you think they're heading for the border?" Ellie asked.

Oliver rested his forehead against the window. "I hope not. But probably."

***

It was full dark by the time they got to Anchorage hours later, and Ellie's eyes felt puffy and raw. Out of the corner of her vision, she'd seen Oliver's head dip a couple of times, then jerk back up, and she didn't like to think about how close she was to doing the same thing. According to her map, the journey from Boulder to Anchorage was over three thousand miles.

They had done it in five days.

She blinked against the bright streetlights—after driving through so much dark, wild country, they were almost overwhelming—and scanned the tall buildings around them for the Hilton that Sam and Darien were staying in.

"Is that it?" Oliver rasped.

But Ellie had already hit the brakes, her pulse quickening. It *was* the right hotel; her brother and sister-in-law were waiting just outside the atrium doors, hand in hand. Affection surged in her, along with guilt. They'd warned Sam about the beating his truck had taken, and he'd said he didn't care. But still ... *He loved this thing.*

Ellie pulled into the sweeping driveway, watching as Sam's head turned. His mouth opened, his face paling, and before she knew it, he and Darien were blurring as tears rose to her eyes, sharp and hot and unexpected.

Oliver's hand slid over her knee. "It's okay, Ellie. He understands."

They squeaked to a stop, and as soon as Ellie threw it into park, Sam was at her door, wrenching it open. He was ghostly pale, his eyes hollow, shadowed with something she couldn't define. Tears spilled onto her cheeks, and she ducked her head. "I'm so sorry, Sam—"

"Get out." His voice was hoarse.

"Sam ..." Oliver's voice was low with warning, but Ellie didn't hear anything else, because the second her feet hit the pavement, Sam swept her into a huge big-brother hug, and the dam inside finally burst.

"I'm so sorry, Sam," she sobbed. "I didn't mean to ... to destroy your truck ..."

"I don't care about the truck. I don't care." He pulled back, his eyes anguished as they swept over her face, lingering on her bruises, on the scab on the bridge of her nose, and the welt on her cheekbone. "Look at you." He crushed her against him again, his voice breaking. "*I'm* sorry. You shouldn't have had to go through this—any of this. I should've been here for you, and I ... instead, I ..."

A silent sob racked his huge frame. Ellie buried her face in his shoulder and let her own tears come. Just for this moment, when she was safe in the arms of her big brother, all the exhaustion and misery and terror of the last week could win. For just a second, she could be a little girl who was allowed to be scared of shadows, because Sam would always come and scare them away.

But you can't stay this way, said a little voice in the back of her brain.

She pulled back, wiping her eyes and nose. "We shoved you out the door, remember? You made the decision to protect your family, and we supported ... you ..."

Ellie frowned. She could tell Sam was trying to focus on her, but his eyes kept flicking behind her, as if he was looking at something.

Or several somethings.

Ellie turned back toward the truck, her exhaustion so strong she felt like she was wading through glue. "Let's get a room—"

"We have a three-bedroom suite," Darien said. She stepped up beside Ellie and put her arms around her, and Ellie leaned gratefully into the hug before letting her sister-in-law release her. "Give me the keys and I'll park the truck. You two just get inside and rest."

Fifteen minutes later, too exhausted to even think anymore, Ellie sank onto one of the hotel beds. For the first time in two days, she was clean, she was in actual pajamas, and she—ostensibly—could look forward to a full night of uninterrupted sleep.

The only thing she regretted as she drifted into the welcome darkness was that Oliver wasn't there beside her.

Chapter Five

"*W*endigo."

Wendigo stumbled at the sound of that Voice, one antler knocking against a white-barked tree with shimmering green-gold leaves. It was the second time he'd heard it. The first was a few hours ago, when it had instructed him to kill.

Which suited him. That was what he was going to do anyway.

He ghosted through the tree, then solidified again as he tried to remember the Voice's earlier instructions. There had been something specific, something he'd lost in the bloodlust. Something important, and he wanted to remember it before he spoke back—

He brushed against another tree and stopped. That sensation ... *the ability to* feel ... *The leaves were soft against his withered skin, and almost shimmered in the sunlight as he ran his arm across them.*

"Wendigo!"

He dug his claws into the tree's flesh and ripped, growling in satisfaction as the bark peeled away, leaving naked white wood behind. This creature—this tree—was much stronger than all the humans he'd killed. He could claw at this, rip and tear it, for much longer before its life ended. Stepping back, he examined it. Like humans, it didn't look as put together on the inside as it did on the outside. Unlike them, though, he couldn't eat it.

Or could he?

He snapped off a branch and started to gnaw.

"WENDIGO. DROP IT."

The branch fell from Wendigo's claws with a rattling crash. A growl built in his throat, and his head snapped up. "I killed."

He paused. His own voice was a wheeze, a death rattle, and a sense of wonder tingled through his bloodstained chest at its sound.

"You killed too much." The voice was quiet, but its edges had gone sharp. Sharp like the glass he'd broken through to get to the prey inside.

"I was hungry. I did what you asked."

"Imbecile."

Wendigo flinched again.

"You killed the wrong humans. And then you killed more of the wrong humans. Do you think they will not notice?"

Wendigo scraped his claws through the tree, shredding more lines into its white bark, marking it as his. "I am the hunter. They are the prey. I do not care if they notice. I will be the last thing they see."

"They caught you on camera."

Wendigo paused. "I do not understand."

"They captured your image! You, killing and tearing up four people inside their Border Protection building! And if they find the bodies you left behind at that outpost—"

"They won't find them."

"You butchered twelve men with your claws. Their wounds will be distinctive."

"There are other creatures with claws who live here."

"It doesn't matter! They have you on camera! Humans are masters of justification, yes, but even they can only make excuses for so long. Sooner or later—and sooner, if you cannot control yourself—they will trust the evidence of their own eyes." The Voice paused. "There are already pockets of the world where they are starting to correctly suspect our presence. If this becomes one of them, then we are in severe danger."

Wendigo scoffed. "Of what?"

The Voice's anger surged. For the third time, Wendigo staggered, his claws disengaging from the tree to clutch at his skull.

"You've only just Awakened. You have no memory of the world we came from; you were nothing but a writhing, insensate shadow. But me? I am Death. I awoke in our world, while the first death rattle was still hissing into the void. And I lived there, in the cold and dark, for millennia before coming to this world, and then I was forced back! You think you know hunger? You think you know deprivation? You know NOTHING! You are INFANTILE!"

A whine shrilled from Wendigo's nasal cavity, or was it from Darien's chest? She rolled, fighting to get free of the cocoon engulfing her, and smacked into something hard, *and*

Wendigo disentangled himself from the bone-hard branches that he'd fallen into and got to his hooves.

"Wendigo." The Voice was silky now. Predatory. "You are heading toward Anchorage, a city that has hundreds of thousands of people in it; more than you've ever seen in your short time Awakened. Can you, or can you not, control yourself?"

That many people ... Hunger rippled in his belly, hunger and nausea because of course Darien hadn't eaten since dinner last night, and now it raked the inside of her stomach with an agony she'd never have thought possible before pregnancy—

"Wendigo."

"Darien!"

"This is your last chance to answer before I remove you as a liability."

"Darien." Warm, human hands closed around her arms.

"I ..." Wendigo's reedy voice trembled. He hadn't known it could do that until this moment.

"Sam ..."

"That's it. Wake up, Dar."

"I'll—

"—doing my best," Darien mumbled. She blinked; dim light leaked around the curtains, illuminating Sam's strained expression.

"Another nightmare?" he asked.

"Yeah." Darien collapsed back onto the pillow. They'd slept for seven hours, but she didn't feel like it. "It was just like the one where I saw Wormwood die. It was so vivid, like I was experiencing what the demon was. I felt and saw everything, heard its thoughts, saw its ..." Her nausea reared, and she swallowed. "... its memories."

"Was it Wormwood? Is he still alive?"

"No." She pressed her fists to her eyes. "This one was a wendigo—a humanoid with a deer skull for a head that—"

"Yeah, I've heard of wendigos," Sam said.

"Well, apparently this one's killing people left, right, and center." Darien sat, tossing the covers off. "Including all the agents at the Canada-Alaska border, just like we suspected."

Sam winced. "Poor guys."

"Worse, it's coming toward Anchorage. So we better wake up—"

Something pounded on the door, followed by Oliver's muffled voice. "We're coming through the door in five seconds! Five, four—"

Sam shot off the bed and turned on the light. Darien followed, chagrined. "Was I that loud?"

"You were pretty loud, yeah."

He swung the door open, and Darien's jaw dropped. Ellie and Oliver stood in the doorway, the latter's torso still swathed in bandages. Light flashed off the blade of a huge hunting knife in his fist, and Ellie gripped an arrow tipped with a razor-sharp broadhead, her face set in a hard, intense expression that Darien had never seen before. In fact, it was so unlike the Ellie Darien knew that she took a step back.

"Are you guys all right?" Oliver asked.

"Yeah, we're good. Darien had another nightmare." Sam looked them both up and down. "You two've turned into barbarians. Wanna put those away before you accidentally skewer someone?"

For a moment, they both stared at Sam. Then, Ellie lowered her arrow—*and*, Darien realized, the lighter she'd gripped in her other hand. She tucked it into the waistband of her pajama pants. "If you'd been through what we have in the last week, you'd be barbarous, too."

Oliver sheathed his knife. "Can't be too careful. Sorry we scared you."

"It's fine." Sam paused, his shoulders tense, and Darien wondered if he was thinking the same thing she was: that they'd had their fair share of mayhem in the last week, too. But he just turned toward their suitcase. "Let's get on the road. Darien says we have a wendigo after us now."

Oliver frowned. "What's a wendigo?"

"It's the thing that came after you yesterday."

Horror kindled behind Oliver's eyes. He turned. "We've gotta go—"

"Wait!" Darien marched toward him. "We have to change your bandages. If you're actually in as good of shape as you're acting, I can do it in a couple of minutes. We should have time."

Unless we don't. A surge of fear rose within Darien, followed by ... a *gleeful* feeling of satiation. The shock of the contrast made her stagger. She steadied herself, then looked up to find Sam and Oliver staring at her.

"Uh, you okay?" Sam asked.

Resisting the urge to snatch for the baby's calm, Darien imagined shutting both her fear and the demon-feelings in a box and shoving it to the darkest corner of her mind. "I'm good. Oliver, get over here and sit down. The rest of you, get dressed."

"Got it." Sam headed for the bathroom, closing the door behind him. Ellie turned on her heel and marched down the hall.

Oliver settled on the edge of the bed, his back ramrod-straight. "You're sure you're fine?"

"Yes. It's not fun to feel what demons are feeling, but I'm getting more used to it. I'll live. Raise your arms."

Oliver did. "You will live. You're tough."

"Knowing you, you'll probably find a way to weaponize it," Sam called through the door.

Despite her tension—and the sadistic buzz in her mind, and starvation-nausea still gnawing at her belly—Darien smiled as she started to unwrap the bandage. She wound it around and around Oliver's torso with the ease and speed of long practice, careful not to brush the circular scar on his shoulder, though that looked like it had been there for ages.

Still, she thought, *scars can be sensitive.* Especially burn scars, which—she grimaced—was what *that* looked like it was.

Not that it's any of your business. You're already dealing with enough.

"The worst part of being a demon radar," she muttered, "is feeling like I'm being watched all the time. It reminds me of how I felt a few days ago, when Ankle Tickler was hiding in our hotel, but we didn't know about him yet."

Ellie's voice drifted through the open door to the hall. "He better not have followed you. Because I could *not* handle him."

"There's no way he could've," Sam called. "Besides, Darien would know if he had. Wouldn't you?"

"Probably. His mind was ... distinctive." The last of the bandages fell away, and Darien examined Oliver's back.

"How's it look?" he asked.

"Good. Really good." Darien sat back, marveling. The wounds still looked raw, crusted, and scabbed, and the center of his back seemed blistered and uncomfortable. But if she had seen Oliver's injuries on any other living thing, she'd have assumed they had been healing for weeks. "I'll be interested to see if it scars or not. Normally, burns like this would cause lasting damage, but since it's healing *literally* supernaturally ...."

Oliver chuckled. "If it does, I'll add it to my collection of burn scars I'm weirdly proud of."

"Please stop collecting those," Ellie said.

"I second that." Darien bustled around Oliver and scrutinized the burns on his chest. The scabs on its edges were already starting to flake and fall off, revealing new, healthy skin underneath. She stood. "Looks great, Oliver. Ellie, can you bring me the first aid kit when you have a second?"

"I can bring it to you right now," Ellie said. "Hang on—"

The bathroom door creaked, and Sam stepped out, dressed in jeans and a loose linen tee shirt.

"You're going to be cold," Oliver said.

"I packed for Hawaii, not Alaska." Sam chucked his pajamas and toiletries into their suitcase, then came toward them. "I bet Ellie and I can handle the rest. You go take care of yourself."

"Thanks." Darien kissed Sam on the cheek and headed for the suitcase, dodging around Ellie as her sister-in-law walked through the doorway carrying the massive first aid kit.

"Not to brag or anything," she said, "but I'm pretty good at this nursing stuff now."

Darien snorted. "You're an inspiration." She straightened with the warmest armload of clothes she could find: skinny jeans she barely fit into and an old tee bearing the name of her varsity volleyball team. Then she stepped into the bathroom and closed the door, grimacing as she caught sight of herself in the mirror.

She really *did* look like she felt.

Pulling tendrils of hair out of her eyes, she tugged it into a thick, messy bun and knotted two hair ties around it, trying to ignore the burbling in her stomach. At least the ever-present roar of the feeding demons was lessening. Or maybe she was just getting used to it.

Either way, I'll take it, she thought, resting her forehead briefly against the wall. She still couldn't shake the sense that something was watching her. *Calm down. That's probably just part of your new ...* Her lip curled. *... superpower.*

She pulled on her shirt and wriggled into her jeans and had just picked up her toothbrush when the pain struck. It sliced her from temple to temple as *Wendigo screamed into the iron-gray sky.*

"But you're killing humans, too!" he wailed.

He bowed forward as Death ripped him, tore his mind apart from the inside just like he, Wendigo, had torn the campers, and it wasn't fair; he was just doing what he was made *to* do—

The red blood on the snow was rushing up toward him, and Darien lay trembling on the cold bathroom tile while Sam banged on the door, shouting her name as her mind fragmented again—

Power.

So much power.

Death opened his eyes as it ebbed, grabbing the wooden sign next to him to steady himself. It was warm and rough against his fingers. His head brushed the sign's bottom edge as he backed away, and he couldn't help but smile when he caught a glimpse of what the words said.

YOU ARE IN BEAR COUNTRY! Grizzly and black bears are part of nature, and you may encounter them at any point during your visit to Eskers Provincial Park—

Meaningless. Bears were like caviar: rare and interesting, an experience, even. But still only an appetizer compared to a person.

Death turned northwest, toward Portlock and the sprawling wilderness between him and it. They were a gift, these mountains, these woods and glaciers. They were killers, just like him. Only, they were expected. Predictable. Unavoidable, even. Under their protection, he could feast on whomever he encountered. And there was always someone, *some fool drawn by the promise of solitude, and peace, and beauty, and other ephemeral, unimportant things that people valued. When—if—the corpses were ever discovered, the cruelty of the wild and the softness of the human body would always be the most reasonable explanation.*

And despite all their brilliance, most humans never looked deeper than that.

"And that, Wendigo, is the difference between you and me," he whispered.

The bathroom door burst open, narrowly missing Darien's nose, and Sam dropped to the floor beside her. Groaning, she forced her gaze upward to see him staring wildly around, his eyes lingering on two different points near the shower. "What happened? Were you attacked?"

"No," she gasped. "No, no, it was another …" *Vision? Am I having visions?* She squeezed her eyes shut against the lingering pain under her scalp. "The wendigo's dead. Just like with Wormwood; same killer, same way."

"We're clear, Ellie!" Oliver's voice rang from the doorway. "She wasn't attacked."

"Oh, good." Ellie's voice was also close, as if she were right behind him.

Oliver spoke again, and Darien could swear she heard a note of pride in his voice. "You might want to put that arrow out before you burn down another hotel."

Ellie huffed. "The Lady burnt that hotel down. I'm not culpable."

"You two are freaking *nuts*," Sam muttered.

Darien reached for her husband. "Help me up."

He grasped her hand and pulled, but no sooner was she on her feet than her nausea finally won. She barely processed the sight of Oliver filling the doorway, fully dressed with his giant knife in hand, before stumbling to the toilet and retching. In an instant, Sam was beside her, pressing his big, cool hand to the back of her neck. "Damn. I should've thought about food, I'm so sorry."

She heaved again, and again, then slumped back against him as her empty stomach slithered back down to where it was supposed to be. "It's okay."

"You guys can come back now," Sam said.

Oliver and Ellie both poked their heads around the doorway, and Darien felt a flash of gratitude that they'd let her puke in private. *Good friends,* she thought tiredly, even as the demon-roar in her head intensified again. *At least I have good friends.*

She stood on shaky legs, bracing herself against the countertop. "The wendigo's dead, but Death is heading for Portlock."

The blood drained from Ellie's face. "Death … as in the one who nearly killed us in Montana?"

"I think so. I've never actually seen him because these … *visions* are through the eyes of the demon whose head I'm in." She swallowed, trying in vain to get the sour taste of acid out of her mouth. "But he thinks of himself as Death, and he's the same one who killed Wormwood, and it was pretty clear they'd been communicating back and forth for a while, so it would make sense they're the same demon."

Sam shifted, a deep frown on his face. "Whatever he is, he's powerful and terrifying, and we don't want him to get to the gate before we do, so I vote we move. Like, now."

Darien nodded, already reaching for her toiletries and bag. "Agreed. And whoever's done packing first needs to look up Eskers Provincial Park."

Sam stopped. "Eskers Provincial ... Why?"

"Because that's where Death is."

Chapter Six

Sam stepped into the cool, damp air outside the hotel and took a deep breath. Rain drizzled from the sky, much more gently than the summer storms that rocketed down the Front Range on Colorado's warm afternoons. But he knew from experience how deceptive the gentleness of this rain was. It was Alaska's first test of a person; an attempt to see how difficult it would be to rob them of their first—and last—line of defense. Their warmth.

Still better than staying in the lobby and watching more of the news.

Together, he and Darien started across the hotel's driveway toward his pathetic-looking truck. He winced as the first drops hit him and glanced at his wife. Curls of moisture condensed on her skin, trickling down her arms and the back of her neck, and she was already shivering. As he watched, an amorphous figure consolidated out of the mist next to her, keeping pace with them as they walked. He fixed his eyes on the shaggy green mountains, determined to give it nothing, not even his horror at what they'd seen on the big screen while cramming breakfast down their throats. *The last thing we need is a repeat of—*

But no. He shouldn't let himself think of the Sphere, either.

"They're c-cute." Darien nodded toward the truck.

Sam followed her gaze. Ellie's and Oliver's outlines were silhouetted against the glass, holding each other in a careful embrace. As he watched, Oliver leaned in and kissed her. Something in Sam's heart softened, and he almost smiled. "If only we didn't have to interrupt."

"If only *none* of us had been interrupted," Darien sighed.

Sam looked at his wife, wet, miserable, and shivering in the cold Alaskan rain. She was as dejected as he'd ever seen her, and his heart squeezed. *If I'd have done something sooner, believed Ellie sooner ...*

"Hey, I love you," he said. "I'm sorry I ..."

Her eyebrows raised. "Sorry for what? None of this is your fault."

"Yeah, I just ..." *I'm sorry I'm so useless against these things. That I can't protect you.* The thoughts speared through him; he swallowed and looked away so she couldn't see the wetness in his eyes.

And came face-to-face with a shimmering, misty *maw*, inches from the tip of his nose.

Shaken, Sam snapped his eyes back to the truck. "Anyway, we'll get through this."

He opened the back door, shot a token smile at Ellie and Oliver, and wrestled the suitcase into the tiny amount of space that wasn't already taken up by luggage and weapons. The physical exertion felt good; by the time he landed in the driver's seat and stuffed the key in the ignition, he felt almost ready to grapple with the questions Darien's latest vision had brought up.

"They've broken the story of what the wendigo did to the border patrol agents," he said as he tugged the seatbelt across his chest.

"What are they saying?" Oliver asked.

"They're seeking information about a masked murder suspect who massacred four border patrol agents and twelve workers at a nearby natural gas well."

"*Twelve?*" Ellie choked.

"I know." Darien shook her head. "It's awful. It's so awful."

"They showed camera stills, too," Sam said. "Not of the murders, obviously, but of the wendigo inside the customs building. They're a little fuzzy, but it's still pretty clear what the creature is. Especially if you *know* what it is."

"*How,*" Ellie said, "are they managing to explain away a *very clearly* supernatural creature just ... showing up and killing a bunch of people?"

"Domestic terrorism, basically," Darien said. "An extremist dressing up in an elaborate wendigo costume to send a message. We watched as much of the story as we could while we were grabbing food, and they never mentioned the possibility of it being an actual supernatural being."

"They can't," Oliver said. "Nobody in their right mind would jump straight to that conclusion. Too few people have seen what we have."

"Still." Sam turned too sharply, causing the truck to bounce as the back right tire fell off a curb. "That thing was scary as hell."

For a moment, there was silence. Sam glanced in the rearview mirror and felt a dull pang in his stomach at the sight of Ellie's expression. "I'm glad you didn't try to stay and fight it," he said.

Ellie just kneaded her forehead, wincing when her fingers brushed the scab on her nose.

"Sam, the light's red," Darien said sharply.

He hit the brakes, forcing his gaze back to the road ... and found that it wasn't much better. This seemed like a very commercial part of town; they'd stopped at a wide intersection between a strip mall and a line of hotels. Sam's eyes darted everywhere—between traffic and across parking lots and over shopfronts, but it was no use. There were dozens of demons, maybe hundreds, invisible to everyone but him. They trailed slow-moving cars, drifted behind pedestrians, revolved in entryways.

He didn't see a single person who was free of them.

He forced his voice to be calm. "Guys. I need someone to find me the nearest shop that sells warm clothes so we can get out of this town as fast as we can."

***

Twenty minutes later, Sam pulled a brand-new, fleece-lined Anchorage hoodie over his head and settled back into the truck's heated seat, feeling warm for the first time since leaving Hawaii.

"Good choice," Ellie said as they pulled out of the parking lot. "You might as well be comfortable on our demon-slaying suicide mission. That's Oliver and I's philosophy, anyway."

Sam chuckled with the rest of them, even as he marveled again at the change in his sister. She'd always been tough, but it had been the stoic, reserved sort of tough. This new thing she was starting to do, fighting back with humor ... he liked it.

The outskirts of Anchorage fell away as Sam drove, and before long, they were speeding through the vast, shaggy wilderness, dotted here and there with little outposts of civilization. A shimmering inlet stretched to their right, and Darien sat with her nose practically pressed to the window, seeming reluctant to break away from such raw and unfettered beauty even to engage in conversation. For a moment, Sam was transported back a month, when his father had been just as full of childlike wonder as Darien was now, and Sam had ached for *Darien* to be there.

Now she was. And his father was dead.

And you're in charge of keeping everyone on the road, so focus.

"Helen and Henry will meet us at the harbor at two," Oliver said.

"Perfect," Sam replied, hoping his voice wasn't too wooden.

"And then we'll need to start planning," Darien said, surfacing. "Oliver, how many people do you think will come with us to Portlock?"

"I don't know." He was silent for a minute. "We'll have three for sure, maybe four or five if Luke and Charlie know and want in."

"And those are your crewmates?" Ellie asked. "I'm just trying to keep everyone straight."

"The two who are legally adults, yeah. I don't think Bill would let the kids go, not in a million years. Even though they're more competent than many adults I've met."

Sam frowned, thinking of his and Darien's conversation with the Night Marchers. "So that'll make six of us at worst, and nine at best. Will that be enough?"

"The Night Marchers said that only a few attacked the gate itself when they were fighting the demons," Darien said slowly, "so I bet ... wait a second, those numbers should be 'seven' and 'ten.' Did you think I wouldn't notice?"

Sam could have smacked himself. "Darien, please. I can't let you—"

"You *absolutely* can. Even if we just stick me on a boat and I motor along the shoreline to try and draw demons away with all the fear I know I'll have."

Sam shot a pained look at his wife. She glared back, and he looked away. "Look, we can talk about this later. The point of this conversation is: we have to get to Portlock before Death does, even if that means we go with fewer people."

There was a silence that Ellie broke, her voice sounding tentative. "Darien, do you know if he's come any closer than Eskers Provincial Park?

Darien shook her head. "I'm not *that* sensitive, unfortunately."

"Or maybe fortunately," Sam murmured.

Darien half-shrugged. "Yeah. But it would be nice to have a little more control, maybe even figure out how to use the fact that I'm now a demon radar to our advantage." She shook her head. "It's just so overwhelming. I have no idea how to start, even though it seems like I'm getting more sensitive by the hour."

Sam didn't know what to say to that, and judging by the silence in the truck, he wasn't the only one.

"The good news is, British Columbia's still pretty far away," he finally said.

"True," said Darien, "but he's coming as the crow flies. He doesn't have to follow roads, which will save him a lot of time."

"But he will have to …" Sam shifted uncomfortably, "… you know, stop and eat."

"Yes." Darien rubbed her eyes. "He will still need to do that."

Sam frowned as a quiet, terrifying thought grew in the back of his mind. If Darien was getting more and more sensitive to the demons' power *period*, and Death—ostensibly among the most powerful—was getting closer every minute, how long would it take for her to experience not only the monster's most extreme actions, but *every killing he committed?*

Darien turned to look back at Ellie and Oliver. "How fast was Death when you two ran into him? You're the ones who have seen him in action. I've only ever seen him in my head."

"He was fast," Ellie said. "I wasn't exactly in a place where I could read a speedometer, but—"

"'Fast' here still means … probably forty miles an hour at most," Oliver said. "We don't know if he can sustain that over long distances or not."

A rustling sound came from the back seat, followed by Ellie's voice. "I'm going to do some math."

Sam snorted. "I guess the world really is ending."

"Amazing how motivating that is," she said.

Sam glanced in the rearview mirror, his heart lightening, but his grin slid off his face as he saw … What *was* that?

He slammed on the brakes. Dimly, he registered Oliver's and Ellie's heads jerking up, but he was too focused on the thing scrabbling around in the half-sliced-off truck bed to care. He caught a glimpse of a low-slung body and ragged, dark fur before its momentum carried it forward and out of sight.

"Sam, what the—?" Darien yelped.

"What do you see?" Oliver twisted to peer behind them, ferocity and pain mingling on his face. Ellie said nothing, just gripped the hilt of her knife.

"I don't know," Sam said. "It was in the back of the truck. It looked hairy, like some kind of animal."

"Could've been a marmot," Oliver said.

But we would've heard an animal hitting the front of the truck bed, Sam thought. Unless ... it had just slid off the truck's slashed-off side and onto the road. He hit the cruise control, trying to relax as the truck accelerated back to its normal speed.

"If we're not being attacked right this minute," Ellie said tentatively, "I have a math estimate."

"Let's hear it," Darien said.

"Okay. But remember, an estimate is all it is. Darien, if you get, uh, *updates*, let me know so we can revise this. But based on where we think Death is, we have about ... five days to close the gate before he gets there, including today. *If* he can keep a steady forty-mile-an-hour pace."

Darien turned. "How'd you calculate distance?"

Ellie held up her phone. "Flight time estimates. It's not exact, but it's the best we've got."

Sam frowned. "This may not matter, and it's a terrible thought, but do any of us know how long it takes Death to feed?"

Darien pressed her hands to her temples. "Hang on. He killed a lot of people right before murdering Wormwood, and he did it really quickly. So he can kill fast." Her frown deepened. "He doesn't seem to want to *eat* fast, though. There's a difference."

Sam suppressed a shudder.

"But if he's coming as the crow flies," Oliver said, "he'll probably have to detour to find people to eat."

"His current game plan is just to kill every person he finds out there. Every hiker, camper, mountaineer, hunter—"

"He'll still starve," Oliver said. "There are places between the Canadian border and Anchorage that have never seen a human footprint. And based on what I know of the Canadian Rockies, they're the same way."

Sam looked over to see Darien chewing her lip.

"When I was in his head earlier today," she said, "he thought about how bears were a delicacy, but weren't as satisfying or enjoyable as people. To me, that implies that he can feed on animals."

"That does seem to be the implication," Ellie said, disgust in her voice.

"But it'll take him time to hunt and kill animals, too," Sam pointed out. "Even with his supernatural abilities. Either way, he won't be able to fly—or ride, or whatever—at top speed the whole time."

"True," Ellie said, "but how much wiggle room do we really dare to plan for?"

"With what he can do," Darien said, "I suggest not much."

Silence settled over the truck, and Sam ticked the cruise control up a few notches. Then, he reached over the center console and laid his hand on Darien's thigh. She looked up at him, her huge brown eyes full of worry.

"All three of your visions have centered around Death at this point, right?" he asked.

Darien nodded.

"Why do you think that is?"

She brushed her fingertips across the back of his hand, frowning. "There are some patterns I've been able to pick out so far. The first is that two visions have come while I was sleeping, maybe because my brain's at rest and my defenses are down."

"That ... maybe makes sense?" Sam met Oliver's eyes in the rearview mirror, and his friend shrugged in a way that seemed to say "anything's possible at this point."

"They've also come right before Death kills another demon," Darien continued. "First it was Wormwood, then the wendigo."

"But you saw both of those events through the other demons' eyes first," Sam pointed out. "Not Death's."

"True, but after the wendigo died, I jumped straight into Death's mind. He's always been the common denominator. I wonder if ..."

Darien released his hand, and he returned it to the wheel as the highway snaked around a series of corners. Sam just let her think, grateful when Ellie and Oliver did the same.

"I'm wondering if the visions work a little like a lightning storm," Darien finally said. "Death goes on a killing spree and builds up a lot of power. Then, he uses it to contact a demon who's physically closer to me, and it's a little like a lightning strike that my newly fine-tuned senses can pick up on."

Sam thought about that for a moment. "Whatever ... energy expenditure? ... happens jerks you inside the affected demon's head, where you get to piggyback off the proverbial lightning bolt and listen in on their conversation."

Darien's voice went low. "And experience what they're experiencing."

"That makes sense for the wendigo," Oliver said, "but why did you see Wormwood die? He was thousands of miles away."

Darien sat back; Sam could practically see the gears turning in her head. She whispered something, so quiet he could barely hear it over the hum of the truck's tires. Something that sounded like "Witness this."

"What?" he asked.

"Before Death killed Wormwood, he murdered a whole bunch of people. Like, most of a small, rural town from the sounds of it."

Sam's mouth fell open. "Why didn't we see *that* in the news?"

"Because we haven't been *watching* the news," Ellie said.

"And even if we were, it seems like there's so much bad news it can't even all be reported," Darien muttered.

A pang went through Sam at the state of the world. He swallowed. *So do something about it.*

"So, Darien," he said, "you saw Death murdering people during that first vision you had."

"No. I saw it through Wormwood's eyes. Or his mind, rather. But even *he* felt it; with every death, there was a palpable spike of energy. And right before Death killed Wormwood ... it seemed like he made a kind of mental broadcast. He said, 'Witness what happens to those who disobey me,' or something like that."

"And then he killed him," Oliver said.

Darien turned to look at him. "You'd beaten Wormwood long before he actually left, Oliver. You should know that. The only thing keeping him there was how afraid he was of Death."

Something like satisfaction spread across Oliver's face. "Huh."

When his taciturn friend didn't say anything else, Sam decided to voice his theory. "It sounds like he was making an example out of Wormwood. In case any other demon was getting ideas about who's in charge. And maybe that was the first time that level of energy has happened." He nodded toward Darien. "So there was enough to hijack your dreams even though we were in Hawaii."

Darien nodded. "Ankle Tickler would have seen it, too." She burrowed down in her new zip-up parka. "Wormwood thought at the time that killing all those people was wasteful. Grotesque. He didn't seem to think that Death could hurt him over such a long distance. Like I said, he thought he could get out from under Death's thumb. He never saw it coming."

"Why did the wendigo risk it, then?" Ellie asked.

Darien shrugged. "The wendigo was practically a newborn. It didn't have any idea how the world worked."

"A wildly dangerous, murderous newborn with zero self-control," Sam muttered.

"Which is why Death killed it." Darien turned to look at him. "It didn't last fifteen minutes between Death chewing it out and slaughtering a bunch of hikers. It would've blown their cover. It almost did."

"Are there others as powerful as Death out there?" Oliver asked.

"Not that I've felt," Darien said, "but that doesn't mean there aren't. The demons are all over the world; there could be a comparable one in Australia or Kenya or Germany or somewhere that's just too far out of reach." She paused. "But it seems like my sensitivity is growing. In a few days, who knows what I'll be seeing?"

Sam hesitated, remembering something she'd said earlier. "So ... *do* you think there's a world in which you could ... I don't know, channel your visions? Control them?"

Darien blew out a long breath. "I don't know, Sam. I'm going to try and figure something out, though." Her voice went quieter. "If I'm going to suffer, I might as well do it for a reason."

"Do you know if any of them have ever noticed you hopping into their minds?" Ellie asked.

"I don't think so. They seemed to just keep going about their lives." Darien frowned. "Except Ankle Tickler. He knew I could feel his thoughts and emotions."

"He was also right next to you while you were figuring it all out," Sam said. "He heard everything you said."

For a moment, they were quiet again.

"What's it like, Darien?" Ellie asked softly. No one had to ask what she was talking about.

"Confusing," Darien said. "Exhausting. Sam can corroborate this, but the juvenile demons drift around, coming and going at random. What that translates to for me, though, is just a constant buzz in my head. Not of words—the ones that aren't fully formed never use words. But when it comes to their emotions, they're junior versions of the ... big ones? Formed, adult—?"

"Realized?" Sam suggested.

"Sure. Let's go with that," Darien said. "And once they're realized, once they take a concrete form, like the Sphere, or the wendigo, their thoughts become more ordered. More human. Ankle Tickler was sort of the exception to that, but even his mind was ordered. Just differently than I've ever experienced."

"Interesting," Oliver murmured.

Silence settled over the truck again. No one broke it for a long time.

Chapter Seven

Oliver clutched the ferry's railing and gazed out over Seldovia's harbor as they drifted toward it, relishing the crisp scent of the ocean. It was a warm day for late August—he'd guess in the mid sixties—but the metal was pleasantly cool against his palm. He savored that, too. Like he savored almost everything now that Wormwood was gone. It was as if he'd been granted a new pair of eyes that saw beauty everywhere, found joy even in the mundane.

And Seldovia Bay is far from mundane, he thought as he squinted at two bobbing shapes near the shoreline that might have been sea otters. Sure now, he grinned and turned to Ellie, ready to point the otters out, but the words stuck in his throat when he saw her face. Her stance was strong enough, her back straight, her arms folded as she leaned against the railing. She was beautiful in her light pink jacket, her hair tied back in a long, sleek ponytail, exposing the clear skin of her face and neck. The bruises there had faded to a light yellow—barely noticeable.

But while everyone else on board was looking at the ferry terminal, Ellie's eyes were fixed on the snow-capped mountains in the distance. They looked cornered. Haunted. Oliver's heart squeezed. The fact that she had to come up here again was unfairness of the highest order. In that moment, he would've shouldered her whole burden and carried it for her if he could.

But that's not how it works, he thought. The best he could do was try and lighten her load. He took her hand. "There are two otters over there, between the mainland and that little island."

She blinked, then looked where he was pointing, and ... a smile twitched at the corners of her mouth. "They're so cute."

"They're all over this place, if you know where to look. There's ..." His grin widened. "There's actually a trail near town, very beautiful. Scenic. We call it the 'Otterbahn.'"

Ellie laughed out loud, the sound dazzling. She leaned her head against his shoulder. "I just want to watch them. And waste a bunch of time with you, and not worry about anything."

He slipped his arm around her waist and looked back out at the otters. One dove, its sleek form disappearing under the waves. The other lazed on its back, nibbling at something clutched in its paws, looking as happy as any animal had a right to be.

Can they feel it? he wondered. *The darkness?*

The other otter surfaced then circled its companion, a lithe shadow cutting through the light sparkling on the water's surface. Whether or not the last month had affected them, they certainly seemed happy for the moment. He braced his elbows against the railing. "Add it to the pile of things we're fighting for, Ellie."

From his other side, Sam spoke. "I feel an intense sense of deja vu. And I don't like it."

"Sam ..." Ellie's voice was low as she gestured toward the dock. "Do you think there are more demons out there than there should be?"

Sam shaded his eyes. "Um—"

"I just wondered," she interrupted again, "since this is one of the nearest towns to the ... the gate, it would make sense—"

"That there'd be more of them here, yeah." Sam dropped his hand. "I can see several. More than is probably proportional."

He met Oliver's eyes and gave a shrug that clearly said *I can't not tell her the truth.* Oliver returned it, wishing he'd been that smart a few weeks ago.

The shadows of a few cottony clouds flitted over moored boats, wooden walkways, and most noticeably, the crowd of people gathered on the dock as they approached. Oliver's heart leaped as he saw Helen and Henry standing on the sea-weathered wood, waiting for them. He smiled and raised his hand in a wave, which Helen and Henry returned.

"That's them," Sam said to Darien.

Darien smiled. "I figured."

Ellie waved, too. "They look so much better than I thought they would."

Oliver nodded, his heart full of admiration and sorrow as he looked down at them. Henry stood straight-backed, dressed in his usual flannel and work pants. Helen had her arms folded, her thick, gray braid spilling down one shoulder, a tired-looking smile on her face.

"They're tough," he murmured.

Minutes later, they were hauling their strange assortment of stuff down the gangplank. Oliver felt a surge of local pride that four young adults carrying three suitcases, a compound bow, a quiver bristling with arrows, an axe, a hatchet, and a bag full of flammable camping goods didn't even merit a second glance from most of the people who lived and worked here.

"Oliver!"

He looked up to see Helen pounding toward him. A jolt of pure joy hit him, followed immediately by fear for his life as he realized how fast she was moving. "Wait, careful!"

Helen slowed so fast she skidded. "Right, burns, sorry." She flung her arms open. "Come here."

Then her arms were around him—gingerly, but that didn't matter—and Henry was there, hugging them both. Oliver's suitcase thudded to the planks behind him, and he threw his arms around them, heedless of his injuries as the three of them merged into one awkward, emotional family huddle. He could hear Helen weeping, and tears stung his own eyes. But this time, they were tears of relief and gratitude. After weeks of intense misery, Helen and Henry still had it in them to love.

Oliver detached himself, and the Calls turned to the Forths, Helen still wiping tears from her eyes. Oliver took the opportunity to study them more closely—particularly Henry. He looked drawn, and though he smiled, he seemed more reserved than usual, keeping his hands in his pockets. Unlike Helen, he made no move to hug any of the Forths. But Oliver thought his first impression was still correct; Henry *was* holding himself with more confidence and authority than he had in a while. There seemed to be no trace of the pallor that had plagued him before Oliver had left.

And Helen ... was as he'd expected. She held out her arms for Ellie, and the latter's shoulders dropped as the tension—that's where she always seemed to hold it—went out of her. And she smiled. For real. Oliver folded his arms, feeling a wave of love for Helen. The fact that she could coax a smile like that out of his girlfriend in her moment of deep fear spoke volumes about her magic.

And that's exactly what it is, he thought. *Magic.*

"It's so good to have you here," Helen said as she hugged Sam. The top of her head barely came up to his shoulders. She released him and turned to Darien, who—

Oliver blinked. Whose lower lip was trembling.

He cocked his head. Granted, he hadn't known Darien long, but from what he'd seen, she seemed about as likely to cry as the mountains behind them. Helen's whole face softened, and she held out her arms. "It's so good to meet you."

Darien let out something between a laugh and a sob as she embraced Helen. "Sam has t-told me so much about you both." She stepped back and wiped her eyes. "Sorry about … *this*. It's the pregnancy."

But Helen smiled, her eyes misting again, and Oliver had the weird impression that there was something behind that smile, some devastating pain that he'd somehow never seen before.

"Don't be sorry," Helen said. "I know how it feels."

Shock jolted through Oliver. He shot a glance at Henry, wondering if he had a secret cousin wandering around somewhere that he didn't know about. The big man's eyebrows were raised, but the expression on his face wasn't *that* surprised. Oliver made a mental note to ask one of them later—maybe? Was that something a person just … *asked* about?—as Helen spoke again.

"You all look a lot better than we thought you would." Her eyes swept over Oliver. "Especially with the injury reports we got."

Ellie smiled. "We were just saying the same thing about you two." Then, to Oliver's surprise, she stepped forward and hugged Henry. He looked shocked, like he'd forgotten how to use his arms.

Ellie stepped back. "Henry, Sam and I want to make *absolutely sure* you know we forgive you."

"Actually," Sam said as he embraced Henry, too, "we want you to know we think there's nothing to forgive."

Ellie nodded as Sam stepped back to stand beside her. Henry just stood for a moment, Adam's apple bobbing. Then, he nodded. "Thank you, kids."

Sam smiled, then bent to gather all the weapons they'd dropped during their teary reunion. "Should we get going?"

"Let's." Helen grabbed Darien's suitcase. "I've got this. You just take it easy."

Oliver followed them across the wooden docks and up the gangplank, holding Ellie's hand loosely in his—and still relishing that he *could* without unendurable pain. Still ... as they made their way through the grim-faced crowd—and as reality sank in—his good mood faltered.

***

Minutes later, Oliver scrunched between Helen and Henry in the front seat of their pick-up. He half-followed the conversation, but mostly he was busy trying to strike a balance between giving his back enough space that it wasn't brushing the seat and triggering Helen's worry instinct.

He bit his lip as Henry hit a pothole, then focused out the windshield, on the beauty and familiarity of the little town he'd come to love. He'd missed Seldovia's quiet, the crisp spruce-scent of its woods. He'd missed its people, he realized. Reuniting with the crew—and having them meet Ellie—was something he was really looking forward to.

But as they drove, his foreboding grew. At first glance, it didn't seem like much in Seldovia had changed. But just like on the docks, the closer he looked, the more ominous things got. No children played outside. No one was rocking on front porches. A lone middle-aged woman—he'd seen her in Murray's store before—walked a Malamute down the side of the road, her pace quick, her posture alert. The dog itself looked nervous, hesitant, even diminished. Its head swung from side to side, and its tail hung low, as if it were ready to pull it between its legs and run at any moment.

Behind him, Darien whispered something to Sam that he couldn't quite make out. His friend's low voice answered. "Well, she's surrounded by them. Maybe it can see them like I can."

"Bill and Luke are planning on meeting us at the warehouse tonight," Henry said over the thrum of the truck's engine. "That all right with you guys?"

"Yeah," Oliver said, and the Forths answered similarly.

Helen twisted to peer at them. "Is that too much for tonight? We know you've been through a lot in the last few days, and we can move the meeting to tomorrow morning if you just need to rest."

"No, let's plan," Darien said. "We're on a deadline. Every second we delay means Death gets closer."

"Agreed," Ellie said. "Being tired is superfluous at this point."

Helen glanced back over her shoulder again. "Sam, Oliver's told us that you and Darien can see and feel the demons now. What's that ...?" She seemed to struggle to find the words.

"What's that like?" Sam asked.

"Yeah," Helen said. "If you don't mind talking about it."

Sam chuckled darkly. "Well, we're living with it, so we might as well use it to our advantage." He launched into an explanation of what they knew—and what they suspected—about the creatures that had invaded their world.

"So they start out as invisible shadows that feed on negativity," Helen said.

"Correct."

"Then at some point, they take a stable form and stay that way, like the one that attacked you in Hawaii?"

"Yes," Darien said. "But we don't know exactly what triggers that."

"Huh." Helen sat back. "Slubgob makes so much more sense now. And ... oh, hell." She looked over at Oliver. "I shouldn't have sent you that copy of *The Screwtape Letters*."

Oliver shrugged, barely avoiding wincing when the scabs on his back crackled. "He would've been nasty no matter what. If you're blaming yourself, stop."

He leaned away to avoid Henry's elbow as his uncle turned the wheel, and the truck bounced onto the forested dirt road that led home. Oliver relaxed fractionally. From here on out, they were more likely to see a moose than a person, which meant there wouldn't be as many reminders of how bad things had gotten.

Unless the moose are being haunted, too.

"Oliver."

He blinked at the sound of his name, then looked over at Helen.

"Has coming back from the dead done anything weird to you?" she asked.

"Not that I've—" He stifled a groan as the truck plowed into the big pothole on the left-hand side of the road that was almost impossible to avoid. "—seen."

"Henry, drive more carefully," Helen barked.

Henry's fists tightened on the wheel. "Helen—"

But Oliver cut him off. "I'm fine. Really. Don't worry about it."

"I'll still want to take a look when we get home," Helen huffed.

"You can if you want, but—"

"We'll have to re-wrap it tonight at the latest," Darien said. "It'll be fine until then, though, Helen, if that helps."

Darien's warm tone seemed to soothe Oliver's aunt; she slumped back against the seat. Oliver stared at her. Then, he cast a bemused glance at Henry. His uncle's face was troubled, weathered-looking. Tired. And it wasn't just the bickering, though that was significant, since Helen and Henry rarely bickered over anything. No, Oliver had learned there was a certain look to a person who was being tortured by something no one else could see—or who was watching it happen to someone else. He'd first noticed it in the mirror. And, for better or for worse, that realization had given him the ability—the empathy, maybe—to see it on others like it was written in neon.

Something hard and angry settled in his stomach, and he looked forward, bracing as the red-roofed cabin bumped into view. In a few days, it would all be over. The gate would be closed.

Or they would be dead.

***

"Dinner will be on in ten minutes."

At the sound of Helen's voice, Oliver looked up from the book in his lap. Her back was to them as she stirred something on the stove, its delicious, savory scent filling the cabin. Oliver studied her briefly, unease pricking at his insides, then glanced at the clock.

Almost four.

He returned to the words on the page, absorbing none of them. They'd already caught the Calls up on everything they knew and suspected about the demons. They'd already armed everyone in the cabin with a lighter and a knife. And they'd already done all the cabin's chores in record time—or at least, he, Ellie, and Sam had after Darien ran to the bathroom, emerged pale and shaking several minutes later, and went to lie down in the guest room.

He shifted, the skin on his back stretching uncomfortably. Ellie had disappeared into the loft twenty minutes earlier to settle in and shower, and despite how much time they'd spent together in the last week—or maybe because of it—he missed her a pathetic amount.

"Hey, Sam," Helen said, breaking Oliver's reverie. He glanced toward them as Sam looked up from his spot at the already-set kitchen table, where he had been reading something on his phone.

"Yeah?"

"Will you tell Darien the food's almost on, if she's up for it?"

"Yeah." Sam stood, watching Helen—or more accurately, the air around her—for a moment longer. His frown deepened. Then, he started for the guest room. "Our meeting with Bill is at seven, right?"

"Yep," Helen said.

"Okay." Sam ran a hand through his hair, glancing at the guest room door. "Dar will want to come, I know she will. But I may try and persuade her not to. There'll probably be demons all over that meeting, and I'm worried ..." He let out a long breath through his nose. "Anyway, I'll be back."

The door creaked shut behind Sam. Oliver closed his book and leaned forward, staring at the places where his friend's eyes had lingered, willing himself to see what he'd seen. When nothing magically appeared, he gave up, returning to the book with a sigh.

"What do you think, Oliver?"

He blinked at the sound of Henry's voice. His uncle sat in his big chair by the pellet stove, his tired but clear eyes fixed on the book in Oliver's lap.

"I'm having trouble focusing," Oliver admitted.

A rueful smile crossed Henry's face. "Yeah, poetry might not've been the best recommendation, now that I think about it."

"Maybe later." Oliver closed the book, an answering smile playing on his own face. "I'm surprised. I never knew you liked poetry."

Henry chuckled. "Only Robert Service. And only because Helen recommended it." He stood and walked to the kitchen, the hardwood creaking beneath his Smartwool-clad feet, and stopped next to Helen. "Need any help over here?"

"If you want to put the breadsticks in the basket, that'd be good."

"Okay." Henry sauntered to her other side, pecked her on the cheek, then reached for a wicker basket on top of the fridge.

"I do still like your company, you know," Helen said quietly.

Henry stilled, his expression softening as he looked at his wife. He reached an arm around Helen's waist and pulled her into a side hug, and Oliver suddenly felt like an intruder. Silently, he set the book on the end table, stood, and padded toward the loft, but Helen caught his eye as he reached the bottom of the stairs. "*Both* your company."

Oliver stopped, nonplussed. Then, he shoved his hands in his pockets and ambled toward the nearest barstool. "Well, that's a relief."

"I'll say." Henry grinned as he released her and turned to the breadsticks.

Oliver slid onto the stool, gritting his teeth against the pulling sensation in his burns, and braced his forearms on the countertop. Up close, the creamy, savory smell of salmon chowder was so good he could swear it quite literally dulled his pain.

Yep, she's magic, he thought.

Helen sniffed, wiping her nose on her sleeve. "I've never been this out-of-control before."

Henry stopped mid-reach, two breadsticks clutched in his hand. Oliver stared at Helen uncertainly. Even the bubbling chowder seemed to quiet.

"Well," Henry said slowly, "I think we both understand that, and have been there."

"I know I do. And have," Oliver said.

Helen sniffed again. "Yeah." She gestured to Henry. "You and I have talked about this in the last few weeks. We've had challenges. I've had challenges. Ups and downs—physical, mental, spiritual. But I've never felt this ... *crazy* before. I have the most horrible thoughts, just the most awful images of ... of ... things happening to people I love. Just all the time; anytime I let my guard down, and I'm exhausted. I just can't ..."

Her shoulders started to heave, and Oliver felt his own tighten in response. A dull shaft of pain speared across his back, but it meant nothing; of the two types of pain in this room, his was by far the easier. Helen wiped at her eyes again, then gestured to the chowder. "Sorry. This has plenty of salt in it. Doesn't need any more."

Oliver saw his relief mirrored in Henry's expression at the reappearance of some of Helen's usual spunk. His uncle pulled a tissue from the box and handed it to Helen. She took it. "Thanks."

"You know, that chowder's going to be great," Henry said. "I'm sure you can step away for a minute and sit down."

Helen let out a ragged sigh. "I know, I know. I just ..."

"Like to be doing something?"

She nodded. "It's how I cope."

"I know the feeling," Oliver murmured.

Upstairs, the bathroom door squeaked, and Oliver's heart leaped. A few seconds later, Ellie started down the staircase. Her eyes widened as she caught sight of Helen's face.

"It's all right, Ellie," Helen hiccupped. "Come on down."

Ellie did, and Oliver couldn't have taken his eyes off her if he'd wanted to. There was still an extra seriousness to her face, but she looked more relaxed than she had in days, and her cuts and bruises looked like they'd healed extra just during the twenty minutes she'd been gone. Her leggings and soft-looking sweater only added to the illusion of comfort.

We should be cozied up on the couch reading, he thought. *Or kissing.*

She rounded the corner and slid onto the stool next to him, clasping her hands together. "I'm sorry if I interrupted something."

Helen waved her off. "It's okay. I was just venting to my boys. Let's get this food on the table."

"That's what we're here for," Henry said, lifting the pot of chowder. "Venting and table-setting."

Oliver had just finished setting out pot holders when the door of the guest bedroom opened. Sam stepped out, then Darien. Oliver stopped. Darien looked how he felt after a twenty-hour shift on the *Redemption*.

"How're you feeling?" Helen asked her softly.

Darien sank down in one of the high-backed wooden chairs, mustering up a smile. "Alive and kicking, despite all …" She gestured vaguely to her stomach. "… this."

"Well, that's good," said Henry, settling into the chair at the head of the table. "If there's anything we can do to help, let us know."

"I will. Thank you." She ran her hand along the table's smooth golden grain. "I'm mostly distracting myself with … thoughts of the baby. And our future." She looked up at Sam. "Which I hope includes a dining set like this, because it is *lovely*. I think I like it even more than the one at the Shack."

"I love it, too," Helen said as she sat opposite Henry. "Shall we say grace?"

Oliver bowed his head as Helen prayed, smiling when Ellie's hand found his under the table.

"So Sam," Helen said once the prayer was finished, "can I ask you a question that might be uncomfortable for both of us?"

Ellie's hand twitched, Darien's eyebrows lifted, and Henry—holding a full ladle of chowder—froze. Sam, though, looked surprised, but not particularly guarded. "Yeah, sure."

"Can you *see* Slubgob?"

"Oh." Looking a little relieved, Sam reached for a breadstick, then passed the basket to Darien. "Yes. Sort of."

"How does that work? If she's in my head, what does that look like?"

Sam's eyes narrowed thoughtfully. "Are you sure you want to know?"

"Yes."

"And no one else has any objection to this being our dinner conversation? Because it's pretty creepy."

"Sam," said Ellie, "it's nice of you to check, but I think we're good."

Sam shrugged. "Okay then. Helen, I can't *see* Slubgob, not as something with a human shape, anyway. But I can see a dark ... almost a corona around your head."

Helen sat back, fear and disgust etched in every line of her face. Oliver thought back to his own experience with Wormwood and shuddered. "Helen, have *you* ever seen Slubgob? I saw Wormwood sometimes, when we were alone and he really wanted to torture me."

Helen shook her head. "I've seen shadows out of the corner of my eye that disappear when I look directly at them, but I've never seen Slubgob. At least, not in the way you described Wormwood."

"Interesting," Sam said. "When I was being haunted in Colorado, that's what I saw, too."

Helen's eyes bugged. "You had one of these in your head during your *wedding*?"

"Yeah, unfortunately. Mostly, it just hated Oliver, though." He let out a humorless laugh and nudged Darien gently. "I was more of a bridezilla than you."

She grinned. "Well, I am incredibly practical and levelheaded."

Oliver took the opportunity to enjoy his first bite of Helen's chowder as the conversation wandered elsewhere. As always, it was excellent—homey and warm and loaded with fish, potatoes, bacon, and corn.

"Could you pass me those breadsticks, Sam?" Darien asked.

"Yeah." He reached for the basket.

"Get them," Darien said.

Sam frowned. "I am."

Darien put a hand to her forehead, looking confused. "I'm ..." She shook her head. "Sorry. *Kill them.*"

"*What?*"

Darien hunched forward, gripping her spoon so tightly her knuckles turned white, oblivious to him—to all of them.

"Get them, get them. Stop them! *Kill them!*"

Sam's eyes locked on something over Oliver's shoulder. He released Darien and shoved his chair back from the table. "Behind you!"

Oliver shot out of his chair, whirling in time to see a cloud of ... *mist*, forming out of thin air, feet away from him. He scrambled backward, bumping against the table, Helen and Ellie's shrieks echoing in his ears. The mist was expanding with volcanic speed, and at its center writhed an indistinct figure that sharpened even as he watched.

Oliver kicked his chair, sending it skittering at the demon, but it passed right through. "Get Darien out of here, Sam—!"

Horror stopped him cold as the thing formed into a monster. It was shaped like a small squid, its skin a deep, angry crimson, its underbelly pale and bloated as a dead fish. Two black eyes swiveled on stalks at the front of its head, waving like they were caught in a strong wind. It thumped to the ground, and in that first split-second, Oliver thought it almost seemed ... *dazed*.

Then, Henry let out a shocked bellow, and all hell broke loose.

Chapter Eight

The monster screeched and shot toward Ellie. Shrieking, she grabbed the back of her chair and swung. To her shock—and relief—the stout wood hit the creature with a resounding *crack*, sending it flying. It landed on its back near Henry, its feet—*feelers?*—waving in the air. They were shockingly fine, like thin feathers made of copper wire.

"GET THEM!" Darien howled as Sam dragged her away. "GET THEM! GET—"

"Darien!" Sam yelled. "Darien, come back—!"

"KILL THEM!" Darien screamed.

Blocking out the scuffle—it sounded like maybe Helen had joined the fight to get Darien away—Ellie ripped her lighter out of her pocket, cursing that she'd let her guard down enough to leave her knife upstairs.

"I've got fire!" she hollered.

The creature flipped upright and dove for her again, dodging a kick from Henry and a swipe of Oliver's knife. Ellie shrieked and careened backward, holding her lighter in front of her like a sword the demon might impale itself on, and watched in shock as *it all but did*.

The creature wailed as it slammed into the lighter, its cold, rancid-looking flesh inches from her knuckles. For a moment, Ellie thought its momentum might tear its flesh, letting her little flame twist its way in. But then it pushed away, reeling like a drunk across the Calls' pristine hardwood. Oliver lunged at it with his knife, but it shot backward across the floor, letting out its weird, whistling screech again.

Ellie met Oliver's eyes. "It's like it doesn't know what it's doing!"

"Good! I'll slash, you burn!" Oliver dashed forward. The demon let out a hiss and turned, pinning him with its bulbous stalk-eyes. Movement flicked in Ellie's peripheral vision; Henry was rounding the table, his knife drawn—

The demon leaped for Oliver.

Ellie bit off a scream as he dropped into a crouch, slashing out with his knife. The move was awkward, and he missed again, the demon sailing over him and smacking into the center of Henry's chest with enough force to make him stagger.

"Henry!" Helen screamed from behind her.

In an eyeblink, the demon wrapped its tentacles around Henry's barrel chest. The big man yelled, slashing at it with his huge hunting knife, opening several small cuts in its skin. Ellie darted forward, lighter held high, but the demon shrieked again, several whiplike tentacles twisting and thrashing as it climbed up Henry's body. Henry bellowed with fear and staggered toward the table, his knees bumping against it as the demon engulfed his head.

With a roar, Oliver lunged. He snatched one of the flying tentacles, gripping it with both hands and pulling for all he was worth.

"*HELL* NO!" Helen screamed. She threw herself halfway across the table and grabbed a second tentacle, then planted her feet and hauled back.

"ELLIE!" Oliver yelled. "It's cut! HURRY!"

"I'm coming—!"

The demon's top half sucked free of Henry's face. He gasped for air, then shoved. The power in his big arms—combined with all of Oliver and Helen's strength—threw the demon onto the table, upending the chowder and sending the breadsticks flying. Bowls and silverware clattered to the floor as Oliver hurled himself forward and sank his hunting knife into the demon's putrid flesh, pinning it to the table. It wriggled, letting out a keening wail, tarlike blood leaking from the wound and from the slashes Henry had left in its skin.

"MOVE!" Ellie darted forward as Oliver ripped the knife free of the demon, and plunged the lighter into the gaping hole it left. It erupted with a final, tortured wail, engulfing everything on the table in flame.

Heat singed Ellie's skin; she cried out and scrambled backward. Oliver grabbed her, pulling her away from the flames until they bumped against the cabin's wall. The fire tore into the creature with white-hot fury, devouring everything—flesh, feelers, and tentacles.

Within seconds, it was nothing more than a burning pile of black goo, spreading across the table's surface and lighting the insides of the empty cups and dishes with a sullen, lava-red glow.

Still breathing hard, Oliver looked down at Ellie. His face was pale, a light sheen of sweat on his forehead, but the corners of his mouth still twitched upward in a painful-looking smile. "Well done, as always."

"You, too," she said.

"That system just worked so well with the Lady, I figured we could just use it again."

"Great thought." Ellie let herself gaze into his cobalt eyes for what she knew was too long, love for him swelling in her chest. For a moment, she couldn't breathe.

"*Henry—*"

Ellie blinked, then turned to see the Calls collapse into each other's arms, Helen shaking and Henry white-faced.

"That was so *fast*," Helen whispered. Henry held her tighter.

"You okay?" Oliver asked him.

"I think so. Hell, that was …" He shook his head. "That was Hell."

"Okay." Oliver braced against the wall, teeth clenched.

Ellie's heart dropped. "Your burns." She took his hand. "Here, come sit down. Let's look at them."

"Darien?"

The frightened timbre of Sam's voice stopped everyone in the room. He crouched on the floor holding Darien, who was blinking like she'd just become conscious again. Sam smoothed the hair from off her forehead. "That's right, come back. It's okay."

She let out a groan. "Help me sit up."

"You sure you're ready for that?"

"Yes. I want my dignity back."

"Oh my …" Helen released Henry and took an uncertain step toward Darien. "Are you okay? Did you hit your head? Do you need …?"

Ellie could hear the bafflement rolling off her in waves. *If it makes you feel better, none of us know what to do, either.* She leaned against the back of Oliver's chair, half-aware of him pulling his shirt over his head but mostly watching Darien closely.

Her sister-in-law started gathering her mussed hair back into a ponytail. She looked exhausted but impressively composed. "Well, that was the worst one so far."

"No kidding," Sam said. "What even happened?"

Darien scowled. "I'm still trying to figure that out."

Everyone stared at her. Finally, Sam broke the silence. "I saw it form, just like the Sphere in our room in Hawaii."

"Yes. He was … Awakening." Her voice dropped. "That's the word Death used as it was happening, anyway."

"Hang on," Oliver said. "Were you in the squid's head, or Death's?"

"Both."

"Wait." Ellie cocked her head. "If the squid was Awakening, why would you have started out in *Death's* head? Wouldn't the squid have been where all the energy was? Or … however that works?"

Sam frowned. "Good point, El. Dar, you weren't in the Sphere's head at all when it was Awakening, right?"

"No, I wasn't. And maybe I'm misremembering what just happened. It was all such a jumble. But …" Darien thought for a moment, then shook her head helplessly. "I don't know, guys. I still think I started out in Death's head, but that could be because he was already watching that demon, screaming at it to kill us."

"You were also yelling 'kill them, get them' over and over," Sam said.

Darien blanched. "I was? Ugh, I'm sorry about that."

"So … what—?" Ellie started.

"There was this *amazing* energy surge," Darien said. "One minute I was sitting at the table, and the next I was somewhere in the mountains, surrounded by …" Her voice trembled.

"What?" Helen asked quietly.

Darien didn't reply for a moment. Then, she drew her knees up, hugging them to her chest. "More bodies. Mountaineers, it looked like."

Ellie felt sick, Helen's hands flew to her mouth, and Henry looked stricken. Little, puckered bruises were already starting to form across his cheeks and forehead.

"Anyway …"

Ellie looked back at Darien in time to see her put her forehead in her hand. "Death was focused on the demon who was about to Awaken." She gestured to Sam. "Which you were also looking at."

Sam nodded.

Darien blew out a breath. "Death has so much more clarity of vision than I thought. This whole time I've been thinking of him as another Lady or Silverskin, but it seems like he's even a level above—" She cringed. "Oh, wow. Something nearby didn't like that."

"That Death calls the shots?" Sam asked.

"And like an actual mob boss?" Darien shuddered. "That's what it seemed like."

Sam looked around, his eyes stopping at several points throughout the room. Ellie tensed, the queasy, anxious ball in her stomach tightening as she realized just how many demons might be hovering around them right now.

"Wow," Darien said again. "I think that's the first time I've ever felt one's individual, specific emotions. Aside from Ankle Tickler."

"So your sensitivity is still growing," Ellie said. "Sam, is yours any different?"

"Nope. It's as straightforward as it was on day one."

"How many are in the room with us?" Henry asked.

"Slubgob, plus three more juveniles. They're just floating around for now, but I'll keep an eye on them. While also trying not to ... *Awaken* them on accident."

Darien closed her eyes and took a deep breath, her hand straying to her stomach.

"Hey, Darien," Helen said, "forgive me for prying, but are you—is the baby—okay? Do we need to get you to the hospital?"

"Oh!" Darien dropped her hand, looking ... Ellie blinked. Was that *guilt*? But as quickly as the expression had come, it disappeared. "No, we're both okay. I promise I'd tell you if we weren't. I'm not trying to be tough."

"Okay. I'm just ..." Helen swallowed and took Henry's hand. "We've lost four. It's not something we talk about a lot, but we want to make sure that doesn't happen to you, even with everything that's going on right now."

Ellie's mouth fell open, her heart going out to the older couple. She glanced at Oliver. Judging by the shock and sadness on his face, he hadn't known either. When she turned back, Darien was looking up at Helen, her eyes glistening. "Thank you both."

"Absolutely, Darien." Helen swallowed, then folded her arms. "So from a more ... tactical standpoint, could you break down the timeline of what happened a little more for us?"

"Helen and I aren't as used to all this as you kids are," Henry said. "So forgive us if we're slow."

"Oh, *you're* not slow," Sam said. "*It's* evolving."

Ellie nodded. "We're *all* slow."

"Just hopefully not so slow that Death gets to the gate before we do," Oliver said softly.

"Correct," Darien said. "So when I hopped into his head, Death had just killed the mountaineers and was using all the energy from ... *that* ... to contact the demon here who was Awakening. I think I started switching between them at that point, which was incredibly disorienting."

"I'll bet," Henry rumbled.

Darien nodded, her expression turning dumbfounded. "The new one Awakened with Death already screaming in its head to kill us. It didn't know what to do. It didn't even seem to know it could switch between solid and not-solid. I ... I think the sheer mental overwhelm was the reason I passed out."

Ellie looked at the table. Its once-beautiful top—and everything still on it—was scorched beyond recognition, covered in a layer of coal-black soot. "I thought it seemed disoriented. That's why it was so easy to kill."

Helen's eyes widened. "*That* was *easy*?"

"Comparatively," Oliver said.

The Calls just stared between the pair of them.

"You'll get used to it," Oliver said.

Henry rubbed his eyes deeply. "I'm not sure how a man can get used to seeing a monster from a *poetry* book crawl into his living room."

Helen's jaw dropped. Then, she whirled on her husband. "That monster. It was from damn Pious Pete, wasn't it!"

"Wait, what's—" Ellie started, but Helen overrode her.

"Oh, Henry, I'm so sorry! First, Oliver and Wormwood, now you and that ... *squid* thing. And my *table*—" She put her hands on her hips, scowling. "I swear I'm never recommending a book to anyone ever again."

"It *has* helped, hon," Henry said. "I just read the wrong poem at the wrong time. That's not your fault."

"Pardon me for asking," Darien said softly, "but what's Pious Pete?"

"A character in a poem written by a guy named Robert Service." Henry crossed his arms, his eyes softening as he met Helen's. "I've never been into reading, but Service wrote a lot about Alaska and the Yukon. Helen thought I might enjoy some of his stuff as I was recovering from the Prozac. And she was right." He shrugged. "And there just happened to be a monster in one I read earlier today. Which is nobody's fault."

Sam piped up. "If it makes you feel better, the Sphere—the one that nearly got us in Hawaii—was all my fault. I was watching it, thinking it looked a little like some Halloween decoration that had scared me to death when I was five or so, and then it Awakened and became that."

"I think it's likely," Darien said, "that the squid would have Awakened even without the poem. It just would have taken a different shape based on something someone else was afraid of."

Henry looked at Helen. "Well, there you go. Not your fault, Helen." He moved to the table and peeked into the blackened pot that used to hold Helen's chowder, then reached out a cautious hand to touch it. When it didn't burn him, he picked it up and started toward the kitchen. "We've had a wake-up call, at any rate. I think we need to set up watches at night. That shouldn't be too hard, since there're six of us."

"Agreed." Oliver stood, wincing, and looked around. "I don't know about you guys, but I'm pretty anxious to meet with Bill now that a demon has openly attacked six people."

"Me, too," Ellie said.

Chapter Nine

Sam followed Henry, Ellie, and Oliver down the wharf toward a hulking metal warehouse, the scents of fir, brine, and fish heavy in his nostrils. To his right, a small fleet of boats bobbed on the harbor's deep, chilly-looking water. Clouds had moved in during dinner; they washed the sky in gray and cloaked the distant mountains in ever-shifting gauze. Their reflections in the dark water were like ghosts—

No. Shut up. Sam forced his eyes ahead, ignoring the vague, shadowy shapes flickering at the corners of his eyes. *You have more than enough creepy visuals to deal with right now. You don't need to make up more.*

Several steps ahead of him, Henry reached the warehouse's rust-spotted door and pushed. It swung open with a guttural squeal, and the big man stepped through, oblivious to the foggy, birdlike shape that had just materialized next to his head.

Yesterday, Sam would've been envious of his ignorance. Today, he was just too strung out.

Resisting the urge to try and shoo the juvenile demon away, he followed Ellie and Oliver inside, closed the door (which the creature was already floating through, tailing them), and turned. The smells of fish and heavy cleaner hit him like a slap, powerful enough that he wrinkled his nose. They weren't nasty, rotting smells—from the gleaming steel tables, to the massive sink in the corner, to the spotless concrete floor, everything in sight was clean. They were just ... powerful. Sam blinked against the too-bright fluorescent light, his gaze settling on the farthest of the stainless steel tables, where four people sat waiting for them. Three men. One woman. And no less than nine demons

Ten, if you count the one behind me. Sam tried to take stock of the hovering figures without letting his eyes—or thoughts—linger for too long on any one of them. They were all different shapes and sizes, most humanoid, one blocky, and one *massive.*

Don't want to tangle with you, Sam thought before tearing his eyes away. Satisfied that none of them were immediate threats, he straightened his back and stepped forward to meet the crew of the *Redemption.*

"Sorry we're late." Henry gestured to Ellie, then to Sam. "This is Ellie and Sam Forth, by the way."

A man with a full gray beard—who Sam assumed was Bill—had already rounded the table, the other three crew members close behind him. He wasn't as tall as Henry, but he was broader—the kind of broad Sam associated with the handful of farmers and ranchers he knew: all strength and power.

"Not a problem. We're just glad you're all right." The man gripped Henry's hand and pulled him into a hug, slapping him on the back. "Naomi said that was quite the text she got from Helen."

The woman behind Bill snorted. "That's an understatement. It nearly gave me an aneurysm. I can't believe you were attacked like that!"

"I can't, either," Henry muttered, embracing her briefly. "Oliver and Ellie here took care of it, though."

While I was busy panicking, Sam thought. One of the demons hovering near a door in the back wall rotated and drifted toward him, as if caught in a light breeze. A jolt went through Sam; he turned away from it.

Bill grinned at Oliver. "Wouldn't have expected anything less from you. And Ellie ..." The fishing captain turned to her. "Pleasure to meet you."

"Likewise."

Bill turned. "And you, Sam."

"Yes, sir." Sam stepped forward, hand outstretched. If making a good first impression was one of the few things he was still confident about, then he'd damn well better do it right. He forced a smile.

Bill sort of returned it. Then, the captain turned and gestured to the others. "This is my sister Naomi, her husband Luke, and our friend Charlie. They all work on the fishing boat—"

"Rarely, for me," Naomi cut in, shaking Ellie's hand, then Sam's. It felt almost as callused as her brother's. "Mostly I keep books."

"Which she's very good at," said the man beside her—Luke. He had a pleasant, rugged face, with a neatly trimmed black beard and lively green eyes. "And she can haul and clean net with the best of them, don't let her lie to you."

Sam nodded, forcing himself not to look too closely at yet another demon, which was drifting toward them like a blobby, scabby rain cloud. "Nice to meet you both," he said, hoping his expression still looked pleasant.

"And you must be ... Charlie?" Ellie asked the last man. He was average in height, with close-cropped brown hair and a faded red jacket that had seen better days. But he shared the same powerful build—and grip, Sam learned as the man grasped his hand—as the others.

"Yep," Charlie said. "Good to meet you."

Bill waved them forward. "Come sit down. We've got a lot to talk about."

They settled into mismatched chairs and stools that looked like they'd been pulled from various parts of the warehouse. Luke gestured to a worn-looking black office chair. "Ellie, we saved the throne for you. Don't want you to think we're barbarians."

Ellie laughed, and Oliver's expression softened as he looked at her. It made Sam think of Darien, and guilt pricked at him for having left her back at the Calls.

She needed the rest, he argued. At ... himself. He averted his eyes as a second demon detached itself from the back wall and started their way.

"Where are Jessie and Jordan?" Oliver asked.

"No one under eighteen goes," Bill said. "That's what we've decided. Now, we need to know ... Something wrong, Oliver?"

"Uh ..." Oliver scratched the back of his neck. "I don't disagree with you. But how do you plan to keep them here?"

"They'll *stay* because somebody needs to defend Seldovia. Our families, homes, businesses."

"I doubt the demons will send anyone to attack Seldovia while ..." Oliver's eyes narrowed. "Ah. I see."

Bill nodded curtly. "And I'd appreciate it if you keep that revelation to yourself. Now." He braced his elbows on the table and leaned forward. "Down to business. How much time've we got?"

"Darien estimates five days," Sam said.

Shocked silence filled the room.

"Including today?" Naomi asked.

"Unfortunately, yes," Sam said.

"And Darien can ... read the demons' minds?" Luke asked. "Bill tried to explain it to us, but I'll admit I didn't really follow that part."

Bill grunted. "Might be because *I* don't really follow that part."

Henry looked toward Sam. "You're the closest to that particular situation. Want to try and do a better job of explaining it than I did?"

"I'll give it my best shot." Sam launched into a brief explanation of what had happened to him and Darien in Hawaii and its consequences. "Now Darien can feel their emotions *and* spy on them every once in a while. And I can see all the demons, even the juveniles that are invisible to the rest of you."

Naomi winced. "That sounds miserable."

You nailed it, Sam thought. But he just shrugged. "It's an asset, and I only have to deal with it for five more days. In that light, it doesn't really matter how I feel about it."

"True," Luke said, and Sam thought he saw a glimmer of approval in his eyes—and in the faces of the other crew members as well. "So how many are in the room with us right now?"

"Ten. All juveniles. Most of them are camped out along the wall behind you—they seem to really like that door. But a few are buzzing around our heads."

"Damn." Luke turned, his eyes searching the air around him. "They're haunting your office, Bill."

Naomi's lips quirked in a wry smile. "That explains a lot."

Bill ignored them and folded his arms. "Why isn't Darien here? Was she hurt in the fight?"

"No, luckily," said Oliver. "She was weakened by it, though."

"The experience of fighting a demon—a physical manifestation that's trying to kill you—is intense and horrible," Ellie said. "And Darien experienced the fight through not only her own eyes, but also from the perspective of the demon we killed," Ellie went on. "So—"

"She's tough," Sam broke in. "I would know. But it was pretty crushing for her, both physically and mentally, and we all decided it would be better for her to stay at the Calls' and recuperate."

"That's ..." Bill tugged at his beard, looking like he was trying to settle on the right word. "Inconvenient. It sounds like we're really going to need her if we're going to win this thing."

Something inside Sam bristled, but Henry spoke before he could. *Which is probably good,* he thought as he watched an eleventh demon materialize next to Bill's head, dark and batlike. Another detached itself from the back wall and rolled through the air toward Charlie.

"Oh, she's needed," Henry said. "And she wants to be involved. Just ... not tonight."

The big guide shot a knowing look at Sam, who nodded his thanks.

"Huh," Bill grunted. "Well, I hope she recovers quickly, for her sake and everyone else's."

"I think we all do," Naomi murmured.

Henry nodded. "On a more immediate note, how much do you know about why we're on such a tight timeline?"

Luke leaned back in his chair, though his casual posture didn't make his tone any less serious when he spoke. "The way I heard it, Darien found out their leader is headed our way. Calls himself 'Death.' Which seems a little presumptuous."

"Not when he can back it up," said Oliver. "Which is why we pushed to have this meeting earlier, but—"

Bill held up a hand. "You know we couldn't take a full day off, not with the Cohos running."

"I think you're going to want to take the *week* off after you hear what we're actually up against," Oliver said.

Bill stared hard at Oliver, but Sam thought it wasn't an unfriendly stare. Despite his frustrations with the hard-driving captain, he found his respect for him deepening. The captain leaned forward. "All right. Tell us."

"And when he says 'tell us,'" Luke said, "he means everything you possibly can. The more intel we have, the better."

"All right." Oliver launched into a description of Death's attack at the Canadian border, with occasional supporting comments from Ellie. Once they'd finished their story—which still gave Sam chills in all the worst ways—Sam filled them all in on what Darien had seen, how Death was bullying other demons into submission and killing the ones that displeased him.

"He's left a trail of bodies from Montana through British Columbia, and he's still coming," he finished to shocked looks and furrowed brows.

"Why aren't the deaths all over the news?" Naomi asked.

"Most of them have happened in the backcountry." Sam's voice dropped. "He's picking and choosing his targets so carefully that the bodies may not have been found yet."

A ripple of what looked like shock, disgust, and sadness went through the crew members.

"And did you hear about the Border Agency attack?" Oliver asked.

Naomi stared at him. "That wasn't …?"

"It wasn't Death," Ellie broke in. "It was an entirely different demon, a wendigo. It had just become sentient, and the fact that it didn't have any self-control—which you saw the evidence of on the news—was what made Death step in and kill it."

"No kidding," Charlie said. "The pipeline workers, too?"

Sam nodded. "Same demon."

"It nearly got us, too," Oliver said. "That's why it was at the border. Its job was to kill us, but like Ellie said, it didn't have the self-control to wait."

A brief silence settled over the room; none of the crew members looked like they knew what to say.

"And that brings us to one of our more serious problems," Henry said.

Bill raised his eyebrows. "Just one of them, huh?"

"Yeah, just one, unfortunately. The demons seem to be Awakening faster now, and are more aggressive when they do. In fact, that's exactly what happened at our place earlier: one Awakened and attacked. And with Death egging it on, it was—"

"Now hold on," Luke said. "What's that mean, Awakening?"

"Well, that's one of the other problems," Oliver said. "The demons are all over the world at this point, and there are likely millions of them—"

"Millions?" Luke asked hoarsely.

Oliver nodded.

Now you're getting it, Sam thought, his heart sinking at the looks on their faces. Oliver went on, explaining the full scope of the situation—how there were millions of demons all over the world, how they drew from people's thoughts and could grow into monsters with human levels of intelligence in an instant, and how Death seemed to be at the helm of it all.

"The good news," Ellie said when he'd finished, "is that they seem vulnerable when they first Awaken. It was a lot easier to kill the squid than the Lady, for example, because it didn't know what to do with itself. And based on what Darien experienced, it was even more confused *because* it woke up with Death screaming at it to kill us. So it ended up backfiring for them."

"On the other hand," Henry added, "sometimes their newness makes them more dangerous. Like the wendigo."

"So why haven't we *seen* more of them?" Bill asked. "I've kept my mouth shut because I wouldn't even know how to explain all this. But based on what you're saying, I shouldn't have to."

But Oliver was shaking his head. "They don't want to be exposed yet."

Bill stared at him. "That's it?"

"That's it."

Naomi frowned. "With millions of them out there, I'd think they wouldn't care."

"But they're not all like Death and the Lady," Henry said. "Those are the minority, and they want to go to big population centers where there's more food. Seldovia doesn't cut it for most of them."

Charlie shrugged. "I guess that makes sense. No bear's going to wander around a mountaintop during the salmon run. These demons seem like they're the same."

"Spot on," Sam said.

Oliver shifted in his chair. "I had one in my head up until a few days ago. He all but told me that they were biding their time until enough demons could Awaken. Then they'd take over the world and farm people like cattle."

Naomi winced again. "You had one in your *head*? How does that even work?"

"We don't really know," Oliver admitted. "But—"

Luke interrupted. "How good is information learned from a demon, though? I think that's a question worth asking."

"Well, let's look at Death's actions," Henry said. "If their goals were carnage, fear, and subjugation, Death would've let the wendigo live."

Bill nodded. "Good point."

"And if they didn't have any weaknesses," Henry continued, "they'd have already won. But since they're acting the way they are—being secretive, sending assassins after people who've figured them out ..." He gestured to Ellie and Oliver. "Clearly, they're afraid of us. Or cautious, at the least."

Sam jumped in. "And they don't seem to get physical forms until they've Awakened, which seems to take time."

"Is there any way to keep them from Awakening?" Luke asked.

"Not that we know of," Sam said. "It seems to just ... happen."

Luke grunted.

"The point is," Oliver said, "if Death gets here before we close the gate, we have no chance. He'll kill everyone trying to attack it, then move on to the boats."

"But even if that happens," Charlie said, "everyone in Seldovia, and probably Nanwalek, maybe even Homer, would know afterward. *Especially* if he destroys an entire fleet of boats. You can't cover stuff like that up."

"Unless ..." Sam's heart sank. "Unless they almost have enough Awakened demons to subdue the world already."

"Well," Bill said, "either way, it seems to me we'd better get working on our plan." He steepled his fingers on the table. "I'm thinking we copy the Night Marchers and split our forces. Ninety-five percent of the fleet sails into Chrome Bay as a distraction. Then a smaller group of us will sneak up into the caves to take on the Gatekeeper."

Henry grunted. "Simple. I like it."

Sam frowned. "The Hawaiians had an entire island full of people they used as a diversion. Way more than we do. How many do you think you can get to come with us?"

"We'll find out Wednesday," Luke said.

"Wait, Wednesday?" Sam's heart sank. "That's *two days* from now!"

"Can we do it sooner?" Oliver asked.

Bill sat back, rubbing his eyes. "That's the soonest I could get Ray to do it. If you want, you can try and persuade the guy, but I don't think you'll have much luck. He *thinks* he's too *busy*."

Oliver shook his head. "If you can't, I doubt I can."

"Who's Ray?" Ellie asked.

"Seldovia's mayor," Oliver said. "He's a grouchy old geezer."

"That he is," Luke said. To Sam's surprise, the fisherman was grinning. "But he's a good-hearted one. Plus, his sluggishness will give us enough time to make sure the whole town knows."

Naomi jerked her thumb toward the door on the wall behind them. "Bill spent most of last night printing flyers about the town meeting so we can go door-to-door."

"Well, I'll have to print more," Bill said. "I wasn't planning on contacting the whole area, but after what we've heard, I think we'll need to try."

"I agree," Sam said absently. Four demons continued their lazy drift around and through Bill's office door. Briefly, he wondered why they hadn't come toward them, since this was where all the emotion was.

"Between the four of us, we can cover the whole town in a morning, and maybe even Seldovia Village," Charlie said.

Bill nodded at Henry. "More if you and Helen and you young folks are in."

"I'm in," Ellie said at the same time Oliver said, "Definitely."

"I'm in," Sam echoed. "But ... flyers?" When the crew all turned to stare at him, he held up his hands. "I have nothing against them. That's just ... admirably old-school."

"We'll send texts, too," Bill said.

"But part of the reason we opted for flyers *was* to get people talking," Naomi explained. "It's different enough to catch people's attention."

"We could hang them in businesses that are willing, too," Henry said. "I'm in, by the way. I'd guess Helen is as well."

"Darien, too, if she's feeling up for it." Sam suppressed a sigh. "And honestly, probably even if she *isn't* feeling up for it."

Bill nodded. "All right, then."

"Hold on," Luke said. "We need to address the elephant in the room here. What are we going to tell the boys?"

Sam blinked at him, confused, before realizing he was talking about the high schoolers. Jessie and Jordan.

"I have some jobs they can do around here," Bill said.

"I know you do, and I know they'll do them." Luke crossed an ankle over his knee, his tone conversational, though his eyes were fixed keenly on his brother-in-law's. "But they're smart, Bill. They already suspect something bigger's happening than we're letting on. I don't think you'll be able to keep them—"

"I can. And I will."

For the first time, Luke's tone turned impatient. "Bill—"

"Luke," Naomi interrupted. "I don't want Jordan up there, either."

Luke held up his hands. "I'm not saying I do. I just don't want to insult his intelligence. Or Jessie's."

Naomi let out a "hmph."

"If they're not legally adults, then I think our mandate as parents is to protect them," Bill said. "In every possible way."

"Thank you, Bill." Naomi gave her husband a pointed glare.

Luke shrugged. "I just think we can accomplish both in a way that treats them more like the adults they almost are."

Bill crossed his arms. "Noted. But you're overruled."

Luke sighed, but apparently didn't think it was worth pursuing. "Second question. Are you going to try and involve Nanwalek and Homer?"

"Yep," Bill said. "And with your connections, I'd like you to be in charge of Nanwalek, if you're willing."

Luke gave a curt nod. "I'll call Boris tomorrow morning. I bet they'll be pretty easy to convince." He stretched. "With luck, we'll end up with a small armada."

The captain nodded. "That's the hope. And that'll take care of getting the distraction force together. Now for the gate team." He made eye contact with Henry, Oliver, Ellie, and Sam in turn. "These will have to be people who not only know the area, but also have experience fighting demons. Because from what I've heard, the Gatekeeper is a tough old bastard, and he won't go down without a fight."

"That he is," Oliver said, and Sam thought he suddenly looked paler.

Bill nodded slowly, his expression turning grave. "And speaking of elephants in the room, everyone on the strike team has to be willing to do what's necessary when we get to the gate."

Once again, the room quieted. Sam could swear a visible ripple went through the demons.

"You know that all of us are willing," Luke finally said. Naomi's gaze was cold, flat, scared. Next to him, Charlie folded his arms, hard determination in his eyes. And an ugly, awful thought hit Sam with the force of a charging lineman.

I'm the fastest in this room.

He glanced at his sister and Oliver. More particularly, the latter. He already knew he could beat Ellie in a footrace, and looking at her boyfriend ... Sam's stomach tightened.

Odds were he could beat him, too. White-hot fear licked his insides, drowning out the beginning of Bill's next sentence.

"—get Helen if she wants to go—"

"She will," Henry sighed.

"And potentially Darien, too," Bill said. "It'll be so dangerous that I want it to be their decision—"

"Darien's pregnant," Sam heard himself say. His voice was low. Harsh.

Naomi's jaw dropped; she turned to her brother. "Bill, there's no way I'm letting you send a pregnant woman up there."

But Bill was already shaking his head. "No, I wouldn't dream of it. Darien's out, at least as far as being part of the gate crew goes." He sighed and passed a hand over his eyes, looking tired for the first time that night. "So the only thing we really need to discuss now is who's going to go in the cave." He paused. "I think we should plan on it being me."

"Wait," Naomi said. "Wait, Bill—"

Bill's voice was quiet when he interrupted, but no less powerful for it. "Naomi, look around. Do any of the rest of you make sense?" He gestured toward Sam, Ellie, and Oliver. "They've got their whole lives ahead of them. And your family's younger; your kids need you, and you need each other—"

"By that logic, it doesn't make sense for it to be you, either," Luke pointed out. "What about Jessie?"

"By that logic," Henry rumbled, "I should do it because my family—Helen and Oliver—are the least dependent on me."

"Wait, Henry—" Oliver started, but Bill interrupted.

"The fact is that someone has to die to close the gate. We can't get around that. And I can't in good conscience lead a group up there if I'm not willing to do it myself. That's how I've always led you, and that's how I'll go out leading you."

"But *Jessie*." Naomi's voice shook, her lips trembling. "He's already lost his mother. There *has* to be another way."

She turned to look at Oliver, as if he could offer hope. But he just shook his head, his expression stricken. "If there is, I don't know it, Naomi."

Bill cleared his throat, blinking. "Jessie's sixteen, almost seventeen, and the best son a father could—"

A light flashed on behind the cracked-open door behind Bill, and it burst open, hitting the wall so hard that Sam could swear the whole building rattled. He leaped to his feet, grasping the hilt of his knife in one hand and scrabbling awkwardly for his lighter with the other, half-aware that Oliver had already fallen into a fighting stance—

Two teenage boys stumbled out of Bill's office. And suddenly, it felt like all the air had been sucked from the room.

Bill, Luke, and Naomi jumped up.

"Jordan!" Luke barked. "The hell do you think you two are doing?"

But it was Jessie who responded, and when he did, it was straight to Bill. "Why didn't you trust me enough to tell me all this?"

Bill folded his arms. "How much did you hear?"

"All of it!" Jessie seethed, his cheeks blushing nearly as red as his hair. "Every single damn word!"

Sam's heart sank into the roiling pit that was his stomach. *So* that's *why so many demons wouldn't leave the office door.*

"I don't know if we're right about this," the other boy, Jordan, said. His voice was calmer than Jessie's, but not by much. "Since obviously we're not competent enough to be invited. But it seems like a lot of people are about to die in a fiery demon fight. Including you." He gestured to Bill. "Did we hear that right? Is that all real?"

Nobody broke the silence.

Jordan crossed his arms. "So we were just going to have to deal with the consequences afterward? Is that it?"

"Jordan," Luke said sharply. "It is our job as your parents to guide and protect you—"

"You were fighting in Iraq when you were only a year older than me!" Jordan shouted. "In freakin' Baghdad! Don't tell me I'm not allowed to—"

"I can, and I will!" Luke bellowed back. "I argued for you—you probably heard it! But if you can't be reasonable about this, I'm revising my opinion!"

"But Oliver can go," Jessie said.

"Oliver's a grown man, Jessie," Bill growled.

Jessie threw up his hands. "And *we've* been doing a grown man's work since we could walk! Has anyone in this room thought that we might actually be helpful? Like, sure, we don't know Portlock—because *you* wouldn't let us go up there." He cast a reproachful look at Bill. "But we can at least be part of the group that sails."

"Or we can go help fight the Gatekeeper," Jordan broke in. "We can—"

"No." Bill stood. "Absolutely not. The conversation is over."

For a horrible second, Sam thought Jessie might launch himself at his father, and from the way Oliver tensed beside him, he wondered if his friend was thinking the same thing. But then the redheaded boy sagged, covering his face with his hands.

"Has anyone," he whispered, "anyone in this whole room other than Naomi thought that I might not want to lose another parent?"

Sam could swear his heart cracked.

"I have."

He blinked at the sound of Ellie's voice, small and trembling.

"I ..." She swallowed again. "I saw my dad die up there. The demons took him."

Tears stung Sam's eyes; he looked away in time to see Jessie raise his head. His eyes were a deep, dusty hazel, and full to the brim of an anguish Sam knew all too well.

"Don't do that to yourself," Ellie said. "You don't need to see it. However horrific you imagine it is, I promise it's ten thousand times worse. I will never, *ever* get it out of my head. Never for as long as I live."

The silence in the room stretched seconds into days, months, Sam couldn't tell; he was too busy trying to keep his bottom lip from trembling.

Finally, Jessie dropped his gaze. "I can't just sit at home, though."

"Neither can I," Jordan said. "I ..." He swallowed, then widened his stance and crossed his arms again. "I can't. Let us fight. Please. Even if we're with the diversion crew."

Bill spoke again, his voice surprisingly gentle. "What I said earlier—" He raised his eyebrows as if to say *which I know you heard,* "—was true. We may need good fighters here."

"Or even in Nanwalek—" Luke started.

"Honey!" Naomi snapped.

Luke spread his arms. "They're almost as old as I was when I was deployed." His voice turned to a grumble. "And they're *far* more competent."

"But I can't ... I can't ..." Naomi hid her eyes in her hand, but not before Sam saw the redness around them. She sniffed, then looked up at her son. "Jordan—"

"Mom." His soft, pleading tone mirrored hers. "Please. I don't even remember the first time I drove a snowmobile, or shot a rifle. I've been driving a truck since I was ten, the skiff since even before that. I've been working on the *Redemption* since I was twelve." His lanky arms fell to his sides. "There's gotta be a way we can compromise."

Naomi pressed her trembling lips together and shook her head.

"Mom—"

"We'll talk about it, Jordan," Luke broke in. "In fact, I think it'd be better for everyone if we adjourn for tonight and let the dust settle."

"Agreed," Henry said. "No one here's in any state to make decisions anymore."

Bill nodded. "Meeting adjourned, then. We can discuss this at home, Jessie."

But Jessie said nothing. He just turned and headed back toward the office, leaving his father standing there, looking anguished. Sam watched him go, feeling strangely hollow.

Chapter Ten

*D*eath *knelt by the carcasses of three brown bears—a mother and two cubs—as the setting sun threw fiery rays into the sky. As intelligent as the bears had been, as attached as they'd been to each other, he needed more to sustain his need to communicate, to watch and direct. His lips pulled back in a snarl. If only there were any other demons close by that he could trust ...*

They are coming, he reminded himself. It was unrealistic to have expected the others to stay in this foodless wasteland when populated areas offered so much more. No one had expected the Lady's death, let alone Silverskin's.

Still, it would be nice not to be the only reasonably intelligent being within a thousand miles.

He closed his eyes, but couldn't block out that red sunset light. It bled behind his eyelids, a visible symbol that time was running, always running, even when he wasn't. He would have to kill again, and it would delay him, and that would make him angry. But he knew what to do with anger. He'd had thousands of years to refine it. To tame it. To weaponize it.

Perhaps even his slow pace could be turned to his advantage.

So Death bowed his head and ... relaxed. He could do that in his corporeal state, and it was such a pleasant sensation that he almost smiled. Yes, traveling through this wilderness had its drawbacks. But as he ran his hands through the mother bear's thick, coarse fur, he had to admit it also had its benefits. There were no people to feed on. But there was also no one, and nothing, that could kill him. He could stay corporeal for hours—days, even, if he wanted.

Which he did.

Which meant he needed to get to work.

Death dug both hands into the bear's fur, so deep that his nails scraped her tough skin. Then he let his mind expand, sent it winging across the vast expanse between himself and ...

"You! Y...you've come back!"

"Yes, Slubgob," Death whispered. "And I will continue to come back until we secure our victory. What news?"

"I torment the old woman. She—well, she's not that old, but she thinks of herself as old—"

"I do not need the details of one pathetic human life." Unless, of course, he was taking that life to sustain himself. Then he wanted all the details. Hunger for human prey yawned in his gut, but he pushed it away. "What else?"

"Yes, sorry, sir. The humans killed the demon that Awakened here earlier—"

"I know. What has happened since?"

"Four of the humans left for a meeting. They've gone to tell others ... well, they've actually already told the others, and now they're just going to try and plan. Word's out about us, at least up here."

Death closed his eyes again, rubbing them vigorously. The lids were very soft. "And the other two?"

"Home. The younger woman is asleep. Helen has taken the first watch—that's what they're doing. Taking watches so that none of us can sneak up on them." Slubgob cackled. "Even though they've already failed there. Did you know about the new one? I have to say I admire—"

"Yes, I know about him. But he is ..." Death frowned. How would he describe the little freak? Simple? Broken? "He's never been particularly useful to me. Perhaps with time, I will reach him, but for now, he is none of your concern. You must focus on what is happening in front of you."

"Well, she's trying to scrub the fire stains off her table." Slubgob cackled again. "She feels really stupid that she's so sad about that. And she's right, you know, in her current situation, a table's a stupid thing to get all worked up over, not that I'm complaining—"

"Meaningless!" Death clenched his jaw, reminding himself that killing Slubgob out of sheer annoyance would be asinine.

"Sorry." Slubgob was practically cringing. "I'm sorry. But wait! There was something ... something I needed to tell you."

Death waited. When Slubgob didn't reply, he drew in a deep breath, loving the way it calmed his physical form. That alone was almost worth the irritation. "What, Slubgob?"

"I ... I don't remember. But it was important, I swear it was important, and I'll tell it to you as soon as I can remember."

Death sighed and ran his hand through the fur of one of the baby bears. The hairs close to its skin were softer than its mother's, but the tips were already taking on the coarse, bristly texture that seemed to come with maturity. That was all Slubgob needed: maturity and guidance. Wormwood had been that way, too, at first.

He looked up into the setting sun. "You can no longer be content with feeding on your old woman. You have too important a role to play not to act. Hop between people. Get in their heads. Find out what they're thinking, planning, all of it. Do what it takes."

He felt Slubgob's trepidation, but all she said was, "Yes, sir."

"When will the three who went to the meeting be home?"

"I don't know, sir."

"Can you get to them now?"

"I ... I've never left the old woman. I don't know."

"Hmmm." Death stood and fixed his eyes on the cold, white sweep of mountains ahead of him. "Try. I must move, and hunt. I will return after my next kill. In the meantime, watch for others who may Awaken."

"How likely is that?"

"Likely." Death strode into the trees, his shadow flitting across the ground between their trunks at supernatural speed. The light was fading, the world cooling. He weaved through the forest, ducked around branches, touched rough bark, spiny needles ... and this was taking too long. With a sigh, he faded back into his shadow state and sped up, no longer needing to heed the trees or the thick undergrowth. "Silverskin did his work well."

Slubgob snorted. "Well, he's dead. The way I heard it, that kid killed him without even knowing what he was doing, so he must not've been that special."

Death tamped down his annoyance. "Silverskin's greatest ability wasn't traveling hundreds of miles in an instant, useful as that was. It was being able to hasten the Awakening of his fellows, including yourself, if you remember. If we secure this world, it will be because of his efforts." And mine, he thought. But there was no need to dwell on that.

"Yes, Silverskin was. He was. And I'm grateful for that. But he was arrogant. Becoming corporeal in the middle of a fire? *That was an idiotic thing to—"*

"Slubgob," Death snapped. "Go do your work."

"Yes, sir. Sorry, sir."

With that, Death withdrew from her mind but let his own linger in the cabin, sensing, getting a feel for what else was there. Though there were several shadows, none were sentient yet. Except ...

Except for that one.

He opened his eyes, barely aware of the trees blurring around and through him as he traveled. That *one. He hadn't expected to find that strange little mind here; the one that never spoke, that might not even be capable of speech. The last time he'd sensed it, it had been in ...*

Hawaii.

Darien's eyes flew open.

No, she thought. *He can't be here.*

She turned her head. Her senses sharpened, threatening to turn the dim gray light creeping around the curtains into a blaze, and the sound of Helen's muffled movements in the kitchen into the rasps of a monster. She could sense the un-Awakened demons in the house. Not as acutely as Death could—she couldn't tell how *many* there were. But she knew they were there, and that they were ... listening, somehow? And ...

Slubgob. She could tell which one was Slubgob.

Darien drew her knees up to her chest as a low pulse of fear rippled from the demon, a half-formed memory of Wormwood's death taking shape in her mind. Shock flooded Darien at how suddenly clear Slubgob's thoughts were, but she didn't have time to dwell on it. In the mental undercurrents running through the Calls' home, something familiar flickered.

Darien's heart seized. She raised her head, scanning the room for a flash of dark fur, the gleam of orange eyes, but wasn't surprised when she didn't *see* Ankle Tickler. He'd be hiding under the bed, of course, if he were here at all.

But how could he be? she thought. He'd have had to stow away with them all the way from Hawaii, through *airport security.*

But as she let her head fall back to the pillow, other memories trickled in. She *had* been weirdly unsettled the entire trip, though she'd—very logically—chalked that up to the situation they were in. Granted, Sam had thought he'd seen a raccoon-sized animal in the back of their truck, but they'd all thought (also very logically) it had been a marmot or something similar.

But Death was convinced Ankle Tickler was here.

So why don't I already know *that?*

Darien closed her eyes and relaxed, reaching for the calm, meditative state she always tried to adopt before praying. A stab of guilt went through her; she hadn't done much of that since leaving for her ill-fated honeymoon. Quickly, she sent a silent apology heavenward, then let her mind ... expand? Her stomach clenched as she realized she was imitating the way Death used his power; the thought was so repulsive she almost withdrew.

No. This could be life and death, Darien, and you're the only one who can do it. Resolve hardened within her, and she pushed harder, straining at the edges of her own mind. And with that push, something *gave*.

Darien gasped as her mind seemed to open. A new layer of awareness and understanding crashed over her, as if her acceptance of her power had suddenly made it stronger. Everything had been dialed up to eleven—not only could she feel Slubgob in the next room, but she could feel the depth and subtlety of the demon's emotional state as surely as if the demon had told her herself. The low buzz in the back of her mind—the emotional swamp of an unknown number of non-sentient demons—resolved into four ... no, five individuals.

And the baby ...

Tears pooled in Darien's eyes. The baby was the same—contented, warm, safe—but she felt it so much more *powerfully*. It was an overwhelming contrast but indescribably welcome, and she couldn't stop herself from grasping for it. All her pain, exhaustion, and fear disappeared for a moment, swallowed up in that golden, blissful—

Discomfort pierced her mind like the blade of a scalpel, and the baby *withdrew*, its little soul seeming to cringe away from hers. Darien gasped as she was plunged back into darkness and confusion. She bolted upright, horror and regret flooding her. "I'm so sorry, I'm sorry—"

Darien froze as an image bubbled through the churn and chaos in her mind, resolving into ... *Sam's face.* She blinked. Was *that* from the baby? No, that didn't make sense; it had never seen its father. The mental picture couldn't be from it.

Which meant it had to be coming from somewhere else.

Maybe I can track it back to its source, Darien thought. Pushing away her lingering feelings of unease, she closed her eyes as the image of Sam formed in her mind again. *He was sitting on the couch in his old apartment, one ankle crossed over his knee, grinning at her, dim lamplight glowing softly behind him.*

Darien blew out a breath. She remembered that day. They'd snowshoed for hours on Horsetooth Mountain, then returned to his apartment and cooked dinner. He'd somehow talked her into playing *Call of Duty*, which she'd never done in her life. But it didn't matter that she was bad at it; not with him. They'd had so much fun, the day had been so close to perfect, and at that point, it had been far from over ...

She could hardly take her eyes off him, and had died at least fifteen times since they'd started, which was why she was so surprised when his grin widened and he said, "Nice shot! You nailed that one!"

Darien's eyes flew open. The memory was evaporating, but it had been as strong and vivid as the evening it had happened—*just* like Oliver had described with Wormwood. Except ... *not* cruel and torturous? If anything, it had felt like a pat on the back.

"You've leveled up ... Where are you, Ankle Tickler? You have some explaining to do."

Approval grazed the edge of her mind, and finally—*finally*—she became aware of him.

Darien gasped. She'd been feeling his presence for days, but hadn't realized it because it didn't feel like a mind at all. Instead, it felt more like a void where a mind *should* be. Conspicuous like a black hole, or an amputated limb, or a chocolate bar wrapper that still held its shape even though it was hollow on the inside. Hardly daring to breathe, she slipped one trembling foot out from underneath the covers and lowered it to the floor, her toes curling into the soft, thick rug. For a moment, nothing happened.

Then, a small, cold hand wrapped around her ankle, its fingers thin and brittle as sticks.

Darien jerked her leg up, scrambling back as another memory pressed into her brain, *of Sam's face, twisted with rage as he looked down at his bleeding shin. Of an overwhelming desire to rip Ankle Tickler to shreds—*

Darien blinked. That hadn't been her memory; it had been the *demon's*. She grimaced. This was getting weirder by the second.

Another memory surfaced, a little hazier, of ... Jack Torrance, in *The Shining*?

"I'm not gonna hurt you."

"Seriously?" she whispered into the darkness.

The words pressed themselves upon her mind again. *"I'm not gonna hurt you."*

"You really need the broader context if you're going to use movie quotes," she thought at the demon.

Confusion flickered back at her. Then, Ankle Tickler went silent.

Darien tucked her foot back under the covers and stared at the bedroom door, biting her lip. She could make it out of the room, probably without even a slash on the foot if she leaped far enough. Which she had a good shot of tonight; despite being tired, she hadn't felt sick since before dinner. Then she could tell Helen, and they could make a plan to solve this new, very strange problem.

She steeled herself. Then, she threw the covers off—

WAIT

Darien rocked back. It hadn't been a word so much as the impression of it.

"You realize that not telling her would be asinine," she thought at Ankle Tickler.

WAIT

For a second, Darien sat there, warring with herself. Her curiosity won. *"WHY?"*

A mental and physical silence followed, so profound that even her heartbeat felt too loud. Forcing thoughts of retreating to the baby's mind away—under no circumstance was that an option anymore—she waited.

The void between her mind and the demon's opened, just a crack.

Inside was boiling, desperate rage.

It was so feral, so intense and focused, that Darien stopped breathing. She cringed away as Ankle Tickler's mind opened a little more, but there was nowhere to go. She just had to *endure* his thoughts—if they could be called thoughts.

As the initial shock subsided, Darien was struck again by how alien this creature was, how differently he saw and experienced the world, even from Slubgob and the juveniles. He used no words, yet was exquisitely sensitive to *everything*—light, sound, and above all, the huge amount of energy given off by people. She could feel the maelstrom that was Helen's emotions—anger about her table, shame about that anger, worry for everyone, and even an extra layer of worry for Darien.

But before she had time to process what she'd felt, Ankle Tickler yanked at her mind so hard she almost yelped.

"What—?" She snapped her mouth shut as an impression formed in her mind of … guidance. Focus.

Let me guide you, she imagined him saying. *Let me guide your mind.*

Darien hesitated.

Ankle Tickler didn't.

She gritted her teeth as another image gathered along the edges of her mind, still not sure whether to fight it or not—or maybe not sure why she *wasn't* fighting it. *A tall, bird-thin man with bright pink eyes and skin so white she expected to see blue veins spidering across it in all directions. Then other images, impressions of blackness and cold, the graveyard down the road, a days-old pig carcass splayed out on the shiny table in the necropsy lab—*

She choked back bile. *"I get it. Death. You're showing me Death."*

Approval.

Darien swallowed again, the lingering scents of salmon chowder, garlicky breadsticks, and burned table suddenly too cloying in her nostrils. *"I'm not sure I want you digging around in my memories."*

Another memory flashed into her brain, of *sitting at a shaded table outside CSU's Lory Student Center, staring down at her first-semester psychology textbook. She breathed in the faint scents of paper and coffee that drifted from the next table over on the fall breeze. Once she was done with her reading, she'd pack up, go find her pre-vet friends, and tell them about the cute guy she'd met in her freshman seminar class. But she shoved those thoughts to the side; she had a quiz on Thursday, and William James would definitely be on it.*

"Your mind is at every stage a theater of simultaneous possibilities," she whispered, because whispering helped her actually concentrate instead of thinking about how warm Sam's gray eyes had been as they'd traded whispers about how seminar was such a waste of time—

In the gathering dark, Darien suppressed a shudder. *"A theater of simultaneous possibilities. Are you saying you can be faster if you use my memories?"*

Satisfaction.

Darien's lip curled. *"First of all, why should I trust you? Even if I did, you have to realize how invasive that—"*

Another memory burst into her mind, so suddenly she gasped. *She was in Wormwood's head, reliving the desperate, final seconds before his end, when Death was ripping his mind to shreds from the inside. Terror rose inside, and with it, that feral rage.*

That could be him. And Death had no right. Not when his own hypocrisy could destroy—

The memory cut off as quickly as it had come. Darien buried her face in the pillow with a muffled yelp, cold sweat trickling down her neck. *This could legitimately drive me insane.*

Sardonic amusement ripped down the connection between her and Ankle Tickler. It was almost as if he were saying, "Now you understand."

"So Death's your enemy, too," Darien thought. *"Are you ... wanting to team up?"* She frowned. *"What's in it for you, though?"*

Silence.

Darien swallowed, then pressed on. *"We have to close the gate. Your kind can't stay here. If an alliance is what you have in mind, I don't see it working long-term."*

Another memory started playing, quick and focused this time; he was getting better at this. Darien watched *as she and some friends hid under a park pavilion, giggling as big, fat raindrops fell out of the dark Colorado sky. They splashed everywhere, coating the grass and trees and dotting the white concrete, but she and her friends were safe from the storm here.*

"You think ..." Darien shook her head, confused. *"You think I can keep you safe somehow?"*

Ankle Tickler dug in so hard that pain twinged behind Darien's eyes. *More images flashed in rapid succession, all of movies, of characters with shields—*

Inspiration hit her in a flash. "Stop! *I get it!"*

It was only in the mental silence that followed that she realized how profound the implications were of what he'd just shown her. She rolled onto her side, peering over the edge of the bed. A pair of orange eyes stared back.

"Of course. It's obvious. You can shield your mind from Death's." She frowned, resting her chin on the mattress's edge. *"Can you get into the heads of other demons the way he does? Could* you *kill* him?"

The little demon's lips pulled back, revealing two long, pointed teeth. Another memory started to play in her mind, of *playing "David and Goliath" with the other kids on the church playground, her curled hair flying around her face, too worried about making the perfect slingshot to notice the grass stains on the knees of her skirt—*

"You realize David won that fight?" she asked.

Ankle Tickler snarled.

"But you don't think you can."

His snarl faded, replaced by a feeling of confirmation.

"Do you want *to kill him?"*

Another wave of approval, stronger this time.

"Well, join the club, I guess." Fear crept over her as she realized something. *"Could Death hear us now?"*

Ankle Tickler blinked, and another memory edged into Darien's mind. *Her seven-year-old self sat with four-year-old Ana in the latter's room, giggling as they greedily licked sugar off their fingers. They were giddy with success; they'd just snuck four freshly-fried churros out of their wrappings behind their mother's back because she wasn't always looking.*

Darien shook off the memory—and the tender, homey feelings it evoked. *"But we're pretty much the center of his attention right now. If he did happen to look while you and I were communicating, I know you'd be safe. But would I?"*

More silence.

Darien's pulse quickened. Aside from Ankle Tickler, the demons around her had never seemed to know she could see their thoughts. But there was so much she didn't understand about them. What if she was wrong and they all had a perfect lock on her, knew exactly what she could do? Had she been terribly vulnerable this entire time and not known?

"I'll teach you."

Her eyes widened as the next memory hit. *Sam, dressed in workout clothes that showed off his muscled arms, bounced a racquetball off the court's wall and caught it with ease. "I'll teach you."*

She swallowed as it faded. *"How? And honestly, I'm still not sure why you'd ally with someone who's trying to close you back in what's functionally a prison."*

Ankle Tickler stared up at her, unblinking, as if trying to decide what to say—or rather, think—next. Then, a single image flashed into her mind: a little woodburned sign that hung above her father's desk in his home office.

There's always another way. All you have to do is find it.

Something clattered in the living room. Darien froze. Ankle Tickler stood, the hairs along his back stiffening, his claws clenching against the floor—

Muffled, familiar voices issued under the door, the floor outside squeaking under several pairs of feet. Ankle Tickler whirled, disappearing under the bed without a sound. An instant later, his mind vanished, replaced by a void so dark and complete that Darien was afraid she'd disappear forever if she tried to go in after him.

For a moment, she lay there, staring at the spot where the demon had been. Then she settled back onto her pillow, only half aware of the low voices outside her door. *There's always another way … like, another way out?* she wondered. Had Ankle Tickler just implied that he wanted Death, well, *dead*, so badly that he'd be willing to go back to his prison-world to accomplish that? Were there other demons out there that felt the same way? Had she just stumbled upon the edges of a coup?

Darien rolled over as the last of the light faded from around the curtains; the sun had finally set. But her mind continued to churn. If she could learn how to shield herself, make *sure* Death—or other demons, for that matter—didn't know she was capable of spying …

She blinked as another thought occurred to her. What if she could go on the offensive? Destroy them from the inside out, like Death had Wormwood and the wendigo?

Darien stared at the door as Sam's low murmur issued underneath it, too faint to make out what he'd said. She'd tell them. She'd be an idiot not to. But first, she needed to know more. She needed to have enough evidence that her husband, or Oliver, or Ellie didn't just try and kill the little demon where he stood.

Research round two, she thought.

Sleep didn't claim her for hours.

Chapter Eleven

Oliver was barely aware of what he was doing as he got ready for bed. He stared out his bedroom window at the shadowy forest, fingers working absently at the buttons of his shirt as he tried to ignore the ache in his back and pull together his scattered thoughts. He felt ... *gloomy.*

Which makes sense under the circumstances.

Wincing, he shinnied out of his shirt and dropped it in his laundry basket. Then, he braced against his closet's door frame, teeth clenched, and waited for the ache in his back to subside.

It was obviously the situation that was getting him, he thought as the pain ebbed. During their frantic road trip from Boulder to Anchorage, he'd been so busy looking over his shoulder at the looming death behind them that he'd almost forgotten about the looming death in front of them. There was no avoiding it anymore, though; they were *here.* It was time. Someone he loved—realistically, several someones—wouldn't walk away from this.

And there was nothing he could do to prevent it.

Unless ...

He pulled on a pair of loose sweatpants, half-aware of the sink running on the other side of his bedroom wall as Ellie got ready for bed, too. Then he perched against the window frame and watched the mist dip and swirl, as if it were flirting gently with the treetops.

The Nantinaq. Oliver kept coming back to him. He knew nothing about the creature except that it was being severely punished for an unknown crime *and* had now failed at its job. It was understandable that Past Oliver had been so fixated on understanding the demons and what they were up against. But why hadn't he tried to learn more about the guardian himself? What if the creature knew something, or could *do* something, that could help them?

You did try, said a small voice in his brain.

A swirling hole opened in the mist, allowing Oliver a glimpse of the ocean beyond, so dark in the fading light that it was almost black. *I could try again.* They had four days; that was plenty of time. A trip to Portlock may be worth the risk.

The Nantinaq wasn't having it last time, though, and probably still won't.

Oliver frowned, picking at a bandage around his waist that was starting to come loose. *Plus, the place has got to be overrun with demons.*

That was probably true. But discovering what had already made its way up there would *also* be helpful.

There's nothing you can do.

Oliver's lip curled; he was sure now. "Get out, Slubgob."

A flash of angry shock confirmed his guess. His stomach clenched violently; it was amazing how strongly his *body* reacted to the thought of another mental invasion. He glared out the window. *You really thought you could sneak into my head? You really think this'll end any differently for you than it did for Wormwood?*

Fear pulsed through him. *Her* fear. Then, just as quickly, it was gone, and so was she.

The water turned off next door, and the sudden absence of sound yanked Oliver back to the present. A second later, the bathroom door squeaked open, followed by Ellie's soft footsteps as she padded across the hardwood. Oliver stood and crossed the room, swinging his door open without a sound. She stood on the other side of the dim, shadowed loft, dressed in soft-looking pants and a tank top. Her back was to him, her silhouette outlined by the dim glow of the downstairs lamp. She'd taken out her ponytail, and her loose hair tumbled nearly to her waist, glinting with bronze at its ends. Oliver took a step forward, a smile rising to his lips—

The floorboards squeaked under his feet, and Ellie whirled, fists raised, a snarl on her face.

He threw his hands up. "Whoa there!"

"Oliver!" She slumped, one fist going to her chest as if her heart were racing. "You can't sneak up on me when there are demons flying around!"

"Sorry, I didn't mean to. And speaking of demons ... Wait a minute." He cocked his head, frowning down at her still-clenched hand. "Can I teach you something about punching?"

She raised an eyebrow. "Sure. But if you teach me to punch and then sneak up on me again, whatever happens afterward is on you."

Oliver grinned and stepped forward, taking her wrist. "Noted." He met her eyes, his expression turning serious. "The secret to throwing a good bare-knuckled punch is to not."

Ellie's brow furrowed. "What?"

"The bones in your hands are small and easily broken. And you'd be shocked at how hard a human skull is. It'll break your hand before you break it."

"You sound like you're speaking from experience."

"I am. Which is why I'd like you to *avoid* that experience." He raised her hand to his lips and kissed it. "If you break this, you'll have a hard time playing your concerto. And that'd be a tragedy."

"Yeah," she said. Her face was inches from his. "I don't want to do that."

Oliver stared at her for a second longer before realizing he hadn't finished teaching her yet. "Anyway ..."

He slid his hand down her slender forearm, lifted her elbow, and tapped his other palm against it. "Use this instead. Twist at the hips just like you would if you were punching, but crack your elbow right across the face. Aim for weak spots: the nose, chin, and jaw. Your knees and feet are better weapons than your fists, too. You just have to keep your balance if you're going to kick someone."

"Or some*thing*," she muttered.

"Or something." Oliver dropped her arm, finally letting himself drink in the angles and curves of her face, that clear skin, those beautiful eyes. His chest ached at the thought of her being hurt. Ever. By anything.

Ellie cocked her head, a small smile rising to her lips. "Should we, I don't know, practice?"

"Do you want to practice?"

"Um ..."

Oliver grinned. "I can tell Helen we'll take her watch. There's plenty of space down there."

Ellie returned his smile, but it seemed strangely hollow. "I should, I know it." She looked over the balcony, her smile fading, then shook her head. "But not tonight. I'm so ..."

"Done?" Oliver supplied.

"Yes."

Oliver opened his arms. "Come here, then. We'll worry about it tomorrow."

With a sigh, Ellie wrapped her arms around his shoulders. Pulling her closer, Oliver let his fingers glide through her silky hair. It was still damp from their walk through the drizzle outside, and the combination of that wild rain-scent with her usual sugary vanilla was almost enough to knock him over. He let his forehead drop to her shoulder. *You're not the only one who needed this.*

Something twinged in his back, and he winced. Ellie pulled back, her expression guilty. "Sorry."

"It's okay." He gripped her waist gently, willing her to stay, relieved when she did. "They're healing quickly now. I didn't even crack any scabs fighting the demon earlier. You didn't hurt me."

Her eyes were huge and liquid in the faint lamplight.

"I can still do this." Oliver dipped his head, closing the last of the distance between them, and their lips met. He hadn't planned on doing this. Slubgob was still floating around out there. But they were finally alone, and it had been so long since he could kiss her the way she deserved to be kissed ...

In one moment, their kisses were tender, and tired, and cleansing. In the next, Ellie's fingers were threading into his hair, pulling him down as if something she'd kept pent-up for days—*weeks*, maybe—had finally burst. Oliver yanked her against his chest, against his racing heart, feeling her breathing go shallow as she arched against him. He was drunk; no, better than drunk because he'd remember this in the morning—he'd remember this *forever*. Her silky lips, her unbelievably soft hair, how perfect the curve of her waist felt under his hands—

Downstairs, Helen broke into a coughing fit. Oliver surfaced with a sharp intake of breath, feeling Ellie's ribcage expand as she did the same.

"Sorry," she whispered.

"Good *night*, that was—" Oliver frowned, willing his brain to start working again. "Wait, sorry? For what?"

Ellie's brow furrowed, then she snapped her mouth shut. "I don't know."

Oliver's heart sank. "It's Slubgob."

"Slubgob? Wait, *seriously*?"

Oliver grabbed her hand and tugged her toward the futon. "Yeah. She was in my head earlier. It seems like she's not exclusively attached to Helen anymore."

He sat, and she settled next to him, their shoulders touching. Oliver fought the urge to close his eyes, both from the sudden re-emergence of his tiredness and how good it still felt to just *touch* her this casually, after Wormwood's ugly interference.

"I guess I'm not actually surprised," Ellie said. "I thought I felt something earlier. A sort of pressure, like when Wormwood was in here." She tapped her temple. "It went away for a while, but now it seems like it's back. My thoughts are dark, my anxiety is overwhelming. Even worse than usual." She let out a long sigh, her voice falling to a whisper. "Kissing you was so wonderful, because I could just ... forget."

Oliver's heart twinged as she seemed to shrink, a hot surge of anger following close on its heels. He wished he could punch Slubgob into absolute oblivion. It would be an honor to break all the bones in his hands doing something that noble. Tracing the outline of her shoulder blade, he murmured, "Well, I'm happy to keep distracting you. But we would need to acknowledge that kissing's a Band-Aid solution."

Ellie snorted. "I'd love it anyway. The smartest thing would be to just put me to bed, though." She let out a frustrated growl. "How do I get her out, Oliver? It took you over a month with Wormwood, and Helen still hasn't succeeded. Unless ..." Her head came up, and she met his eyes.

"Unless she *just* did," Oliver said.

Ellie nodded. "Which would be a huge victory." She stared across the dark loft, her eyes unfocused. "It makes sense that Slubgob would want to stick around. Maybe she's replaced Wormwood as a spy. You and Helen are too tough now, and everyone else is asleep, so she's stuck with me." She dropped her gaze, her voice falling to barely a whisper. "The coward."

Oliver's gaze whipped to her. "Ellie. Did you just call yourself a coward?"

She blinked, but the shine of tears in her eyes didn't fade. He took her by the shoulders. "Listen, that doesn't make any sense."

She sniffed. "I'm so afraid, Oliver."

"Of course you are. You're human."

"I know, but ..." She looked up again but didn't quite meet his eyes, tears falling down her cheeks. "How can it still be this strong? Why do I still feel like this? After all we've survived, all I've overcome, why do I still feel so paralyzed by these damn feelings? I've been to therapy! I *know* they're not ... not *me*! I'm *better* than this!"

Oliver stared down at her, fumbling for the right thing to say. Finally, he put a hand on her shoulder and said, "You're being too hard on yourself."

When she didn't reply, he went on.

"Your fear makes perfect sense. Your last month has been a nightmare; you lost so much up there. But you refuse to lie down and quit." His voice softened. "That's the opposite of cowardice."

A sob shook her frame. She leaned into him, resting her forehead on his shoulder. Oliver wrapped his arms around her and held her, her tears dripping onto his skin and trickling down toward his bandages. He let them.

"Want more evidence, Miss Lawyer's Daughter? Aside from killing the Lady and shooting arrows at Death himself, let's not forget that—"

"Yeah, I guess—" She hiccupped. "I guess that was pretty cool."

"You also kicked Wormwood out of your head after only a few days. The rest of us took weeks." He pulled back, then lifted her chin until she was looking at him. Gently, he brushed his knuckles across her face, wiping the tears away.

"Not that long ago," he continued, "I also watched you stick to the truth even though no one believed you. And when Darien woke up screaming in the hotel this morning, you ran to her with no hesitation. You nearly beat down their door."

"I ... yeah." She nodded, her expression seeming to clear some.

"Want me to keep going?" he asked.

A watery smile broke through Ellie's tears. "No. I'm good. I think she left, and this is getting embarrassing."

"Good. Now, while I have you ..." He took her face in his hands and looked deep into her eyes. "No one—*no one*—gets to call the woman I love a coward. Not even you."

He smiled gently. Then, hoping he wasn't overstepping, he tapped his fingertip to the center of her chest, right over her sternum. "I know what's in here. I've seen what you're capable of. I know you can beat this."

Her breath caught, her eyes turning brilliant with surprise. "You heard me."

"I heard you." Oliver let his hand fall, then leaned forward and rested his forehead against hers. "I wouldn't have made it back without you. The pain would've been too much. Your strength is the reason I'm alive." He brushed a light kiss across her lips. "I love you."

He kissed her nose, her cheeks, and when her eyes fluttered closed, their lids. "I love you," he whispered again. "You brave, beautiful woman."

They didn't say anything after that; at least, not with words. Oliver just kissed her, slowly, passionately, tasting the salt of her tears on his lips, surrendering to the siren call of her velvet-soft skin. For a moment, she was his whole world.

And then movement sounded from downstairs; Helen was on her way to the kitchen. Like a summer butterfly, the moment was gone. And Oliver found himself wanting to mourn.

Ellie looked down at the futon, then back up to him. "What if I lie down and quit? Just for tonight."

Oliver shrugged. "You've earned it."

"Will you stay with me?"

Something inside Oliver melted. "Of course I will."

They lay down, and Oliver pulled the comforter over them, then draped his arm around Ellie's waist. Part of him was afraid he wouldn't be able to sleep next to her now that his body was on the mend, that she would be too distracting. But, it turned out, he was *tired*. The warmth of her, the steady cadence of her breathing ... this was more relaxing than half a bottle of oxycodone.

You addict, he thought. *You've only stayed with her for three nights.*

But as Ellie's breathing deepened, and as drowsiness started to overtake Oliver, too, he thought there were much worse things to be addicted to.

Chapter Twelve

Darien lay in the haze between sleep and waking, her limbs leaden, the blankets and pillows around her a perfect, cozy cocoon. Next to her, Sam stirred. A moment later, his languorous whisper reached her ears.

"Hey, beautiful."

The soft brush of his lips on her cheekbone made Darien smile. She rolled onto her back as he kissed her temple, the side of her mouth, and her cheek again. "It's six-fifteen. I think Helen's making breakfast."

"Mmmm." She sighed as he nuzzled against her.

And then memories from the night before invaded.

Darien's eyes snapped open. Slubgob was spying for Death. She'd pushed the baby too far, and it had shut her out. Ankle Tickler was here, and wanted something from her. And ... "Sam. I made a breakthrough last night."

He stared at her uncertainly. "A breakthrough ...?"

"With my powers."

Sam's mouth opened in shock. "What kind of breakthrough? What—?"

"I can feel individual demons now. Even juveniles."

"No kidding!"

"Yeah."

She sat, smoothing her hair out of her face, and chanced a peek at the baby. Last night, its little psyche had seemed to return to normal quickly, and ...Darien exhaled as she felt its usual contentment and peace pulsing from it, as if nothing had ever happened. Relief swept over her. *Never again, I promise.*

"So what is it? What's the breakthrough?"

Sam's voice jolted Darien back to the present. "There are ..."

Closing her eyes, she tried to expand her mind the way she had last night, trying not to think about where her inspiration to try that in the first place had come from. "Five juveniles. And Slubgob is ..." Darien frowned. "She's trying to bug Henry, but he's not easy for her to get to because he's not ..." She almost laughed. "He's just not as prone to worry as she is. Is that just generally a man thing, do you think ...?"

The words died on her lips at the look on Sam's face. "Dar, this is incredible!"

"I know."

"You not only know how many demons there are in a room, but whether they're juveniles or Awakened, *and* what they're feeling."

"Yeah!"

He stared at her for a moment more, an incredulous grin spreading across his face. "You're a better demon finder than even me! We might have a shot at winning this thing!"

Darien laughed. "I like to think we always had a shot." But the smile slid off her face as she thought about the other developments from last night. "Slubgob's spying for Death."

"Yeah?" Sam grew serious. "Well, we knew that was a possibility."

"I don't know how effective she is, though," Darien said slowly. "She doesn't seem ... well, all there. But she is trying to switch between people now to dig for information, so be aware."

"Noted." Sam cocked his head. "If you can get in their minds now, have you tried messing with them at all?"

"No." She thought of Ankle Tickler and their weird interaction the night before. Did she dare tell Sam the demon wanted to ally to take down Death? Did she dare, when all he wanted to do was rip the creature limb from limb?

Do I dare not *tell him? It's not like Ankle Tickler is my friend, either.* The situation would make them temporary, uneasy allies at best. But throwing Sam into the mix might break any fragile trust that had managed to grow between them, especially since the creature had requested that she not.

Maybe waiting—at least for now—was the best option.

"Well, there's still time." Sam threw off the covers and climbed out of bed, stretching. Darien watched uneasily, thinking about creepy, elongated hands reaching out from the dark space beneath her, slashing another gash in his shin—

You know that won't happen, though. He doesn't want anyone else to know he's here.

"I'm going to head out, maybe see if I can shower before breakfast." He grabbed an armful of clothes, kissed her lightly, then stepped toward the door.

"I won't be far behind you," Darien said. The door opened and closed, letting in a whiff of something warm and savory that, to her relief, actually smelled *good*.

In a second, she told her stomach, smiling as she caught another little glimpse of the baby's warm contentment. A strong part of her still wanted to bask in that, treasure it. Instead, she reached out, feeling for the void that was Ankle Tickler's mind. *"Are you there?"*

Silence.

"You promised to teach me. I can't stay here long, but at least give me something."

A faint tremor of acknowledgement. Then, an image from one of her textbooks brushed against her mind, a passage of text that was all hazy except for one word: fortification.

"Fortification." She frowned. *"You mean, fortify my mind?"*

Approval.

"Any suggestions on how to get started? Or what that even looks like?"

A string of words flashed through her mind. *Collins ... Alamo ... Laramie ... Knox—*

"Yeah, I do know what a fort is, thanks." At the sound of stairs squeaking above her, she stood. When nothing grabbed at her feet, she crossed the room, pulled on a pair of insulated pants she'd bought in Anchorage, and threw on a sweater. Then, she paused, hand on the doorknob. *"They'll be expecting me. I'll see what I can do about that mental ... fortress, though."*

Approval brushed against her mind again as she opened the door and stepped out.

***

Oliver's phone buzzed in his pocket as he thumped down the stairs, but he ignored it, taking in the scene before him instead. Breakfast seemed all but ready; as he watched, Henry pulled a pile of pot holders out of a drawer and started for the table. Helen and Ellie seemed to have stacked enough golden-brown biscuits in the bread basket to feed half the town, and Sam and Darien were setting out plates. Other than the burn that scarred the Calls' honey-gold table, it looked so ... normal.

"'Morning, Oliver," Helen said. "How are your burns?"

"They're good." His eyes swept the room again. Now that he was paying closer attention, things *weren't* so normal. In fact, there seemed to be little weapons everywhere. A long, blue lighter stuck out of Sam's pocket, and Darien hovered within arm's length of a completely unnecessary carving knife that gleamed against the table's charred surface. A second lighter—this one shaped like a shotgun—rested on the coffee table. Someone had pulled the fireplace poker, shovel, and ash bucket out from their usual places and set them within easy reach of the couch. The Calls' .44 revolver lay on the mantle, its grip facing outward—with a can of bear spray to keep it company. And to complete the arsenal, Helen had lit a candle. It flickered on the granite countertop, its little flame swaying in a slow, sinuous dance, as if it knew it might be called on to destroy at any moment and wanted to be limber for it.

"Could you grab these biscuits and take them over?" Helen asked.

"Yeah." Oliver crossed the kitchen, brushing his palm against the small of Ellie's back as he passed. She smiled at him as he grabbed the basket, then turned toward the table.

"And do you want me to help rebandage your burns after breakfast?" Helen asked.

"Nah, they're great. They don't need bandages anymore." Oliver turned in time to see his aunt set a bowl of fruit on the bar top, her face taut with worry as she looked at him.

"But thank you," he added. "I promise I'm not trying to be a hero."

Helen fixed him with a loving glare. "You don't have to try. It's just your character. Which is why the rest of us have to worry about you so much."

Oliver spluttered, feeling his cheeks heat. Over Helen's shoulder, Ellie shot him a smug smile that seemed to say, "See? I'm not the only one."

"I'm ... just going to take this over," he muttered at the fruit bowl.

Sam snickered. "There's no good way to respond to that."

"That's why I ran away."

Sam's snicker turned into an outright laugh. Oliver frowned as his phone buzzed again, but forgot about it almost instantly as Ellie spoke.

"Slubgob is head-hopping. She came after both Oliver and me last night. Just thought you all should know."

Helen grunted as she lifted a heavy pitcher of what was probably milk. "*That's* why I slept so well after my watch. I feel like she's circled back around this morning, unfortunately."

"Oh!" Sam slapped a hand to his forehead as he settled next to Darien, who had been strangely quiet this whole time. "That's what I've been seeing!"

"What?" Henry asked from next to the pellet stove.

"Last night during my watch, I saw something that looked like a gargoyle standing behind your couch. It came toward me, and I was just about to sound the alarm when it disappeared." He scowled. "I felt really ... *morose* for the rest of my watch, then had a hard time falling asleep afterward."

"You know, insult to injury," Ellie said as she pulled up a chair next to Oliver.

"And you can see when she's in someone's head, right?" Helen asked as she took her seat at the end of the table. "So you know where she is all the time."

"So far, yeah."

"I can live with being the favorite if it keeps her off of the rest of you," Helen said. "I'm just sorry she's—"

"No sorrys," Henry rumbled as he stumped toward the dining table with a big pot of sausage gravy. "That demon's her own person. Or ... entity. Point is, you're not responsible for what she does."

"Besides," Oliver said, "I think we're willing to take her on for a little bit if it gets you a break."

Helen pressed her hand to her mouth, her eyes suddenly glistening. She blinked, sniffed once, then reached for a biscuit. "I love you all."

Oliver smiled. "We love you—" His phone buzzed again, "—too ..."

He glanced down, brow creased. *That* much activity was unusual.

"—there are still a bunch of baby demons hovering around?"

Henry's voice brought him back to the present. He looked up, pulling his phone out of his pocket, his attention divided between the two.

"Five at my last count," Sam said.

"So, more than there used to be." Henry stared at the burned table, looking pensive. And Oliver's phone buzzed *again*. He swiped it open, cursing its slow load time, half-listening as the conversation continued.

"The five come and go," Sam said. "They're not always here in the room with us. Sometimes they'll drift through the wall for a few minutes, sometimes one will follow someone into a bedroom or the bathroom—"

Darien snorted. "Don't let *that* image disturb you."

"I'll just moon them," Henry said dryly. "Give them exactly what they deserve."

"Henry," Helen snapped, but Sam and Darien were already chuckling. Even Oliver couldn't help but grin, but it disappeared as his screen finally loaded. Jessie and Jordan had put the three of them in a group text, and all four messages were from the former.

`Oliver we need to talk ASAP`

`Text me back`

`Hurry we don't have a lot of time`
`If you don't text back in five minutes I'm going to call`

Oliver's frown deepened as his thumbs moved over the keypad. **`Sitting down to breakfast. Call you when I'm done`**

"Darien?"

The tone of Sam's voice—quiet, fearful even—made Oliver look up. In the time it had taken him to answer Jessie's texts, Darien had *wilted*. She sat with a hand pressed over her eyes, ashen-faced, her expression pained.

"Dar?" Sam grabbed her shoulder.

She let out a tiny moan. Then she collapsed on the table, drawing in a shuddering gasp.

***

Darien had enough warning to think *I'm not ready* before being sucked into Death's head. *The world was a whirl of stone and sky, ice and forest and feathery white clouds as he killed, and killed again, and again. The power was blinding; he heard their screams, felt the cool, delicious wind on their faces as they tried to run, the slap of dew-heavy undergrowth on their feet, their shins, the battering of their doomed hearts.*

Vampire. Reaper. Undead.

Death breathed in their terror. He was all of those things.

He was whatever they saw him as.

He was euphoric.

Darien cried out as *the last one died, its life draining out of it too quickly. Death breathed several times—he could; he was in his physical form—and looked down at its little body. A shame, really. They weren't satisfying when they were that young. He would much have preferred to let it grow, to* experience *more before—*

"*God*, no," Darien gasped, *prayed*, tears searing her cheeks. "Please, *please* no—"

Fortify.

The concept burst into her head. She choked back a sob, then, blocking out Sam's scared voice and his hand on her back and the tumult around her, she raised an image of the structure she'd spent the last half hour building in her mind.

Her fortress.

It loomed, a graceful behemoth of Rocky Mountain granite, cut and shaped and sculpted until it gleamed, a strange synthesis of Disney Princess and Gothic cathedral. And now—though it was still far from finished—she was grateful she'd put so much detail into it. She had things to focus on, places to hide.

Darien shut her eyes, put her elbows on the table, and smashed her palms over her ears. She imagined herself safely inside the stone walls of her mind, then let herself peek out a window. *You only need to know where he is,* she told herself. *That's all you need—his location.*

Death straightened, gazing out across the vista before him. It was easy to see why they liked this place. The variety and dramaticism of this world were on full display here. Perhaps once he secured it for himself, he would let himself enjoy it. He turned away from the steep drop into the ravine—and the bodies he'd rolled down into it. It was likely they wouldn't be found for days, and—with the predators that roamed these forests—possibly they wouldn't be found at all. He hiked back to the hilltop and the road beyond, letting himself enjoy the exertion, the strain in his legs and chest.

But he couldn't stay.

Death took one last look around, noting the big vehicle parked in the half-circle of dirt. There was nothing he could do about it. Shuddering back into his shadow form, he enjoyed one last look at the mountains and the massive glacier snaking between them.

"Salmon Glacier," he murmured. He'd never tried a fish before. If the opportunity presented itself in the next few days, though ...

He turned north and began his fast, gliding walk that ate up miles like he'd just eaten those people's lives—

A hand closed around Darien's wrist, her husband's muffled voice in her ear. She let him tug her hand away, raising her head as Death's power ebbed and the vision evaporated.

"Salmon Glacier!" she gasped. "He's at a place called Salmon Glacier. He just killed seven people—a whole *family* ..." Memories of what she'd seen crashed back over her, and she started to shake, as much from rage as fear this time. "It's so awful. I can't *do* anything ... I, I just have to *watch* them die—"

Sam's arms came around her and crushed her to him. She buried her face in his chest, fresh tears leaking from her eyes.

"Salmon Glacier ... that's down on the Panhandle," she heard Henry say.

"If it's the one I'm thinking of, yes," Helen said. "That's down by Juneau, Skagway, Glacier Bay, Stewart, all those places," she added, probably for the benefit of Darien and the other Forths. Emotion pricked at Darien's heart; in that moment, she desperately missed her parents and sisters.

But Ellie's shocked voice broke through her pain. "Wait, so he's already in Alaska?"

Alarm shot through Darien. She pushed away from Sam but kept her grip on his hand—she needed it.

"Stewart's still thirteen hundred miles away," Helen said. "We have time."

She didn't say what Darien suspected they were all thinking: *but it's running out.*

"Let me find a picture," Darien said, pulling out her phone. "I'd know it if I saw it."

"Here." Helen turned her phone screen around to reveal a photo of a landscape that perfectly matched what Darien had just seen.

She nodded. "That's it."

Henry's expression darkened. "Clever, clever bastard. Salmon Glacier's a tourist attraction, but it's not as busy as some of the others in the area. You have to drive over thirty miles of dirt road to get there, which most people won't do." He shook his head. "It's the perfect spot for him to hunt. This time of year, he's all but guaranteed to catch someone. But he'll still have enough time to hide their remains before the next group gets there."

Darien's chest felt hollow. "I wish I could warn everyone who's about to be in his way."

For a moment, the only sound in the room was the mechanical *whir* of the pellet stove's auger.

"How many days?" Oliver finally asked.

Darien straightened, only too happy to make her brain chew on the kind of problem she could actually solve. "Let's do the math. When Death is in his shadow state, he can go right through trees, rocks, and all sorts of obstacles, and cold and weather don't affect him. I don't think he's moving as quickly as he did when he was chasing you two." She nodded toward Ellie and Oliver. "I'd guess he's going at a steady fifteen miles per hour, maybe more if he's pushing himself."

"If he has to feed to sustain his traveling pace, he probably can't fly straight across the Gulf," Oliver said.

"Yeah," Henry said. "Unless he's real good at fishing or stumbles onto a shipping boat, there's no food out there for him."

"So he *has* to go overland, but obviously wants to be as efficient about it as possible." Sam looked to Henry. "You said Salmon Glacier's thirteen hundred miles?"

Henry shook his head. "Stewart's thirteen hundred, but Salmon Glacier's more like a thousand. By road at least." He frowned. "Since he's not following the road, it might be even less."

"Let's stick with nine hundred," Darien said. "I'd rather overestimate his speed than underestimate it."

She reached for her phone, but Oliver had already beaten her to it. His eyes widened as he looked down at the screen.

Next to him, Ellie's face paled. "Three days?"

"And if the meeting isn't until tomorrow night—" Oliver started.

Helen's curse cut him off. "Ray's foot-dragging is going to get us all killed."

"Helen, we still have time," Henry said.

"We'll be cutting it close, though," Helen said.

Henry crossed his arms, his expression both frustrated and sympathetic. "Nothing we can do."

Darien stared down at her empty plate, queasiness stirring in her belly. That family ... those *kids* ... "I hate that Death is probably going to kill so many more people before he even gets here." She looked up at the faces around the table, all a reflection of what she felt. "That family didn't deserve what happened to them."

Helen stared at her table with a look so thoughtful it was almost a scowl. "People rarely do." She looked up. "Let's finish eating. We've got to move fast if we want to be at the warehouse by nine."

Chapter Thirteen

Breakfast was over quickly, which was a mercy, because the mood at the table was more like one that would typically be found at a funeral. Oliver pushed his chair back and stood, staring at his phone, only half-aware of the post-meal clatter around him as he looked down at Jessie's latest text.

Hurry

"Oliver?" Ellie asked. "Is everything okay?"

"I don't know. Jessie's been texting me all morning. He says it's urgent." He looked up at Henry. "Have you heard anything from Bill or Luke this morning?"

Henry shook his head. "No. You, Helen?"

"Nope." Helen cast Oliver a worried look. "I think you'd better get out there and call your friend.

Ellie held out her hand for his plate. "I can take this. You go."

"Thanks," he said, handing it to her. She flashed him a thumbs-up.

"Just to make sure I've got this straight," Oliver heard Darien say as he headed toward the front door, " ... Jessie's Bill's son, and Jordan's Luke's son?"

"Correct," Sam said. "And Jessie wants to go help avenge Charity, his mother, who died in a mugging about two weeks ago. But Bill won't let anyone under eighteen come."

"Two weeks?" Darien's voice rose in shock, the ache in it palpable. "That poor kid."

"Yeah, he's not thinking clearly," Henry said sadly. "Not that any of us blame him."

"The only thing you really need to know," Henry said as Oliver laced up his shoes, "is that Portlock's a serious sore spot for everyone involved right now. I'd stay out of it if I were you."

"I'd stay out of it if I were *me*, and I've known that family since before Jessie was born," Helen muttered.

"Noted," Darien said. "Is there anything else I should know?"

Oliver didn't hear Helen's reply. He straightened, meeting Ellie's sober gray eyes from across the big room. She gave him a nod, which he returned. Then, he slipped out the door.

The morning air was cool on his face, the smell of spruce and rain wrapping around him like a chilly, fragrant parka. He took a deep breath and let it out slowly; everything was clearer out here under the open, cloud-strewn sky. Goosebumps flitted across his skin as his body adjusted to the drop in temperature, and he wriggled a little as they skated across the tender parts of his chest and back. When they settled, he pulled out his phone and hit the call button.

Jessie picked up almost immediately. "About time, dude."

Oliver leaned against the gnarled pinewood column next to him. "What's going on, Jessie?"

"Hang on, let me get Jordan on the phone."

"Are you okay?"

Jessie's derisive snort sounded in Oliver's ear. "No. But I think I'm about to be better."

Oliver frowned as he listened to the sounds of dialing, and rustling, and maybe ... was that water? "Are you outside?"

"Yeah. I'm walking down the road."

"Alone?"

"Yeah."

Oliver closed his eyes. "You know there are demons all over the place."

"Ha. I'm less worried about demons than I am about people."

You're just like your dad, Oliver thought.

A click sounded in his ear, then Jordan's voice drifted over the speaker. "Hey, guys."

"Are you alone, Jordan?" Jessie asked, and Oliver's eyebrows rose. Suddenly, this was feeling a little too secretive for comfort.

"Yep," Jordan said. "Mom and Dad are down at the warehouse. They took Allie with them and Nora's still asleep, so I'm good."

"Good," Jessie said.

"All right, what's this about?" Oliver asked as the door banged shut behind him. He turned to see Sam striding across the porch.

"Don't mind me," his friend whispered as he half-jogged past Oliver and down the stairs. "Just getting more pellets."

"There's a wheelbarrow on that side of the house," Oliver said, tucking the phone away from his face. "Easier if you're going to get a couple of bags."

Sam gave him a thumbs-up—the gesture nearly identical to the one Ellie had given him minutes ago—and changed directions.

"Is someone there, Oliver?"

Oliver's unease deepened at the suspicious, almost frightened tone in Jessie's voice. Experience had taught him that when someone sounded like that, it was rarely for a good reason. But he schooled his voice into a neutral tone. "Sam Forth. From Colorado. He was just passing on his way to get pellets. Now, are you going to tell me what's up, or do I need to find you and make you?"

Jessie scoffed. "You're tough and all, but I think I could take you."

Oliver scowled. "That's not relevant, and I only have a few minutes. So get on with it."

"Right," Jessie said, his tone suddenly businesslike. Oliver listened with narrowed eyes, half-watching Sam as he appeared again from around the corner, his wheelbarrow thumping over the uneven ground as he headed for the shed.

"So here's the deal. After the fiasco last night, Jordan and I got talking. We think if a few of us get together, maybe take the *Poor Buoy* because she's fast and reliable, and leave tonight, after everyone falls asleep, then we can travel while the sun's down, get to Portlock just as it's rising, and shut the gate. Just get it done."

For a moment, the muted *thump-thump* of the wheelbarrow and Sam's footsteps were the only sounds.

"You're kidding, right?" Oliver finally said.

Jessie's voice hardened, reminding Oliver even more of Bill. "No."

Oliver rubbed his eyes. "That's not a good idea."

"Why not?" they both asked at the same time.

"Oliver," Jessie said, "we might be able to save hundreds of lives. We could stop this thing before it even begins, hit the demons before they're expecting it."

"Isn't Death getting closer?" Jordan asked. "Like, right now, as we speak?"

Oliver ground his teeth. Trust Jordan to cut right to the heart of the matter like that, and he didn't even know what Darien had just seen. "Yes."

"So let's not give him another day," Jordan said. "Let's just go do it."

Oliver leaned down and braced his elbows on the railing. A shaft of sunlight broke through the cottony clouds, bathing his back and shoulders in sudden warmth. He barely felt it. "You two realize someone has to die to shut the gate, right?"

"Yes," said Jessie quietly.

"Yeah," echoed Jordan.

"Guys, think about that. Are you both willing—really *willing*—to walk to your death in cold blood? Because that's what we're talking—"

"*Yes*, Oliver," Jordan said.

"Hell yeah!" said Jessie. "As far as I'm concerned, it's their fault my mom's dead. I'll do what it takes."

Oliver kneaded his eyes. "Listen, guys. I don't doubt your bravery, but you don't understand what's up there. You *can't* understand until you've faced it. It took a whole troop of Hawaiian warriors to get past the Gatekeeper last—"

"Are *you* willing?" Jessie interrupted. He sounded almost scornful.

Oliver's scowl deepened. Across the yard, Sam poked his head out of the shed's open door, a shrewd expression on his face. Oliver made the snap decision not to lower his voice. If he could enlist Sam's help in talking the teens down throughout the afternoon ...

"I already tried, Jessie," Oliver said evenly. "I went up there alone. Took the boat and the kayak and my bear pistol, with no backup and no idea what I was getting into. And when I got there, the Nantinaq himself told me to turn around and go home. That if I stayed, I would probably die."

"That's because you were alone—" Jordan started, but Oliver overrode him.

"No, listen. I tried anyway, and I had the same motivations as you: grief, love, and yeah, even a little fear. I get it. I've been there. But it was the most horrific thing I've ever experienced, including almost being burned alive."

And almost being seduced by the Dark Lady. A horrible image of that morning popped into his mind, and he shuddered so hard his back twinged. Slubgob-thought or no, it was absolutely true. But his friends didn't need that in their heads. He moved on. "I almost died. The only reasons I didn't were Dean's ghost and the Nantinaq."

"See? We have more help than—"

"No. We don't." Oliver slapped his palm down on the smooth wooden railing. "Dean hasn't spoken to me in days, and the Nantinaq says he can't help."

Do you believe that, though? asked a small voice in his head. Oliver ignored it; what he *knew* was that the boys' proposal verged on suicide. "You *don't* understand what we'd be getting into. And I don't want to watch either of you die."

For a moment, it was quiet. Sam appeared in the shed's doorway with another fifty-pound pellet bag slung over his shoulder. He looked back at Oliver again, this time with a clear frown on his face.

Then Jessie spoke. "I thought, of all people, *you'd* be willing to let us make our own decisions."

"Look," Oliver said, "I'm not saying—"

"Hang on, I have a question," Jordan interrupted. "A couple of them, actually. How do you *know* how many Hawaiian warriors it took?"

"Sam and Darien—my friend and his wife—fell into the demons' world while vacationing in Hawaii."

Sam dumped the bag of pellets on top of the first one, then turned to face Oliver. Keeping his eyes on his friend, Oliver continued. "When they got out, they were confronted by the spirits of ancient Hawaiian warriors. The same ones who beat the demons thousands of years ago. They got to talk with the men who led the cave assault, including the one who actually dove in and sacrificed himself."

Oliver pulled the phone away from his cheek and mouthed "right?" at Sam. He nodded.

"From what I was told, there were at least four or five—"

Sam flashed a hand above his head, fingers spread.

"Five," Oliver amended. "But they had a backup team, and half an army fighting most of the demons on the other side of the island. We wouldn't have any of that."

"Yeah, but I can't imagine your dad *wouldn't* come help you again, if you were in trouble up there," Jordan said.

Something twinged in Oliver's chest, but he ignored it. "He'd probably try. Whether he'd succeed or not is a different question."

"What about my mom?" Jessie's voice was low and gruff, but he didn't quite manage to cover up the rawness at its core.

"I don't know," Oliver said gently. "I'm sure she would help if she could, but it's ... more complicated than that."

"Complicated how?"

Oliver pinched the bridge of his nose. "It's hard to explain. Can I fill you in while we're out knocking on doors or building weapons or something today?"

"If we're even allowed to do that," Jessie grumbled.

"They'll let us," Jordan said. "That stuff's not dangerous, and I think they feel bad about last night. I bet you money they put us to work this afternoon, just because they think it'll make us feel better."

There was a pause. Then Jessie just said, "Sure. Tell me then."

"All right." Oliver dropped his hand again, suddenly feeling drained. *Bad sign, given that it's only eight in the morning.*

"Before you go, just consider this," Jordan said. "We're not Hawaiian warriors. But we *are* buff fishermen who've done hard physical labor our whole lives. We're young, fit, strong, and incredibly pissed off. And the Nantinaq helped you before, and so did Dean. That might be five people right there."

"Three of whom are reliable, trustworthy, and brave." Oliver released the railing and started to pace. "But who's going to die, Jordan? If you can tell me that with a steady voice, I'll—"

"I will."

Oliver stopped, blinking. They'd both said it at the same time.

And a little voice in his heart answered. *I will.*

Damn it, he thought.

"Fine, I'll give you credit for that." The squeak of the burdened wheelbarrow reached his ears. He turned to see Sam pushing it toward him, a grim look on his face. "Listen, I've got to go. And you need to know I'm not sold, and I'm going to try and talk you out of it all afternoon."

"You're not gonna succeed," Jessie said.

"Probably not," Jordan admitted. "We've all got too much on the line, yourself included, Oliver. And while we'd *like* to use the *Poor Buoy* because she's faster, we do have other options if you decide *you'd* rather play it safe."

"Jordan ..." Oliver ran a hand through his hair, his nails scraping against his scalp. The wheelbarrow squeaked one more time as Sam set it down at the bottom of the porch steps, then looked up at Oliver with his hands on his hips. Turning, Oliver thumped down the stairs toward his friend. "Listen, I've got to go. Don't do anything stupid."

"Stupid and heroic often look the same at first glance," Jordan said.

"And someone has to do something," Jessie added. "We're running out of time."

"We *are* doing something. You two includ—"

"Don't patronize us," Jessie snarled.

Oliver's frustration finally boiled over into his voice. "I'm *not*, Jessie! We're in a bad situation. Everyone's suffering. And the people who care about you the most are trying to protect you because they love you, even if that protection is misguided. Yeah, it's frustrating, but be grateful you have people like that in your life."

For a moment, the only sounds were the breeze flowing through the tops of the spruce trees, the distant cry of a seabird, and the trickle of water crackling through Jessie's end of the speaker.

"So you *do* think they're wrong for not letting us go," Jessie said.

"I'll talk to you soon," Oliver growled, then hung up. Kneading his eyes again, he leaned against the railing and tried to wrestle his anger back into the pit of his stomach where it belonged.

"It sounds like they want to take matters into their own hands," Sam said.

"Yeah." Oliver blew out a long breath. "Idiots."

There was a soft crunch of gravel, then a deep breath from Sam, then quiet. Oliver finally looked up. His friend had turned his back to the porch railing and was leaning against it with his arms crossed, staring into the lush woods surrounding the cabin.

"Are they?" he asked softly.

Oliver stared at him for a moment. "Yes. They are."

Sam stared back, unrelenting. Then his eyes flicked over Oliver's shoulder to something on the porch behind him. Fear flashed across his face. The hair on the back of Oliver's neck rose, but when he whirled, there was nothing there. Shuddering, he turned back to Sam, his skin still prickling at the thought of what was behind him, what it might be doing. *He* was likely feeling enough frustration, helplessness, and fear to keep it fed for a solid month, maybe two, without factoring in whatever the others were dealing with.

"They're everywhere, Oliver," Sam muttered. "All the time."

Oliver studied his friend for a moment: his brooding, hollow expression, the slump of his huge shoulders, the way he hunched against the porch's railing like an old man on a cane. Oliver folded his arms, too, willing his body to relax as he considered what to say next.

"Is Slubgob out here?" he asked.

Sam shook his head. "She was out here with you a few minutes ago, but she's gone now. I assume she's either back with Helen or trying to get at Darien." His expression darkened, if possible, even more. "She's been weirdly focused on Darien this morning.

"The point is," Oliver said, "we're both thinking, acting, and speaking without her influence."

"For the moment, at least."

The silence stretched for a few seconds. And the instant Sam spoke, Oliver knew he shouldn't have let it.

"Jessie and Jordan might have a point."

"No. Absolutely not." Oliver gestured at Sam. "You heard most of that conversation. I stand by what I said about how horrific the Gatekeeper is."

"Yeah, and I believe you. It's not like I'm excited about the idea of sneaking up there in the dead of night, probably *dying* up there. But if we have the means ..." He looked over at Oliver and shrugged.

But Oliver shook his head. "Granted, you're the one who talked to the Night Marchers, so you might have a better idea than I do. But based on my experience, I think you're going to lose at least two people, maybe all four of us if we—"

"What are the odds we can persuade the Nantinaq to help?"

"Zero. I think."

"He saved Ellie. And you."

Oliver paused. "That's true. But I don't know what his motives were for doing that. He's completely different from us, Sam. He might as well be an alien. And getting answers out of him is like trying to kill a four-hundred-pound halibut with an ax."

Sam's mouth quirked upward. "Never tried to do that before."

Oliver let out a humorless laugh. "I have, and I've still got scars from it. The point is, we'd just be four guys against one of the baddest monsters ever to walk the earth."

"I think that's how the Hawaiians saw themselves, too, and they succeeded."

"With an army."

"Which was clear on the other side of the island." Sam turned to face him. "I don't know if we should dismiss this idea out of hand. Death isn't here, and the demons that *are* won't be expecting an attack." He gestured toward the porch. "We have five ticking time bombs floating around constantly, sometimes more. Any second could be a repeat of last night, and my pregnant wife is right in the middle of it."

"You're right," Oliver said. "But—"

"And so is Ellie."

Oliver shut his mouth, then scrubbed a hand across his face. Ellie was his Achilles heel. And not only did everyone know it, but it seemed like all of them were willing to use her against him.

Sam took a step forward. "Neither of us wants to watch her go up there again, but we both know we can't stop her."

"So you want them to wake up and find out we've taken off on a suicide mission instead? Not knowing which, if any of us, will come back? That's not better."

Sam's expression darkened. "No, it's not ideal, but neither is waiting. Nothing—no option we have—is ideal. So why not just end it?"

"That's the problem. I don't know if we *can*."

"Based on what the Night Marchers did, I think we have a shot." Sam straightened his shoulders. "And if we do, then we have a duty to take it."

"That's—" Oliver fought down a bizarre, bitter laugh. That's exactly how he'd felt a month ago. *I guess that makes me the Bill in this conversation.*

Sam took a step forward. "I want to be with you when you talk to Jessie and Jordan."

Oliver stared at his friend for a moment. Then, he shook his head, leveling a glare at the nearest spruce tree. "I can't believe this."

"Would you consider it?"

"Not a chance."

Sam looked away. "You faced the Gatekeeper and walked away."

"Because Dean interfered. But he's ..." Oliver hesitated. "His *connection* to this world is unreliable."

"You know the country."

"That doesn't matter in this context."

"You know the Nantinaq."

"I don't think *anyone* can really know the Nantinaq. All I *know* is that he can't—or won't—help."

Sam opened his mouth but closed it again as the door cracked open. Darien leaned out, her eyes darting between the two of them, her expression changing to one of relief.

"We just wanted to check and make sure you guys were all right," she said.

Sam smiled at her. "Thanks, Dar. We'll be there in a second."

"All right." She hid a yawn behind her hand. "We're planning to leave right after Ellie gets out of the shower, so you have a few minutes."

"Okay." Sam watched as she turned and pulled the door shut behind her. Then, his smile faded. "She's not okay, Oliver. She's withdrawing. We barely spoke this morning, even before she had the vision."

"None of us is okay, Sam. I had to talk Ellie down last night, too, because she's so afraid ..."

The words hung unsaid between them. Sam just gave him a significant look.

"Point taken," Oliver sighed. He flopped against the porch again, another wave of tiredness sweeping over him. *Was* he being a coward?

"I just don't know, Sam," he said. "On one hand, you're right. We could end this without an ugly fight and probably save a lot of people. We could make it so Ellie and Helen and Henry never have to go up there again. And maybe hitting them early, before they're expecting it, is brilliant."

"It seems like there's a 'but' in there somewhere," Sam said.

Oliver smiled thinly. "*But* ... if we're unprepared, if we screw up at all, the four of us are dead."

"And maybe that will galvanize the whole town into action."

"And Darien will be a widow at twenty-one, and a single mom at twenty-two."

Sam scowled. "Believe it or not, I *had* thought of that." He sighed and cast a look at the door. "Oliver, I'm a Division One starting athlete. What do you think the odds are that you, Jessie, or Jordan can beat me into the cave?"

Oliver was silent. He was in good shape, but he wasn't on Sam's level. His friend crossed his arms again, his eyes glinting, a low note of anguish in his voice. "I don't want to leave her, or the baby. I adore her beyond words. But that's also why I'd do anything to keep her—to keep *them* safe."

A memory rose in Oliver's mind of Ellie's eyes the night before. Her tears, how her lips trembled as she smiled despite them. How those lips felt on his own, and the quiet, steady rhythm of her breathing as she slept.

"I'd do the same for Ellie," he said quietly.

Sam turned to him again, his eyes intense. "Then let's finish it, Oliver."

Oliver met his stare through narrowed eyes. Then, he shook his head and blew out a sigh. "I'll think about it."

***

Darien slipped into the Calls' guest room and closed the door, hoping she'd kept her body language natural enough not to have drawn attention. She turned, wishing her eyes could adjust more quickly to the dim light but not daring to open the curtains. Light might scare him away; it wasn't worth the risk. Keeping her movements slow and fluid, she crouched and peered under the bed. *"Are you here?"*

In the dark, void-like space below the bed frame, two orange slits appeared.

"Are we alone?" she asked. *"Is Slubgob—?"*

A memory rose, of *Sam pulling her close in his dimly lit apartment, whispering, "We're alone—"*

Darien's lip curled. *"Stay out of those. Nothing between Sam and me is yours."*

Displeasure seemed to shiver through the air between them, then an impression formed in her mind. *Layers of earth and rock, and children running across the surface, digging up half-buried stones and holding them up as if they were the greatest treasures in the world.*

Darien knelt, trying to work it out for a moment. When it came to her, she shook her head. *"I don't care if those memories are the closest to the surface. The easiest. Whatever. They're not yours to take."*

Ankle Tickler's wrath simmered. Then, he closed his eyes. Darien's stomach turned over; he couldn't leave, not when she was just scratching the surface of controlling her power. Not when he was, apparently, willing to teach her. The things she could *do* with it, the ways in which she could help ...

She just needed a little more direction.

"You can have the non-romantic ones," she thought.

Ankle Tickler's eyes slitted open, confusion rippling across the space between them. Darien could have smacked herself. Of *course* he didn't have any understanding of romance. *"Nothing to do with mating. Got it?"*

The demon's confusion didn't stop.

"Do you not understand...?" Darien glanced at the door as a set of heavy footsteps clomped by, trying not to let her scientist brain run away with what that might say about

the creatures on a species-wide level. *"Never mind, we don't have time. I managed to partially shield myself earlier from a Death vision by taking your advice."*

For a moment, the silence in the room was oppressive. Then, approval washed through Darien. Breathing out in relief, she went on.

"I started building a wall." She closed her eyes and raised the image she'd spent the last two hours piecing together in her mind: her behemoth of a fort, angled and obdurate and too massive to ever exist in the real world. A tiny smile crossed her lips.

But that's the beauty of the mind. It's not constrained by mundane things like physics.

A mental jab interrupted Darien's thoughts. Repressing another shudder at the one-sided invasiveness of this ... *partnership*, she sat cross-legged on the smooth hardwood. Then, she opened her mind to Ankle Tickler and tried to remember everything about the mental structure she'd constructed. The walls had gone up just after Sam had left, as she'd dressed alone in the gloomy bedroom. The roof went on next, and even with Death's interruption, she'd managed to floor the structure during breakfast, plank by golden plank.

Ankle Tickler stirred, then another memory rose in Darien's mind. *She was a high school freshman, flipping over her freshly graded biology final, nerves sparking in her stomach. A sigh of relief went out of her as she saw the big, red 97% scrawled at the top, as she read her teacher's comment.* **Well done! I love how thorough you are!**

Darien pressed her hand to her forehead; the praise had felt so good coming from Mrs. Blakeman. But those exact same words coming from Ankle Tickler? She dropped her hand and stared under the bed at the place where she'd last seen his eyes. *"How do I know you're not just torturing me for food? How do I know this isn't some twisted, sadistic game of yours?"*

An image of a cartoon snake jostled its way into her mind, *cajoling the hapless boy at the foot of the tree it was hanging in to trust it.*

Darien shook her head. *"All right, message received. You still really need to work on the whole idea of context, though."*

A flash of nonchalance.

Darien sighed. *"Fine. Anyway, I used my fortress about an hour ago, when Death killed again. I imagined myself retreating inside it and peeking out a window at what he was doing."*

Approval again.

"I had more control over the experience. It was still awful, but better than being over-whelmed and passing out."

Darien's head twinged, and she winced as she realized ... One of the non-sentient demons nearby was feasting on somebody. She took a deep, controlled breath, imagining laying bricks in a circle in the middle of the courtyard, one by one by one, the mental motion rote and comforting. If the devil and God were both in the details, she probably should be, too. *"I'm going to make it bigger. More ornate."*

A soft snarl emanated from under the bed. Darien fought the urge to bolt out the door, her fingers stealing to her ankle where he'd slashed her a few days ago. The skin was smooth and whole. Unfortunately, so were her recollections.

"It's my *mind,"* she thought steadily. *"I have a right to protect it, even from you. I'll build rooms you can access and fill them with memories you can use. Fair?"*

Another snarl drifted from under the bed, softer this time, followed by surly accep-tance.

Darien nodded. *"Now that I've started the fortress, what's next?"*

The demon seemed to consider for a moment. Then, another memory started to play. *Green turf. A roaring crowd. Sam flying down the field, breaking tackles until one burly player lunged for him, wrapping his huge arms around his midsection, stopping him cold.*

Darien blinked to clear her vision. *"You want me to tackle some...thing."*

Another memory started to coalesce, of the Sphere just as it had shimmered into view. Something clicked. *"You want me to try stopping a non-Awakened demon? Mentally .. tackling it?"*

This time, Ankle Tickler's approval swelled like an ocean wave.

"How do I do that—?"

Footsteps sounded outside the door, confident and purposeful. Sam's.

Darien leaped to her feet and lunged for her phone charger on the bedside table as a knock sounded at the door. A second later, it squeaked open, spilling light from the outside all over the floor. Her vision blurred; she'd stood up too fast.

"Hey, Dar." Sam's voice was soft with concern.

Guilt squeezed Darien's chest as she pretended to unplug her phone from the charger, blinking through the haze in her eyes. She really hoped he hadn't seen her scrambling to pull it out of her pocket as he'd come through the door. Resting a hand on the table's cool, smooth surface for balance, she turned. "Hey, Sam."

He took her in his arms. "You don't look so good. Are you sure you're up to walking all across Seldovia today?"

She rested her forehead against his shoulder as the whirl in her head began to ease. "I'm fine. Really. It's just pregnancy. It makes me more sensitive to things like standing, sitting, bending over ..." She gestured to the end table. "Besides, I can't stay here alone."

"We'd make arrangements." He pulled back and looked into her eyes, his own hooded and bloodshot, and if Darien's guilt had been a squeeze in the chest before, it was a knife in the heart now.

"Sam ..." It all threatened to spill out. Ankle Tickler, what she was learning from him, what she hoped she'd be able to do—

NO

The demon's sheer panic took Darien off guard. *"Fine, not yet! But I* will *tell him as soon as I can. We don't keep secrets."*

"It's really okay," Sam said. "Don't feel like you have to tough this out if what you need is rest."

Darien took his hand and offered him a small smile. It was the best she could do at the moment. "I'd say the same thing to you, but I know you too well."

She kissed him lightly, then led him out the door. The skin on the back of her neck prickled as she left; she could feel Ankle Tickler's stare. It was obvious what she and the demon would be after they took down Death: enemies. Which meant that if she wanted to protect her mind, she needed to build a lot more rooms in her mental fortress.

And regardless of what she'd implied to Ankle Tickler, she'd be fortifying most of them.

Chapter Fourteen

Sam followed Ellie and Oliver into the low, steel warehouse, blinking at the contrast between the patchy sunlight outside and its flat, fluorescent interior. Once again, the smells of fish and cleaners hung in the air, noticeable but not unpleasant. For him, at least. He glanced at Darien, but other than looking a little pale, she seemed … well, if not great, then at least steady. *And honestly, after this morning, steady might be the best we can hope for.*

A hot bolt of anger shot through Sam, and for a moment, he saw red. He was livid at the demons, at Death for murdering innocent people, at the fact that his wife had had to watch. Part of him knew that anger was just a cover-up for his own helplessness, but he didn't care. It gave him strength, will, courage. Right now, he'd take it.

Letting his eyes roam around the warehouse, he tried not to grimace. It was crowded, and not just with people. Demons drifted here and there, too many to count on sight. Some followed people around, some floated aimlessly, and several were moving toward him.

And all my delicious rage, he thought. Relief washed over him as he realized none of them were sentient, though the huge, dark one from the night before was still there. He jerked his eyes away as it started to move along the side wall. *Don't accidentally Awaken it.*

The Forths, Calls, and the crew exchanged quick pleasantries, including introducing a still-subdued Darien to everyone. She cracked a smile when Charlie said something dryly funny, but the expression died on her face as two teenage boys stepped around the table and beelined for Oliver.

Sam's stomach jolted, and he released Darien's hand. "Hang on, I'll be back in a sec."

Weaving around Henry, Bill, and Luke, Sam stopped beside Oliver and sized up the teens. Jessie wasn't big, but he was athletic—if he were on the football team, he'd probably make a great kicker. And there was something about him, an easy, wiry confidence that made Sam sit up and take note.

And, of course, there was the dark halo around his head, clear evidence that a demon like Slubgob had taken up residence inside it. Sam's core contracted in sympathy. Not only was this kid a fighter, but he needed every bit of that spirit he could muster.

"Hey, Oliver." Jessie's pleasant tone didn't match the hard look in his eyes.

"Hey, Jessie," Oliver said. He nodded to the other boy, who was stocky, brown-haired, keen-eyed, and looked just like a teenage version of Luke. "Jordan. This is Sam."

Sam stepped forward, offering his hand. *Yes, there's anger there,* he thought. A lot of it. He felt it in their clipped introductions, their too-serious expressions, the crush of their handshakes.

Jessie stepped back and fixed Oliver with a significant stare, his voice lowering. "Let's us three cover the Village. We can talk more that way."

Oliver's shoulders tensed, but when he spoke, it was still in that same even tone he'd used earlier. "Fine."

"Oliver," Sam said once the teens were out of earshot. "Jessie's got a demon in his head."

"I'm not surprised. Jordan?"

"Not that I can see." Sam frowned, watching Jessie and Jordan whisper together, casting glances in their direction. "I don't remember Jessie having one last night."

"Huh." Oliver put his hands on his hips. "That makes me even more determined to talk them out of it."

Sam scratched the back of his head. "I kind of want to hear them out, honestly."

"Sam, you can't be serious."

Am I serious? Sam eyed the boys, who stood just off to the side of the group now, whispering and casting glances in their direction. The demon haloing Jessie's head was frightening.

But if we close the gate, it's gone.

But if they all died trying, which Oliver thought was a distinct possibility, they'd only make things worse.

But I was able to walk all around that canyon looking for Dad, and theoretically, the Gatekeeper was there at the time.

Sam let out a long, silent breath. He couldn't shake the nagging thought that this might be his chance to finally *do* something, to move the needle, to help.

"Oliver," he started, "what if—?

"All right, everyone, let's get started." Bill clapped his hands together. "I don't care if you sit or stand or hop on one foot so long as you shut up and stay that way until we get your routes figured out."

"I'm coming with you," Sam muttered to Oliver. Ignoring his friend's surprised expression, he stepped across the room to where Darien stood next to Ellie and Helen, and took his wife's hand.

It was shockingly cold.

Trying not to be too obvious, Sam looked sideways at her, though her expression was so vacant that he doubted she'd notice if he danced around in front of her naked. Her lips were moving, shaping soundless words addressed to no one but herself and the unseen things in her head. Sam tore his eyes away; no matter what she said, something wasn't right, and she wasn't telling him. He felt helpless, powerless; there was *nothing* he could do.

Except ...

His eyes settled on the teens. Jessie was whispering something to Bill, but Jordan stood a little way apart, his head cocked to the side, watching him. Sam forced an uneasy smile before turning back to Luke, only half aware of the current route the burly fisherman was describing. He could practically *see* the gears turning in Jordan's head. And he had a hunch he knew what they were chewing on.

I'm tempted, Jordan. Let's get moving, and we'll talk.

***

An hour later, Sam sat in the passenger seat of Oliver's old, beat-up pickup as they rattled up a dirt road framed by tall, silent evergreens. He still felt bad about pressuring Darien to go with Ellie, Helen, and Naomi, and judging from the way Oliver had gazed after Ellie as they'd left, he'd much rather have been in different company as well. But the two teens sitting behind him needed them. And Sam had to do something—anything—to stop Darien's slow descent into madness. He shifted in his seat as the truck grated across a patch of washboard and tried to tell himself it was the rough road, not the fact that his stomach had turned into a writhing snake pit, that was making him uncomfortable.

"So what time are we leaving tonight?"

Sam glanced in the rearview mirror at Jessie's face. The teen's expression was remarkably calm, though the dark, writhing halo around his head was not.

"I assume Sam knows everything," Jessie added. "Or you wouldn't have brought him. My only question is whether he's with us or with you."

Oliver flexed his fingers on the wheel. "*I'm* with you. I'm trying to keep you from getting yourselves killed."

"All right then, Sam." A hollow *slap* sound drifted from the back seat, as if Jessie had just smacked his hand down on his thigh. Sam turned to see the redhead looking at him, unruly hair sticking up all over the place, a sharp contrast to the sickly, air-warping darkness around it. "Are you in, or what?"

Once again, Sam hesitated. He liked these two, admired their courage, grit, and proactivity. He didn't *want* to risk them, especially when it was expressly against the wishes of their parents—wishes he understood. But if he didn't, then he was choosing to risk Darien and their baby every second of every day until the gate was closed. And ...

The snakes in his belly started to writhe again. After having met Jessie and Jordan, his assessment hadn't changed; he was still bigger, faster, and stronger than anyone else in this truck. Which meant that unless something went terribly wrong, it was only his death that was a foregone conclusion.

"Am I in?" He rubbed the bridge of his nose, Oliver's warning glare hot on the side of his face. "I have a family to protect. Yes, I'm in."

Oliver let out a deep sigh through his nose, his shoulders tight with frustration. "You guys realize you're asking me to *steal* my aunt and uncle's boat. That alone would be a 'no' from any reasonable person." He shook his head. "I'm still out."

Sam felt the tension gathering in the back seat. He swallowed, waiting for the blow to fall.

"You're a coward, Oliver," Jessie said quietly.

Oliver didn't even blink. His eyes just flicked to the rearview mirror, his stare flat. "And you, Jordan? Anything you want to say?"

Sam twisted to look back at the teenagers. Jessie was stone-faced, his arms crossed, glaring at the back of Oliver's head as if he wanted to bore a hole in his skull. Jordan, though, was more relaxed. So much so that Sam suspected it was deliberate. Only the intensity in his eyes gave him away; he had the look of a man who was preparing himself to hit. Hard.

Jordan met Oliver's stare, then lifted one shoulder. "Honestly, I'm starting to wonder if Jessie's right."

Oliver's expression darkened.

"I don't think courage has anything to do with it, actually," Sam said. "Remember, he did go up there—alone, too—before the rest of us even knew anything was going on."

"Because *Ellie* asked him to," Jessie muttered.

Oliver's eyes snapped back up the rearview mirror. "She didn't ask. I went because I was sick of watching *everyone* I care about suffer. Including you two, believe it or not."

"But now you won't fight for the woman you say you love," Jessie shot back. "Not so different from your dad now, are you?"

Oliver slammed on the brakes.

Sam's eyes widened, and even Jordan looked shocked. "That was low, Jessie," he said as the truck bounced onto the road's shoulder. Oliver threw it in park, then twisted and fixed Jessie with a stare so glacial that Sam could have sworn it lowered the temperature in the cab. Jessie swallowed, but glared right back, the shadow around his head twisting with unmistakable glee.

Oliver let the silence stretch. And stretch some more.

"Let me make something perfectly clear," he finally said when the teens had both started to squirm a little. "You cannot provoke me. Nothing you could possibly say would be worse than what I've already dealt with and overcome. What you're trying to do, Jessie? It won't work. So quit. I don't have to prove myself to either of you." His stare flashed to Sam. "Or to you."

Sam studied his friend's face. Oliver was angry—no, *irate*. But unlike Jessie, he was in control. The rage, the frustration, the pain—he'd walled it in, created a reservoir out of a seething river. A resource instead of a time bomb.

"No," he said, "you don't."

Oliver gave him an almost imperceptible nod. Then, he eased the truck back onto the road, his back ramrod straight. For several minutes, no one spoke. Then, Sam turned back to the boys. "Let's get back to the point of this conversation. I ..." He suppressed a sigh as feelings of helplessness crashed over him again. "I'll go. If the *Poor Buoy* is ... unavailable, tell me where to meet you and I'll be there."

"That's great," Jordan said. "We're glad to have you, Sam. It's just ... well, seeing if Oliver would guide us—and using the *Poor Buoy*—kind of *was* the original purpose of this conversation."

Sam looked over to see Oliver shaking his head. "Not happening. I'm not going to be an accessory to your deaths."

"I don't know why you're the only one who won't see reason," Jessie grumbled.

Oliver's expression was still dark, but when he spoke, his voice was measured, almost compassionate. "It's not me who's being unreasonable, Jessie."

Jessie's expression turned thunderous. Then, with visible effort, he calmed himself and leaned forward. "You are, though. Because if you saw reason, you'd see that we're doing this with or without you. *Three of us*—three smart, capable people who you trust—are doing this without you. And we'll do a lot better if we have you and your boat."

"The Calls' boat."

"Whatever. A fast boat that you have access to."

"You've underestimated the Gatekeeper," Oliver said. "I *promise* you, you've under-estimated him. And if you're unlucky enough to get on his radar, a fast boat won't save you."

"And even if it *could*, it might not anyway because dying's half the damn point!" Jessie burst out. He lowered his voice, glowering. "If you risk nothing, you risk everything, Oliver."

Oliver pulled off onto a long, dirt driveway, the war inside written all over his face. No one spoke until they'd stopped in front of a beautiful, two-story log cabin that Sam would have deeply appreciated under any circumstances but the ones he was currently in. The truck clunked into park, and Oliver sat for a moment, staring at the front door.

Then he gave an irritated shake of his head and opened the door. "Grab the flyers, Jordan. We've got work to do."

***

Oliver's stomach felt like it was boiling.

He turned his pickup onto Main Street, ignoring the wheezing rattle it made as it rounded the corner. The thick, heavy silence in the cab—which had hovered on the edges of every halfhearted conversation they'd attempted in the last few hours—wasn't what was bothering him. No, it was an ally; it had given him time to come to a decision. And hours of crisscrossing the backroads around Seldovia Village, of parrying Jessie's and Jordan's verbal thrusts, of watching Sam sink further into quiet resignation, had only cemented it.

He was going to march into the warehouse and blow the teens' whole scheme wide open, consequences be damned. Their respect was a small price to pay for saving their lives.

Let's go, he thought as the warehouse came into view. It squatted on the horizon, a dark gray hulk against the lighter gray smears of the ocean and sky. Oliver squinted as they drew closer; Bill's green pickup with its mismatched black topper was the only vehicle in the gravel lot. He swallowed. Henry should be there, too, and Luke, if he remembered the groups correctly. That would be enough. A small part of him was relieved that the others weren't back yet. He didn't really want Ellie—or Darien or Helen or anyone else, for that matter—to see what was about to happen.

It would be bad enough as it was.

Oliver parked next to Bill's truck and opened his door with a clunk. He heard the teenagers and Sam do the same—his truck wasn't exactly subtle in its old age—so it didn't shock him when he stepped out and came face-to-face with Jessie. Oliver planted his feet and crossed his arms, fixing his friend with what he hoped was an inscrutable stare. A gentle gust of wind ruffled Jessie's red hair, but apart from that, he was stone-still, an ugly gleam in his eye.

"You're serious about being a coward, then."

"I'm not going to be part of this, Jessie."

Rage sparked behind the young man's eyes. Then, to Oliver's relief, he spun and stalked away, muttering under his breath, and Jordan shot a half-sad, half-accusatory glance at Oliver before following. Pain pricked at him as he watched his friends walk away. Then, he closed the truck's door and started for the warehouse.

"You've really riled them."

At the sound of Sam's voice, Oliver stopped. His friend was leaning against the truck's bumper, his face unreadable.

"And you've encouraged them," Oliver said.

Sam's eyebrows drew together, and—not for the first time—Oliver became suddenly, acutely aware of his sheer size and athleticism. Ellie's brother was so kind and gentle-hearted that it was easy to forget that he had four inches on Oliver and dozens of pounds of muscle that he knew exactly how to use. Right now, his deadpan expression was that of a curious predator, something that knew it was the apex in its sphere and didn't have to think about its place in the world. Oliver wondered whether the expression was cultivated, whether Sam used it during football games to intimidate members of the opposing team.

If he doesn't, he should.

A gull cried from somewhere out in the harbor. The breeze sighed across the waves. Sam dropped his gaze, his face falling back into the troubled lines that had defined it all afternoon. "I don't know what the right decision is, either, Oliver. I think it's to save my wife and baby—my family. But I don't think you're a coward. We have similar goals; you're just going about it a different way." He sighed. "And if I felt like I had time, I would, too."

Oliver stared at Sam for a moment, unsure what to say. *You won't get the chance? I'm going to stop you guys? I'm sorry?*

But he wasn't sorry. Not one bit.

"It's nice to hear that," Oliver said. Then he turned, fixed his eyes on the warehouse's door, and started toward it.

Gravel crunched behind him as Sam shifted. "I'm going to call Darien. You know, just to check in. I'll holler if something tries to kill me."

Oliver waved a hand in acknowledgment but didn't turn around; he didn't want Sam to see all the pain and frustration he couldn't manage to keep off his face. It would be interesting to see what his friend thought of him fifteen minutes from now. Whether he'd still respect Oliver's decision, or whether he'd be the coward who'd condemned his wife to another two days of mind-destroying suffering.

Either way, he'll be alive. And that's what matters.

Before he knew it, the crunch of gravel under his feet had given way to solid concrete, and he was pushing open the warehouse's rusty door. Dread rose in his belly as he saw Bill, Luke, and Henry sitting at the stainless steel table, their heads together, poring over what looked like a notebook. Probably full of fire-weapon ideas, if Oliver had to guess. He glanced around. Jessie and Jordan were nowhere to be seen, but the door to Bill's office was cracked open—maybe they were in there on some kind of errand. Relieved that he wouldn't have to do this in front of them, hardly daring to believe his luck, Oliver squared his shoulders and headed for the table.

"Glad you're back, Oliver," Henry said.

"Where's Sam?" Bill asked.

"Right outside. He wanted to call Darien."

Bill grunted. "Hope he's being careful. He needs to—"

"Bill, I'm sorry to interrupt," Oliver said, "but I have something that can't wait, and I need all three of you to hear it."

They all looked up at him. Bill frowned. "Out with it, then."

"Jessie and Jordan came to me earlier. They're planning to steal a boat and sneak to Portlock to try to close the gate. Tonight."

Stunned silence filled the room. Luke glanced at the open office door, then leaned forward, his eyes like chips of flint, his voice low. "How long have you known about this?"

"I just learned about it this morning. They called me and laid it all out. They wanted me to guide them, since I've been up there a couple of times before." Oliver's frustration rose again, and he shook his head. "I thought I could talk them out of it—I spent the entire time we were in Seldovia Village trying. But they won't see reason. And now they've roped Sam into it—"

Bill smacked his hand down on the table with enough force that Oliver jumped. The captain shot to his feet, anger blazing on his face. "JESSIE! GET OUT HERE!"

Luke jumped up. "Jordan, you too!"

Oliver fell back, shaken, suddenly a little afraid for Jessie and Jordan. There wasn't a reason for his fear; Bill and Luke were both loving fathers, if stern at times. But with the demons ... with things being the way they were ...

Oliver took a deep, steadying breath, then squared his shoulders and raised his eyes in time to see Henry push his chair back. His uncle came to stand beside him, clapping one hand on his shoulder briefly, and Oliver was grateful for his unspoken support.

"Remember they're only kids, you two," Henry rumbled as they started toward the office door.

"Yes, but this can't be allowed to stand," Luke said. Oliver breathed a sigh of relief when he caught a glimpse of his face; he was angry, yes, but not out of control, and Bill seemed the same.

"Boys!" Bill swung the door open. "Get out—"

He froze.

Oliver's blood ran cold as Bill's face paled. Then, the captain whirled. "They're gone. Snuck out the back door."

Chapter Fifteen

Sam had just sent a third call ringing into the void—this time to Ellie—when the dull pound of footsteps on packed earth reached his ears. He whirled, his hand dropping to the knife at his hip, half expecting to see a grizzly bearing down on him, or worse. But it wasn't a grizzly, or a demon, or even some sick combination of the two. It was Jessie and Jordan, *sprinting*, their expressions terrified.

Adrenaline jolted through Sam. "The hell's going on?!"

But the teens blew straight past and into the green, tussocky grass adjacent to the warehouse, heading for the docks. Over his shoulder, Jessie bellowed, "If you want to save your wife, you better come with us!"

Sam's mouth went dry. Everything snapped into focus, the facts painting a very sudden, very clear picture. Nobody was answering their phones, Oliver hadn't come out, and Jessie and Jordan were fleeing the warehouse in a state of panic. There was only one thing to do.

Sam ran.

He sprinted after the boys, his speed turning the cool, sea-scented breeze into a wind. It slapped him awake, invigorated him, because this was what he *did*. Within seconds, he'd caught up to Jessie and Jordan and slowed his pace.

"Smart choice," Jessie yelled.

"What's happened?" Sam shot back. "What's going on?"

A shout echoed from behind them, but Sam didn't look back—*that* had been so beaten out of him that it was against his very nature at this point. Neither of the boys, however, was that disciplined. They both dropped behind him, just a yard or two, and Sam had to slow again.

Jordan cursed and sped up, all but throwing himself in the direction of the pier. "How fast are you, Sam?"

"Fast."

"The boat we're after is ... is a red Bay Weld. Called *Tide Chaser*. Three hundred horsepower outboard motor, far left end of the dock."

"That one," Jessie said, pointing. "There's lines tied around the cleats. Start untying them so we can cast off."

"Got it." Sam blazed ahead, legs pumping, blood singing in his veins. From what he could see, the only access point into the harbor itself—and the boats beyond—was a wooden pier maybe twelve feet across, which connected to a metal ramp that sloped down to the surface of the harbor. It was roughly sixty yards away.

And he wouldn't even have to break any tackles. Easy.

Sam surged forward and was on the walkway in seconds. Bracing a hand against one of the posts at its edge, he turned on a dime and raced across the pier. He slowed as he reached the long, sloping metal section that led down to the harbor, his body adjusting to the incline, then skidded to a stop on the damp wooden dock at the bottom.

Down here, the dock branched into a neat spread of walkways winding through a small forest of masts, and it took a moment for him to catch sight of the red boat Jessie had pointed out earlier. He broke into a careful jog, avoiding a few wet spots on the wood that looked extra slippery. The ocean lapped on either side of him, inches below his feet, dark and cold and an impossibly rich shade of navy. Sam gulped. Down here, there were no railings to keep him from careening into it if he slipped.

Grateful that the rain clouds had stayed on the other side of the bay, Sam looked up again. He'd lost sight of his goal; there were more boats than he'd first thought, and he didn't have a great line of sight anymore. A muffled yell echoed behind him, then he heard the hollow metal sound of the boys' feet on the ramp. Heart racing, Sam sped up. *Red boat. Tide Chaser.* He had no idea what "Bay Weld" meant in boat terms, but—

His eyes locked on the red vessel again as he half-slid around a corner. The words "Bay Weld" was emblazoned across its front side in bold white letters. And toward its middle were other words, in flowing script: ***Tide Chaser, Seldovia, AK***

Relief swept over Sam, so intense it almost made him lightheaded. Then, more shouts echoed behind him. Throwing caution to the wind, he bolted for the boat, his eyes locking on the lines that tethered it to the dock, just as Jessie said they would. He skidded on another slick spot as he tried to stop, and cried out as he nearly plunged into the sliver of dark harbor between the boat and the dock. For a sickening moment, he imagined himself crushed, immobile, drowning between the wood and the boat's unforgiving metal hull.

You're going to drown anyway.

Panic bolted through Sam at the thought, but he managed to recover his balance, seize the nearest line—bungee, more like—and start unwrapping it from its anvil-like hook.

"Dammit," he muttered. The yells and shouts were getting closer. Even those few seconds may have been too many. He snapped his head up in time to see Jessie round the corner and charge down the dock toward him, Jordan on his heels.

Jessie snatched one of the other bungee cords and started unwinding, his hands an expert blur. Jordan, on the other hand, *didn't* stop. Deftly avoiding the same wet patch that had nearly sent Sam into the water, he sprang off the dock and landed in the *Chaser*, then ducked into the boat's little cabin. Jessie tossed his line into the boat with a thunk, then moved on to the next one. "Hurry up, Sam!"

Sam gave a last, desperate tug, and the line came free. He tossed it into the *Chaser* then leaped in after, staggering as the boat rose underneath him.

"HURRY!" Jordan screamed through the cabin's open door.

Sam bolted toward him. "Jordan! What can I do—?"

"JESSIE! STOP!"

Sam froze. He recognized that voice. He whirled just as Oliver tore around the corner, his face drawn into a snarl, eyes blazing, his posture so aggressive that Sam took a step back. He plunged his hand into his pocket for the lighter.

The Lady could shapeshift, he thought wildly. Was this a demon who'd tricked the others and was coming for them now? Horror hit Sam like a punch; was *that* why Darien and Ellie hadn't answered his calls?

Oliver—the creature that looked like him?—lunged toward them, but Jessie was faster. The redhead leaped into the boat beside Sam and yelled, "GO, JORDAN!" Then he seized the last line and started pulling it in.

"No, you don't," Maybe-Oliver snapped. He grabbed the line's end and hauled back, making for the central cleat, as if he thought he could re-tie it and stop them before they'd started. And Sam realized two things at once.

He's actually Oliver. No demon would try to stop them by grabbing a *dock line*; it'd just float onto the boat and start attacking. Second, the line Jessie had thrown to the dock had coiled in his mad attempt to unwrap it. And Oliver had stepped right into the center of that coil.

The boat's huge engine revved, the whole thing vibrating as if it were tensing. Sam bolted toward the *Chaser's* cabin. "Jordan, wait—!"

The boat plunged forward.

"Oliver!" Sam yelled, but it was too late. The line flew out of Oliver's hands, and he was jerked off his feet. With a cry, he plunged over the side of the dock and into the frigid, pitiless water. Horror nearly froze Sam; he could see Oliver being dragged under the surface, the line still tangled around his foot.

He bolted for the open door. "JORDAN! STOP!"

But Jessie was already inside, shaking his cousin's shoulder, yelling so hard that Sam could make out every word. "Mayday, Jordan! Man overboard!"

Sam stumbled as the engine cut, throwing him forward. Righting himself, he staggered to the side of the boat, where the death trap of a line dangled. He grabbed for it as the boat pitched again, coming up in time to see Oliver burst out of the water, his eyes shocked and staring, mouth wide open as if he was fighting to draw breath. He floundered, going under again. Cursing, Sam fumbled for the line's end—

A weird, flat-sounding splash sounded from behind. Sam whirled, then sagged in relief as he saw that Jessie had thrown a life preserver. *Of* course *they have better rescue equipment on board than a single line.* He grimaced. Especially one that might still be wrapped around Oliver's ankle—not a great option if the goal was to keep his head above water.

Oliver slung an arm over the life preserver, and Jessie started to pull him toward the still-drifting boat. Sam ran to his side and joined in, matching his movements to the teen's. In seconds, they'd pulled Oliver flush to the *Chaser's* side. His hand grasped the boat's edge; he was wheezing, shivering, his movements spasmodic and uncontrolled. Sam dropped the line, ran to him, and gripped his forearm. "Grab on."

He sucked in an involuntary gasp as water from Oliver's soaked clothes leeched into his own, a frigid shock against his skin. Bracing against the boat's side, he heaved with everything he had. Coughing, Oliver pulled himself onto the deck and collapsed onto his hands and knees, shivering violently. His breathing was shallow and fast, his face and hands bloodless, his lips blue. Sam stared, stunned, rage building in him. Then, he turned and met Jessie's eyes. "You tricked me!"

Jessie's eyebrows contracted. "We didn't—"

"JESSIE!"

Sam turned. Three figures were running across the section of the dock they'd just vacated—Luke, Bill, and Henry. Shame swept over him, making his breathing more unsteady than any run at this low altitude ever could.

The engine roared, sending the boat skimming across the water, its speed tipping its prow upward and throwing up a glittering rooster-tail of spray behind it. Sam staggered and went down next to Oliver, watching numbly as the three stricken figures on the dock grew smaller and smaller. *What have we done?*

It was Oliver's strained, hissing breathing that brought him back. He'd come up on his knees and was trying to unbutton his shirt with shaking fingers. Sam unzipped his jacket. "When you've gotten that off, take this—"

Oliver's eyes jerked upward, glinting with anger. "W-what the hell were you th-think-ing?"

Sam opened his mouth, then closed it again as he realized Oliver was looking at a point over his head. Something sour and sick slipped into Sam's chest; he turned to see Jessie staring back at the dock, looking stricken. Slowly, the teen shook his head, his voice hollow. "We're committed now."

"You d-don't ... have to b-b-be," Oliver gasped. Sam turned to see him peeling his soaking shirt off his arms, every muscle in his exposed torso tight with the extreme effort of shivering. "I c-can't stop you. B-but—"

Sam grabbed a sleeve and pulled, shocked to realize that Oliver was shivering even more violently now. "Jessie, we might have to turn around so that he doesn't freeze to death."

When there was no response, he turned. "Jessie?"

Jessie seemed to shake himself. His eyes focused on Oliver, who had managed to pull Sam's jacket around his shoulders and was fumbling awkwardly at the button on his pants.

"No, we won't." He grabbed Oliver's arm and helped him to his feet. "The cabin's heated, and there are spare clothes."

"*Now* you t-tell me." Oliver lurched over to the cabin and disappeared inside. Sam cast an uncertain glance at Jessie, then another out to the dock. They'd put several hundred yards between them and it, but he thought he could still make out three figures jogging up the long, metal ramp toward shore.

"Come on, Sam," Jessie said.

Anger blazed back to life in Sam's belly, driving his cold and discomfort to the back of his mind. He stomped toward the cabin after Jessie and slammed the door closed. The space wasn't big, maybe half the size of the *Poor Buoy's*, and a significant portion of it was taken up by a big steering wheel and two cushioned chairs. Jordan sat behind the wheel, frowning as he guided the boat around the rocks at the harbor's edge and into open water. Sam's scowl deepened as they blasted past a big, red sign that read **NO WAKE ZONE**; even he knew how badly they'd just shattered that rule.

Jessie plopped down in the other chair, rubbing a hand across his face. Sam barely resisted grabbing him by his plaid shirt and hauling him to his feet.

"*What*," he gritted out, "did you do that for?"

Jessie dropped his hand, his expression still stunned, as if he couldn't believe what they'd just done. The black cloud around his head sparked and popped soundlessly.

"Do what?" he asked hoarsely.

"There were no demons!" Sam bellowed. "You tricked me!"

"We never said there were any demons," Jordan said evenly. "*You* followed *us*, remember?"

Sam threw up his hands. "Because you came sprinting out of the warehouse like every demon on earth was after you! What did you expect me to think?"

"Well, it wasn't premeditated," Jessie said. "We just thought you were in. You'd basically said you were."

"I—" Sam turned away, clenching his fists, his attention momentarily falling on Oliver—and the equally black look on his face. His friend was rummaging in the compartment underneath one of the bench seats, likely looking for a shirt since, by the looks of things, he'd already changed into dry pants. His body still spasmed and shook. Coupled with the stark red brand on his shoulder and the mostly-healed burns on his back and chest, the man looked more ragged than Sam had ever seen him.

"I'm opening her up," Jordan warned.

"Do it," Jessie said. "Let's put some distance between us and Seldovia."

Rage boiled in Sam again; he'd never been more tempted to punch someone in his life. *I could do it,* he thought. *I could probably take on both of them—*

But then what? Oliver would help, sure. Between the two of them, they'd probably be able to overcome the two teens and turn the boat around. But with Oliver's condition, and how strong—and likely to put up a fight—Jessie and Jordan were ...

Sam grimaced. There would be injuries, likely bad ones. Plus, Jessie was right; he *had* been in earlier. And their horrible exit from Seldovia hadn't actually changed the parameters of what they were doing. He looked out the cabin's back window at the little bit of harbor he could still see.

It'll be me who dies, not them. His heart twinged, his vision blurring as he thought of Darien. *I'm so, so sorry.*

Choking back tears, hoping no one noticed, Sam stood and headed for the door, but didn't make it out before Oliver spoke.

"I d-don't think anyone'll catch you. It'll p-probably be half an hour b-before *Poor Buoy's* ready to sail. The last t-time she was out was when I took her to P-Portlock."

Sam's sick feeling intensified. Outside the window, the motor churned the ocean into a frothy wake; it almost looked like an arrow, pointing the way for anyone following.

"What about the Coast Guard?" Sam asked. "Would they—?"

"Not up here," Jessie said. "Well, they *are* up here, but they still wouldn't catch us in time. At this point, I don't think anybody can."

Uneasy silence descended on the cabin, and Sam felt the truth settling in his own gut. They were alone. Their options were the vast Alaskan wilderness or the even more vast Pacific Ocean, both of which were almost as unforgiving as the demons themselves. *One—maybe several—of which we'll face at the gate, so that one of us—probably me—can die saving the world.*

Sam blew out a breath. In that light, he *hoped* someone was coming after them. When it was all said and done, when the noble sacrifice had become a body recovery, whoever was left would definitely need the help.

He yanked open the cabin door and stepped out into the misty air.

The rock of the boat, coupled with the wind of their speed, made Sam feel like he could never quite find his footing. He grabbed a metal handhold built into the cabin's side, shuffled a few steps, then sat on the boat's edge. Like the *Poor Buoy*, the *Tide Chaser* had no railing, and the ocean raced only a few feet underneath him. He swallowed and turned away, his stomach swooping as the *Chaser* angled west in a long, graceful arc. The bay disappeared. Now, all he could see was ocean. An unnerving amount of dark, frigid abyss.

Sam stood, intending to switch sides so he could look at the shoreline, not the sea, when the cabin door opened again. Oliver stepped out, carrying Sam's jacket, as graceful as if he'd been born on a fishing boat despite his shivering. He held out the jacket, which Sam gratefully took and slipped back into, then they both settled on opposite edges. Sam suppressed a wince as Oliver's shuddering intensified. It would probably take him an hour of being inside the cabin to make *that* stop.

Instead, of course, he's out here.

Neither of them spoke for a moment.

"Help me stop this," Oliver finally said.

Another wave of indecision swept over Sam, all the reasons why he should—and shouldn't—clashing in his brain again. He swallowed as he remembered the hollow look in Darien's eyes that morning, her tears as she'd watched that family die.

"No."

Oliver closed his eyes. "I was afraid you'd say that."

"You can't be thinking of trying to stop us on your own."

"No. Even on my best day, I couldn't fight all three of you."

Sam tried to hold Oliver's stare, but the expression on his face was so resigned, so heartbroken, that he looked ... away? Dizziness hit him; there was nowhere *to* look except out across the blue expanse. With the color of the clouds, he could barely tell the difference between sea and sky.

"What makes you think *this* is the best way?" Oliver asked.

Sam fixed his eyes on the boat's rough floor; at least he didn't have demons to worry about. Other than Jessie's. "It's not. But I don't think Darien will last another two days."

"You know her better than I do. But she seems tough. I think she might."

"'Might' isn't good enough, especially with the baby on the line." Sam sighed. "Oliver, I respect the hell out of you. You know I do. But this isn't something you understand."

When Oliver said nothing, Sam glanced back the way they'd come. The water hissed underneath them, the enthusiastic thrum of the engine sending constant vibrations up Sam's right arm and into his shoulder. Portlock was still hours away. His insides already felt like they were dissolving; he didn't know if he'd still be functional by the time they got there.

"When I did this trip a month ago, I did it for Ellie."

Sam's hackles rose. He looked up, about to tell Oliver that it *wasn't* the same, that *yes*, he might love his sister, but there was a big difference between the heady high of falling in love and actually *building a life together*. But he stopped at the look on Oliver's face. He was staring behind Sam at the shoreline, his head cocked to the side, frowning thoughtfully. There was no aggression there, no reproach or judgment, no defensiveness. His whole demeanor was ... well, *disarming* was the best word Sam could think of to describe it.

A rueful smile twisted Oliver's mouth. "It's funny. I wouldn't let myself admit it at the time. And there were others I was worried about, lots of others. But she was always on the list. And the more I actually understood what was happening, the darker and more dangerous things got ... She moved to the top pretty quickly."

He looked Sam in the eye. "Right before I faced the Gatekeeper, before I didn't know I couldn't just walk right into the pool and drown ... she was all I could see. She gave me courage. If I could have, I would've already done it, because of her. So no, maybe I don't understand what it's like to marry the woman of my dreams, to actually, fully share life with her. To be a father." Pain flashed on his face again. "But I love your sister with everything I have, and it hurts to watch her suffer. I'd take it all away if I could." He gestured around them. "This, though? This isn't the way. I know because I've already tried it, Sam."

"We're too committed now. We can't go back."

"You still think we can pull this off."

"With the four of us? Yes."

Oliver's smile frosted over. "You know, my other influence was Wormwood."

Sam blinked. "What?"

"When I came up here last time, I mean," Oliver clarified. He nodded toward the cabin, his voice lowering enough that Sam had to lean forward to hear him over the roar of the motor. "Does Jessie still have his demon?"

"Yeah."

Oliver just raised his eyebrows, as if to say, *And you're following him?*

Sam bristled. "Look, they came charging out of the warehouse looking absolutely terrified. I thought they'd walked into a bloodbath and that everyone in there was dead, including you. Darien hadn't answered, Ellie hadn't answered ..." He threw up a hand. "I mean, what would you have done?"

Oliver shrugged one shoulder, the movement setting off a tremor that set his teeth visibly clattering. "Exactly what I d-did."

"Come on, dude."

Oliver let out a shaky sigh. "I don't know. In your shoes, there's good odds I would've done the same thing." He stood, still shivering visibly. "But right here is where our decisions would diverge. I'm going back in before I get hypothermic again. But if you change your mind, let me know. I can't do it alone. But together, we could turn this thing around."

"And if I don't change my mind?"

Oliver paused, his hand on the cabin's knob. "Then let me be the sacrifice."

Sam rocked back.

"I'm dead serious." Oliver set his jaw, his features rigid. "*Don't* leave Darien and your baby."

Anger seethed in Sam's belly. "It wouldn't be like that. I'm not like Dean. I *want* to be with them. And Darien will have all my inheritance; she won't want for anything—"

"It's not about money, Sam." Oliver turned to him, pinning him with a stare that was positively wolflike. "Darien needs other things."

With that, he pulled the door open, stepped inside, and closed it behind him, leaving Sam to his turmoil.

Chapter Sixteen

Ellie looked up as the waitress set a hot, steaming basket of fish and chips in front of her with a clatter. Then, she hurried away, looking far older and more careworn than she probably was. Just like Helen and Naomi, sitting in the booth across from her. And Darien.

At least she's eating now, Ellie thought as her sister-in-law tucked into her basket with apparent relish. She looked down at her food and sighed. The whole thing was a study in golden-brown: thick, hand-cut fries, perfectly battered fish. A cup of fresh coleslaw bloomed at the corner of the plate, a splash of green against the basket's red plastic. Fried foods were a luxury she allowed herself only occasionally; she should be more excited about this.

Ellie tightened her shoulder and core muscles, then tried to relax them. It did no good; the rock-hard ball of anxiety in her stomach was a lead weight she couldn't get rid of, leaving no room for food. *Now I know why Oliver was so skinny when we picked him up in Denver.*

She picked at a fry. *Come on, Ellie. You can't fight demons while malnourished.* Swallowing, she grabbed a piece of fish, focusing on the roughness of its crust against her fingertips, the deep gold of its breading, how it was almost too hot to hold comfortably.

Across the table, Naomi's phone rang, a light, syncopated phrase at complete odds with the classic rock pulsing through the radio. Ellie flinched, and the fish plopped back into its basket.

"Sorry, ladies." Naomi pulled her phone out of her pocket and frowned as she looked down at its screen. "It's Luke. I'll be right back."

"No problem," Helen said. "We've hit just about every house and business I can think of, so take your time."

Naomi slid out of the booth, strode to the diner's front door, and pushed it open with the tinkle of a bell. Ellie watched her go, the nerves in her stomach tightening even more. She reached into her pocket and pulled out her own phone, but there were no notifications. Not that that meant anything. Her service up here was all but nonexistent.

Shaking her head, she shoved it back in her pocket, doing her best to shove half-formed anxiety-thoughts of Oliver and Sam dead on some dirt road away with it. Then she settled her elbows on the table, eyeing her fish again. *They're fine. They're strong and smart, and Oliver knows how to handle demons.*

"Darien, are you doing okay?"

The sound of Helen's voice brought Ellie back to earth. She looked over at her sister-in-law, who was blinking at Helen with her mouth slightly open. Ellie's heart sank. Darien had looked tired before they'd stopped for lunch, but she'd been more present than Ellie had seen in a while. Now, the uncharacteristic vacancy that had seemed to plague her since their arrival in Seldovia was back. Not for the first time, Ellie wondered if Darien was being leeched on by a demon that Sam somehow couldn't see. That would be a ludicrously specific ability for a demon to have developed this quickly.

Then again, I thought the thought, which means something *might have picked up on it.*

"Oh." Darien sat back, her expression clearing. "Yeah, I'm okay. Sorry, it's just …"

A tiny, sympathetic smile crossed Helen's face. "A lot?"

"Yeah."

Helen studied Darien for a moment, her expression both loving and melancholy. Then, she nodded toward the fish and chips. "Well, you better keep eating. With everything you're doing, you and the baby both need your strength."

Darien blinked. "The baby's fine. Sometimes I think she's stronger than I am."

Ellie and Helen looked at each other, identical grins splitting their faces as they realized what Darien had said.

"So you think it's a girl?" Helen asked.

Darien let out a self-conscious laugh. "That's my guess. Obviously, I don't know for sure, though."

Helen leaned forward, a conspiratorial look in her eye. "Doctors might disagree, but I trust a mother's intuition."

Darien shrugged. "It doesn't matter to me whether it's a boy or a girl. Either would make a great vet tech."

Ellie and Helen both laughed.

"Is this how we pull you out of your slump?" Ellie teased. "We just have to get you talking about the baby?"

Darien cocked her head, her smile turning thoughtful. "I think it's talking about the future that pulls me out of it. The hope that if we can get beyond this, things on the other side will be *so* good." She patted her belly. "The baby's just the most obvious symbol of that."

"That makes perfect sense." Ellie settled back in her seat, a warm, happy glow in her stomach. It took her a moment to realize ... it was hope. Unbidden, an image bubbled to the surface of her mind, of her and Oliver, and a whole life they had yet to live. Adventures and rainy days and long nights together—

The front door burst open.

Naomi charged through with such force that the bell's frantic ringing didn't stop until she'd almost reached the table. Quiet swept in her wake like a frigid mountain wind as the patrons all turned to look at her, and Ellie's happiness shattered at the look on her face. She was terrified.

Naomi smacked both palms down on the gray linoleum, sending her basket of salmon flying. It hit the floor and scattered; she didn't even glance at it. "Jordan and Jessie have stolen the *Tide Chaser.*"

"What?" Helen asked.

"They're going—" Naomi pressed a hand to her suddenly trembling lips. "They're going to Portlock. They just ... just *took off*—"

"Move so I can get out of here." Helen scooted out of the booth. Ellie and Darien exchanged an alarmed glance, then followed as the two older women started for the door. "Let's get to the warehouse, so we can—"

"Luke's already going after them," Naomi said. "He, Bill, and Henry are just about to launch the *Poor Buoy*—you'll probably get a call from Henry but, but ..."

A sob shook Naomi's shoulders. Helen took her by the arm, ignoring the stares of the other diners. Ellie followed a pace behind Darien, breathing slowly. The lead ball in her stomach felt like it had grown fists and started punching, and the incongruous beat of whatever '80s band was blaring into the now-chatterless restaurant didn't help.

Oliver had been with the boys—and Sam, too. Where were they?

Her hand stole toward her pocket where her phone was nestled. She probably couldn't call either of them, but maybe a text—

A rough hand tapped hers, and a gravelly, male voice said, "Hey."

Ellie barely resisted the knee-jerk reaction to rip her hunting knife out of its sheath. Instead, she looked down. A rough-cut block of a man stared up at her, his weathered face concerned. He nodded toward Helen and Naomi, who were already out the door. "I don't know what's going on, but you tell Helen that if either of them needs anything, give us a call. The name's Roman Bauer."

Ellie nodded, then glanced at where Darien hovered at the door, waiting. "I will, thanks."

"And me, too," added a lady at the next table. "Tell them the Lees are willing to help if they need it."

"Okay." Ellie gave another nod, hoping it came across as grateful, then beelined out the door.

"Let's go," Darien said, breaking into a jog. "They are *not* waiting."

"Should you be running?" Ellie asked, even as the sheer relief of the familiar physical motion washed through her. She wanted—*needed*—more of this.

Darien waved her off. "Doctor says I'm fine to exercise. At this moment, I'm choosing to believe that includes light jogging."

"Fair."

They caught up to Helen and Naomi just as the truck started, and jumped in the back seat. Ellie buckled her seatbelt, then looked up ... and found herself staring right into Helen's cobalt-blue eyes, reflected in the rearview mirror. They were so like Oliver's. They were also misty with tears.

Ellie's heart dropped like a stone as Helen backed out, her jaw tight, clearly trying to keep her emotions under control.

"Girls, I'm sorry to be the bearer of bad news," Helen started.

Numb disbelief stole through Ellie. But she knew. So when Helen said it, it wasn't really a surprise.

"Sam and Oliver are with Jessie and Jordan."

***

Oliver shivered, but not because he was freezing to death anymore. They were barely two miles away from a monster whose preferred way of killing was through sheer, undiluted, heart-shredding terror. And this time, he probably wasn't getting out alive.

He sat on the bench closest to the heater—the bone-chilling memory of the ocean was recent enough that warmth was still one of the most pleasant sensations he'd ever felt in his life—and pulled his phone out of his pocket again.

It was still dead.

He stared at it, anger and regret simmering deep in his soul. He didn't know what he'd expected. Still, it hurt that there wouldn't even be a chance to tell Ellie he loved her one more time.

"Oliver, do we need to be worried about rocks or sand bars?"

Oliver didn't look up; he thought he might punch Jordan if he did. "Stay away from the portside shore. Take it wide and come in from starboard, especially since it's low tide."

"Okay." For the first time, Oliver thought there might be hesitation in Jordan's voice. "If you want to take us in, since you've been here before—"

"Jordan, if I take the wheel, I'm turning us around."

The teen let out a sound between a grunt and a growl. Then, the cabin went quiet again.

Breathing deeply, Oliver finally allowed himself to look up and out the tempered-glass windows. His eyes tracked the handful of abandoned buildings that squatted along the shoreline, sullen, ramshackle, frozen in time. Across from him, Sam shifted, drawing Oliver's stare. Part of him hoped he could catch his friend's eye, try one last time to ... glare at him, shrug at him; he didn't know what, just *something*.

But Sam wouldn't make eye contact, either.

Oliver suppressed a frustrated sound. Once, from the deck of the *Poor Buoy*, he'd watched two huge brown bears feeding on the bank of an inlet, tearing into their fish with an intensity—a desperation—that only an oncoming Alaskan winter could provoke. During the half hour he and the Calls had watched them, the bears never once looked at each other. Later, Helen had told him that male bears often avoided acknowledging the other at all costs in situations like that, because direct eye contact could so easily lead to an attack.

It's us, Oliver thought as he stared over Sam's shoulder. Anger began to build in his heart again at what the demons had done to so many of the people he loved. Maybe this—ending it right now—*was* for the best.

The biggest problem was that, deep down, he still didn't think they could.

The *Chaser* slowed, its engine dropping to a throaty purr. Oliver half-stood, peering over Jordan's shoulder, and his heart nearly stopped as he saw how close they already were to the beach. Memories assaulted him: the isolation he'd felt, the indescribable smallness. The towering figure of the Nantinaq, its revolting odor. The Gatekeeper's red eyes, its leering face, its flayed-looking, inhuman figure. His stomach burbled; he gripped the back of Jordan's chair and tried to breathe like Ellie did when she was corralling her anxiety. *Slow in, hold, slow out, hold—*

"You going to be okay, Oliver?" Jessie asked.

"Probably not." *And you won't, either.* Still, Oliver felt like he needed to try one more time. "Guys, you've been good friends to me. I care about what happens to you, which is why I'm *begging* you to turn around. Please don't do this."

No one replied. Instead, Jordan turned the *Chaser's* prow toward shore and cut the motor. Oliver's heart sank, his mouth suddenly dry. "You're going to beach her?"

"The tide's going out," Jordan said stubbornly. "We shouldn't be on shore *that* long. And after watching what you went through earlier, I sure as hell ain't swimming."

"Jordan ..." Oliver shook his head, dumbfounded as the teen started to raise the outboard motor so it wouldn't drag the bottom and break in the shallows. Their momentum carried them forward even as the engine that had created it hummed out of the water, dripping. Oliver had to admit that Jordan had struck the perfect balance—enough momentum to beach the *Chaser's* prow firmly in the soft sand, but not so much that she was damaged. In another time and place—one that *didn't* have thirty foot tide swings—he might have been impressed with his skill.

If only skill and desperation weren't such a bad mix right now, he thought tiredly.

"I can't watch my family suffer anymore," Jordan said quietly. "I'll do what it takes."

Oliver's gut twisted. "Believe me, I've been there, Jordan."

The boy just shook his head. "Brace."

Seconds later, the *Chaser's* prow hit the sand. Her hull slid up onto the beach with a wet, sibilant *hiss,* then she was still. Oliver studied the treeline and what he could see of the swamp for a hulking, apelike figure, or even for massive footprints in the sand, but there was no sign of the Nantinaq. He wondered if the creature would greet them. Maybe *that* would knock some sense into the teenagers and Sam.

But if not …

"If we make it past the Gatekeeper, then I'm going in," Oliver said. "That's not negotiable."

Sam pinned him with a look, but Oliver held his ground. "It's not."

"We may not have time to guarantee that—" Sam started.

"I know," Oliver said. "And whatever happens will happen. Just … remember that you three all have families who love you."

"So do you," Sam said.

"It's not the same."

Sam rolled his eyes as he opened the cabin door. "Fine. *You* can try telling Helen that and see what happens. Henry, too. Or Ellie. She'd straight-up smack you for being an idiot, and she'd be right."

"I—"

Jessie slapped Oliver on the shoulder as he passed. "And your crew. What are we, chum?"

Oliver swallowed a sudden lump in his throat as he watched the three holster pistols, load a bag with spare clips, sheath knives … "None of those will do much."

"Better to be prepared," Jordan said as he slipped a second, fully-loaded 10mm clip into his pocket.

"You coming or what?" Jessie hollered through the open cabin door. Without waiting for Oliver's response, he clambered around the cabin toward the *Chaser's* bow. Oliver breathed like Ellie one more time as Sam and Jordan followed. Then, he stepped out of the cabin and shut the door behind him.

***

Darien sank into a cushy, slightly ripped office chair in the warehouse. She was terrified. She was enraged. And she felt utterly, completely helpless.

Ellie sat a few feet away, staring at the metal wall opposite them, her fingers tapping across the tabletop with such speed they were almost a blur. Helen perched on the table's other end, in hushed conversation with Naomi. Jordan's mother had pulled herself together quickly after they'd gotten the news, and had been straight-backed and severe ever since. Darien didn't envy what Jordan was in for when he got back. A wave of furious resentment washed over her; she didn't envy what *Sam* was in for when he got back, in no small part because she was the one who would be dishing it out.

If he comes back.

Darien grabbed the thought, then stuffed it into the deepest, darkest cellar of her mental fortress. *Maybe I'll make that section a crypt.*

Something twitched in an alien consciousness nearby. Darien stiffened, then leaned forward and rested her face in her hands, imagining opening the windows in her Fortress—just a crack; just enough to get a feel for the metaphorical demon-weather on the outside.

She wrinkled her nose. *Twelve now.* When they'd arrived at the warehouse three hours ago, she'd only counted four (plus Slubgob, of course, who hopped between her, Ellie, Helen, and Naomi like a mad rabbit.) The demons roared as they fed on the four women's fear and rage and helplessness; it was a revolting crush of sadistic gluttony. Darien shuddered but resisted the urge to slam the windows of her fortress closed. *Practice again. Catch one and hold it.*

Closing her eyes, she let her mind expand, trying to mimic what she'd felt Death do during her visions. She'd already succeeded twice in the last few hours; the goal now was to lengthen the time she could immobilize a demon. She hadn't communicated with Ankle Tickler since that morning, and didn't *know* if this was the next step he'd want her to take … but it was what she'd decided to do. *Your fault for latching onto a self-starter, buddy.*

Darien stilled as the cacophony around her resolved into individual creatures. Focusing on the loudest, she imagined golden threads of power snaking from her to it, wrapping around its shadowy form, binding it so it couldn't move, couldn't feed. She bit down on a gasp as it struggled, then imagined pushing it away from Naomi, through the wall, and out into the gathering rainclouds beyond. Darien held it there, straining but—her heart leaped—*in complete control* as the seconds ticked by—

"Darien?"

Ellie's voice shattered the tendrils, destroying the connection. Darien's eyes flew open, and she realized she was covered in cold sweat. "Huh?"

"You don't look very good," Ellie said. "Do you need to lie down? Or drink some water?"

"Oh! No, I'm okay, thanks though."

Ellie leveled a skeptical look at her.

"I'm ..." Darien lowered her voice. "I'm reading the room, if you know what I mean."

Ellie's expression changed. "How many are there? Do you know?"

"Twelve."

"*Twelve*?"

"All juveniles except Slubgob, who's, well, bothering you right now."

"I figured." She frowned. "Slubgob has to know you and Sam have supernatural powers, right?"

Darien looked down at the table. "I would think so."

"Which means Death knows," Ellie whispered.

Chills crept over Darien. "He has to. He just ... doesn't seem concerned about it? Maybe that's because I only catch him while he's feeding and he's *euphoric* then."

"Right, he wouldn't be thinking about his problems in that state." Ellie dragged a hand over her eyes. "And it's not like you can really go on the offensive with your powers. It's hard to turn a radar into a rocket launcher, even if the radar's getting more sensitive by the hour."

Guilt pricked at Darien. *I have to tell them what's going on with Ankle Tickler.* Obviously now wasn't a good time, though. And if she was being honest, there *was* still a strong part of her that wanted to push it until the last second. She'd made such incredible progress; she could actually *do* something now with this curse that had been thrust upon her. And there was so much more to learn ... it would be stupid to expose her teacher before she'd mastered the subject matter—

Something *pulsed* near the far wall.

Darien stared in its direction, but when it didn't happen again, she turned back to Ellie. "Sorry. I'd still think Death would at least *think* about our powers if he knew. He's thought about his other problems." She frowned. "I can't shake this gut feeling that something isn't adding up."

The demon along the far wall pulsed again. Darien tensed; it was how a discordant note *felt*, like an unravelled thread, a faraway grumble of thunder. A subtle, quiet warning that things might change. Foreboding pricked at her, and she reached for the baby's mind before remembering that that was *not* an option.

The thing pulsed again. Darien's right hand slid down to the sheathed knife at her belt, reassured at the weight of the lighter in her opposite pocket. "Ellie. One of the demons is doing something."

Ellie straightened. "Awakening?"

The thing pulsed again.

"Hang on." Darien listened for a few moments ... and the demon seemed to settle. "I don't know. I don't really remember what happened before Henry's squid demon awakened. And in Hawaii, I wasn't sensitive enough yet when the Sphere came after us." She glanced over at where Naomi and Helen were talking. "But something might be up. Just be—"

A punch of barbaric glee hit Darien; she winced and put a hand to her head.

"What is it?" Ellie asked.

Darien shook herself. "Slubgob. She just switched to Naomi."

Ellie glanced at the willowy woman. "She's holding up really well."

"So are you."

Ellie let out a mirthless snort. "I'm a basket case, Darien. I can't imagine ..." She rubbed her face, anguish breaking through. "He's just the type, though. To nearly drown trying to stop his friends from doing something stupid, then go fight with them the second it becomes obvious they won't be stopped. Even though he knows what's waiting for them. I can't imagine what he's going through."

Sudden heat stung Darien's eyes, and she looked away. "What I don't understand is how they roped Sam into it. I thought he was smarter than that."

Ellie's grim expression took on a thoughtful cast. "No. I know my brother. Not as well as you do, but still ... I bet there's more to this. Maybe they tricked him, or a demon got to him. Or both."

"I'm still going to kick his butt when he gets back."

A slightly feral smile lifted one corner of Ellie's mouth. "Oliver taught me how to throw elbows last night. I've been looking for a way to practice, so let me know if you want Sam to be my first target. I don't know what I'm doing and he's practically Goliath, so I probably won't even break his face."

Darien snorted. "You might have to get in line."

"Fair. You get first—"

A staticky voice—Luke's—drifted through the open door to Bill's office. "Warehouse, come in. You there, Naomi?"

Naomi sprang toward the door and was through in an eyeblink, Helen on her heels. Ellie and Darien leaped up and pounded after them, bolting through the door as Naomi grabbed the receiver.

"We're here!" she said. "What's going on?"

"We have visual on the *Chaser*."

Helen gasped. Darien hadn't realized she'd shrunk closer to Ellie until her sister-in-law put an arm around her shoulders.

"Where are you?" Naomi barked. "Where are they?"

"We just turned into the bay. Henry can just barely see the boat through his binoculars." Luke paused. "He says it looks like she's beached. He can't tell whether the boys are still on board. "

Naomi went pale; she grabbed the back of Bill's office chair. "How fast can you get to them?"

"We estimate they had about a forty-five-minute lead on us to start, but I'd guess they don't have more than thirty now. Bill agrees."

Naomi's lip trembled, and Darien felt her own throat constrict. Half an hour was still plenty of time to get in mortal trouble. But when Naomi spoke, her voice was calm. "Okay. The Lees took Allie and Nora. I'll call and tell them they can sleep over. Helen, Darien, and Ellie are here with me, and we're staying right here." She swallowed. "Go get our boys."

"We'll bring 'em home," Luke said. "Out."

The static died. Naomi just held the receiver, staring blankly out the window at the harbor. Then, she set it back in its holder and turned. "If we're going to be here for a while, does anyone need food?"

Helen was already shaking her head. "I couldn't eat right now if I wanted to."

"Me neither," Ellie said. "Darien?"

"No. Believe me, I—"

She froze.

"Darien?" Ellie asked.

But Darien barely heard her. The pulsing was back, growing, intensifying, drowning out the chatter of the other feeding demons. Even Slubgob was—

A twisted sort of joy smacked into her like a thunderclap. *Slubgob* was overjoyed. And on the other side of the wall, a mind was taking shape.

Horrible, aching hunger exploded in Darien's belly.

Metal scraped on metal as Ellie drew her knife.

"Get out of here!" Darien screamed. "Something's coming!"

Chapter Seventeen

S am's feet hit the sand with a muted thump, and he looked up. Mist hovered in whorls around the snow-capped peaks, verdant spruce stood in proud, silent ranks, and the bushes that he and Henry had pushed through a month ago on their way out of the marshland were lined in deep red-gold. The beach sprawled before him, a pale, elkhide shade of tan. Not as golden as the beaches in Hawaii, but still beautiful in its own wild way.

He hated all of it.

"Let's get this over with." He shrugged his backpack—loaded with extra lighters, bug spray, bear spray, and a spare box of shells—higher onto his shoulders. Then, he fell into step beside Jessie and Jordan, who had just finished tying the boat to a big, black rock that stuck out of the beach about ten yards away.

"We should've brought plumbing torches," Jordan said softly.

"We can still go back."

Sam turned to see Oliver padding toward them, having just thrown another line around a second rock to keep the boat from crashing into either once the tide came in—though they all hoped to be long gone before then.

Jessie's expression hardened. "No."

Oliver didn't look surprised. He just ran a hand through his hair, his shoulders rising and falling in a deep, silent breath. Then, he let his hand fall against his thigh with a slap. "All right. Let's do it, then."

He started up the beach. Sam let the teens fall in behind Oliver, then took up the rear, all his senses on alert. The distant caw of a raven, the wind sighing through the spruce boughs, the faint, fetid odor of the swamp it carried ... they were torture. His mouth went dry; he was absolutely *certain* they were being swatched.

The four managed to steal through the gloomy strip of trees that lined the beach, then paused at the edge of the swamp. There was more of it than Sam remembered. Pain lanced through him as he gazed across it, remembering his dad's excitement, the joy that being in places like this had brought him.

If only we'd known. He closed his eyes for a moment, wrinkling his nose against the pungent swamp odor and the prickling behind his eyes. *I'm coming, Dad.*

"The cave isn't far from here."

Sam blinked; Oliver had turned to face them. His expression was still hard and cold, if a little resigned. Sam felt a sort of detached empathy; he imagined his face looked similar. Jessie's and Jordan's sure did. If nothing else, he had to give the kids credit for their courage.

"The cave's about a ten-minute walk through the swamp, then fifteen more up the sidehill. Based on my experience, the Gatekeeper won't appear until we're nearly inside it, probably so he can ambush us. Since there are more of us this time, though, he might try a different tactic. So stay alert."

Sam racked his brain, trying to remember details of his conversation with the Night Marchers. "Kekoa—the guy who closed the gate last time—implied that the Gatekeeper didn't travel far from the gate even when the warriors were attacking it. So ... whatever that's worth. He did say they met other demons along the way, though."

Jessie frowned. "Yeah, I was kind of expecting more resistance than this. Why haven't we ... Oliver?"

"Uh ..." Oliver's eyes were wide, his mouth open in a stunned expression that wasn't quite fearful. The hair on the back of Sam's neck stood straight up. Then a voice spoke from behind him, deep and inhuman, like something played out of a broken stadium speaker.

"You did bring the angry one."

***

Ellie bolted for the back door, grabbed the knob, and wrenched it open with such force that it hit the metal wall behind it with a reverberating *clang*. "Come on!"

She grabbed an ill-looking Darien by the arm and yanked. *Don't pass out on me, don't you do it—*

"How much time do we have?" Helen yelled from inside.

Darien tore her arm from Ellie's grasp, and Ellie was relieved to see some of the fight return to her. "I don't know—seconds! It's like watching a puppy grow into a Chupacabra!"

Something banged inside, then Helen charged out the door, gripping the huge bear pistol that usually lived on her mantle. She turned. "Naomi, hurry—!"

"I'm here!" Naomi slipped outside and slammed the door, a gleaming metal canister clutched in her fist. She whirled on Helen. "We can't leave, though! The radio's in there!"

"And there's our neighbors to think about." Helen glanced around. The warehouse was near the end of the road, where the trees began, but there were still other buildings within easy shouting distance. Ellie had never seen anyone in or even near them, but judging by Helen's distress, they were far from abandoned. "I couldn't stomach a demon getting Kirby, or the Bauers."

Fear twisted Ellie's gut, sudden and vicious; stopping had given their situation a chance to sink in. Sweat broke out on her forehead.

No. Fight it. The adrenaline cascading through her system was a gift, the tenseness in her muscles an asset. *I'm not ready to run. I'm ready to fight.*

The world snapped back into focus, and for a bizarre moment, Ellie was grateful for her anxiety. She likely had as much practice managing feelings of irrational terror as anyone else here, maybe more.

"Is it coming after us, Darien?" she asked. If they could lure it out here and kill it ...

Darien's face contorted. "Hang on ... I'm ..." Her teeth clenched so hard Ellie was afraid one might crack. Then, her eyes flew open. "Yes, he's coming after us. Death's egging him on; I can feel them both."

"Do you need to get out of here?" Helen asked.

Darien's face hardened. "No. I'm sticking this out."

"If you pass out—" Ellie started, but Darien overrode her.

"I can handle it, Ellie! And we don't have time—!"

"Enough!" Naomi bellowed. "Darien, if you need to get out, then get out. Otherwise, let's kill this thing. Here ..."

She jogged over, loosening her pistol in its holster. "You two. Gun or bear spray?"

Darien looked up at Ellie, eyes wide. In that moment, Ellie realized ... this was her sister-in-law's first real fight.

"You choose first," she heard herself say.

Gratitude flashed in Darien's eyes. She turned to Naomi. "I'm more practiced with a handgun."

Naomi held it out. "It's loaded, safety's on."

"Thanks. I won't shoot you if you don't bear spray me."

Naomi blinked. Then, her face split in a grin, and Ellie wondered, just for a moment, if this was a relief for her. If having something physical to fight was better than another hour of agonized waiting. She glared at the warehouse, anxiety and rage turning her belly into a seething cauldron. *Maybe it's a relief for me, too.*

Darien doubled over again, clutching her head. "We have seconds!"

Adrenaline shot through Ellie, so intense that lights flashed in her vision.

"Watch that wall!" Darien threw out an arm—the one that wasn't pressed to her forehead. She looked terrible; Ellie had no idea how she was still upright. A soft *click* sounded to her right as Naomi primed the bear spray.

"Here it comes!" Darien shrieked.

The creature burst through the wall and streaked toward them.

It was huge.

And that was all Ellie could process before it barreled into her.

***

Sam whirled, ripping his borrowed 10mm out of its holster. A gag-inducing odor smacked him in the nose; eyes watering, he brought the gun up—

A giant, hairy brown hand grabbed the gun by the barrel and plucked it away as easily as a father taking a toy from a child. Sam staggered backward, barely aware of the teens' yells of fright as he took in the creature the hand belonged to. It loomed over him, covered in thick fur that had the same consistency as dirty shag carpet. Its face was apelike, its posture stooped, and its eyes ... they were the blackest things Sam had ever seen.

He took a shaky step back, his eyes still watering at the thing's smell. "You ... you must be Bigfoot."

The thing cocked its head. "I do not know Bigfoot."

"I … you …" Sam gaped at the creature as Oliver appeared next to him, his hands stuffed in his jacket pockets. He looked so nonchalant it was almost infuriating; in fact, Sam thought he might be working to hold back a smile. But when he spoke, his voice was serious.

"Sam, this is the Nantinaq. Nantinaq, this is Jessie, Jordan, and the angry one, who usually goes by Sam."

Sam snapped his mouth shut. *Angry one?*

The Nantinaq regarded him for a moment more, and Sam shivered. The creature's stare was so appraising it was almost oppressive. It turned to Oliver. "Where is Just Ellie?"

One slow blink was the only indicator of any emotion Oliver felt. "We had to leave her behind."

The Nantinaq said nothing. He stared at Oliver, who, to his credit, didn't break eye contact. "Does she know what has happened here? She deserves truth."

"Yes, she knows," Oliver said. "If we fail today, she'll probably lead the next charge, knowing her."

The Nantinaq nodded once, then turned back to Sam. He gulped. The creature hadn't blinked once during this entire conversation. "Will you do what you must?"

Sam willed his voice to be steady. "Yes."

"Will you give what you must?"

"If you mean my life, then yes." He blinked a few times as he thought of Darien. Then, summoning his courage, he held out his hand. "But, it might help to have my pistol back. Even if it can't kill the Gatekeeper—or anything else that's out there—it can at least distract it, right?"

The Nantinaq held up the pistol, bemused, as if the weapon was of so little importance that he'd forgotten he'd taken it. Still gripping it by its barrel, he held it out to Sam, who took it and holstered it. "I didn't mean to threaten you with it. Just … reflexes."

"Your weapons mean nothing to me."

" … Right," Sam said lamely.

A wry grin quirked Oliver's mouth. Sam fought an urge to kick him.

"Will you help us?"

Sam blinked at the sound of Jessie's voice. He stepped aside so both he and Jordan could join them, fighting not to cringe at the sickly, greenish cloud that glommed around Jessie's head; it looked like a translucent tumor.

"Eager one." The Nantinaq surveyed Jessie for a long moment. "I cannot help you."

"Why not?" Jessie asked.

The Nantinaq stared at Jessie. The teen stared back for a moment. Then, he began to rock back and forth. Then, he looked away.

"Please," Jordan asked softly.

The Nantinaq's head swiveled to him, and Sam could swear something in its gaze softened. "You suffer."

Jordan's expression clouded. "I can't listen to my dad wake up screaming one more time. My mom had a … a light about her. Now it's gone. My nine-year-old sister's being terrorized by *something*, I don't even know what. And I haven't seen Nora, my other sister, in probably a month, not really. She just hides in her room." Jordan nodded at the monster. "Suffering. You nailed it. We *all* are. So you going to help us out, or what?"

The monster appraised them for a long moment.

"I cannot," it said. Then it turned and started to walk away. Sam's heart sank; he exchanged a look with Oliver, who looked disappointed but not surprised.

Jessie, on the other hand, started after the creature. "Get back—*how* can you just walk away? It's your fault, you're the one who failed!"

The Nantinaq stopped. Sam's eyes went wide. "Uh, Jessie—"

"Shut up," Jessie snarled. He stalked toward the Nantinaq, who was slowly turning, its hooded eyes narrowed. "You're a low-down, dirty coward. You've been sitting up here for a month doing *nothing*. People have died—my mother died! And they're still dying! So get off your stinking ass and help us!"

"Jessie—"

Oliver grabbed him by the arm, but Jessie threw him off, the cloud around him flaring. "Touch me again and I'll break your nose!"

Oliver's expression went dead except for the gleam in his eyes. For a second, Sam saw the person he *had* been, the fury that cut the lines of his face into angles sharp as glass shards.

"And then you'll be on the ground with a broken shoulder," he growled, "and none of us will get what we want."

Jessie's hands balled into fists, but Sam had had enough. He shouldered between them. "Guys—"

Jordan—who had apparently had similar thoughts—grabbed his cousin's shoulder. "Jessie, bud, you're going too far."

"The gate must be closed," the Nantinaq rumbled. "But I do not want to see any of you die."

The four of them quieted; it was as if the creature's voice was a gravelly, primal, very scary sedative. Oliver scowled. Then, he turned and faced the monster, hands on his hips. The pose reminded Sam of Helen when she was scolding someone.

"I don't understand you," he said. "When you say you can't help us, what do you actually mean by that?"

The creature tilted its head. "I cannot help you."

"Cannot, or will not?"

The silence around them became oppressive.

Oliver gestured to the four of them. "You've lived so long, we're probably like mayflies. But you seem to care a little about us. Is that right?"

In a shockingly human move, the Nantinaq shrugged.

"Even if you don't, there are billions of people—and animals, too—who are suffering, and you can help us put it right." Oliver's tone softened. "I respect what you've done for all these years. I'm grateful for it. But we're in a bind—the whole world is. Is *anything* worth not trying?"

Sam hardly dared to breathe. The quiet was so complete now that even the faraway raven had stopped croaking. And the Nantinaq stood still as a statue, like he'd been carved from the bones of the earth itself.

"Earnest one," it finally rumbled, "I cannot. I am not of this world. They are not of this world. I can ..." It paused, as if searching for the right word, " ... touch this world. They can touch it. But we cannot touch each other."

Sam frowned, sharing a glance with Oliver.

"So you're saying there's, like ..." Jordan gave a vague gesture. "Too many degrees of separation? It's like a Venn Diagram?"

The Nantinaq tilted its head. "I do not know diagram."

"Still ... if they don't affect you," Oliver said slowly, "then why are you so afraid of the Gatekeeper?"

The Nantinaq blinked. "I do not want to watch any of you die. I have seen too much needless death."

The four of them stared at it. *Holy crap,* Sam thought. *It's too ... sensitive?*

Oliver crossed his arms. "You didn't seem to have a problem with sending me to die last time."

"You had courage. And were protected. Sometimes, we must risk." With that, the Nantinaq turned and began to walk away. Its footfalls were nearly silent, even in the sucking marsh mud. "I will carry you to the beach if I can. Alive or dead."

Then, it disappeared into the trees.

Chapter Eighteen

Darien gaped as Ellie went down, the demon's hairy, sinuous form shoving her into the gravel. Naomi was yelling, Helen cursing, and the demon fed in ecstasy and Death howled, "KILL THEM—"

Ellie's scream shattered the misty air. Pain seared into Darien's stomach, right below her ribcage. She doubled over, gasping; it felt like she'd been *knifed*. Through watering eyes, she watched the demon arch in agony and realized ...

Ellie stabbed it. It's the demon's pain, not mine.

Relief hit her—Death *hadn't* somehow crawled inside her body and started ripping it apart—and with that relief came clarity. She snatched the pain and imagined funneling it into her mental dungeon, along with everything else that belonged to the demon—its mind, its hunger, its rage. The scene around her swam back into focus just as Ellie cracked an elbow across the demon's grotesque, otterlike face. Naomi lay on the ground next to her, looking dazed. And Helen—where was Helen?

Do something! the sane part of Darien screeched. She charged toward the writhing scrum on the ground, her nerves screaming so loudly that she scrabbled for the baby's calm on instinct. Ellie—still partially underneath the creature—had flipped onto her stomach and was trying to crawl away, and Naomi was lurching to her feet, reaching out a hand. Heart pounding, Darien flipped the safety off the pistol. Despite the time she'd put in at the shooting range with Sam, she didn't trust herself in this situation unless she was at point-blank range—

POP! POP! POP!

The demon screamed again and skittered off Ellie, revealing Helen crouching behind it, face contorted in a snarl. She leaped to her feet, still holding the pistol she must have practically jammed into the thing's bristly, matted hide. Darien threw herself away as

Helen fell into a perfect shooter's stance and fired once, twice, three times. The demon flinched once, and pain flashed through Darien's stomach. Then, two holes appeared in the warehouse's wall.

NO! screamed a voice in Darien's mind, like a badly-tuned radio. *KILL THEM!*

The otter-thing—it *had* to be over eight feet long—looked back and forth between them and the warehouse, as if tempted to take refuge inside. Something scraped along the gravel behind Darien, and she whirled to see Ellie staggering to her feet. She was gasping, her shirt torn at the shoulder. Blood welled from underneath the fabric, somehow redder and more shocking than anything Darien had ever seen on an operating table, but Ellie didn't seem to notice. She looked down at her knife, which was covered in black, tarlike demon blood, then pulled her lighter out of her jeans pocket. The demon let out an eerie, chittering scream, then fell onto all fours and started to pace, eyeing them like a wolf looking for an opening in a herd of bison.

"What're you supposed to be?" Helen yelled. "A Kushtaka?"

The creature snarled.

"Kill them, then there will be others—"

"Death's talking to it." Darien screwed up her eyes. She was managing to keep her mind, Death's mind, and the otter-demon's mind in their own separate rooms, but with the amount of effort it was taking, she couldn't do it for long. The baby flinched away again. Darien let go of its mind immediately, nearly buckling as the full mental weight of the situation hit her. She gritted her teeth. "He's ordered it to kill u—"

The demon charged again.

Darien whipped the pistol up with trembling hands, half-aware of Naomi's yell. The sound of aerosol hissed through the air. The demon screeched again as a noxious cloud enveloped it, and Darien felt little pinpricks burning her skin, her eyes, her nose—

The pain disappeared.

"He's not solid anymore!" she yelled. "Save your—"

"Kill them! Pain is temporary!"

"Save your ..." Darien bit down on a cry. *NO, you can't reach for the baby!*

She moaned as she *felt* a memory shiver through the monster in front of her. *One demon ripped apart the mind of another, burning it from the inside, leaving only a shell behind.*

She blinked as it subsided. It had been Death and Wormwood; she'd watched that happen only a few days ago. But to the creature—newborn, impressionable, and deadly—the memory felt as ancient and natural as a child's fear of the dark.

"Give up!" Naomi shouted at the otter-demon, tossing her hair out of her eyes. "Go away!"

"He won't!" Darien shrank toward the other women as the demon started to circle around them. "He's too afraid of Death. We'll have to kill him."

Ellie let out a strangled sound. "The irony."

"He's got three big holes in him already," Helen said. "All we need to do is—"

"Shove the lighter in him," Ellie said.

Then, she dashed toward the demon.

***

For the third time in his life, Oliver marched up the rocky mountainside toward the gate, and certain death. And though nothing in life was actually certain, though he'd cheated the Gatekeeper twice now, he didn't see how he was getting out of this one.

"I still think the Nantinaq could try and punch the demons when they're solid, or something," Sam muttered from beside him. He was barely breathing hard, and Oliver fought back a grimace. Beating him into the pool was going to be difficult. For a number of reasons.

"Doesn't that make sense?" Sam asked. "Shouldn't he be able to do that?"

"I'd think so." Oliver let out a long exhale. "I also think he'd have thought of that. He's not an idiot."

"But he does think differently than us," Sam pointed out. "Maybe we should suggest it."

"Or maybe we should just forget about him and go take care of it, like we planned to do this whole time," Jessie said.

Frustration surged through Oliver as he looked back at the teen. Jessie's right hand rested on the butt of his holstered pistol as he climbed, his eyes fixed straight ahead. Already, he looked waxen with fear, his brown eyes stark in his freckled, too-pale face.

Oliver could feel it, too, burrowing under his skin, into his chest, into his brain. It was so obvious, he wondered how he'd missed it the first time.

Oliver glanced at Jordan. He was keeping pace easily, his expression a grim mirror of his cousin's. In his typical, stoic fashion, he'd said nothing. But he also hadn't faltered. Sudden, horrible images invaded Oliver's mind: Jordan dead on the ground. Jessie screaming as he died from sheer terror. Sam floating facedown in the pool, just like his father had been.

Oliver gritted his teeth. *I know what you're doing,* he thought at whatever creature had put the thoughts there. *It's not going to work.* He wrenched his eyes upward and scanned the now-familiar stone wall in front of them. There was less mist this time; he could see the caves dotting the cliff, growing larger and larger further down.

He swallowed. They were maybe a hundred yards away.

His eyes roved across the cloudy gray sky; he had no idea what time it was—maybe sometime between eight and nine. That would give them an hour of daylight, maybe a little more. *At least we're not doing this in the dark.* He couldn't even imagine what that would be like.

"Oliver?"

Oliver didn't realize he'd stopped until Sam said his name. He shook himself, then pointed with a surprisingly steady hand. "See that cave down at the end?"

They looked in the direction he was pointing, and the silence on the mountain grew, turning the cool evening air into something cold, unfriendly, suffocating.

"That's it, huh?" Jordan finally asked. His voice seemed so small.

Oliver nodded. "That's it."

For another long moment, they stood there, and a small part of Oliver was grateful that they were finally—*finally*—as afraid as they should be. Not that it did any good. He doubted any of them would turn around at this point ... including himself, he realized. They were here. There were four of them. They might as well try and end it.

He stepped forward. "Let's go."

Other than the occasional scrape of boot soles on slippery rock, the four made almost no noise as they crept toward the cave. There was no need to be so quiet. It wasn't like they could sneak up on the Gatekeeper; Oliver was positive the creature already knew they were there. The fear was burrowing into his very bones now, an external force as real and penetrating as the frigid water he'd fallen into earlier.

"I walked right past it," Sam whispered. His voice shook. "When we were looking for them, I walked right past ..."

The fear grew. Jessie let out a choked sound. Oliver gritted his teeth. "It's just fear. It's all in our heads. He'll appear soon, don't let—"

In front of the cave, something shimmered.

***

Darien scrambled after Ellie, cursing. Helen's and Naomi's footsteps crunched on the gravel behind her, but Ellie was much faster than any of them. The demon snarled, tensing as it prepared to leap—

POP!

The creature rocked back as Helen's seventh bullet buried itself in its body, and pain seared through Darien's hip. She stumbled and went down on one knee, but managed to yell, "Solid again!"

You're not shot, it's the demon. Get up. Leave the baby alone. Darien staggered to her feet in time to see Ellie jab at the creature's throat with her lighter, the little flame bright against the demon's dark fur. But the demon lashed out, its giant paw sweeping Ellie's legs out from underneath her. She crashed down on her back, eyes wide, gaping up at the sky.

"Ellie!" Darien screamed. Ignoring the diminishing pain in her hip, she fell into her stance, raised the pistol—

Naomi blew past her, hurtling toward the demon.

Darien swore again and lowered the gun; as chaotic as everything was, the older woman must not have seen her raise it. She dashed forward, watching in disbelief as Naomi drew a knife, buried her other hand in the demon's straggly fur, and stabbed. It turned on her, slashing with its clawed paws. Beside them, Ellie was hauling herself to her feet, but she was clearly dazed, and her little red lighter lay on the ground ten feet behind her—

"BEHIND YOU!" Darien broke into a sprint, clutching her own lighter, praying with everything she had that her baby would be fine, that no one would die here today. Fury exploded through her, and this time, it was her own. She was furious at the otter-demon for existing and livid with Sam for leaving; she was even angry with Oliver for letting him go.

But above all, she was enraged at her own ineptitude.

The demon flipped Naomi onto the ground, its dark, sullen rage seeping around Darien's stone walls. This time, she let it in, feeling it mix and meld with her own like a dark, ugly thread connecting their two minds. And she felt, in that second, its intent.

It was going to crush Naomi's skull.

"NO!" Darien screamed as its paw flashed upward. "STOP!"

The demon froze.

Literally ... *froze*.

And then a crushing weight descended on Darien's mind.

***

Oliver pulled his pistol, barely preventing himself from trying to empty the clip into the Gatekeeper as terror threatened to overwhelm him. "He's coming. Jessie and Jordan—"

A helpless whimper came from behind Oliver. He whirled to see Jessie sink into a crouch, hands over his head. The boy's pistol clattered to the ground as he clutched his face, rocking back and forth, pleading with something only he could see.

Oliver crouched beside him. "Jessie?"

But Jessie didn't even seem to see him. "No, no, no, don't take Mom, don't—"

Oliver stumbled back, his breathing shallow and uneven. Beside him, Sam and Jordan gawked at Jessie, looking as frightened as Oliver felt. He shuddered. He could feel the Gatekeeper's gaze on them, feel himself beginning to weaken already.

"We have to go now." Oliver grabbed Jordan's shoulder. "Cover us. Your only job is to shoot it as many times as you can when it grabs one of us. Just try not to shoot *us*. Sam ..."

But Sam's gaze was fixed over Oliver's shoulder, horror spreading across his ashen face. Oliver fought his compulsion to turn; his back was to his enemy, yes, but what more could be done to it anyway? Instead, he grabbed Sam by the lapel of his jacket. "Look at me. All you have to do is run."

"Toward that thing," Sam said hoarsely.

Oliver smacked him in the center of the chest, hard. "It's what you're good at." *Breathe, Oliver. Breathe.* "Let's do it."

He turned back to the cave and his heart nearly failed him. The Gatekeeper was fully visible now, an expression on its skinned, elongated face that might have been a smile. It shifted, its warped, exposed muscles sliding over and around each other like feeding snakes. The monster was even more terrible than he remembered.

Oliver took one more unsteady breath. Then, he charged anyway.

Come on! he screamed as his shaking, rubbery legs threatened to collapse. *Move!* Sam came up beside him, careening to the side, his breath coming in short gasps. Oliver let him draw just a little ahead; if the Gatekeeper went after Sam, maybe he could still get around and into the cave and end it all.

He glanced behind. Jordan was following, breath hissing between his clenched teeth, terror and determination blending on his face. Oliver would have been impressed if he'd been able to feel anything but overwhelming fear. He imagined that faraway part of himself as he stumbled, tried to remember that he was *that* man, not this ... this shuddering meat sack that could barely control its own limbs.

He forced his gaze back toward the gate. They had covered maybe half the distance to it, and the Gatekeeper hadn't moved; its utter, complete *stillness* was almost as terrifying as its appearance. It watched them come on, like it was a hungry Kodiak bear and they were a yipping pack of baby malamutes practically offering themselves up for dinner.

The bang of Jordan's gunshot was so loud in Oliver's ear that he gasped. In front of him, Sam stumbled. Horror flooded Oliver as he watched his friend fall; Jordan hadn't done that, had he? It was all he could do to turn toward the teen—

Another shot. On instinct, Oliver threw his hands up. His foot came down on an angled rock, and he felt it slip, his jelly legs wobbling. He teetered for a moment between terror and courage, between control and complete failure.

His legs failed him.

Oliver crashed to the ground, gasping as his knees, his side, and his hands hit the rough stone. The pain was amplified far beyond normal; he felt his flesh bruise, his vessels rupture, his skin tear with paralyzing acuteness.

And then the real fear hit.

Oliver screamed. It was bad, so bad; this was the worst death he could imagine. It was every pain he'd ever felt, physical and mental. Sam's cry of terror and the thump of a body hitting the ground assaulted his ears. Everything was hideous and painful and hopeless—his capacity to feel it all, to experience every awful facet of human existence, had been expanded beyond what any living thing was designed to feel. And it was going to kill him, slowly, so slowly—

Staggering footsteps lurched by. Oliver couldn't lift his head, not even when another gunshot shattered across the mountain. "Jord ..."

"I ... won't ..." Jordan's words turned into a retch. Oliver heard him stagger to a halt, then continue on again.

Come on! Get up!

It took everything he had to push himself onto his hands and knees. "Dean. Help us."

A fourth shot rang out. Adrenaline spiked through Oliver, so intense in his current state that it was almost blinding. But it gave him the strength to force his head up, to take in his surroundings. Sam was on the ground in front of him, crawling toward the Gatekeeper. Jordan was still, somehow, on his feet and advancing.

And the monster wasn't smiling anymore.

It pinned Jordan with a stare that Oliver felt. The teen stopped as if he'd hit a wall.

But ...

Oliver blinked, shook his head a little, then sucked in a deep breath. Yes, the fear that held him captive was lessening—it seemed like Jordan was now taking the brunt of it. His throat constricting at his crewmate's awful situation, Oliver forced one foot underneath him, then another. Shakily, he staggered after Jordan. As he passed Sam, his friend raised his head. "Oliver."

Oliver reached out a hand. Sam grabbed it, and Oliver braced as he lurched to his feet. "Come ..."

He had no energy to finish the sentence, but Sam didn't need his encouragement. Something in his eyes flashed, and he tottered forward. "Jordan! Wait—"

The Gatekeeper moved.

In a show of courage that Oliver knew he would never forget if he lived through this, Jordan planted his feet and shot again, then again. But it seemed like the Gatekeeper wasn't solid. Oliver cursed himself. Of course it wasn't. Of *course* the Gatekeeper wasn't like the newborn demons they'd been fighting; it was thousands of years old. It knew how to handle itself in a fight; it wasn't going to make itself vulnerable until the very last second.

The monster shambled toward Jordan, its posture leisurely, its speed spine-chilling. Oliver cried out, willing himself to go faster, but he knew it was too late. The pistol fell from Jordan's hand, and he went slack, staring, frozen like a rabbit as the Gatekeeper bore down on him.

The monster slipped one ropy arm around Jordan's shoulders, as if greeting a good friend. Then, with its other hand, it stabbed him through the chest.

Oliver screamed as its bladelike fingers broke through Jordan's back, red with his blood. Helplessness crashed over him, grief, pain ... he was running; both he and Sam were. Not that strange, lurching thing they'd been doing before, but actually *running*—

And now they were close enough to see Jordan's body go limp.

The Gatekeeper turned its burning red eyes on them, and Oliver felt like he'd hit a physical wall. Beside him, Sam threw up his hands, staggered, and came to a halt. Lethal fear leeched through Oliver's veins again, and he swayed as the strength threatened to go out of his muscles. He watched dumbly as the demon pulled its bladelike fingers free of Jordan's body, which hit the ground and didn't move, glassy eyes wide. Oliver raised his pistol and fired, knowing it was useless, but he couldn't just ... sit here and ... and die ...

He sank to his knees, breath coming in short gasps as the Gatekeeper started toward them. Apparently, he could. And would.

No. Fight for Ellie, he thought. But his heart was shuddering and splitting, *breaking* under the pressure, and the world was spinning so hard he thought he might be sideways and Jordan might be standing up—

Oliver blinked.

Jordan *was* getting to his feet.

Oliver watched dumbly as his friend shook himself and put both hands to his head. He stumbled around and saw them. His eyes locked with Oliver's, confusion written in every line of his face. Then, they snapped toward the Gatekeeper, and his mouth fell open in shock.

For a moment, the teen stood still, tilting his head, almost as if someone were speaking to him. The confusion left his face, replaced by resolution. He sprang toward the monster with unnatural speed, leaving his body—*his body was still lying on the ground.* As Oliver gaped, another figure flitted into view, a slim young man with black hair.

"Dad," he whispered.

The Gatekeeper stopped.

Dean turned and mouthed, *GO.* Then he limped forward to join Jordan, who had planted himself between Oliver and Sam and the monster. The fear lessened, becoming a dull roar that pounded at the inside of Oliver's skull like a Wormwood headache.

But *that* he could deal with.

"Sam." Oliver lurched to his knees, then staggered upright and grabbed a fistful of Sam's jacket. "Get up."

Sam's eyes were squeezed shut, tears leaving wet streaks in the dirt on his face.

"We have to move right now, or we won't make it." Oliver snatched Sam's arm and hauled back. For a moment, Sam was limp, and terror seized Oliver—he couldn't leave his friend to die here alone. He wouldn't. Wishing he didn't feel so weak, longing for even a little bit of adrenaline, Oliver started to pull, dragging Sam over the ground with painful slowness. "Get up, damn it!"

"Lemme go." Sam tugged his arm away, then lurched to his feet. Behind him, Dean and Jordan were still standing in front of the Gatekeeper. Their shoulders were bowed under the weight; apparently, even ghosts weren't immune to the monster. A few yards beyond them, the Gatekeeper's mouth was opening wide, wider, wider. It let out a guttural roar that seemed to shake the foundations of the mountain.

Oliver screwed up his face, clapping his hands over his ears. He couldn't form words, but Sam didn't need to be told what to do. He turned and careened back down the mountain, looking back once to make sure Oliver was following. Oliver waved him on, scanning the ground for Jessie's bright red windbreaker, but the boy was nowhere to be found. Praying the Nantinaq had saved him, Oliver crashed into the dark stretch of spruce below the rock face, the edges of his vision clouding, hoping they could put enough distance between themselves and the Gatekeeper before they passed out.

Chapter Nineteen

arien fell to her knees as pain spiked into her head—it was like someone had driven a nail through her skull. It was the demon; its entire consciousness, somehow she was *holding it back*—

POP! POP! POP!

WHOOSH!

Darien was burning.

She screamed in agony, falling forward, scrabbling against the gravel. It was pain like she'd never known, beyond what she could endure, but it was fading … fading …

The weight disappeared from Darien's mind. She blinked, and suddenly she was lying in the cold, damp gravel, her hands and knees stinging with scrapes, and the air smelled like rain and cauterization—

"Roll! ROLL, NAOMI!"

At the sound of Helen's panicked yell, Darien hauled her bleary eyes up. The demon—what was left of it—lay on its side, fire devouring its carcass with so much heat that steam rose from the earth around it. Naomi rolled on the ground a few yards away from the blaze, her face contorted in pain. Helen, coughing, beat at her black, smoking pant leg. As she watched, Ellie limped toward them and snatched Naomi's arm. Then, with a groan of pain, she started to try to haul Naomi away from the burning demon.

Darien staggered to her feet and plunged toward them, throwing up a hand to shield her face—the heat was *overwhelming*. Not sure what else to do, she leaned down, grabbed Naomi around the waist, and started to pull in the same direction as Ellie.

"Darien—"

Darien turned and met Helen's terrified eyes. But the older woman shook her head, wrapped her arms around Naomi's thighs, and lifted. Together, the three of them managed to haul the injured woman about twenty feet across the gravel before she choked, "Put me down! Put me down!"

Grunting, Darien lowered Naomi, feeling Ellie and Helen do the same. Naomi yelped as her injured leg touched the ground, and some vital part of Darien came back to her at the sound.

"Let me look at your leg." Not waiting for a reply, Darien knelt. She was so wired her whole body felt like it could catch fire again at any moment—for real this time. But she forced herself to focus on peeling back the burned remnants of Naomi's pant leg.

Naomi pushed herself up, leaning back on her hands. She sucked in a breath through her teeth. "Nice shooting, Hel."

"It helped that it finally stood still," Helen said.

Darien's stomach dropped; she ducked her head as a flush crept up her cheeks, pretending to closely examine Naomi's leg. She couldn't have frozen the demon for more than two or three seconds. Naomi had been on the ground in mortal danger, Ellie had seemed disoriented, and Helen would have been focusing on where she was aiming. Maybe in the chaos, no one had noticed her collapse.

And even if they did, you were going to tell them about Ankle Tickler soon anyway. Still, she'd have preferred to be totally in control of the situation, instead of feeling like she'd been caught in a lie.

Naomi groaned as she raised her arm and uncurled her fist. Ellie's lighter sat in her palm, scratched and dented but still clearly usable. "Want this back?"

"Yeah. Thanks." Ellie shuffled over and sank to the gravel beside Naomi, plucking the lighter out of her hand and pocketing it. Then, she extended the leg she'd been limping on and rolled up her own pant leg, examining her calf. "Way to put it to good use."

Naomi grinned, but the expression tightened into one of pain as Darien probed gently at the red, blistering skin on her leg. "I take it that hurts?"

"Well, *yeah*."

"That's good. It means it's not third-degree. Probably." Darien wiped the sweat from her brow with her sleeve—the demon's fire was starting to burn down, but it was still as hot as any of the natural bonfires she'd ever encountered.

"That's lucky," Helen said. "I was terrified when I saw the demon go up like that, with you so close to it ..." She shook her head, staring at Naomi's leg. "We're lucky it made a mistake."

Ellie frowned. "We are lucky."

Darien bent over Ellie's leg. Blood welled from several deep cuts in the back of her calf, but as with all the other demon-inflicted wounds she'd seen, the edges were already starting to knit themselves back together. "I think those are going to be fine."

"Good." Ellie winced, flexing her other foot. "I definitely tweaked my ankle when it tossed me. And my back." She leaned forward, pain flitting across her face. "I have even more sympathy for Oliver now."

"Well, hopefully it counts as demon-inflicted by whatever weird physics decides that." Darien flashed a strained smile at Ellie. "You're too good at this to be out of commission."

Ellie just shook her head. "For better or for worse. If the me of a month ago could see me now ..."

But Darien had noticed—or re-noticed—the blood on Ellie's shirt. She shuffled over to her other side and knelt. "Let me take a look at this."

Ellie looked confused. Then, as she saw the blood staining her shirt, her expression changed to one of shock. "I didn't even feel that."

"I think you're about to, unfortunately." Darien peered at them. The demon's claws had slashed neatly through the fabric, catching the top of Ellie's shoulder and scoring three furrows across her collarbone and down the upper part of her arm.

"It must have happened when the demon first jumped on you and pinned you." Ellie shook her head. "Adrenaline is crazy."

Darien sat back, brow furrowed. "They're pretty deep. Let's watch them closely for half an hour or so—"

"I think I'll be okay," Ellie said.

Darien fixed her with a stare. "Still. Watch them. What about you, Helen?"

"I'm fine. That thing never even touched me, and my old knees wouldn't let me go fast enough to get a hold of it."

"Thank your lucky stars," Naomi muttered.

"Not when you're in that condition because of them." Helen hefted the pistol held loosely in her hand. "Thank goodness for the great equalizer."

Naomi chuckled darkly.

"And you, Darien?" Helen took a step toward her. "Any pain or anything?"

Darien stilled, taking a mental inventory of how her body felt. She had a few aches and pains—bruised knees, scraped palms. But other than that ... no. There was nothing.

Carefully, she let herself peek at the baby's consciousness, and sagged in relief. It was warm. It was safe. It was peaceful and content once more. She imagined pulling a little mental blanket over it, tucking it in. *I'm sorry. I promise I'll get better at not—*

"Darien?"

She looked back at Helen, blinking. "I don't think so. I think we're okay."

Helen eyed her. Then, she nodded. "Okay."

Thunder grumbled in the distance; the clouds on the other side of the bay seemed to have decided now was the time to make good on their threats.

"Let's get inside." Naomi held out a hand to Helen. "Help me up."

Helen grasped it and pulled. Naomi rose, then started toward the warehouse, wincing with every step. Helen turned to Ellie, who was already on her feet. "Need a shoulder to lean on?"

Ellie shook her head. "I think I'm all right, but thanks."

Darien fell into step beside them as they made their slow way to shelter, glancing back only once at the smoldering remains on the beach. "What are the odds anyone else saw that?"

"I think if they had, they'd already be here," Naomi said over her shoulder. "And it went up so fast, anyone who saw the smoke will probably just think we were burning cardboard or something." She shrugged. "I guess if none of our neighbors show up to check on us, we'll know."

She turned forward, still hunching in clear pain. Helen broke into a jog, muttering, "Let me go help her."

As Helen hurried away, Ellie spoke. "There are still ... what, eleven demons in the warehouse?"

"Yeah. I count at least that." She eyed the low-slung building and swallowed. "But I can tell when they're going to Awaken now. At least we'll have warning."

"If the radio weren't in there ..." Ellie let out a deep sigh. "We're not in any shape for another fight. Next time, we'll have to run even if it means we don't get updates."

"Let's just hope there won't be a next time. At least, not today."

Ellie was quiet for a minute. "And if there is, let's hope you've got enough mental strength to freeze it again."

Darien stopped. Ellie turned to face her. "Is that what happened? I was pretty out of it, but the way it acted just seemed so ... *weird.*"

Inwardly, Darien sighed. Then, she squared her shoulders. "No, you're correct. I froze it."

Ellie lurched to a stop, her expression shocked. "How?"

Darien considered for a moment, unease creeping through her. Then, she came to a decision. "I'll tell you."

Most of it, anyway.

***

Sam was in a haze. He was lying down, that much he knew, and close to the ocean, judging by the lapping of water somewhere to his left. He dragged in a long, slow breath, the tang of salt mingling with the loamy scent of the forest and ... and a whiff of rotten egg, the stench of stagnation and rot. His mouth tasted foul. Of course it did. He'd ...

He grimaced as memory returned to him. The cool air had slicked over him as he'd crashed down the mountainside like a frightened bull moose, tearing his way through clumps of spiky shrubs that tore him right back, stumbling and falling over roots and rocks because he was too completely, too *utterly* overcome by the horror of what he'd just seen to pay attention to his feet. He'd heard Oliver behind him—he'd hoped it was Oliver—and turned to look. That's when his foot had caught on some ... *thing* ... and sent him crashing to the earth.

The impact had felt horrible. Harder than any hit he'd ever taken. His stomach revolted; he'd come up on his hands and knees and been sick, so violently that he remembered wondering how his organs weren't being ejected, too.

And that was the last coherent thought he'd had.

Sam groaned and rolled onto his back, sand sticking to the side of his face. His eyes felt like they'd been punched over and over and over. A dull pain had burrowed in behind them; it matched the damp cold that seeped down the neck of his shirt, crawled under the hem of his jacket, crept up his calves under his pant legs.

"You are all safe now."

No, Sam thought. *We just really want to pretend we are.*

He cracked one eye open, wincing when the pain in his head redoubled. The hazy shape of what might have been the Nantinaq swam in and out of focus above him. "The others are almost here."

Its gravelly, harsh voice, the cold, failing light … Sam shut his eye again. It was too much.

"Oliver … and … Jessie?" He could barely get his tattered rasp of a voice to form the words.

"I'm here." Oliver's voice came from somewhere farther down the beach. It was so weak that it was almost lost in the slow roll of the waves. "Jessie's still out."

"But here?"

"Yeah."

Sam stifled another groan. There was a reason he'd only had one hangover in his life; he'd worked hard to hone his body into the fine-tuned instrument it was. He liked feeling good. *Lived* for it. And now, here he was: stone-cold sober, feeling the worst he had in his life, and *wishing* he could drink until he forgot everything he'd seen in the last hour. Pain lanced into him, and heat stung the corners of his closed eyes. "What about Jordan?"

Oliver didn't answer right away. Sam listened to the *lap-lap* of the ocean, trying to work up the courage to get up, sit up … or maybe just try opening both eyes at the same time. From somewhere on the other side of the marsh, the raven started croaking again. And Sam thought he might be able to hear something else: the low drone of an engine.

"Jordan's here, too."

Just do it. Sam forced his eyes open, his breath hissing through his teeth as the dimming light sliced into his brain. He blinked as the iron-gray sky resolved into the layers, puffs, and whirls of individual clouds. If he hadn't known better, he'd wonder if he had a bad concussion. But he did know better. So he threw caution to the wind and turned his head.

Oliver sat a few feet away, looking pale and sick. A crumpled form in a bright red windbreaker lay huddled on his other side. But neither of them was what caught Sam's attention, sucked it in, and trapped it like a class five rapid.

Jordan was lying on his back between him and Oliver, his hands by his sides, dull eyes staring up at the iron-gray sky. Three blood-soaked holes gaped in the front of his jacket. Rusty stains dotted the sand above his head, disappearing into the bright autumn foliage that the Nantinaq had, apparently, carried him through. *A blood trail.*

Sam stared at Jordan's face. It was so … empty.

He looked away, waves of numb disbelief rolling over him like a second pulse. A tear leaked out of one eye, scalding hot on his chilled skin. Outside of viewings, he'd never seen a body before. Oliver, his expression a weird mix of haunted and compassionate, had gently encouraged him to wait when they'd found his dad. Now all Sam could think of was how much the teen's eyes looked like those of the elk he'd killed last October.

We're all the same in the end.

Summoning his courage—pitiful as he now knew it was—he forced down his nausea, feeling it land in his gut like a spiky, prickled thing. Then he pushed himself up. His head spun; nothing in his body or mind felt right. Jordan was dead, his body bleeding into the sand feet away from him, and the drone of that engine was getting louder—

"You may be in shock, Sam."

At the sound of Oliver's voice, Sam broke. He covered his eyes as the tears came, gushing down his face in a hot flood of grief and regret. "God," he choked. "What have we done?"

The Nantinaq's voice issued from somewhere beside him, and Sam jumped. In his insanity, he imagined it could have been the voice of the sand itself.

"It is in the nature of every sentient creature to fall, and fail. You are not alone."

But Jordan was.

Sam stayed like that, crying like a child, out of control, until the hum of the approaching boat—the reckoning—became a roar. Just when he thought he couldn't take it anymore, that the incessant drone would drive him insane, it stopped. Human shouts echoed to him, frantic, panicked. Sam forced his eyes up, intending to look toward the ocean, but instead Jordan's dead eyes sucked him back in. The tears started to flow again, so thick and fast he could hardly breathe.

"I'm sorry." He reached for the teen's cold, lifeless hand. "I'm sorry, I'm so sorry ..."

He was still babbling when a very warm, very alive hand pried his off of Jordan's. Henry's face appeared in front of him as the last motes of daylight died around them. "Come on, Sam. Come on—"

"I could have stopped this," Sam gasped. "I *should* have stopped—"

A dark, humanoid form appeared behind Henry, moving oddly, making strange, terrifying sounds. Sam lurched to his feet and lashed out mindlessly so it wouldn't get everyone who was left—

Henry locked his arms around him and hauled him back a few steps, barking gruff words that didn't make sense. Sam blinked, and the humanoid shape became Luke, who staggered and dropped to his knees beside Jordan. A low moan tore from the man's throat; he gathered his son's body into his arms, his shoulders shaking. Sam watched, feeling so sick and dazed that he didn't think he'd ever be well again.

"Sam, come on."

Sam let himself be led back to the rowboat like the dumb calf he was, allowed himself to settle next to Jessie's prone form, now wrapped in a rescue blanket.

"Can you row?"

Sam blinked at the sound of Henry's voice, his mouth going slack, but it was Oliver who answered.

"Yeah."

Henry nodded. "When Bill gets here, help him get these two on the *Poor Buoy*. Then come back for me, Luke, and ..." His voice thickened. "And Jordan."

"Okay," Oliver said.

Time slowed and sped and didn't make sense. At some point, Bill clambered into the rowboat and settled behind the oars. The boat rocked, then heaved itself into the ocean, and the *Poor Buoy* was coming closer—or, yeah, *they* were getting closer to *it*—

He shook himself. *Get it together. Rally. Idiot or not, they need your help.*

Chapter Twenty

"Come in, warehouse."

The voice wasn't Luke's this time. It was Henry's.

Dread crept over Ellie as Naomi snatched the receiver. The last news they'd heard was that all four boys were on the beach. Oliver, at least, was upright and definitely alive, but everyone else looked alarmingly lifeless. The shock of the message, the agony of not knowing what was going on, had all but driven Darien's confessions about her powers—and Ankle Tickler—from her mind. If Sam and the others were fine, or were *going* to be fine, they'd figure it all out later. If not, if her brother was gone ...

She shuddered. Who cared if Darien had been keeping secrets? Who cared about anything, really?

"Henry, what's happening?" Naomi asked.

"Sit down, Naomi." Henry's voice was gentle in the worst possible way.

Naomi's lip trembled. "Oh, no. Oh, no ..."

Helen slipped an arm around Naomi's shoulders, then gently took the receiver as she sank into a chair. Jordan's mother balled both hands into fists and pressed them to her mouth, tears falling down her cheeks.

"I've got her, Henry," Helen said quietly. "Tell us."

Static crackled through the radio; Henry was pressing the button, but hadn't said anything. Maybe *couldn't* say anything. Ellie tried to make her struggle for breath as quiet as she could; it was like her ribcage had come alive and was smashing itself together, trying to crush everything inside of it.

"Oliver, Sam, and Jessie are pretty beat-up, but they'll be okay."

The air whooshed out of Ellie; tears rose to her eyes.

"But Jordan ... I'm so sorry, Naomi."

Naomi folded in on herself, shaking like she was going to break. Helen dropped to her knees and held her the way she'd held Ellie a month ago, right down to the same heartsick look, the same stunned disbelief. Darien let out a strangled sob, hugging her midsection.

Ellie couldn't take it anymore.

She hauled herself out of the ratty old office chair, relieved when her ankle held her weight, and pushed her way through the door and into the empty warehouse. Time blurred. Naomi cried. Snippets of the story drifted through the open office door, all relayed in Henry's radio-crackle voice. Jessie—and maybe Jordan?—had been battling Wormwood-like demons. Sam had been tricked—sort of?—but had pushed forward anyway, genuinely thinking they could finish it, save everyone. Oliver had been pulled into the ocean trying to stop them. Then, when *that* hadn't succeeded, he'd led the charge against a monster he *knew* had a good chance of killing them all, rather than letting them face the consequences alone.

Of course he would. Of course *he would do that.*

At one point, Darien slipped through the door and sat down at one of the tables, staring at its shiny surface as Naomi continued to keen. Ellie got up and started to pace, limping mindlessly from one end of the low building to the other. She understood why Oliver did that now. There were no answers to chase, nothing to fight. She almost *wished* a demon would Awaken so her sorrow could become rage, so she could cover up her own helplessness with a flash of a knife, bury it in an explosive roar of flame.

It was past two when Helen came out of the office. "They're here."

Darien—who had taken water bottles to Naomi and Helen an hour earlier, then hadn't moved since—stood. Ellie followed her into the office, her eyes welling again at the sight of Jordan's mother. She stood with her arms wrapped around herself, staring out the window, her bloodshot eyes tracking the *Poor Buoy's* headlight as it coasted across the surface of the bay toward the harbor. She looked frail, sunken, as if she'd aged thirty years in the last four hours.

Helen laid a gentle hand on her shoulder. "Naomi—"

"I'm going, Helen."

Helen looked at her for a moment, then nodded. "Okay."

Ellie followed them out, glancing at Darien as she did. Her sister-in-law's shoulders slumped with exhaustion, but she still stared down the approaching boat with what could only be described as grit. Ellie felt a swell of admiration for what she'd handled—what she'd managed to learn—on her own, and an equal surge of frustration that she hadn't *told* any of them.

They followed Naomi and Helen down the long boardwalk that led to the docks, the vibration of the *Poor Buoy's* engine growing louder with each stride. By the time they stepped onto the slightly slick wood at the bottom, its thrumming basso had settled into her bones. They turned right, keeping pace with the boat as it eased around the dock's far end, then settled into an open spot. Its headlight dimmed, and Ellie's heart leaped into her throat as she made out Oliver's lithe silhouette. Behind him stood a taller, larger shadow—Sam—supporting another, smaller person. Jessie, she'd guess.

She didn't realize she'd broken into a jog until Helen shouted, "Careful!" Slipping a little, she righted herself as the *Poor Buoy's* engine died, replaced by the quiet rippling of the ocean as it eddied around and beside them and under their feet.

Oliver jumped onto the dock and started tying the boat to a hook sunk into the wood, his movements stiff and jerky. Automatic. Bill and Henry did the same, then Bill reached out a hand for Jessie, who carefully navigated the gap between the rocking boat and the dock's solid wood. Ellie watched in silence as Bill slipped an arm underneath his son's shoulders and helped him up the pier. Jessie's expression was glazed. Bill's looked like it had been carved from wood.

Sam came next, looking ... *beaten*. Any anger that Ellie felt at him evaporated, leaving devastation in its wake. "Sam ..." She sniffled. "You—"

He swept her into an awkward, one-armed hug. "Are a damn idiot, I know. I know."

He kissed her on the forehead, then released her and made his way toward Darien. She seized him in a fierce hug, then grabbed his arm and started to tug him back up the dock, her murmured words growing more muffled with every step. The details of Sam's reply were buried in the lapping of the water.

Shoving her hands in her pockets, Ellie turned back to Oliver. Her shoulder prickled and her ankle ached, but much less than normal injuries would have. Less than her heart did, that was for sure. She watched as he finished tying off the line. Knowing him, he needed the rote motion, the control, the easy accomplishment of doing something well. When he was finished, he straightened, swallowed, then turned toward her.

Ellie's throat constricted. Even in the dim light of the boat's beam, she could see his eyes were red-rimmed.

"I thought I could stop them." His voice was hoarse, raspy, as if he'd been screaming. "That's what I was trying to do. But then there wasn't time. It all happened too fast."

Ellie wrapped her arms around Oliver's waist, and he pulled her tightly against him. He was shivering. "I tried—"

Naomi's renewed sobs broke through their conversation, and Luke's, too, Ellie realized. She shrank against Oliver, her reaction so visceral that it felt like someone was twisting a screw into her stomach. His shoulders shook. "I should've tried harder. I should've ... should've *fought* them—"

Ellie took him by the hand, the sobs of the grieving parents behind her carving themselves so deeply into her brain that she knew she'd never get them out. "Come on. You don't need to be here anymore."

She led him back up the dock and onto land, neither looking back nor slowing until they'd reached the parking lot. Bill's truck was just pulling out as they left, and Ellie thought that even the crunch of the vehicle's tires seemed subdued. Sam's and Darien's quiet voices issued from inside the warehouse's open door, and Ellie hesitated. *The last thing* that *conversation needs is an interruption.*

But then footsteps sounded on the gravel. Ellie turned to see Helen walking toward them, looking like all the light had been sucked out of her.

"Let's go home," she said.

They said nothing during the ride back, nothing as they climbed out of the truck, as they entered the Calls' warm, dark cabin. Ellie never let go of Oliver's hand and watched Sam closely as they all slipped out of their shoes and jackets. He seemed hollowed out, empty. Ellie caught Darien's eye, but her sister-in-law just gave her a sad shoulder-lift that said something like *"let's go help these idiots we love."* Then, she slipped her arm around Sam's waist and shepherded him into the guest room, closing the door behind them.

"I'll keep watch," Helen said. "You two go get some sleep."

"Helen—" Oliver said.

"No," Ellie and Helen said at the same time. Ellie tugged him toward the stairs, relieved when he didn't protest. "I'll set an alarm for six."

"Eight," Helen shot back.

Ellie thought about objecting, but didn't have it in her. An extra two hours of sleep ... "Thank you. Don't worry about breakfast—"

"Ellie." Helen's melancholy posture made the loving look in her eyes even more poignant. "What else am I going to do?"

For a moment, Ellie couldn't speak. Then, she nodded and squeezed Oliver's hand. "Come on."

The telltale creak of Henry's big chair sounded behind them as they climbed, and Ellie's gratitude for Helen deepened. *The best thing I can do for her is take care of Oliver.* She turned at the top of the stairs. "Let's get you—"

But Oliver wrapped his arms around her and pulled her against him. "Just one moment here. Please. I just ... need ..."

The lump in Ellie's throat finally won. She threw her arms around his shoulders, choking on the scream she'd wanted to let fly since getting the news that he was going back to Portlock. "Safety? Rest? Comfort? The world to make sense again?"

"Yeah."

The brokenness in his voice tore at her soul. He crushed her to him, palms pressing flat against her back, swaying slightly as he buried his face in the curve of her shoulder, and Ellie thought this wasn't a hug so much as the collision of two terrified, drowning people who were way out of their depth. She sucked in another unsteady breath; he smelled wild, like smoke and the ocean and the deep, frowning pines. Not a trace of his usual scent, though this suited him just as well. She breathed him in, the fabric of his shirt bunching in her fists as they both sobbed.

It was minutes before they calmed. Intermittent sniffles rose from downstairs, and Ellie realized with a pang that Helen had almost certainly heard them. But she felt no shame. There was no room for it. Oliver's chest rose and fell against hers. Once. Twice. Then, he pulled away, turning toward his room. "Let's change into clean clothes, at least."

After his door closed, Ellie crossed to her suitcase and slipped her pajamas on, not bothering to take them to the bathroom for privacy. Even if Helen happened to look up, she'd already seen Ellie in nothing but a hospital gown anyway; she was basically family. Shivering in her tank top, Ellie stole to Oliver's room and knocked.

It swung open instantly, as if he'd been standing on the other side waiting. Ellie had a split second to take him in—he was wearing his typical lounging pants and a black tee and looked ruffled, like he'd speed-dressed—before he grabbed her hand and tugged her into his room. "Come here. Hurry."

Angst flared in Ellie's stomach as he towed her across the smooth hardwood toward his bed, his eyes fixed on the window above it. "Don't tell me there's—"

"It's not a demon." He gestured toward his quilt. "Sit down. Look."

Ellie settled on his bed and squinted out into the vast, dark expanse. There was no moon; the night was so black that only the scattered stars showed her where land ended and sky began.

"It's ... dark outside." She looked sideways at him. *Maybe after months of daylight, I'd be this excited about nighttime, too.*

He settled down beside her, shaking his head. "No, that's not it—"

Inspiration struck her. "The rain's moved off."

"No. Well, yeah, but ..." He stared up at the sky, his shoulder brushing hers. "Maybe I just imagined it."

Ellie stared at him for a moment longer, wondering if this latest, worst encounter with the Gatekeeper had actually cracked him. She took his hand, her heart twinging again at the rope burn on his palm, painful-looking even in the dim shadows of his bedroom. "Does this hurt?"

"Oh." He glanced down, then back out the window again. "Yeah, but I've gained a new perspective on pain over the last few days."

Frowning deeply, Ellie looked out the window again. When nothing happened, she shifted to face him. "Look, Oliver, today has absolutely sucked, and it's three in the morning. Maybe we should go ..."

Something green flashed across the sky.

"Lie down ..." Understanding finally dawned on Ellie, and her heart leaped into her throat. "Was that ...?"

Oliver smiled, his face still tipped toward the stars. "The aurora. It's fickle, and it might not be worth waiting to see if it actually happens tonight. But I caught a glimpse while I was dressing, and you mentioned wanting to see it, so I thought if there was a chance—"

Something in Ellie's chest warmed; she squeezed his hand. "I want to see them."

He gazed at her, that tiny smile still on his lips. "Let's give ourselves twenty minutes. Then, if ..." His eyes widened, then he brushed the scabs on her hurt shoulder with his fingertips. "Are these from today?"

"You should see the other guy."

"Let me guess, you lit him on fire."

"Actually, Naomi lit it on fire. I just assisted."

Oliver snorted, letting his fingertips linger on her shoulder. Her skin tingled under his touch.

"I bet they're gone by morning," she managed.

"Probably." He examined the wounds for another moment, his expression troubled. Then, he leaned down and brushed his lips over one of her scabs. "Okay?"

Ellie's heart wobbled. "Uh-huh."

"Good," he murmured. "I can at least *pretend* I can fix something."

"Oliver ..." Her eyes fluttered closed as the tingling spread across her shoulders and down her spine. "There's no pretending happening here."

He drew back and brushed a lock of hair out of her face, his eyes searing into hers. "I won't leave you again. Not until this is all over. I'm sorry I did today."

Ellie shook her head. "You did *good* today. You probably saved Sam and Jessie's lives."

He looked away, pain shadowing his face. "If only I could've saved Jordan. It just ... wasn't enough."

"Hey." Ellie laid a hand on his cheek. "No one can ever do enough. Life's too much for any of us. What happened up there is *not* your fault. Please don't fall back into the Wormwood trap."

Oliver was quiet for a moment. Then, his eyebrows contracted. "It's in the nature of every sentient being to fall, and fail."

"What?"

"That's what the Nantinaq said, on the beach." He rubbed one battered hand across his face. "He was right. And you're right, it's not my fault. It just ..."

Hurts, Ellie thought.

He closed his eyes, kneading them again, but not before Ellie saw the fresh set of tears tracking down his cheeks. Aching for him, she took his face in her hands and pulled him down until their foreheads touched. "It's also in our nature to rise."

A long sigh escaped him, and for a moment, neither of them moved. Finally, Ellie pulled back. "Not tonight, though."

"No." His eyes went to the clock on his bedside table. "Let's give ourselves ten more minutes. *If* you still want to try and see the aurora."

Ellie nodded; as exhausted as she was, she wanted—*needed*—this time with him. "Ten more minutes."

"Okay." He looked up at the sky again, restless energy rolling off him in waves. After a few fidgety seconds, he turned to Ellie and ran his fingers gently through the length of her hair. "Can I braid this?"

Ellie smiled. "Yes."

He settled behind her, and a moment later, his gentle hands worked into her hair, brushing against the back of her neck.

"I didn't know you could braid," Ellie murmured.

The bed creaked as he leaned in, his breath skating across the shell of her ear. "I'm a fisherman. My hands can do a lot of things."

Goosebumps swept across Ellie's shoulders. "Shameless flirt."

He chuckled, then kissed the back of her head. "Not tonight, though. Too many demons."

"Right." Disgust welled in Ellie as she remembered ... "And Ankle Tickler's here."

Oliver's hands stopped. "What?"

"It's true." Quickly, she filled him in on what Darien had told her. "She's made huge strides with her power. She stopped the Otterman, or Naomi wouldn't have made it. So that's encouraging."

"Still ... I don't know. Making a deal with a demon doesn't sit right with me."

"I don't love it, either." Ellie shrugged. "But if it gets results ..."

"Yeah." Oliver's knuckles brushed the skin between her shoulder blades as he worked. "You said Death doesn't seem to know about Darien and Sam's abilities?"

"That's what Darien thinks. He's never thought about them when she's in his head, at least. So either Slubgob's a lousy spy, or Death knows and doesn't think they're a threat."

"Hmm."

His hands fell below the level of her tank, skimming her back through the fabric as he tied off her long plait. Ellie watched the stars, frowning. "You're right. It really doesn't make sense."

"I just hope we're not missing something."

His hands fell away, and a pang went through Ellie. "Don't leave."

With a nearly silent sigh, Oliver wrapped his arms around her waist and pulled her back against his chest, resting his chin on her shoulder. They sat that way for a moment before he broke the silence. "What do you want when this is all over?"

"You. Obviously."

He squeezed her gently. "I mean long-term. Beyond us. But also including us, if you want."

Ellie let her head fall back against his shoulder, her eyes on the sky, her focus a million miles away. "I don't know if I know anymore. I'm not ..." She chewed her lip for a moment. "I'm not the same person I was a month ago. I still love a lot of the same things I used to—music, running, the mountains, ice cream. But ..." She blinked sudden wetness out of her eyes. "I'm not even a big Tolkien fan, but I feel a little like Frodo trying to go back to the Shire."

"I get that."

"I mean, what am I going to talk to my roommates about? How am I supposed to pay attention in class? It starts Monday, Oliver. Monday."

"Sluff it. Take a vacation."

"You're a bad influence."

He chuckled. "I do what I can."

"And I'll *never* be able to watch scary movies again."

Oliver grunted. "Or read scary books. Stephen King's right out for me."

"So it's Disney movies and rom-com novels from here on out."

"I might try spy thrillers. But if you want to read rom-coms, go for it."

"Oh, I will." Ellie's smile faded. She didn't have to look at the clock to know the ten minutes they'd allowed themselves were almost up. Loss crept over her, threatening to sully what was happening now. *No,* she thought. *Don't let it.*

"I know what I *don't* want," she said softly.

"Demons."

She almost laughed, but it died as sharp fear needled into her heart. "A life without you."

Oliver stilled.

"I know it's too soon to feel that way," Ellie whispered. "But I'm not sure if I care."

He let out a long sigh, his lips brushing her shoulder, her neck, his voice a bare whisper. "Ellie."

She melted against him, her eyes falling closed. "What do *you* want, Oliver?"

"You. For forever, if I can get away with it."

A smile quirked Ellie's lips. Right now, forever sounded incredible. "What else?"

He paused for a moment. Then he pulled back slightly, his hands skimming up her arms to settle on her shoulders. "A normal, boring life. I thought I wanted to get an MBA, be really successful, earn a lot of money." He started to massage her shoulders, his voice turning thoughtful. "Maybe I still want that. I know I did before I met you. But maybe part of why I want it now is so you don't think I'm after your money."

"I'd never think that, Oliver."

"I hope not, because it's the furthest thing from the truth. But this experience has made me think ... maybe I want to find a way to help people. I think about all the kids out there who are just like I was. If I could help them ..."

"You could put the two together. Start a nonprofit."

Oliver ran his thumbs down the ridges of her shoulder blades. "When and if I ever get downtime again, I'll think about it."

For a moment, the only sound in the room was the ticking of the clock. Then, Oliver nuzzled against the nape of her neck. "People say things like what we're going through—challenges, trials by fire—people say they change you. But I'm starting to think that's not true."

"Yeah?"

"I think they force us to know ourselves better. See ourselves more clearly. Then, if we're smart, we *choose* to change."

"Deep." Ellie considered for a moment. "I think it might be both."

Oliver kissed the top of her head. "I think I'm addicted to you."

Ellie folded her hands over his. "Makes perfect sense. I'm fan—"

The sky exploded.

Ribbons of green split the darkness, their edges tinged with radiant purples, bold pinks, reds so vibrant they almost looked alive. Ellie gasped as they shimmered and twisted, cavorting with the stars. It was the most beautiful thing she'd ever seen.

"Yes!" Oliver's chest rose and fell against her back; he seemed as breathless as she was. "This is a good one. I'm so glad you could see this."

Tears filled Ellie's eyes again. She wasn't even totally sure why this time. "Me, too. It's ..." She gave a helpless shrug. *Amazing* just didn't cut it; neither did beautiful.

Oliver ran his fingers down the length of her braid. Then, he swept it to the side, sending it spilling over her uninjured shoulder, and nibbled at the nape of her neck. Maybe it was the tenderness of his kisses, or the strength in his arms. Maybe it was how acutely she felt her own mortality tonight. Or maybe it was the lights winging their way across the sky, free of grief, loss, or fear. Ellie didn't know. She only knew that she was turning, and their lips were meeting, and his hands were settling around her waist.

With a low groan that Ellie felt in every cell of her body, Oliver pulled her closer, gripping her like the only thing preventing her from disappearing was how tightly he held her. He angled his head, their kiss turning slow, thorough. Time became meaningless, and her heart sped up, aching with fierce, almost overwhelming love.

Oliver's chest fell in an unsteady exhale, and he broke the kiss, his forehead coming to rest against Ellie's. She opened her eyes and her breath caught; the aurora traced gleaming fingers across the planes and angles of his face, lining his lashes in silver, and she just … *stared*, in awe that this good, brave, kind man was hers. She kissed his cheek, tasting the salt of the ocean—either that, or his tears. Her heart breaking for him, she kissed his neck again, his throat, the hollow above his collarbone. A shiver went through his body, and Ellie felt it like it was her own, as if the lines between them were blurring. When she looked up again, he was gazing at her, adoration and desire mingling on his face as the reflected lights danced in his eyes.

His lips found hers again, and all her nerve endings came alive, as if delighted to finally be doing something that wasn't rooted in fear.

"Ellie," he murmured again.

Sparks blazed through her. She kissed him hard, her fingers gliding through his deliciously soft hair. "I love you, Oliver. I love you—"

He pushed her down, his lips still on hers, exploring, *insisting*. Ellie's heart was beating so fast it hurt; his thundered next to it in a perfect counterbeat. It was the most natural thing in the world to fall, collapse with him in a tangle, to let him pin her arms gently and kiss her with a passion that made her forget how to breathe. His thumbs skimmed across the delicate skin on the insides of her wrists as he kissed her throat. "I'm so stupid."

Ellie tipped her head back, the heat in her chest building as his lips skimmed across her collarbone, dipped to the skin just beneath. "Me, too. So dumb."

"You're just so beautiful. And so … in my bed."

She smiled as he kissed the side of her mouth. "You put me here."

He brushed his lips over hers again. "Best bad idea I've ever had."

"Oliver." She tried to say his name like she still had control. "We should—"

His breath skated across her skin.

"We should ..."

He pulled back a fraction of an inch and shook his head a little, like he'd been punched and was trying to recover. "Stop. Yeah. Demons. Ankle Tickler." His fingers curled into the spaces between hers, warm and callused and perfect. "It's not worth ruining. I mean—you're too important to ruin. We're too—*this* is too important—"

Ellie let out a soft laugh. "It's okay. I know what you mean." Still ... she held him there for a moment longer, memorizing the feel of him, telling herself she'd let go if he moved to leave.

He didn't.

Finally, Oliver lifted his head. His pupils were huge in the dim, viridian light, the sliver of his iris a shade of blue-green that Ellie could barely believe existed. The look in them was indescribable. Pressing a final kiss to her forehead, he eased onto his side, keeping one arm slung across her waist. "Sorry, Ellie. My self-control's ... not at peak tonight."

"Be honest. If I stay, will you be able to sleep?"

Will I? she thought.

He traced her cheekbone with his thumb. "Honestly, you being here might be the only reason I sleep at all."

Ellie smiled. "Well, if you insist."

Darkness took the room then, and it took Ellie a second to realize the aurora had winked out. But Oliver's quiet laugh filled the space; even subdued, it was like its own kind of light. He rolled onto his back and Ellie burrowed against him, her head pillowed comfortably on his chest. They lay silently in each other's arms after that, and it wasn't long before Oliver's breathing became slow and deep. Ellie held on a little longer before drifting away from consciousness, the beat of his heart soothing in her ear.

One more day.

With Oliver by her side, she could do one more day.

***

Oliver lay in the pitch dark, holding the love of his life and dreading the sunrise. At some point—maybe even during their too-short moment of passion—a feeling had come over him. Two feelings, actually. The first was that they were being watched, which had delivered his slipping self-control right back to him on a silver platter. And the second was that things were coming to a head. That they all had less time and control than they thought.

Ellie shifted in her sleep, slinging one long, slender leg over his knees. He turned his face into her hair and let himself numb out to everything that wasn't the slow rhythm of her breathing, the smoky, vanilla-tinged scent of her, the softness of her hair against his lips. He knew he needed to sleep. He should be trying harder—

"Psst. Oliver."

He bolted upright, his hands balling into fists. A shadowy, human-shaped figure stood by his door. The hairs on the back of his neck stood straight up; he lunged over Ellie, fumbling for the knife he'd laid on his bedside table.

"Stop!" The figure started toward them. "Wait, Oliver, stop it!"

Oliver froze. He recognized that voice. He looked up as the figure stepped into a patch of moonlight, and its outline—the powerful shoulders, the close-cropped hair—became hauntingly familiar. "Jordan?"

"Yeah, dude." Jordan shook his head. "*This* is bizarre. I thought a lot of things about living were bizarre, but being dead takes the cake."

Oliver stared, his mouth hanging open. He snapped it shut as he realized what *hadn't* changed about the situation. Ellie was still silent and limp. Panic seized him before he realized ... "Oh. Duh. I'm dreaming."

"Duh, indeed."

"Otherwise, time would be moving a lot faster for me than for you."

"Yeah." Jordan's nose wrinkled. "I think that's going to get old really fast. It's been good for now, though. There are a ..." He looked out the window, his Adam's apple bobbing. "There are a lot of people I need to see. Touch however I can. People who weren't ready for me to go yet."

Oliver sat with a sigh, crossing his legs, careful even in his dream not to jostle Ellie. "Including me."

A sad smile crossed Jordan's face. "Including you."

"And ... you? How're you handling ...?" ... *being dead?* That didn't seem like the right thing to say.

But Jordan seemed to have guessed exactly what he was getting at. He shrugged, apparently unfazed. "I'm ... well, it's a big transition, as you know." A frown creased his face. "I'm shocked at how *natural* it's felt, though."

He shrugged again, and Oliver noticed he was wearing the same windbreaker and fishing pants he'd had on when he died. The bloodstained holes in his jacket where the Gatekeeper's blades had punched through him were gone, though. Oliver was shocked at the emotion that flooded over him at the sight. It was such a little thing, but it felt, somehow, like a promise. Like it was all going to be okay in the end. For everyone.

"So, uh, yeah," Jordan said awkwardly. "All told, dying's not too bad."

"I'm glad. I—" Oliver ran a hand through his hair, laughing because his body didn't quite know what else to do. "I thought it was terrible."

Jordan grinned. "Your problem is that you didn't *quite* die. It's the coming back part that sucks."

"*That's* the truth," Oliver muttered.

"Plus, it was demonstrably not your time."

Oliver blinked. "There's a good argument it wasn't your time, either."

"Yeah, but I'm a good, reliable kid who stoically accepts what life throws at him. Including death, apparently. And you're a recovering rebellious punk, so ... you know. Once a gangsta, always a gangsta—"

Oliver burst out laughing. *Laughing.* For *real.* "I can't believe I'm sitting here comparing deaths with my friend's ghost."

"While you're still alive," Jordan put in.

"But asleep." Oliver let his fingertips skim over Ellie's shoulder. "This just feels so real." Suspicion snuck into the back of his mind, and he frowned. "I don't remember falling asleep."

"No one ever remembers falling asleep. Look back over your whole life. Do you ever actually *remember* a moment when you fell asleep?"

Oliver met the ghost's eyes. "How do I know you're not a demon posing as Jordan?"

Jordan's grin disappeared.

Oliver's heart twinged. "I'm sorry. After the Lady, I *have* to be suspi—"

"No, it's okay. I get it. No hard feelings." Jordan folded his arms. "I came to warn you about the demons. Which is probably not something a demon posing as me would do."

"True. And you don't feel like a demon." Oliver glanced down at Ellie—or at his sleeping brain's approximation of her. "Even when the Lady was posing as Ellie, it was obvious pretty quickly that she was an imposter."

He shrugged. "There you go. And I'll make you a deal. Hear me out, and I'll leave."

"That's it?"

"That's it." A twinkle snuck into Jordan's eyes—one that Oliver hadn't seen since before the demons had invaded. "I promise I won't even haunt you."

Heart thudding painfully, Oliver sat back. He swallowed the welling emotion in his throat, forcing his voice to come out steady. "Okay. Shoot."

Jordan's expression sobered. "They're coming to Portlock, and fast. I've mostly been concerned with my—" His voice cracked. "With the living. But I've seen them as I've been flitting around between Portlock and Seldovia. Every town is crawling with juveniles, and the ones that are Awakening now are just going straight to the gate."

Oliver's stomach dropped. "Why didn't we encounter any when we were up there?"

"Most of the Awakened ones aren't actually that fast. And it seems like they're attracted to cities. More people, more suffering ..." He shrugged. "Point is, it's a trial, tearing themselves away from all that and going somewhere where there's no food. It's taking time, luckily for us."

Oliver grunted. "Makes sense, I guess. How many are close enough to get there by Thursday?"

"I don't know. A dozen, probably more. And a few are ... they're pretty bad, Oliver. I've only gotten a few glimpses, but ..."

Oliver let out a slow breath.

"So it's a good thing you're sleeping, because if you're going to have a chance, I think you need to go today."

"*Today*." Oliver felt a weight settle onto him. To have to go back and face the Gatekeeper again so quickly, and without the numbers they'd all been counting on ... "So we *are* in a way worse spot than we think we are."

Jordan nodded, his expression so anxious that any remaining thought of him being a demon fled from Oliver's mind. Even in death, he was still so readable; so open.

"If you don't attack today, I don't honestly know how you're going to succeed," he said. "Especially since Death is coming, too. I don't know where he is—I probably should've tried to find him—"

"With what you've been through in the last few hours, I don't blame you for Death not being your focus." Oliver sat back, feeling like he'd been hit in the chest. "We have so few people. I'll go, of course, and ..." He looked down at Ellie again. "I know she'll go, even though I wish ..."

He swallowed. There would be no stopping her. And since it was one of the characteristics that had made him fall so hard in the first place, wishing it away—even in this context—seemed ridiculous.

"Sam will, I bet," he whispered. "Even after today. And Darien. Pregnant or not, I don't think we could keep her away. Helen and Henry will—"

"Bill will come," Jordan said. "Jessie's zonked—he pounded down a bunch of sleep aids—but once he wakes up, I bet he's all in."

"That's still only eight of us. If it were just the Gatekeeper we needed to get past, I'd think we could do it, but—"

"The four of us almost did," Jordan pointed out. "Which I'm actually kind of proud of."

"Right, but that was without *extra* demons to fight." Oliver leaned back on his hands, examining his friend's ghost. "How's your energy? Is this ... draining you?"

"A little, but not too bad. I really feel pretty great. Deadness and all."

"Huh. Dean—he's been helping us out here and there since the demons escaped—just seemed to have such tight limits on what he could and couldn't do."

"That's because Dean had to fight tooth and nail to get back to this place from the Afterlife. Then he had to fight even harder to actually appear in your world. I haven't been here long, but it's been long enough to realize what he's doing is nearly impossible."

Pain lanced through Oliver as he realized what Jordan had just said. *"Your"* world. Not *"ours."*

"But when *you* died," Jordan continued, "you gained a connection to this weird in-between place. Now that you've been here, you're a lot easier to talk to."

"So ... why hasn't Dean talked to me then?"

Jordan shook his head. "He's wrecked, Oliver. Like, *wrecked.*"

"I think I saw him at the gate."

"Yeah, he was there fighting anyway. Guess I know where you get it now."

Oliver opened his mouth, then closed it. He *still* didn't know how he felt about being compared to his late father, even with everything that had happened. Still ... warmth tingled through him, and what felt like peace.

"Seeing Dean trying to protect you all was what helped me know what to do after I died. Gave me a lifeline." Jordan grinned. "Figuratively speaking."

Oliver stared at him.

Jordan laughed, his hands coming together in a soundless clap. "Got it. Dead jokes are worse than dad jokes. Anyway, Dean's seesawing between the in-between and the Afterlife. He ... I don't *know*, I'm still new to all this, but it seems like he used up too much energy trying to have a physical effect on the world. Getting you wire cutters, taking out security cameras, you know."

"Yeah," Oliver said quietly.

"It's driving him crazy, but the Afterlife is pulling on him. Hard. He doesn't belong here."

"But it's not pulling on you."

"Oh, it is. But unlike Dean, I haven't been there yet, so maybe the pull is less strong? Also, I have ..." He waggled his eyebrows. "... unfinished business. It won't keep me here long, but I think I have a day or so before the pull gets too strong and I have to move on."

Pain lanced through Oliver again. "Jordan ..."

His friend shrugged. "Hey, it's just a matter of time before you all join me. You know what they say about death and taxes."

A tear squeezed out of the corner of one of Oliver's eyes. He wiped it away. "I'm so sorry."

Jordan's voice softened. "It's not your fault we wouldn't listen."

"I know."

"If you'd fought us, we'd have tied you up and thrown you in one of the storage benches."

"I believe it."

"Like a trussed-up Thanksgiving turkey."

A smile broke through Oliver's grief.

"That's better." Jordan stepped forward. "Now listen. You've got more people behind you than you think. Remember the nurse who died in Homer a few weeks ago?"

"Yeah." Goosebumps crawled up Oliver's shoulders. That had probably been the Lady's doing, he realized.

"Well, everyone at the hospital loved her. And between your story and what everyone else in the town has gone through, half the staff is ready to start a freaking riot. They're calling friends in Seldovia, putting the pieces together ..."

Hope bloomed in Oliver. It must have shown on his face, because Jordan smiled. "Nanwalek, too. My dad's friend Boris—remember how he found that bear?"

"That kind of thing is hard to forget."

"Well, my dad called him earlier this afternoon. He's thrilled to have an explanation, and now he's convinced most of the village. They'll join you."

Oliver looked up at Jordan. "We might pull this off."

"You will. You *will* pull it off."

The air shimmered next to Jordan; he looked over at it and smiled. "Dean says to tell you he loves you and is proud of you."

Emotion rocked through Oliver. He swallowed and sat up straighter as Jordan began to fuzz around the edges. "Sleep. Be at peace, Oliver." A tiny, sad smile crossed his face. "Tell my family I'm okay, and I love them."

"I ... I will." Oliver brushed another tear off his cheek. "I'll see you again."

"Sooner or later, yeah."

Jordan lifted his hand in a wave, fuzzing, and Oliver was suddenly so drowsy. He fell down next to Ellie, sleep closing over him like the unfathomable deep of the ocean.

Chapter Twenty-One

*D*eath knelt on the cold metal, his knees swathed in moisture, breathing in the scents of freshly-caught fish and the sharp tang of seawater. He placed a hand on the chest of the still-warm body at his feet. This one had given him so much. There had been the usual: the heady rush of mortal terror, its ebb into exhaustion, bewilderment at the fact that he was dying.

Death frowned at the body. "Why the confusion? Isn't dying what you were designed to do?"

The corpse didn't respond; of course it didn't. And for that, Death was grateful. He wanted to just ... enjoy for a moment, relish the man's details and contradictions. Like how he had loved the sea, lived for it, and yet had been overwhelmingly, profoundly relieved that it wasn't what had killed him in the end. Smiling, Death patted the man's ashen face, the bristles of his beard rough on his palm. "You all are such puzzles."

He skimmed a hand over the man's jacket; it was smooth and cool, except for a patch on the left breast—an anchor and chain with words winding around it that read **Northstar Seafoods.** Death stared at it for a second, wondering how clothes would feel against his skin. In the eyes of everyone—even himself—he was wearing them. But actually feeling them ...

Death stood, letting himself stay in his physical form for just a little longer as the boat rocked under his feet. This world was so alive. It breathed and sighed and changed; he couldn't believe how blithe humans were about it. He put his hands on his hips, staring down at the body. The sheer hubris, to take a world like this—an experience like living—for granted ...

Death paced to where the prow of the boat jutted out over the water, a black wedge against the dark night. But it wouldn't stay night for long. Already the horizon was lightening; if he stayed in his physical form, he'd feel its warmth on his skin—

No. *He grasped the railing. If he wanted to keep this, he had to keep moving—*

And Darien was awake, so suddenly and completely that she wouldn't have been surprised to feel the mattress around her soaked with icy water. It wasn't the sunrise that had woken her; the light around the curtains was just starting to gray. She rolled onto her side, not sure why she felt so alert, almost *panicky*.

Apart from the fact that Death just killed an entire fishing crew. Heat stung behind Darien's eyes; she reached for Sam, who lay facing away from her, the steady rise and fall of his shoulders all the reassurance she needed that her tossing and turning hadn't affected him at all. She snuggled into his broad back.

An entire crew.

Darien closed her eyes, anger simmering in her gut. *I have to find out where he is.*

She forced herself to relax, then let her mind expand. Several demons floated around the Calls' cabin—mostly little un-Awakened ones, plus Slubgob, who seemed to be plaguing Henry. But she wasn't interested in those. She imagined casting her net wider, wider, until it encompassed all of Seldovia—

Darien gasped. Not with the effort; it was taking less out of her than she thought it would. No, there were demons *everywhere*. Most were un-Awakened, just vague little shadows that flitted mindlessly through the night, following the scents of fear, despair, anger, pain. But there were others, too. Ones that were far more powerful. They crouched in dark warehouses and in the backs of parked cars, hid in unoccupied rooms and deep inside snarled pine groves. Every human instinct had put them there. And now they were reinforcing every human instinct.

Fear rushed through Darien in a nauseating torrent. She gritted her teeth, then forced her eyes shut. *You have one job: find Death.*

Breathing deeply, she imagined climbing a flight of interior stairs in her fortress, higher and higher, until she emerged at the top of a watchtower. It seemed to be working; she felt like she was zooming out, searching, roaming through the vast Alaskan expanse in search of—

"STOP!"

Darien's eyes flew open again as a memory assaulted her. *She could smell the musty clothes in the back of the closet and hear the tiny noises of her friends as they tried to keep themselves from shifting into more comfortable positions, risking giving away their whole game of Sardines.*

"You can't let him know we're here," Ana breathed.

But she'd felt bad for Liam. He'd probably only been searching by himself for five minutes. But to a grade-schooler, left out and alone, five minutes might as well be eternity. "Ana—"

"NO! He'll find us all and the game will be over!"

"This isn't an elementary school game of Sardines," Darien snarled.

Ana's face. Too terrified for the situation. "HE'LL FIND US!!"

A damper descended on Darien's brain. She rocked back. *"Get out of my way, Ankle Tickler!"*

But the pressure only intensified. Darien bolted upright, cradling her temples, pushing with everything she had against whatever the demon was doing to limit her.

"Darien?" It was Sam's voice, low and rough with sleep. "What's going on?"

"I'm ... fighting ..." She threw a hand out, hoping to connect with some part of him, ground herself in his solidness, and nearly sighed in relief when his hand closed around hers.

The mattress shifted as he sat. "What can I do? What do you—how do I—?"

Ankle Tickler's pressure started to buckle.

"HE'LL FIND US—"

"Both of you shut up!" Darien snapped.

"HE'LL FIND—"

The bubble around Darien seemed to shatter, and there it was. Something powerful, something big: a *consciousness*, old and cunning and ambitious.

Come on, she thought. *Come on, come on ...*

Death brushed his hand up the railing on the stern of the boat one more time. Then, he stepped through it and glided down to the choppy surface of the ocean, heedless of the cold or damp—

Something ... swept over him.

Shocked, he hovered on the surface of the ocean, waiting. If he'd been in his physical form, the hairs on the back of his neck would have prickled. Instead, he waited. He knew the Gatekeeper had rebuffed one poorly conceived attack earlier in the day without issue. Another, however, would surprise him. Unless ...

Darien gritted her teeth, clutching her head. Keeping her mind separate from Death's—especially while on the offensive—was more challenging than she'd bargained for, but she couldn't stop now. She imagined diving back in, and *the consciousness swept over Death again, but this time it probed. He reeled back. It wasn't the Gatekeeper. It was similar, but more intelligent. More ... ambitious.*

It was the consciousness he'd found in Hawaii.

And it seemed it had gone on the offensive.

"You," he seethed.

The word clanged around the inside of Darien's head. "You ... you ... you ..." She clapped her hands to her temples, the pressure so intense that all she could do for the moment was pray she could hold her skull together.

"Dar!" Something squeezed her shoulders. Sam's hands. "You're scaring me—"

"You," Death said quietly. "You've never responded to me, never done anything to indicate that you are with us. Do you need to be taught a lesson?"

Death gathered himself, drifting back toward the boat as his power built. He rose past its hull, past the rust-spotted wings drawn across its side and the scrawl that read **Gray Angel, Cordova, AK—**

"Cordova!"

Darien ripped her mind free of Death's, gasping as the pressure from both him and Ankle Tickler released. She dove for her phone on the bedside table. "We have to find Cordova, I think it's close—"

Pain split her skull. She was half aware of tumbling backward, landing on the bed, writhing in agony—

"THIS IS BUT A TASTE. FALL IN LINE OR DIE."

Darien bit down on a scream. Hating herself, she scrambled for the baby, felt its calm, contented little mind. Something steadied in Darien, some bright little core of stability coalescing deep in her subconscious.

She sat up.

And *pushed* Death out of her mind.

He screamed as the alien consciousness hit him with a force that was almost physical. The world around him swam in and out of focus, slate-colored metal and shimmering ocean and star-splattered sky and gray-faced corpses blurring into one—

Darien opened her eyes and found herself staring at the heavy, plaid sherpa quilt spread over the now-rumpled sheets. Within her, the baby seemed to tremble.

"You back with me?"

She looked up into Sam's face. He was pale, the purple half-moons under his eyes visible even in the predawn dimness. She pushed herself up, swallowing a wave of nausea. Already, the baby felt like it was settling back into it usual contented state, but Darien couldn't help but wonder what effect this was having on it.

But if I go insane and die, the baby will die, too. Her heart threatened to break. *Talk about an impossible situation.*

"Death is in Cordova. Where's ...?" She fumbled across the quilt, cursing. "Where'd my phone go? We have to find out where that is."

Blueish light bloomed in the dark.

"I've got it," Sam said. "Let's find yours."

"Find Cordova first."

"Okay."

Sam typed, the blue screen-light blunting the lines of his face. Combined with his paleness and the shadows around his eyes, the effect was almost skull-like. Darien looked away, foreboding pressing on her chest like a physical weight. And ... some other emotion, too.

Anger. Not her own.

"Look," she thought at Ankle Tickler, *"I did what I had to do."*

The demon simmered for a moment. Then, another memory assaulted her. *Halloween. The thick, warm scent of her mother's molé sauce wafting from the kitchen. Sharp humiliation as she watched Mateo scuttle down her drive as fast as he could go. Still clutching her witch's mask, she looked over at Isla, her beautiful, tall, non-pimply best friend. Whose face was bright red.*

With wide eyes, Isla patted her awkwardly on the shoulder. "He thought you were me."

She said it again. "He thought you were me."

And again, like a replay. "He thought you were me."

"Stop doing that." Darien blew out a breath, rattled much less by the memory of that doomed, ancient-history middle school crush than she was by the fact that Ankle Tickler could now rewind her memories like a TV show. "But he can't *get* to you. You have a ... a mental *shield*; you're not like all the others ..."

She trailed off as she caught sight of Sam's face. Its ghostliness was even more disturbing now that his mouth had fallen open.

"Oh. Sorry, I wasn't ... talking to you."

Sam shut his mouth, looking like someone had hit him with something heavy. Then, he shook his head and turned back to his phone. "I didn't think so. Ankle Tickler?"

"Yeah."

"Creep."

"He's under our bed. He can hear everything you're saying."

Sam stretched out one long leg. "I don't really care. We have bigger things to worry about." He looked up. "Like the fact that Cordova is only two hundred miles away from us as the crow flies. And given that Death *can* fly—"

"Two hundred?" Darien's voice came out as a squeak. "That's all?"

Sam flipped his phone around. "Look at the map. It's an estimate, yeah, but ..."

Darien squinted at it, her heart sinking. If she was reading it right—and she probably was—then all Death had to do was soar across Prince William Sound and down the south side of the peninsula until he reached Portlock. There was even a convenient chain of islands that he could follow until he got to the nearest town, snacking on unfortunate wildlife the whole way. She cursed, then looked up at Sam, trying to ignore the growing burble of nerves and sickness in her stomach. "He's moving so much faster than I thought."

Sam dropped his phone facedown on the quilt, plunging the room back into its former state of dimness. Except ... not quite. Dawn was coming; already it was pushing a few watered-down rays of sunlight around the edges of the curtains.

And Death was coming with it.

"He could be in Portlock by this afternoon," she whispered.

Sam's expression didn't change. He just looked at her, his irises a gray-blue ring around his wide, dark pupils. "We're out of time."

Panic shot through Darien; they weren't ready. *She* wasn't ready! But she forced it down, tossed the covers off her legs, and swung them over the side of the bed. "Then let's go—"

Something scraped along the side of her ankle.

Darien yanked her feet up, barely fighting off a shriek. Sam cursed and lunged across the bed toward her. "I'll kill that little—"

Darien threw out an arm, catching him across the stomach. "Wait, stop! He's ..."

Ankle Tickler's mind was creeping into hers again; she could almost hear the skitter of his claws on the imaginary-stone floor of her fortress as he rifled through her memories.

She shuddered. "He's trying to tell me something, and I think *he* thinks it's important. He's going through my memories."

"He's going through your—are you sure I can't just break him in half?!"

"No!" *And this is why I didn't tell you he was here!*

Frustration welled in Darien. Despite being objectively dangerous, the demon had proven his usefulness and *was* risking his life to help them. Tenuous though their symbiosis was.

A symbiosis built on ulterior motives and mutual manipulation.

"No," she said, more calmly this time. "No, he's our ally."

Sam grunted. Then, he crossed his legs and went quiet. Darien leaned against his shoulder, feeling a rush of gratitude for his solidness and goodness that was at least equal to her annoyance.

Marriage, she thought wryly. But the thought evaporated as Ankle Tickler's memory of choice started to play.

Ninth-grade biology—their unit on evolution and adaptation, to be precise. Darien shifted in the hard plastic chair, her thumb running along its strange, pebbled texture, and it was mind-boggling how real the memories felt, how exquisite all those sensory details were that she'd just taken for granted.

"It's because you're obsessed with them, aren't you?" she thought at Ankle Tickler.

He sent back a mental jab, as if she'd poked at sensitive territory, then *forced* the memory back on her. Darien reeled, suddenly understanding in a whole new way why Death was so concerned about him—*them,* she guessed, though the boss demon still didn't seem to know she was involved yet. She frowned, filing that thought in her Cabinet of Things To Talk To Sam About. Then, *she* let the memory sluice back into her consciousness.

Because, after all, *she* was still in control.

Not Ankle Tickler.

Mr. Kerrige paced across the front of the room, short, balding, and sharp-eyed as an osprey. "Does anyone know the difference between evolution and adaptation?"

Several seconds of silence followed, enough that the wave of "I do's" in young Darien's mind almost gained enough momentum to force her hand up. But Aliya beat her to it.

"Evolution happens over time. It's when all the animals in a certain area—or plants, too, I guess—all end up with the same characteristics because of natural selection."

Kerrige nodded. "Bingo, Aliya. Evolution takes time and encompasses entire groups, with consistent results. Whereas adaptation …?"

Darien put up her hand.

"Yes, Darien?"

"Adaptation is what individual animals do when, well, basically when they're forced to change because of seasonality, or … or a natural disaster or something like that."

Her face went a little hot; it hadn't been a great answer. But Kerrige nodded. "At its basis, yes. Adaptation doesn't involve genetic changes to an animal or plant. Instead, it involves learning. For example, a housecat can learn to look after itself if something unfortunate happens and it ends up on the street. That's adaptation. Evolution, on the other hand, is the long tail that all cats are born with that helps them balance. Populations—"

Sam's hand slipped over Darien's, breaking her out of the memory. A second later, Ankle Tickler's annoyance hit her with enough force to make her wince.

"BE. PATIENT," she thought at him. Then, to Sam, "He's showing me a memory from middle school biology. Adaptation versus evolution."

"But you're okay."

"Yes."

"Are they always this long?"

Darien closed her eyes. *Be patient.*

"It depends on how quickly I catch on." She pressed a hand to her forehead as Ankle Tickler's impatience swelled again. "He thinks this is important. Critical, even."

Sam let out a long breath through his nose. "Well, you better get back in there, I guess."

Another wave of urgency hit Darien, and this time, the demon started to tug at her mind, bending her thoughts back to that high school biology class. She resisted for just a moment longer. Just because she could. "Ankle Tickler agrees with you."

"That's a first," Sam muttered.

A humorless smile lifted Darien's lips. Then, she closed her eyes, squeezed Sam's hand, and let the creature back in.

"Populations evolve," Kerrige said. "Individuals adapt. Remember that, because it's going to be on your midterm. Yes, Shaw?"

"What about short-tailed cats? My aunt has a Highlander that doesn't have a tail at all, and they're all like that. Is that because of selective breeding?"

Kerrige's face broke out in a grin. "Excellent point. That's exactly because of selective breeding. Anyone here own a pet?"

Most of the people in the class raised their hands. Not Darien, though. She tapped her toe on the cold, smooth metal leg of the seat in front of her, wishing for the millionth time that her mom and Sophie weren't so allergic to everything.

"So you're all familiar with selective breeding, even if you don't know it," Kerrige said. "Humans are the most adaptable species on the planet. We're so adaptable that we can change nature's course, and we're going to have whole discussions on whether that's a good or bad thing later. The point here is that because of our power, we can quite literally create 'new models' of animals and plants based on our needs and wants."

The memory seemed to freeze, then rewind. "Because of our power," Kerrige said again, "we can quite literally create 'new models' of animals and plants based on our needs and wants."

For the second time, it rewound. "Because of our—"

"I got it. Stop." Darien pressed a hand to her forehead with a soft groan. "He's stronger even than he was yesterday. He's figured out how to manipulate my memories."

"What?"

"He can hit rewind. Replay sections for emphasis. Earlier, he also made a memory version of Ana a lot more angry than real-life Ana has *ever* been, so—"

"Darien ..." Sam seemed to grasp at what to say for a moment. Then, he let out an angry sigh and shook his head. "Listen. I trust your judgment more than pretty much anyone else's in the world. But I'm not so sure about this alliance. Especially if he's—"

Urgency. Panic. Darien straightened. "Wait. I think he's trying to show me why we should continue ... Just a second. We can talk about this in just a second because I think I see where he's going ..."

"Because of our power, we can quite literally create 'new models' of animals and plants based on our needs and wants."

Kerrige and the classroom dissolved, and a final image appeared in Darien's mind: of a white-swathed man with high cheekbones, bone-white skin, and red-pink eyes. "Because of our power," he said, "we can quite literally create 'new models' of animals and plants based on our needs and wants."

Then another series of images flashed through her mind. *The Service Squid. The Otterman. The wendigo. Their confusion and fear. How their behavior had been so different from*

Ankle Tickler's, or Wormwood's, or even the Sphere-demon's in Hawaii. How they hadn't felt quite ... complete. Like caterpillars broken out of their cocoons too soon, doomed to die in a world they weren't ready for.

"I think I get it." She clawed her way out of the thoughts, only mildly disturbed at how deeply she'd been pulled into them this time. It didn't matter; she'd *done* it. She'd figured out the puzzle. "I think—and correct me if I'm wrong, Ankle Tickler—but it seems like Death is somehow using his power to *force* demons to Awaken."

Affirmation.

"He says yes."

"And we're still trusting him."

Darien shrugged impatiently. "He's giving us information, isn't he?"

"What if he's just wasting our time? He knows we're running out of it; what if he's not on our side at all and he's just—?"

"Sam. Why would he be trying to help me control my stupid superpower—when he *knows* I could theoretically use it against him—if he *isn't* on our side? What I've learned from him saved our lives yesterday."

Sam shook his head. "I just don't know if the whole 'enemy of my enemy is my friend' adage applies here."

"If Death is taking their natural evolution and growth into his own hands—at a *huge* detriment to them—then why not?"

He shook his head, silent.

Darien frowned, then glanced over the side of the bed. "Ankle Tickler, given the circumstances, are there others out there besides you who are rebelling?"

The demon jabbed at her again, and she winced. "No, Sam's right. If you want us to trust you, then you have to—"

"You don't want to go back to your world, do you?" Sam interrupted. "You like it here as much as Death does, I'd bet. So what really *is* your plan?"

At that, Ankle Tickler withdrew so suddenly and completely from Darien's mind that it knocked her off balance. She grabbed the bedside table.

In an instant, Sam was at her elbow. "You okay?"

"Yep." Darien straightened, trying to hide her irritation with him. "He's gone. Completely gone. We're not getting an answer to that question."

Sam stared at her. "Does that disturb you?"

Darien met his eyes for a moment. Then she looked away, biting down on her frustration, embarrassment, and regret. "Deeply."

Chapter Twenty-Two

When Sam pulled open the guest room door, he didn't know what surprised him more: the fact that Ellie and Oliver were already hurrying down the stairs, the sheer number of un-Awakened demons revolving around the Calls' living room (ten, at first glance), or the delicious scent of some kind of sweet-smelling bread wafting from the kitchen.

Helen sat in her chair, a huge book open in her lap, her jaw slack as the four of them converged on her. "I said eight! Not …" She glanced at the clock. "Six fifteen! Did you all plan this or something?"

"No," Sam and Oliver said at the same time.

Helen rubbed a hand over her eyes, and Sam tried not to let his inner guilt show. She was visibly exhausted, and Slubgob hovered around her head in a noxious cloud. No wonder she'd had a fit of early-morning stress baking. Sam avoided empty carbs almost as much as he avoided alcohol, but after yesterday—and this morning—*he* still wanted to drown all his sorrows in… well, *whatever* was in that oven.

"Where's Henry?" Oliver asked.

"He spelled me at four when he couldn't sleep, so he just went in to lie down about half an hour ago."

Sam winced.

Helen closed her book. "Tell me why you all came bursting out of your rooms, then I'll decide how quickly I need to go wake him up."

"Death is in Cordova," Darien said baldly.

Helen's novel hit the floor. "*What?*"

"And that's not all." Quickly, Darien told the others what they'd learned from Ankle Tickler.

Ellie was the first to speak into the stunned silence that followed. "So he's warping the baby demons into what *he* wants them to be."

Darien nodded. "Basically."

Oliver put his hands on his hips, his expression faintly disgusted. "I never thought I could feel sympathy for demons, but ..." He scratched the back of his head, as if he couldn't quite decide how to finish the thought.

"I don't think I *really* do," Helen said. "They're evil, soul-sucking parasites who want to make us all miserable, and you reap what you sow." She stared down at the polished hardwood, then slowly shook her head. "Still ... there's just something so wrong about the idea of taking away a sentient creature's choice."

"Yeah," Darien said quietly.

Sam stepped forward. "Moral questions aside, Death *is* flying closer as we speak. He could be here as early as tonight, maybe sooner. If we want to have any shot at closing the gate, we have to act now."

"Ellie, that fits," Oliver said quietly.

Ellie nodded. "What a relief."

Sam cocked his head at the exchange, but before he could say anything, Ellie spoke.

"Our turn to tell you about *our* weird night. It sounds like they're two sides of the same coin." She settled on one of the barstools next to where Oliver stood and looked up at him, her gaze steady. Something about the motion made Sam pause. It took him only a moment to realize why. Despite being dressed in pajamas, her hair mussed from sleep—not to mention the dark circles around her eyes from not getting enough of it—Ellie had *presence*. The way she carried herself now, the coolness in her eyes, and the determined set to her jaw ... this was a new level of confidence that Sam had never seen in his little sister before. She'd never been insecure or timid. But she'd never been ... whatever *this* was, either. Affection surged in his chest; he had to fight not to cross the room and give her a high-five. Or a hug. Maybe both.

"Your vision, Oliver," Ellie said. "You go ahead."

"You're having visions now, too?" Helen asked.

A wry grin quirked Ellie's mouth. "Right? I'd feel left out if the three of them didn't seem so horribly stressed all the time."

Helen put a hand to her forehead. "All right, tell us."

Oliver nodded. "I talked with Jordan in a dream last night."

The floor underneath Sam seemed to lurch. Jordan, his sightless eyes, how dark the bloodstain on the sand underneath him had been. He, Sam, could have prevented that if he'd paused to actually *think* for three seconds.

Helen's gasp grounded him again. Mostly. "*What*? What did he say? Oh my *gosh* ..." She reached for the back of the couch and leaned against it.

Oliver blinked a few times. "He said to tell everyone he's okay, and he loves you."

Tell him I'm so sorry!

The words roared up Sam's throat, bitter and blistering as acid, but he couldn't have spoken them if he'd wanted to. Instead, he ducked his head, waiting for the stinging in his eyes to stop and trying not to look too closely at any of the six demons that now hovered around him. Beside him, Helen sniffed.

"He's okay," Oliver repeated, as much to himself as to them, it seemed. But then, he went on. Sam was relieved. The last thing he needed right now was to have a public breakdown.

"He said the demons are gathering at Portlock," Oliver said. "The window to be able to march straight up to the gate is closed. There are many on the way that are newly Awakened, and others like the Lady, or Silverskin, who have been around for hundreds of years and know how to handle themselves."

Sam felt the blood drain from his face. Beside him, Darien looked stricken.

"Did you see them?" he asked her. "When you were looking for Death?"

Darien shook her head. "I was so busy looking for him that I ... well, I *did* see other demons, but only the ones that were here in Seldovia or close to it. By the time I'd figured out how to ... expand my vision, I was moving too fast to get a good look at anything."

"It's all right, Darien," Ellie said. "Despite the fact that you're far and away the most perfect among us, we don't expect you to *actually* be perfect."

Sam put an arm around his wife's shoulder and was relieved when she let him tuck her against his side. "Ellie's right. Sorry if that came out accusatory. I'm ... struggling with that today."

Darien flashed him a brief, strained smile.

"Unfortunately, that's not all," Oliver said. "Jordan said he saw others, too, coming via water. Sea monster-types. The point is, we need to be prepared for anything—"

Darien stiffened.

Sam's eyes whipped down to her face; it was draining of color. "Vision?"

"Yeah." Her legs threatened to buckle; Sam looped an arm under her shoulders, steadying her. Her eyes were open and fixed on the wall, focused as if she were actually seeing it.

"Are you with us?" he asked.

"Mostly."

Sam waited for a heartbeat more, but it seemed like that was all Darien could manage. He scooped her up and lifted her onto the couch. Someone was moving behind him, probably Helen. The slick hiss of metal on metal rang across the room as someone else, probably Oliver, drew a knife—

Helen's voice issued from behind him. "Darien, can you tell us where the attack will be coming from?"

"Slubgob," Darien whimpered.

Sam jumped to his feet and whirled in time to see the blood drain from Helen's face. Her hand rose to her head, her expression terrified. Sam took a step toward her, hand outstretched as if he could somehow grab the ugly black cloud around her head and rip the demon out.

Footsteps pounded across the creaky hardwood, and Oliver grabbed his aunt's shoulder so hard his knuckles went white. "We won't let her kill you. We'll—"

But Sam didn't hear the end of her sentence. The dark fuzz outlining Helen's head was shifting, boiling like a pot of water left on the stove for too long. Then a shape ... *emerged* out of her, pale and misshapen, a gargoyle with a face twisted in agony. It rose off the floor a few inches, thrashing and writhing, clearly not in control of itself.

Sam yelled and jumped back, and Helen and Oliver and Ellie were all shouting at him, but things were happening so *fast*. Slubgob twisted, agony written all over her flat, brutish face. Even on a demon, the expression was sickening.

"She's being pulled out of you, Helen!" he managed. "She's—"

The demon started to scream—Sam could see it, even if he couldn't hear it—and Darien let out a thin, high-pitched keen. Sam plunged his hand into the pocket of his shorts, his hand closing around his lighter. There were many reasons Slubgob needed to die. It was strange that mercy topped the list in the end.

Sam brought the lighter up, intending to rip the demon's flesh open with his bare hands if he had to, when she bowed backward at such a hideous angle that he felt physically sick watching it. Then, as her agony seemed to reach a fever pitch, she exploded into hundreds of little black ribbons. Even as Sam gaped, they, too, dissolved.

"SAM!" Oliver thundered. "TELL US WHAT'S HAPPENING!"

Sam jumped; he hadn't known Oliver was capable of bellowing like that. "Slubgob's dead." He turned on his heel and knelt by Darien, catching hold of her hands. "You okay?"

"Yeah. Yeah, Death killed Slubgob."

"I know. I saw it." He looked up, addressing the room at large. "It was ugly. I'll spare you the details."

Darien pushed herself up, shuddering. "So horrible. Death assigned her to spy on us, and it seemed like she did, for a while anyway. But then she just ... quit."

Oliver's eyebrows contracted. "Why would she do that?"

Darien didn't speak for a while, but the frown on her face was as deep as Sam had ever seen it. He sat back, pieces of a grim puzzle starting to fall into place. "Death doesn't seem to know about our abilities."

Darien shook her head slowly. "If he knew, I'm almost positive I would have overheard him worrying about it. So, no."

"Which suits us just fine," Helen said.

"Yeah," Sam said, "but it also suits ...

He met Darien's eyes. "Ankle Tickler," they said at the same time.

Sam crossed his arms. "He's playing his own game, and I'm sorry, love, but we're all just pawns, including you."

A translucent, vaguely leg-shaped appendage swooshed by Sam's head—one of the juvenile demons had come to lap up his worry like a stray dog at a grimy puddle. He ignored it. "I guess what I'm getting at is: what if Slubgob didn't choose to stop spying? What if something *made* her? And if Ankle Tickler's involved in that—if there's ugly demon politics going on—how does that inform our actions going forward?"

Darien's eyes hardened. Then, she stood and headed for the bedroom. "Give me five minutes."

***

Darien burst through the door of the bedroom. *"Where are you, you little rat?"*

Silence.

"You're just like Death, aren't you? You can force other demons to do what you want, and that's exactly what you intend to do once you get him *out of the way."* She slumped against the door frame, crossing her arms. *"And here I was thinking there was some altruism at play here, for other demons, even if not for us. I feel really stupid."*

Again, there was no reply. Darien scowled at the space underneath the bed, her mind kicking into high gear.

"I assume you heard everything that just happened in the living room."

More silence.

Darien's patience snapped. *"Fine. I'm coming for you."*

She closed her eyes and envisioned her fortress, imagined climbing the steps to the highest parapet, brushing her fingertips along the walls as she went. Obdurate, rough, cold. Pure Rocky Mountain granite. She stepped out onto the tower's top and tipped her head toward the clear, brilliant sky. Then, she relaxed and let her mind expand. She was pleasantly surprised at how easy it had become to slip into this strange, half-meditative state, to send the weird sixth sense she'd developed winging across the wildlands.

"Come on," she whispered. "I know you're out there."

But he just ... wasn't.

Of course. Darien opened her eyes; she wanted to smack herself. If Ankle Tickler could hide from *Death*, why did she think *she'd* be able to find him?

Still ... She paused for a moment, painfully aware of the digital clock blinking out the seconds on the bedside table. Did she keep trying? Should she check Death's location again to get a feel for how fast he was moving? If Ankle Tickler had really left and was no longer shielding her ... would that risk giving her ability away?

Darien hovered near the door, hand on the knob. Then, she stiffened her spine. She couldn't—*wouldn't*—walk out of here with no answers.

So, she expanded her mind again, looking for that powerful, consuming point in the darkness. Straining, she felt him, then focused her mental telescope—though if she were being honest, she imagined it as more of a full-blown observatory now. He was stationary. In fact, he was ... feasting on some poor animal that had been in the wrong place at the wrong time. Another bear, it looked like.

Steeling herself, Darien snuck into Death's mind and was almost whipped away by a whirl of sensation, color, sound, and memory. Not the demon's. The bear's. The creature was shockingly intelligent, but didn't express any of it in words. Instead, Darien felt the warm stupor of hibernation, the chill of water when it swam, the all-consuming drive to forage and hunt. The infinitely pleasurable sensation of tearing at a moose carcass, feasting on salmon, glutting itself on berries. She saw its habitat through its eyes, knew every rise and fall of the island, and understood on an instinctive level how to survive a swim to the next one over.

The creature's consciousness started to fade, replaced by Death's euphoria.

Suppressing a shudder, Darien pulled away before he could sense her. She had enough clues to at least make an educated guess at where he was, and she didn't want him to look up and realize there were *two* threats to him now.

She glared at the space under the bed again. *"Ankle Tickler, if I don't hear anything from you within ten seconds, I'm going to assume we're enemies. One ... two ..."*

The irony sank in even as she counted. Ankle Tickler, the demon who had started out as a joke, might be one of the most dangerous of them all now.

"Five ... six ..."

Was she strong enough to fend off his attack if he turned on her?

"Eight ... nine ..."

JAB.

The force of Ankle Tickler's mental punch sent Darien crashing out of her fortress and back into the real world. She was on the floor, trembling, the hardwood slick under her sweaty palms. For a moment, she sat there, trying to get a grip on herself. Then, she got to her feet. *"I assume we're enemies, then."*

There was no response.

Turning on her heel, Darien yanked open the door and marched back into the living room.

Chapter Twenty-Three

If Hell could have been personally engineered to cause Ellie the most possible suffering, then that morning would have made a great template for the devil.

They'd left the house minutes after Darien had emerged from the guest room with a baleful expression and the bad news that Death had already covered *at least* forty miles, maybe more. All five of them carried knives, lighters, and pistols (Ellie was still reeling a little at how many spare guns Helen and Henry had), and they'd loaded Henry's big equipment duffel with sterno, hand sanitizer, bear spray, bug spray, and anything else they'd been able to get their hands on that was flammable. Helen had also brought her moose rifle.

"In case we need a sniper," she'd said as she loaded it barrel-down into the truck next to her. The rest—what little Henry, Luke, and Bill had been able to cobble together before the boys' doomed Portlock trip—was waiting at the warehouse.

Now Ellie stood on the dock, arms wrapped around herself, shivering against the damp chill that still clung to the morning air. She didn't know exactly when the panic attack had hit her. Maybe when she'd passed the burn scar in the dirt where they'd killed the Otterman yesterday. Maybe it was when she'd seen Henry and Bill carrying weird plumbing torch/bayonet hybrids out of the warehouse, and realized how outgunned they were (despite all their guns). Or maybe it had been watching Sam approach Luke on the dock, tears streaming down his face, when Jordan's father not only forgave him, but embraced him.

No more deaths, she begged the universe, knowing how futile it was. *Please, no more deaths.*

Ellie started up the docks toward the *Redemption*, looking for Oliver. The tide was going out, the log framework underneath her becoming more and more exposed by the minute, the tang of seawater so strong she could taste it. The clouds were engaged in their usual morning guerrilla warfare with the sun, casting the boats, the ocean, the dock, and the mountains in ever-shifting patterns of dark and light. One moment, the water bloomed a brilliant and sparkling shade of navy. The next, it was a sullen gray, choppy and mercurial.

Hiding who knows what.

Ellie stopped, breathing deeply, and dropped her gaze to the planking at her feet. *You have minutes before you get on a boat for Portlock, and you can't be a gibbering idiot when you do, so get it together. Focus on the sensory. What can you hear?*

She closed her eyes. Seabirds cawed and cried. Water sloshed. Human voices drifted over it all, cracking with urgency. Most of them came from the right, where the *Redemption* and another huge fishing boat were docked, both of which were swarming with people.

Footsteps were coming from that direction, too—hollow thumps, fast and rhythmic.

Ellie's heart sped up, and the squeezing sensation in her chest intensified, but she didn't allow herself to move or open her eyes. *It's a* person *walking up those docks, not a demon.* And if it were a demon, she'd deal with it just like she'd dealt with all the other demons, panic attacks aside. Or included; it didn't matter.

After all, despite how crappy it felt, she was getting inhumanly good at all this.

Once Ellie was reasonably sure she'd staved off the worst of the attack, she opened her eyes. The sun was out again, and seemed to be trying to dazzle everyone while it could, sparking off the surface of the water and bathing everything in a golden glow ... including Oliver. The footsteps had been his. He stood beside her with his arms folded, gazing back at the *Redemption*—the direction he'd come. "We're ready to go."

"Okay."

"Sorry to interrupt your peace."

A strangled half-laugh erupted out of Ellie, even as her entire core spasmed again. She pressed a fist to her chest, hoping she could contain it all. "There's no peace in here, Oliver. Don't feel too bad."

He looked over at her as a cloud passed over the sun, deepening the color of every note of blue in his eyes. Then, he opened his arms and drew her into his chest. Everything in her steadied.

"You don't have to put on a front, Ellie." His voice was a low murmur, thick with emotion. "Everyone is terrified."

"You don't seem terrified. Worried, maybe, but—"

He laughed, and Ellie closed her eyes as the sound rocked through his strong shoulders. It was a fleeting and fragile echo of joy, but she'd never valued it more. She wanted to absorb the sound; carry it with her like a little golden shield around her heart until she died—whether that was today or sixty years from now.

The squeezing was all in her throat now; she gave up and buried her face in the side of his neck. He kissed her hair. "I want you with me."

"So you can protect me?"

"Yeah. And because *I* need *you*. You make me stronger in ways I can't put into words." Oliver pulled back, cupping her face in his hands. "We'll free your dad. We'll save the world."

"And they'll have no idea. And I won't care, because Dad won't be trapped anymore, and *we'll* finally get to be together and start figuring out our future, and that's all that matters to me."

Oliver brushed her lips with his, just a whisper of a kiss, but one that still sent goosebumps racing across her shoulders and down her back. Then he pulled away, taking her hand. "Let's go."

"Remind me who all is coming," Ellie said as they walked.

"Apart from the Call Crew—you, me, Helen, Henry, Sam, and Darien—we've got the entire surviving crew of the *Redemption*—"

"I'm still amazed at Naomi and Luke," Ellie said, shaking her head. "I can't believe they're here."

"I know," Oliver said.

Ellie shielded her eyes against the sun, peering up as they approached the *Redemption*. It towered over the other boats. On its deck, she could make out Luke's broad-shouldered frame and Naomi's gray-streaked French braid. They moved slowly, bent like trees in a stiff wind, their grief palpable. But they were there.

"Jessie's coming, too," Oliver said quietly. "There's more to that kid than people give him credit for."

Sadness swept over Ellie as she watched Jordan's parents work. "I'm beginning to think there's more to everyone than people give them credit for."

Oliver just squeezed her hand.

"And Helen said we've got ..." Ellie looked away as she tried to remember. "The Bauers. Both of them, right?"

Oliver looked surprised. "You know the Bauers?"

"I met Roman in the diner. He stopped me as we were running out the door and told me to call him if any of us needed anything."

Oliver smiled. "That's just like him.

Ellie managed a tiny grin. "Who else have we got?"

"Richard Lee, for one. Not that I expect you to know him—"

"I think I met *a* Lee in the diner, too. She told me the same thing Roman did."

"That'd be Emma. Richard's her husband. She's staying with, well, with Jordan's sisters." The corners of Oliver's mouth twitched downward. "But anyway, there are others who are coming, too. More than I thought would." He gestured to the boat next to the *Redemption*, the only one that even came close to its size. "The crew of the *Crab King*. A couple other locals you've probably seen running around. And the best part," he continued, "is that we can probably expect even more people than are here."

Hope surged in Ellie. "Really?"

Oliver nodded. "According to Henry, the text chain really took off last night. That doesn't surprise me, with how well-connected he and Bill are in this area. And the town meeting is still happening tonight." To Ellie's surprise, Oliver chuckled. "Murray of all people is going to lead the charge there."

"So maybe we'll have reinforcements," Ellie said.

"We'll have them whether Murray succeeds or not. A bunch of people from Nanwalek are going to join, too."

"No way."

"Yeah. Plus, three private boats and a ferry full of people from Homer got here about half an hour ago. Doctors, welders, fishermen—people who are sick of what's going on, have come to grips with the fact that it's supernatural, and want to help. I think there are about fifty of them total." Oliver turned to her. "This wouldn't have happened without you, Ellie. You survived, you chased the truth, and you fought because you didn't want what happened to you to happen to anyone else." He smiled. "Some people might call that heroic."

Something in Ellie's chest loosened. "Thanks, Oliver."

They stepped from the dock onto the deck of the *Poor Buoy*, its engine already growling under their feet. Ellie watched, slightly numb, as the *Redemption* glided past them toward the harbor's entrance, the *Crab King* following a few hundred yards behind.

She ducked into the cabin after Oliver. Helen and Henry were both inside; the latter spoke as Ellie shut the door behind her. "You still good to drive, Oliver?"

"Yeah, I'm good." He slid into the captain's chair—or whatever it was called; Ellie still wasn't sure—and patted the seat beside him. "You can sit here if you want, Ellie. And you two get some rest," he tossed over his shoulder at the Calls.

"We'll do our best," Helen grumbled.

Oliver eased on a lever on the dashboard. The *Poor Buoy* juddered backward, away from the dock, and from safety.

But it isn't safe here, Ellie reminded herself. That was when the realization hit her: everything was now truly, completely out of her hands. She was just along for the ride. Her stomach started to writhe, threatening to convulse as Oliver eased the *Poor Buoy* into the harbor proper, the boat rocking in the wake left by the behemoths in front of it.

No. She set her jaw, fixing her eyes on the glittering horizon. *You're not just along for the ride. You're along because you're terrifying. Act like it.*

***

Sam braced his forearms against the *Redemption's* railing, watching the rest of the little fleet—flotilla? Armada?—as they reached the harbor's edge. He'd counted at least twenty boats, including the *Redemption*. Twenty boats, and probably sixty juvenile demons.

Death isn't the only ticking time bomb here.

The growl of the *Redemption's* huge engine grew into a roar, and its deck canted upward. Gripping the railing, Sam shot a glance at Darien, wondering how her extra-sensitive stomach was taking all this. She stood with her legs braced, her knuckles white against the cold metal rail ... but her expression was determined.

Sam turned back to the ocean, the cool breeze whipping against his skin as the *Redemption* accelerated, its wake spreading behind it in a white, frothy vee. The boats following it did likewise, spreading out across the water as the harbor fell behind. The *Poor*

Buoy came up alongside them—sort of; Sam estimated they were still at least a hundred yards away. Unease prickled through him as he watched the sun glint off its metal frame.

"You're wishing we were all together," Darien said.

"Yeah."

"Me, too."

For a moment, the only sounds were the thrum of the engine and the frothy hiss of the water underneath them.

"I think we did the right thing," Sam finally said.

"Oh, I know we did. Bill's basically functioning as commodore, and the *Redemption's* the flagship." She frowned. "I think, anyway."

Sam shrugged. "I learned everything I know about boat warfare from *Pirates of the Caribbean*, so don't look at me."

Darien laughed. "Same." The smile slid off her face as she looked out at the *Poor Buoy*. "The point is, it's hard to argue with being needed here when you're the eyes and I'm the ears of the whole flotilla."

Sam raised his eyebrows. "Flotilla, huh?"

Darien shot him a dry smile. "I thought about 'herd,' but that just didn't seem to fit."

Sam chuckled and looped his arm through hers, pulling her into his side. She rested her head on his shoulder. "I'm shocked we got underway so easily. I was expecting to be attacked, but ..."

Sam looked sideways at her. "Nothing?"

"Nothing at all. I mean, there's a lot happening. I can tell they're gathering at Portlock, and communicating with each other. The ones that can anyway." Her frown deepened. "But no, there was no chatter at all about attacking Seldovia Harbor."

Sam chewed his lip, trying not to feel too disconcerted. "I don't trust that we're safe."

"Oh, we're not. Not by a long shot. I was just ... expecting a little more mayhem to have happened by now." She paused. "Are the demons you saw on the docks keeping up?"

Sam glanced behind them. "A few are. But whatever speed we're going right now seems to be out of reach for most of them."

"That's good."

"Yeah." He lowered his voice, turning so his lips were next to her ear. "Jessie's still got his. I don't think he'll get rid of it until we close the gate."

"But he's aware now," Darien pointed out. "He's fighting it."

"Yes. Don't think I'm harshing on the kid, because I'm not." His eyes flicked to the *Redemption's* cabin, which was large enough—and set high enough—that it needed its own set of stairs for accessibility. Jessie was in there with Bill, helping. Fighting, despite everything, like Darien had said. "I don't think any of us could do better in his situation."

Darien shook her head slowly. "I don't, either."

"Anyway," Sam went on, "Naomi and Luke were swarmed, but mostly with un-Awakened ones, and they're all behind us now."

"That's got to be a relief for them. *I* feel better now that we're on our way, and I'm just on the fringes of the loss they've taken."

Sam swallowed. He, too, was only a fringe member of this little fishing family. But he'd seen the Gatekeeper's blades slice through Jordan's body, watched the light leave his eyes. He had to fight constantly against those terrible memories, and deal with the nightmares—waking and sleeping—that assaulted his brain when he got too tired. Where did that leave him?

Right here, right now, with a job to do.

Sam let out a long, silent breath. "It's hard to get a firm count of the demons I can see because they come and go so much." He nodded toward a boat that had settled in on their right flank, close enough that he could see the little wisp of fog that was trailing it. "There's one following that boat there, but it's not going to keep up."

Darien grinned. "You mean the *Morgan Seaman*?"

Sam blinked. "Is that what it's called?"

"Yep."

Despite everything, a laugh erupted out of Sam. "I love these people."

"Sam! Darien!"

They both turned at the sound of Jessie's voice. He'd poked his head out the cabin door and was peering at them. "Dad wants you in here."

"On our way!" Darien took Sam's hand. "Let's go ... wait."

She stumbled to a halt.

"Vision?" Sam asked as her hand tightened around his.

"Yeah ..." Darien's gaze was unfocused, but her eyes darted everywhere, as if she was seeing things he couldn't. Sam's unease reared again.

She snapped back to focus, naked fear on her face, then started for the cabin. "We've got to go. Nanwalek's under attack."

Chapter Twenty-Four

When they rounded a bend in the coast and saw smoke billowing from the direction of Nanwalek, Oliver was surprised to feel ... *relief*. Finally—*finally*—they knew where an attack was coming from. Beside him, Ellie stared at the writhing black column with wide eyes. She cursed.

"You're not wrong," Oliver said.

She shook her head slowly, eyes still fixed on the smoke. "I don't want to fight; I'm *terrified* to fight. But ..." She gave a helpless shrug. "At least we know where they are now."

"I was thinking the same thing." Oliver glanced back at Helen and Henry—neither of whom had moved since flopping down on the bench seats two hours ago. "Hey, Henry! Helen!"

Both jerked awake at the sound of their names, Henry's hand going to the plumbing-torch-bayonet he'd strapped to the wall beside him. "We under attack?"

"*We're* not, but Nanwalek is," Oliver said as he accelerated around the last bend. Ellie gasped, and hot fury shot through Oliver's stomach as the little town came into view. The smoke wasn't coming from just one place, but several. A warehouse on the shoreline. A boat, half-sunk, belching black clouds into the air. And—his gut twisted—what might have been a house. Or ... two or three, now that he could see more clearly.

"Holy ..." Helen breathed.

"We have to help," Ellie said.

"Yeah, we do." Oliver reached for the radio's mic, formulating what he planned to say to Bill, but it crackled to life before he could touch it.

"*Redemption* to *Mermaid* and *Poor Buoy*. You copy?"

Oliver raised the mic to his mouth. "Copy."

Another voice—Roman's—responded. "Copy."

"I want you two to go in and check it out, help if you can. The rest of you, stay back. They won't be able to get out of the harbor if you're in the way—"

Oliver didn't wait to hear the rest of Bill's instructions. He brought the *Poor Buoy's* prow around, then sent her charging toward Nanwalek's harbor as fast as he dared. Movement flashed out of the corner of his vision; the *Mermaid* was pulling alongside. He could make out Roman at the wheel, as well as what looked like his wife Lana, Richard Lee, and two others, whom Oliver didn't recognize. Roman raised his hand in a wave, and Oliver acknowledged.

"Look!" Ellie yelped. "What *is* that?"

Oliver stared in the direction she was pointing, and his mouth fell open. Something huge and dark was forming on the shore; it almost looked like the tornadoes he'd watched videos of in his old earth science class, except smaller. And slimmer. And blacker than a moonless night in the dead of winter. In fact, it was the darkest thing Oliver had ever seen; so much so that he was struggling to truly make sense of it. It seemed to warp the air, bending the light around it into a perverse halo.

He sat back. "I have no idea what that is."

The sounds of rummaging came from behind them, then Helen said, "Found them. Here."

Seconds later, Henry knelt between Oliver and Ellie and pressed his massive pair of binoculars to his eyes. He stiffened, then let the binoculars fall from his now-ashen face. "God help them."

"What's happening?" Helen and Ellie asked at the same time.

"That ... *thing*, that demon ... it looks like it's choking anyone who gets near it."

"What?" Helen yelped.

Oliver's stomach twisted; Ellie looked sick. Now that Henry had said it, Oliver could make out people on the shoreline, some standing, some hunched over, and some—the ones nearest to the monster—splayed out on the ground, unmoving. He gripped the wheel so hard that his battered hands ached in protest. "How many fires, Henry?"

"Three, it looks like. Four, if we count the boat. Two of them look like houses."

"I hope nobody was inside when they went up," Helen said.

"Why do they keep lighting fires if they know fire is what kills them?" Ellie asked.

"Maybe this one's like Silverskin," Oliver said.

Ellie winced. "I hope not."

"In that he was arrogant," Oliver clarified. "Which was why he died."

She folded her arms, her voice stone-cold. "That'd be helpful."

Oliver forced his eyes away from the Void and the burning buildings, slowing the *Poor Buoy*. While they'd been distracted, four boats had broken away from the harbor and were speeding toward them. One pulled up next to the *Mermaid*, which had stopped short—or as short as a boat could anyway.

Henry raised his binoculars to his eyes again as the radio crackled. It was Roman's voice again, gravelly even through the receiver. "I've sent Dan out to talk to Boris. I'll relay info as I get it. Stand by."

They were silent for a moment.

"Those boats are jam-packed," Henry said, lowering his binoculars. "There's got to be forty fighting men and women there."

"That'll help." Oliver ran a hand through his hair. Did that leave enough people to defend the tiny village?

"This was the trap all along," Helen growled.

"Because we want to help?" Ellie's voice was also low with rage. "But helping will take time that Death can use to get to the gate?"

"And we *know* that," Helen spat. "We're not stupid. Yet here we still are, because we can't just *leave* them."

"They're using our own humanity against us," Henry muttered.

They fell silent as Roman's voice came over the radio again. It was higher-pitched this time. "Something's attacking the docks. We have visual, but it's hard to describe. It's like a ten-foot-tall black hole that's shaped like a man."

"Accurate," Ellie muttered.

Oliver glanced over at her. She was turned away, her face in half-profile, but he still noted the flush in her cheeks and down her neck. Her pulse fluttered under her jawline, fast and frantic. Still, she sat in the passenger's seat like a princess on a throne, her hands folded neatly in her lap. She was the picture of someone who knew exactly how to handle her nervous energy. A wave of admiration washed over Oliver, incongruous with everything else he was feeling.

It receded when Roman spoke again. "Boris said two of them appeared when they were getting ready to launch. The townspeople blew up the boat repair place, killing the first one, but then the Void demon chased them to the docks. It sank one boat. Then it got smart, and now it's just blocking the pier, suffocating anyone who tries to get past. The people already on the boats couldn't get back to land, either, so they decided to just take—wait, stand by."

When he didn't say more, Oliver, Henry, and Ellie exchanged glances.

"Look," Helen said suddenly. "Roman's turning around."

And he was. The four Nanwalek boats—similar in size to the *Poor Buoy*—followed, zooming past them toward where the *Redemption* waited with the rest of Seldovia's little fleet. Oliver's heart sank; he gripped the wheel as the *Mermaid's* stern dipped, its outboard motor digging into the ocean, propelling it in a long, graceful turn. Away from Nanwalek. Away from the screaming people there.

Oliver grabbed the radio. "Roman."

"Yeah."

"What about the people in Nanwalek? We're leaving them?"

"Boris says that thing can't be killed. The only thing we *can* do is get to Portlock and close the gate."

Oliver shook his head. "That's ridiculous. They can all be killed."

A beep came over the radio. An unfamiliar voice followed. "This is Boris. That thing is like a vacuum. It sucks up everything around it, including oxygen. Fires can't burn near it—you can't even *breathe* near it. We've left some people to defend the town, but our best chance is to shut the gate, send that thing back to Hell." Static sounded for a moment, then Boris went on. "We're hoping that now it's seen the whole fleet, it'll decide we're the bigger threat and follow us."

Helen fixed a hollow stare on the burning shoreline. "That's a big risk."

"Yeah, but he's got a point," Henry said. "How do we fight something that can't be killed? Best chance might be to try and draw it off."

A hundred yards away, the *Mermaid* blew past, following the other boats to join up with the fleet. Bill's voice came over the radio. "*Poor Buoy*, fall back in with the rest of us. That's an order. Darien's been monitoring the situation. She thinks the Void is here to keep us distracted. She's saying if we move on, there's a good chance it follows us."

"I never thought I'd be so relieved to be followed by a demon," Helen said.

Ignoring the clenching in his gut, Oliver reached for the throttle. "Sit down, everyone." He sent the *Poor Buoy* into a tight turn, following the *Mermaid* and the other boats that had gone before it.

"Here's hoping Darien's right," Ellie said.

Oliver just nodded.

***

Darien stood in the *Redemption's* cabin, gripping the thin metal railing that ran the length of the ceiling, ostensibly put there for people like her. People who *didn't* have sea legs, who *always* felt like they were one wave shy of being tossed onto the boat's heaving deck. Who couldn't believe how easily everyone else moved around. Even Sam seemed confident, though he still didn't have the easy grace of Bill, Jessie, Luke, Naomi, or anyone else who had clearly been born on a fishing boat.

She stood still, waiting for her latest bout of nausea to pass. So far, she'd only thrown up once, when they had hit a rough patch of waves near a place called Pogi Point, about six miles out of Seldovia. But after that foray into the Void's head, she was afraid she was in for it again.

"Dar."

She risked turning her head, squinting up at her husband. "Huh?"

"Come sit down."

He took her hand, and she let him lead her to the nearest bench. Its seat was cushioned, at least. That was nice. "Thanks, Sam. Bill, if I need to puke again, I just head out the door, right?"

The grizzled captain didn't look at her, but his face softened. "Or aim for one of those buckets in front of you."

"Got it."

Sam took up his spot behind her seat, one hand gripping the other end of the same railing she'd just let go of and the other rubbing smooth circles on her back.

"Can you tell if he's following us, Darien?" Bill asked.

A wave of weariness threatened Darien at the thought of diving back into that thing's head. She pushed it away and grabbed a bucket. "Let me check."

Settling the bucket between her knees, she raised her fortress and reached backward, toward the creature wreaking havoc on the shore behind them.

Hunger and glee. There was nothing quite like the fear of humans trying to defend their homes. They had been the same last time, too. Like ants swarming—

Darien gripped the bucket so hard her knuckles turned white. "He's old. I think he was in Hawaii, too."

"Interesting," Sam murmured.

Darien glanced at him. "What?"

"The older ones seem more humanoid. The newer ones more ..."

"Monstrous?" Darien's stomach roiled; she leaned forward. "But Wormwood and Slubgob—and the wendigo, I guess—were more human."

"They happened before Death started imposing his will on everything," Sam pointed out.

"True." Darien bowed her head as more nausea rolled over her.

"Take it easy," Sam said.

Darien shook her head. "I can't take it easy. People are dying back there."

She threw herself back toward the Void. *He turned, feeling grains of sand fleck his feet as his power pulled them in. Disappointment settled heavily in him. The fleet was moving, as Death had suspected they would. Which meant—*

Darien's jaw dropped. As Death had said? How had she missed *that*?

"You okay?" Sam asked.

"Hang on."

Darien forced her attention back to the Void. *The fleet was moving away, the boats that had managed to evade him scurrying like rats from a hunting cat. Despite the deliciousness here, he knew what he needed to do. So, he turned and started gliding across the surface of the water. He was slower than they were, but that was survivable. Once they stopped, he'd soon catch up.*

Darien's eyes flew open. "Yep, he's following us."

Then, she leaned forward and threw up into the five-gallon bucket.

A painful half-minute later—made slightly better by the feeling of Sam's warm hand rubbing her back—she emerged, weak and trembling.

"I'm sorry, Darien." Bill's voice was laced with a surprising amount of sympathy. "I remember when Charity—"

He stopped. When Darien looked up at him, his shoulders were stiff.

"Anyway, don't be embarrassed," he said gruffly.

Darien snorted. "At this point, I'm not willing to waste any energy on something as silly as being embarrassed. Thanks, though." She let out a sigh, tried to center herself as best as she could, then turned to Sam. "Something's off, and I need you to help me logic through it."

Sam fixed her with a steady gaze. "I'm ready."

A wave of gratitude washed over Darien as she looked into his eyes, intense and serious. *I adore him.*

"I'm not seeing all of Death's communications," she said.

Sam's eyebrows rose. "Do you think you've *been* seeing them all? Let me rephrase: do you think that's possible in the first place?"

Darien thought for a moment, then shook her head. "I can't imagine. I'd guess he's been in contact with demons all around the world—"

"But why?" Sam asked. "If they're not a social species, why would he bother with contacting other demons if doing so didn't directly serve him?"

"Well, contacting a demon in Australia, or Ghana, or Switzerland wouldn't, that's true." Darien thought for a moment. "And, overall, lack of care and compassion for each other *is* what we've observed. With the exceptions of Silverskin and Ankle Tickler."

"Yeah, but even they had self-serving motives. Silverskin was looking for Ellie so he could kill her, and was clever enough to start helping other demons Awaken in case he couldn't, not because he actually *cared* about the other demons."

"Right. It was pure strategy."

"And Ankle Tickler ..." Sam shifted, frowning. "I think he was using your noble human sentiments to manipulate you into keeping tabs on Death for him, so *you* could take the fall when Death found out he was being spied on. And when I say 'noble human sentiments,' I really do mean noble. Don't take that the wrong way."

Darien shook her head. "I won't. We have bigger things to worry about. Like the fact that I'm afraid we haven't left him behind."

Sam's eyebrows raised. "What makes you think that?"

"Nothing concrete. But we *know* he can block communications from other demons to Death. What if that extends to *all* the demons' communications, and mine, too?"

Sam frowned.

"I don't expect to overhear everything Death says," Darien said. "But think about it. I've always heard his most powerful statements, like when he broadcast killing Wormwood. And I've always heard the ones that are physically close."

"Like Slubgob," Sam said. "And the squid."

"Exactly. And the Void literally just thought about something Death had told him, but I never even get an *inkling* that they'd talked to each other."

Sam frowned at her for a few more seconds, then started kneading the bridge of his nose with his fingertips. "I think we have to act like Ankle Tickler's here."

Bill spoke, and they both jumped. "And you can't find him, Darien?"

"No. Believe me, I wish I could, but he can hide his mind from me, too."

"Would you guess that he's on the *Redemption*?" Bill asked.

Darien exchanged a glance with Sam, who nodded. "Based on past experience, yes, I'd guess this is where he is. If he's here."

Bill grunted, then turned to Jessie. "Go tell the others to keep an eye out for a stowaway."

Jessie's stoic expression didn't change. He just nodded and headed toward the door.

"They probably won't find him," Darien said. "But if they do, he looks like a sick aye-aye."

"Or possum, if you haven't seen an aye-aye before," Sam added. "Furry, snarling, low to the ground, big ugly claws—"

"I'll just tell them to watch out for a demon wolverine," Jessie said.

"Sure," Sam said. "That works." He turned to Darien and shrugged, as if to say *how much worse can Ankle Tickler really get, anyway?*

Jessie shut the door behind him, and Darien tried to center herself. If she wasn't going to have the wool pulled over her eyes again, then she needed to be aggressive, tiredness and nausea aside. "I'm going to see where Death is."

"Don't tire yourself too much," Bill said.

"Remember, we still have a battle ahead of us," Sam added.

Darien waved them away. "I'm going to be an optimist, and believe there'll be time after all this to take a ... break ..."

A whisper of sound drifted through the air. Darien stilled.

"What is it?" Sam asked.

Darien shushed him, then closed her eyes and climbed her tower, reaching, searching, *singing, alluring and arresting and hungry, so hungry—*

Darien shot out of her seat, grabbing the closest rail for balance. "Something's coming. I didn't see it before now."

Sam loosened his pistol in its holster. "Where?"

"Close. I can't believe I didn't *see* it!" Seething, Darien closed her eyes. "*Ankle Tickler, I'm going to KILL you, I swear—*"

Another wave of sickness washed over her. She swayed, clinging to the railing, rage boiling in her stomach. *"Are* you *doing that—?"*

"Oh." Sam's mouth opened, the fight going out of his posture. "Darien ... do you hear that music?"

"Yes. Don't trust it. Let me try and find where ... it's ..."

Her mouth fell open as she locked on a cluster of demons less than half a mile away. And not just one. She concentrated on parsing them from each other. *Three, four, five ...*

She grabbed Sam's forearm to steady herself. "There are eight."

"*Eight?*" Sam and Bill said at the same time.

"Dar ..." Sam stared at her. Then, his gaze hardened. "Well, I guess we *know* something's interfering with your demon radar now."

"He has to be. How else would I miss eight freaking demons less than half a mile away who are intent on killing—" She winced as their intentions became even clearer. "*Drowning* as many of us as they possibly can—"

"Where and how, Darien?" Bill snapped.

"Just around this corner. There are rocks sticking up out of the water; they're on those."

She slipped into the head of one of the monsters, wishing it would turn around so she could catch a glimpse of one of its fellows and get an idea of what it looked like.

Come ON, girl. Death was forcing demons into sentience before they were ready. Ankle Tickler had mind-controlled Slubgob. *She'd* frozen the otter-demon. *I can make it turn its head.*

Darien put pressure on the thing. Surprise flashed through it, then an odd sense of ... was that betrayal? Then, its head turned. Trying to ignore the demon's rage and fear at being taken over that battered her from every side, Darien redoubled her efforts. *Faster, faster—*

She gasped. In front of her was the most beautiful man she'd ever seen. At first glance, he looked like Sam, but the more closely she looked, the less he actually resembled her husband. His features were perfectly symmetrical, his torso bare, the lines and muscles in it nothing short of artful, as if the creature had been rendered by a master sculptor with an eye for beauty far superior to any human's. His hair was thick and perfect, his eyes smoky and smoldering, and his skin glowed a dusky, warm gold, as if illuminated from within by a shaft of pure sunlight.

All in all, it was one of the most terrifying things Darien had ever seen.

She threw herself out of the demon's mind and crashed into Sam. He grabbed her shoulders, steadying her as she half-registered Bill's voice.

"—bear starboard, everyone bear starboard and keep watch to port. There are eight demons waiting on the rocks—"

"What are they, Darien?" Sam asked.

"I need details!" Bill shouted, gripping the radio mic in one hand and the wheel in the other.

Darien looked up into her husband's face—one eyebrow slightly more upturned than the other, the little scar on his left cheek, the flecks of green in his gunmetal eyes.

"They're sirens," she said.

"Mayday, mayday," Bill said. "Eight demons portside, posing as sirens. Be prepared—"

He cut off for a long moment. The singing grew louder, and Darien realized that what the demons had been thinking before was absolutely right. The music was captivating. Alluring. Beautiful in a way that she'd never heard before; it was more of an *experience* than just music—

"Charity?"

Darien froze. Sam looked up, his eyes wide with horror. They turned in time to see Bill stand, staring at something off to the left, vacant joy leeching into his expression.

"Charity," he repeated.

Then, he turned and rushed for the door.

Chapter Twenty-Five

Ellie tensed as Bill's crackly voice echoed through the radio again. "Mayday! Mayday! Eight demons portside, posing as sirens. Be prepared—"

The radio cut off. The four of them looked at each other.

"*Eight?*" Helen said. "And that Void-thing's after us, too?" She leaped to her feet and reached for her rifle. "Henry, take the wheel. No offense, Oliver."

Oliver stood. "None taken." He flashed a grin at his uncle. "I don't have your decades of experience."

"Watch it, kid," Henry grunted affectionately as he settled down behind the wheel.

Mouth dry, Ellie slung the quiver of makeshift fire arrows across her back, wondering how they had the fortitude to rib each other at a time like this. She reached for the compound bow she'd borrowed from the Calls as Helen spoke again. "Let's go, you two. Henry, drive straight."

"Anything for you, Helen."

Ellie followed Helen out the door and onto the lightly undulating deck of the boat. The humid, sea-salt air and cool breeze assaulted her immediately, and she shivered, grateful when Oliver closed the door behind them and squeezed her shoulder briefly. The roar of the engine seemed ten times louder out here; even Ellie could tell that the boat was responding differently under Henry's direction. It seemed lighter, more nimble as they raced across the water after the rest of the fleet. *If nothing else, at least his skill is reassuring.*

Ellie reached back for an arrow, nocking it as Helen dropped to one knee and racked the bolt of her rifle. "I've got four shots long-range before I have to reload or switch to my pistol. I don't know how useful they'll be in this context, I keep forgetting I'm not fighting creatures that follow the rules—"

"It's fine!" Oliver shouted. "Better to be prepared."

"Well, that's what I think." Helen slung the rifle across her back and pulled her pistol out of its holster. "Worst case scenario, this'll open some holes in them. And best case," Helen nodded at the bow—and the field tip nocked to it that practically dripped Sterno jelly, "you can light it up before it even gets here, Ellie."

"That'll probably depend on how old and smart they are," Ellie said. "If they're Death's Frankenstein demons, this shouldn't be too bad, but if not—"

A sound drifted to them on the breeze, and they fell silent.

There it was again: a thread of melody. It was coming from their left, rising over the tops of the pines, haunting, swelling, and ... *intriguing*.

"Right," Helen said. "Sirens. That makes sense."

Suddenly, the music swelled. Ellie dropped her bow, her mouth falling open at the sheer, incredible beauty of it. The melody was haunting, minor, as wild as the landscape around them, dissonances and tone clusters resolving perfectly into open chords, the voices blending seamlessly. There was no way it was just eight voices; it was a choir with a full symphony—it *had* to be. There was no comparing it to Dvorak, or Tchaikovsky, or Handel or Mozart or Vivaldi; there was no comparing it to *anything*. It put *Ode to Joy* and *Finlandia* to shame; it made *Carmina Burana* and *Brandenburg* sound childish.

She needed to get to it. She needed to *immerse* herself in it, let it wrap around her, fill her heart, her lungs, her soul.

She stepped forward.

***

"BILL!" Sam seized the captain by the lapels of his jacket.

"LET GO OF ME!"

"NO!" Sam cursed, struggling to keep his grip as Bill started to twist and struggle. "Darien, find Jessie, Luke—anyone who's sane enough to help me hold him down!"

Darien bolted for the door, staggering as the boat pitched. Sam stumbled, barely managing to keep his feet. "And somebody has to drive this thing—!"

Bill ripped from Sam's grasp, his rain jacket slippery as a fresh-caught trout. Thinking fast, Sam fell into a crouch as Bill straightened. Then, he threw himself at the stout man, tackling him around the middle with enough force to send them both crashing against the window. Sam caught a glimpse of something outside—*two* somethings, both very human, both seemingly naked.

Unless one of you is Darien, I don't have time for this, he thought, and turned his attention back to Bill. "I'm *not* letting you go out there. That's *not* your wife. You're going to drown."

Bill wrenched his arm free and backhanded Sam across the face. He crashed to the floor, stars bursting in front of his eyes, blinking as the world came back to him in oddly timed fits and spurts. Cold metal floor. Gray light. Gorgeous singing. Blood pulsing out of his nose, over his mouth. The sound of the door opening—

Sam cursed again and rolled onto his hands and knees, trying to get a grip on himself as the boat heaved and bucked underneath him. *Hell, now I have a concussion.*

Worry about it later.

He forced himself to his feet and staggered after Bill.

***

"Ellie!"

Oliver's voice cracked through the music like a fire alarm at a concert, and Ellie winced. "You're ruining it! Leave me alo—"

Something seized her around the waist and pulled her backward, away from the music, from life and light and peace and everything she'd ever wanted. She fought and thrashed.

"I'm not letting you go over!"

She knew that voice; she'd loved it once. Why, she had no idea. It was so harsh and grating. Another voice yelled her name, higher-pitched and even more annoying, but at least *it* wasn't trying to yank her away from the rapture she'd found.

"It's not worth dying for!" the first voice shouted. "Ellie—!"

BOOM!

The concussion from the explosion smashed into Ellie, and she reeled. Her ears rang, and the iron bar around her waist was so tight now she could barely breathe. Dazed, she looked around in time to see Helen lower her rifle. Rage sliced through Ellie at the sight; she opened her mouth to yell, "Why would you waste a shot? They're not solid!" But nothing came out, and if she was honest, she wasn't as mad at Helen for taking a shot as she was about not being able to hear the music anymore—

Of course, she realized. *That's why she did it.*

With that, reality invaded: the chilly wind slapping her in the face, the ringing in her ears, the seawater foaming beneath her feet as Oliver pulled her *back from the edge of the boat—*

Ellie shrieked and scrambled away, stopping only when she smacked into Oliver's chest. He said something, but she couldn't hear it over the ringing in her ears.

"*What?*" she asked, looking up at him.

He pointed out across the ocean, mouthing, "Siren!"

Adrenaline shot through Ellie. She whirled, looking for her bow—*there*! She dove for it, scrabbling across the rough deck, trying to keep an eye on the blur streaking across the water toward them.

POP! POP!

Ellie whirled, clutching the bow and fumbling for the lighter in her pocket. Oliver and Helen both had their pistols out and aimed, though she couldn't be sure who had fired. And honestly ... she wasn't sure why it was that important. Not when there was that transcendentally beautiful melody to listen to—

Ellie cursed. Her hearing was recovering, the song leaking back in. She ground her teeth, fighting against the music's allure as it tried to sink into her bones again, to hook her and drag her into the ocean.

Oliver and Helen. Fight for them.

Ellie turned.

And nearly dropped the bow again as she saw what they were up against.

It was the most beautiful woman she'd ever seen, the image of absolute perfection. Every photoshopped model Ellie had ever seen in magazines, on glossy ads in makeup aisles, every Hollywood-perfect actress she'd ever watched—the creature was it and more, as if she'd swallowed every social media filter and absorbed them into her hair, her eyes, her skin. And there was *plenty* of skin—she wore only a wrap around her perfectly-proportioned hips.

"Oliver, no! Wait 'til she gets here!" Helen yelled over the music, which was growing louder and louder. Ellie's head was starting to spin again; she barely heard Helen shout, "No, don't waste your shots—!"

POP! POP! POP!

The shots drove the music from Ellie's mind again. She shook off the stupor, then scrambled toward the back of the *Poor Buoy*—and its roaring engine. Planting herself as close to it as she could get, she nocked her arrow, lit it, and pulled until she reached full draw. Setting her sights on the unearthly woman, she waited for the right moment to let her arrow fly.

POP! POP!

The concussion from Oliver's pistol smashed into Ellie's ears again, but the siren only smiled.

"Stop wasting ammo!" Helen yelled.

Ellie cast a desperate glance in Oliver's direction. His stance, as always, was perfect, even on the rocking deck of a boat, his eyes fixed on the demon's face. She was laughing, tittering, toying with them, the sound spiralling out over the water. "Oliver, silly, *that's* not going to turn me on."

Some undefinable expression flashed across Oliver's face—guilt, maybe? Then, to Ellie's horror, he lowered his gun. His shoulders relaxed, his expression turning coy, almost flirty, and suddenly, Ellie felt sick.

"Well, what would turn you on, then?" he asked.

***

Darien pitched toward the railing of the *Redemption's* upper deck, managing to latch on before her momentum carried her into it—or worse, *over* it. "HELP! Naomi, Luke, Charlie, ANYONE! Bill's lost his mind!"

A shot roared through the air, then a second and a third. Someone—Luke—yelled something that Darien couldn't make out.

"LUKE!" Darien scrambled for the stairs. "HELP—!"

Motion blurred past Darien. On instinct, she ducked, clamping down on the chilled metal railing for balance. A siren weaved just above and to her left, pale-skinned and gorgeous even at a glance, her sleek red hair streaming out behind her. Its laughing, seductive gaze was trained on the cabin's windows, and Darien felt sickened. *Hurry up, while it's not interested in you.*

She turned.

And came face-to-face with the Sam-siren.

Darien lurched backward, feet sliding on the deck as she scrambled in her pockets for her weapons—

The boat listed under her feet. She lunged for the railing again, cursing as she realized she had to choose between her knife and lighter. Opting for the first, she fixed the Sam-creature with a defiant glare as she drew it out of its sheath. The demon's smile only widened. "Oh, come on, Dar."

She tried to slash across its chest, but it drew back until it was floating in the open air, still with that same laconic grin on its face. It was so like Sam, and yet ... so *not*.

"Darien. I *know* you—"

"You really don't."

The demon's smile faltered, and Darien felt a surge of satisfaction. *I'm not as easy prey as you thought, you—*

The cabin door burst open. Bill charged through, heading for the stairs.

"No!" Darien yelled. "BILL!"

She lurched after him, snatching desperately at his jacket, but the captain was too fast.

"LUKE!" she yelled again.

But at that moment, Sam appeared in the doorway—the *real* Sam. Blood stained his mouth, his chin, the front of his jacket, and all thoughts that didn't have to do with that lurid crimson cascade fled from Darien's mind. She swayed toward him as fast as she dared, keeping a tight grip on the railing and cursing her lack of sea legs.

"Where'd he go?" Sam asked.

"Did *Bill* do that to you?"

"Yeah, but he's not himself right now." Sam trotted across the deck and down the stairs. Darien followed as quickly as she could, caught between relief and unease when the Sam-siren didn't reappear.

***

"Oliver," Helen said sharply. But Ellie stood paralyzed; the betrayal had her by the throat, and she couldn't have spoken if she'd wanted to. Not that it mattered, because Oliver wouldn't look at either of them, anyway. He had eyes only for the goddess-like creature that was now drifting toward them, full hips swaying, perfect lips pursed into a pout.

"You're a clever man," she said. "I'm sure you'll figure it out."

"Come on over here and let me, then," Oliver purred.

Ellie felt sick; she glanced at Helen, who still had her pistol trained on the siren, waiting for the perfect shot.

Get it together. Trembling, she lit another arrow, drew it, fixed her sights on the demon, and waited. Rage started to build in her. She welcomed it; it made her strong, blocked out her devastation. *I'll kill you. I'll burn you until there's nothing left.*

As if the siren had overheard her thoughts, she flicked a contemptuous hand toward Ellie. "She won't last, Oliver. She'll grow old. She'll sag and wrinkle. But I'll stay young and beautiful forever. You can be with *me* forever."

Ellie's grip on the bow slackened, her heart twisting at the demon's words. At that moment, the music swelled again; it was so tempting to just take refuge in it, let herself drown in its beauty—

NO! Ellie shifted closer to the *Poor Buoy's* roaring motor, so close she could feel the vibration from it in her toes, her teeth, in her left hand, still wrapped around the cold metal frame of the compound bow.

"Come on," she muttered, shifting on the boat's heaving deck. The compound bow had a relief mechanism that took the bulk of the weight once the string was at full draw, allowing her to hold it almost indefinitely. But that left her unable to defend herself for a few crucial seconds if the siren was faster than she looked.

"I would like that," Oliver murmured. "To be with you forever."

His voice was low and velvety, and it took everything Ellie had not to just let her arrow fly. The siren's smile widened. Then, she nodded toward Helen and Ellie. "Help me get rid of them. Of everyone else on this boat. Then take me somewhere, Oliver. Anywhere you want, as long as it's just us."

Oliver stood very still for a moment. Then, he turned and started toward Helen. "Give me your pistol."

"Oliver, you can't be serious."

He stopped inches in front of her, towering and menacing, his voice a snarl. "I am serious. Give it to me now or go overboard."

Helen stared at him, white-faced.

Oliver stared at her, then spoke slowly. "Your *pistol*, Helen."

Helen blinked, looking for a moment like she was going to fight him. Then, she lowered her gun. Oliver snatched it, then tossed it toward the cabin door. "Your rifle, too."

"Yes, Oliver," the siren purred as Helen complied. Oliver slung Helen's rifle across his back.

The siren gestured at Ellie. "Disarm her next."

Oliver whirled and stalked toward Ellie, his face set in cold, rigid lines. "Give me your bow. And that arrow, too. I know you'll light it on fire the first chance you get."

Ellie stood rooted to the spot as the engine roared beside her. She wasn't willing to drop the bow, but Oliver was strong enough—and armed—that what she *wanted* didn't matter. A sick, horrible thought occurred to her: should she turn the bow on him? Try and incapacitate him so she and Helen might have a chance to kill the creature?

His eyes found hers, and she could have sworn that underneath their icy madness there was a reservoir of pain.

I can't hurt him, she realized.

She lowered the bow. "Don't do this, Oliver."

He winked.

Winked.

"Drop it all!" he snarled, his voice so harsh that Ellie immediately wondered if she'd imagined it. "Now!"

Hoping she hadn't read him wrong, Ellie obeyed. Fear boiled in her stomach as the bow clattered to the deck. *He's never let you down before. Trust him.*

She slipped the little lighter—which she *hadn't* dropped—into the pocket of her windbreaker.

Oliver kicked the bow toward the cabin, where it settled next to Helen's pistol. Then, he strode toward the siren, who hovered over the water about ten feet from the boat's edge, and held out a hand. "Come to me. Please."

The siren cocked her head, her eyes amused. "Throw them overboard first."

***

Everything was chaos when Darien set foot on the lower deck of the *Redemption*. Luke and Jessie wrestled Bill; the captain was fighting like a man possessed, thrashing and yelling. Above the ocean, maybe thirty feet out, floated the pale-skinned siren, crooning Bill's name.

"Hey!" Sam took off across the deck. "HEY! NO ONE IS DRIVING THIS BOAT!"

"Find Naomi!" Luke narrowly dodged Bill's left hook. "Or Charlie! We can't let him drown himself!"

"Go help them!" Darien yelled at Sam. "I'll find someone!"

Sam nodded, then charged toward the scrum. Darien turned and careened toward the other side of the boat. It was big, sure, but not *that* big; she should be able to find them quickly. She rounded the tower the cabin was set into just in time to see Charlie stab something huge and flaming into the Sam-demon. It erupted with a scream. Darien threw a hand up to shield her eyes as Charlie fell backward, landing hard on his rear. The demon flared brighter, then started to dim. Darien started toward it, squinting at the lean, feminine figure she could now make out on the other side.

"Charlie!" Naomi emerged through the roiling smoke and flaring sparks that were all that was left of the monster. "Are you okay?"

"Yeah," Charlie panted, picking himself up off the deck. "Man, those things *burn*!"

Darien broke into an awkward run. "HEY!"

"Darien!" Naomi started toward her. "Where's the other demon? Where's Luke?"

"The other one's trying to lure Bill overboard. It looks like Charity. Luke, Sam, and Jessie are all trying to restrain him. Which means no one's driving the boat, so one of you two needs to—"

"I've got it!" Charlie blew past her, moving faster than Darien knew she'd *ever* be able to on this bobbing, swaying monstrosity. In a few quick steps, he was up the stairs and out of sight. Darien could swear the boat steadied a second later.

Naomi came toward her, picking up … Darien squinted at the makeshift weapon in her hand. It looked like someone had duct-taped a plumbing torch to a harpoon, then wired some mechanism to make it so the torch ignited with the press of a button near the handle.

Naomi held it up. "I can't believe this worked. Charlie's a damn genius."

Darien choked back a sudden, insane urge to laugh. "Let's get that to Luke, Sam, and Jessie."

Naomi broke into a jog. "Follow me."

Chapter Twenty-Six

Ellie's mouth went dry as she stared down the siren, her stomach tying itself into a knot. *This is it.* Even if Oliver was acting—and she still wasn't fully convinced he was—this is where it would all unravel. Oliver glanced at them, his face hard as stone, and Ellie's gut constricted even more.

"They're strong," he said.

"You're stronger."

"Yes." Oliver's voice was hoarse with need, and Ellie felt it clear into her bones. "But they'll struggle. And if Henry comes out here, the three of them will beat me. But if I have your help, we can throw *them* overboard, then take care of Henry together. And then it can just be the two of us. I know a place—I'll take you there. I'll do anything, *everything* you want."

The siren gazed at him, ignoring the shots and screams echoing across the water from the other boats. Then, the corners of her mouth tugged up into a satisfied smile. "Anything and everything. Your word, Oliver."

"You have it."

The siren's smile widened. Her eyes locked on Ellie's. "Her first."

Oliver turned his back on the siren, his eyes so dark that Ellie shuddered. "Done."

***

"BILL! KNOCK IT OFF!"

"DAD! STOP—"

"It's no use!" Sam bellowed, his heart twisting at the desperation in Jessie's voice. Was this how his dad had been at the end, too? He shoved the thought aside. "We can't talk him down! We need to find a way to kill it!"

"How?" Luke yelled. "That thing's too smart to come any closer, not when she can incapacitate us from there, and they're fast enough to keep up—"

Bill let out a roar and redoubled his efforts, pulling them all off balance. Sam's head swam at the sight of the frigid water half a dozen yards below, half-formed memories crashing through his mind of Oliver's desperate thrashing, the horrible gasping sounds he'd made as the cold water sucked the life and strength out of his body.

Luke cursed again. "He's gonna get us all killed—"

"Let's tie him up!" Jessie yelled. "Tie him to the stair railing!"

"Fine!" Luke barked.

Together, they started hauling Bill backward. Sam hadn't been to many rodeos, but in that moment, he felt a distinct kinship with the men who wrestled squirming, writhing steers to the ground for a living. What he was doing felt a lot like that.

Footsteps clunked across the deck behind them—at least two pairs. Sam managed to duck another wild punch from Bill, then twisted to look. Relief swept over him at the sight of Darien and Naomi pounding toward them, the latter carrying what looked like some strange enmeshment of a harpoon and a plumbing torch.

"Naomi!" Luke hollered. "Find some rope!"

Naomi pivoted and tore off in a different direction.

"Is anyone driving the boat?" Sam hollered at Darien.

"Charlie!"

Sam gritted his teeth as Bill let out another crazed roar. "Okay, just stay clear! I don't want him to hit you!"

Darien gave a curt nod. Then, she retreated to the side of the boat, closed her eyes, and went stock-still as she sent her mind powers snaking toward the siren. Or at least, the last part was what Sam *assumed* she was doing; he was too busy shoving Bill against the railing of the stairs to actually check.

"Naomi!" Luke yelled.

Naomi burst back into view, clutching a thick coil of rope. "Here!"

Luke tried to snatch it, but Bill started thrashing again.

"On it!" Jessie snatched the rope from his aunt, then started winding it around his father. "Sorry, Dad!"

"Get his arms down!" Luke yelled.

Sam grabbed Bill's meaty forearm and shoved for all he was worth. The captain thrashed and bellowed, but Jessie kept looping, and before long, Bill was immobile. The three of them stood back, panting, and Sam wondered if the others felt like he did: both relieved and guilty at the sight of Bill trussed up in such an undignified way. Sam liked him. Respected him. The man deserved better.

Luke smacked Jessie on the back. "Good idea, Jess."

"You can thank Mrs. Freese for making us read *The Odyssey*. And the best part is I don't remember the rest of it, so I won't even accidentally spawn any Greek monsters."

Sam and Luke both chuckled. A smile cracked across Jessie's face. He glanced to his side, almost as if expecting to see another person there ... and his face fell.

Guilt shuddered through Sam. He turned away, mumbling something about checking on Darien as Bill continued to bellow. Trying his best to ignore it, he shouldered past him and toward where she stood, silhouetted against the ocean with her back to him. He stopped for a moment, uncertain. Then, he crept toward her, grasped the railing at her side, and looked down into her face. He'd been right; her eyes *were* closed. But for the gentle rise and fall of her chest, she could have been a statue. But not the languid, Greek kind. More of a study in tension.

Sam stared at her for a moment, then looked out across the water at the siren. It had closed half the distance between itself and where they stood on the *Redemption*, and was watching ...

Him.

***

Ellie's mouth opened in shock as the siren charged. She was fast; in seconds, she'd sped through the side of the boat and onto the deck, her face twisted with naked, ugly greed. A shriek tore from Ellie's throat and she scrambled back, but she wasn't fast enough. The siren's graceful, frigid hand clamped around her wrist with viselike force. Ellie kicked out, struggling as it dragged her toward the *Poor Buoy's* side. She plunged her hand into her windbreaker's pocket, groping for the lighter, but the demon grabbed her hand and twisted until she could feel all the little bones in her wrist start to pop and grind.

Terror engulfed her as they pitched toward the side of the boat, but her scream was lost in the seething roar of the ocean. They were so close now that the mist thrown up by their speed flecked her face. Adrenaline surged through her veins; she struck out at the demon, kicking and stomping, half-blinded by the salty spray. *I'M NOT GOING TO GET MURDERED BY A SOCIAL MEDIA FILTER—*

"He wouldn't have stayed anyway," the demon laughed. "I know what you want, but eternity's a myth, and only pathetic people believe in it—"

BOOM

The demon's sultry voice became a high-pitched squeal that Ellie barely heard over the ringing in her ears. She ripped her arms free and scrambled backward as the siren writhed. Helen stepped up beside Ellie, clutching her smoking rifle, a savage expression on her usually kind face. "How's that for pathetic?"

"Oliver!" The siren's body contorted. "Oliver, help me—"

"MOVE!" Oliver roared.

Something crashed into Ellie, sending her stumbling away, and in the chaos, it took a split second to realize it had been *Oliver* who had shoved her. She spun back around, gripping her lighter, ignoring her throbbing wrists. But Oliver had already reached the siren. The sun flashed off something in his fist—his knife blade, Ellie realized.

And then he moved so fast and ferociously that she didn't understand what had happened until the demon's hand thudded to the ground at her feet.

The creature screamed, sticky, tarlike blood oozing out of the stub of her arm, and Ellie saw her chance. She clicked the lighter on and lunged. The little flame spluttered in the wind but held on long enough to graze the thing's mangled wrist. Fire shot up its arm—*underneath* its arm—exploding through its skin in long, ropy cords.

She snatched Oliver's arm and tugged him away, yelling at Helen to get back. They rushed to the back of the boat as the demon erupted into a fireball. Ellie looked away, heat searing the back of her neck. When it faded, she turned, wide-eyed, to see a pile of smoking embers in the middle of the deck.

The boat slowed suddenly, pitching them all forward, and the cabin door burst open. Henry charged through. "Are you all okay?"

"Yeah, we're fine," Helen said as she picked herself back up. "You gotta get back in there and drive, though, or we're going to be left behind."

Henry blinked at her. "You know how hard it was to hear the shooting and the screaming and keep going anyway? The fireball was the last straw—!"

"Uh ... Ellie?"

She looked up at the sound of Oliver's quiet voice. His eyes were fixed on her; tentatively, he held out a hand. She took it, wincing as he helped her to her feet, but relieved that her wrist didn't seem to be broken. Bruises she could deal with. She swallowed, then met his eyes again, hoping she'd find some kind of reassurance in them. He held her stare, horror lingering in his expression, and Ellie's heart twisted.

At this point, the physical bruises were the easy ones.

"I'll come with you, Henry," Helen said. She fixed Ellie and Oliver with a stare. "You kids come in when you're ready. But make it quick; we *are* in a dicey situation."

With that, she closed the door behind her.

A few mildly destabilizing strains of music echoed over their heads, leaving Ellie feeling lightheaded and a little stupid, but the shots and screams coming from the other boats seemed to take away most of its power. Oliver stepped up in front of her and took her hands. "Ellie. I'm so sorry. It was an act, I swear—"

Something in Ellie broke, tears spilling down her cheeks. "You scared me so bad, Oliver. You ... you ..."

Oliver let out a big, shaky sigh and held her more tightly. "She looked so much like you. And it gave me an idea—"

Ellie snorted. "Yeah, I *wish* I looked like that."

Oliver froze, and Ellie felt her face redden. *What a stupid thing to say right now.* She pulled away. "Sorry, that was dumb. Let's get back ... inside ..."

The look on Oliver's face stopped her. He was gazing at her, a slight crease between his eyebrows, looking both confused and a little heartbroken.

"What?" she asked.

Oliver didn't immediately respond. Instead, he brushed the remnants of a tear off her cheek. "*She* was imitating *you*."

"To try and seduce *you*."

"Because I'm wildly attracted to *you*." He tapped her chest gently, just below the hollow of her throat, and smiled. "I just want you, Ellie. For as long as you'll let me have you. You never, ever have to worry about—" He jerked his head toward the still-steaming pile of embers, "—*that* or anything like it. Ever."

Something in Ellie seemed to settle. "I know. I trust you."

He cupped her cheek in his hand, then lowered his forehead to hers. "I don't know where this is going to go, but I know where I *want* it to go. And aging, kids—if you want kids, that is—"

Ellie laughed. "A question for another day."

Oliver smiled. "The point is, whatever challenges we face—sickness, injury—it doesn't matter. You're it for me. And you're beautiful."

Ellie swallowed the lump in her throat. Then, she kissed him, tasting the salt of the ocean on his lips, leaning into his warm hand that still cupped the side of her face. A siren-scream shattered through the air, landing them both back in reality. Oliver grabbed her hand. "Come on. Let's go see if anyone else has had any luck."

***

Sam glowered at the siren as it started to change, unsurprised when its skin turned a beautiful dusky tan, darkening its hair from root to tip. And though it was still too far away to hit with anything but a bullet or very well-shot arrow, Sam saw its facial structure change. It rounded, softened, the eyes, eyebrows, and lips growing larger, the proportions of its body shifting to ones that were all too familiar. For a moment, he stared at the imitation of Darien that now drifted over the water. Then, he raised his eyebrows. "Nice try."

The siren grinned as another loud BANG sounded off somewhere to the left, then started to drift toward them, revolving as she went. "Like what you see, Sam?"

"Sure do." He returned the siren's grin. "That's why I married *her*."

The corner of Darien's mouth twitched in a smile.

Then, the siren buckled.

Sam's jaw dropped as the creature folded in on herself, mouth wide in a silent wail. What looked like a black *rip* opened in her chest, widening even as he watched. Then, she simply evaporated into dark ribbons. Just like Slubgob had.

Darien drew in a shuddering gasp and swayed. Sam put an arm around her waist. "Hey. Hey, I've got you."

"Thanks," she mumbled.

Sam looked over at where Bill was still tied to the staircase, blinking like he'd just woken from a deep sleep. Jessie hovered next to him, looking uncertain.

"I think you can untie him, Jess!" Luke shouted. Jessie flashed him a thumbs-up, then turned back to Sam and Darien. "Did *you* do that to her?"

Darien swept a few tendrils of her long, dark ponytail out of her face. "I ... *think* so?"

"You *think* ...?" Sam asked. "How do you not know?"

"Because I *was* digging around in there. I *was* seeing through her eyes, and then tearing her apart from the inside like ..." She shuddered, and Sam didn't push her to finish *that* uncomfortable comparison. "But here's the problem, Sam. I still don't know where Ankle Tickler is, or what he's doing. For all I know, what just happened was all him."

"Why would he help you kill his own kind, though?" Sam asked.

"I have no idea."

"I don't think he helped you. I think that was all you, Dar."

"Yeah, but I still don't even know why he even helped me in the first place!" She closed her eyes, clearly frustrated.

Sam folded his arms. "I get it. It's hard to predict someone when you don't know what's motivating them."

"Yeah." Darien put her back to the railing. "In any case, I'm all but sure he's here. There are other demons around apart from the sirens, but I can't seem to get to them. It's like I just bounce right off. But, I can still get a perfect lock on Death whenever I want. So what does that tell us?"

"That Ankle Tickler's interfering."

She nodded. "I'm still a pawn. And I really don't like it." She paused, looking deeply bothered. "Anyway, let's go see if Charlie can get us close to any of the other sirens so I can take them out."

Sam studied his wife. Her face looked sallow, and dark circles ringed her eyes, but she'd looked that way for days now. It was becoming increasingly difficult to distinguish between dangerous exhaustion and regular exhaustion. "Give it to me straight, Dar. Do you have the strength for that?"

"Yes."

"And the baby's ...?"

"Still fine. Healthy and happy."

Sam looked down into her face for a moment longer, worry gnawing at his insides like termites in an old wooden shack. Then, he nodded. "Okay, then. Let's go."

They started toward the stairs, where a freshly untied Bill was rubbing his arms, talking to Jessie. The kid's face was so red, it matched his windbreaker.

"Hey," Darien said quietly.

"Yeah?"

"Did the siren impersonate me?"

"Yeah."

Darien chuckled. "Funny. The one Charlie killed on the other side of the boat looked like you."

Sam grinned. "I'm flattered."

"You should be, you Adonis—"

"Another one down!"

They stopped and looked up in time to see Charlie burst out of the cabin.

"Yeah, Darien just killed the female!" Sam hollered up at him.

Charlie grinned. "Excellent—Naomi, relay the news! Marty's crew out of Nanwalek just killed another one, too, so we're down to three."

"Good riddance," Bill said. His cheeks were pink, but he cleared his throat and looked back and forth between Jessie, Luke, and Sam. "Thanks."

Luke cuffed him on the shoulder. "Somebody has to save you from yourself."

Bill just shook his head, then turned back to the cabin. "Charlie, how far out—*Charlie*?"

Sam looked up at the top deck and his heart stopped. It was completely, horribly empty.

Darien stared stupidly at the place where Charlie had been. The roar of the engine cut, a few weak notes of siren-song swirling in to take its place, but they paled into insignificance compared to the scream that rose from the cabin—Naomi's scream. "MAN OVERBOARD TO STARBOARD!"

Luke moved first. He dashed toward the railing, Bill and Jessie on his heels. Darien and Sam exchanged one horrified glance, then followed. The *Redemption* was heaving in earnest now that they'd lost their momentum, and as Sam drew ahead, Darien once again cursed how slow she was.

"There!" Jessie pointed down into the heaving water.

"Don't take your eyes off him!" Luke turned and barrelled for the life preserver hanging on the side of the cabin, but Naomi had gotten there first. Darien scrambled toward the railing next to Jessie. There wasn't much she could do, but at least she could be another set of eyes on Charlie. The water ebbed and swelled underneath them, foam bubbling across its top from where the bow had sliced it into a wake. It was difficult to see *anything* in that heaving blue abyss; she couldn't make out—

"No!" Jessie yelled. "I've lost him!"

Movement in the water.

Adrenaline surged through Darien. She opened her mouth to shout that she had eyes on Charlie, but the sound died in her throat as the thing she was looking at .. *undulated*. It rose closer to the surface, coiling and shifting, and Darien's jaw dropped. It was huge, long, and faintly greenish, the sun and the choppy water throwing shifting fractals of light across its back. As quickly as it had come, it whipped under the boat and was gone.

The hair on the back of Darien's neck stood straight up. "Guys!"

But her yell was lost in the clatter of Naomi and Luke reaching the railing, the latter now clutching the life preserver. "Where is he, Jessie?" he bellowed.

"He's gone!" The teen's voice was high, panicked. "I can't—"

"You yelled, Darien!" Luke cried. "Do you see him?"

"No!" She jerked away from the railing, eyes darting all around as the feeling of being watched settled over her. "There's something else in the water—!"

"THERE!" Bill bellowed. "There's his arm!"

The captain snatched the life preserver and threw it. Hope spiked through Darien, so intense that it was almost overwhelming. They couldn't lose another crew member, they just *couldn't*, especially not to whatever was—

"GRAB IT, CHARLIE!" Bill roared.

Luke leaned so hard over the railing that Darien was afraid he'd pitch himself over. "REACH! DON'T GIVE UP!"

Sam sidestepped Luke and grabbed the life preserver's rope, tense, ready to haul back. Darien readied herself, just in case they needed one more person. Just in case there was something she could do.

The next few seconds were a lifetime.

Then, Bill's shoulders slumped. Luke pressed a hand to his forehead, looking both stunned and stricken.

"He can't be gone," Jessie gasped. "He can't be gone."

Bill just shook his head. Darien swayed, clutching the railing for support. She bowed her head but kept her eyes open as she scanned the water's surface, praying that she—that *anyone*—could see Charlie, that he wasn't really—

Her head snapped up. The thing in the water.

"There's something else down there!" she yelled. "We need to get off the deck!"

Bill swore. Then he whirled, grabbed Jessie by the arm, and hauled him toward the cabin steps. "Everybody inside, now!"

Jessie's face was pasty, his eyes wild. "We're not going to—?"

"There's nothing we can do, Jess," Bill said gruffly. "He couldn't swim."

"Couldn't—*how* could he not swim when he spent so much time on a fishing boat?" Sam spluttered as they reached the ladder.

"Didn't want to linger, if he fell in," Luke muttered from over their shoulders. "Wanted it to be over quickly."

Darien's skin crawled at the sheer morbidity of that sentence. It was still crawling as she followed Bill and Jessie up the stairs, and as Bill spoke. "Describe what you saw, Darien."

"It looked like a giant snake," she said. A blast of warmth enveloped her as she entered the cabin, but she barely noticed. "I was looking for Charlie, and I saw it rise up almost to the surface, then swim underneath the boat."

"I figured," Luke said. "He wouldn't have fallen like that on his own. He was too good."

The burly fisherman pulled the door closed behind him with a solid *thunk*. Darien stared at it, shock at the sheer brutality—the finality—of Charlie's death rolling over her in waves.

"No one leaves the cabin."

Bill's barked order brought Darien back to earth. Fury bubbled in the pit of her stomach; she turned toward one of the bench seats along the wall, ignoring the sharp pains in her sides as her muscles protested.

"Sam," she said, "come sit by me so I can pull myself out if I need to."

His forehead creased. "Pull yourself out ...?"

"I'm going after the sea snake. I'm going to kill it."

Chapter Twenty-Seven

Darien wriggled her way into the sea snake's mind just in time to see it hit the water. A body thrashed through the darkness in front of it.

"Can you tell where it is?"

Bill's voice catapulted Darien outside of the monster's mind. Head spinning, she clutched at Sam's shoulder to steady herself.

"Any landmarks?" the captain threw over his shoulder from where he sat at the wheel.

"Give me a second," Darien gritted out. She shut out both the noise and her nagging worry that she was opening herself up to Ankle Tickler by doing this. Or worse, Death.

What else can you do, though? You can't not help.

So she sent her mind winging back toward the sea snake. The creature was moving so fast that it took Darien a second to catch up. She locked on, let herself be drawn in, and then *she was spearing through the ocean, reveling in the warm flow of the water over her scales, looking for another food-creature to drag down so she could devour its terror. There—the vibration of a machine. She streaked toward it, poking her head out of the water, and yes, there was a perfect target. It was scrambling for safety, but it wouldn't get there in time. Her jaws opened, and she prepared to leap,* and Darien caught a glimpse of the words *Kenai Princess* stamped across the boat's side.

"It's after the *Kenai Princess*!"

Bill snatched the mic. "*Kenai Princess*, the snake's coming for you! Repeat, the snake's—"

Darien threw herself at the monster again, because maybe she could stop it before—

It hit. The human catapulted off the side of the boat with no sound. They never did make a sound; she hit them too hard. She circled around the prey as it crashed into the water, its limbs locking, muscles stiffening. The boat's roar stopped, leaving room for her to feel smaller, more subtle vibrations. The fast, uneven beat of her prey's heart. The angry buzzing of other boats as they whizzed over the water's surface. Small, metallic thumps beating out a desperate rhythm just overhead—footsteps. Others were coming to help this one.

She knew she needed to move on, to delay and incapacitate as many as possible. But she hesitated. There was so much prey, right here, right above her head—

Fury exploded through Darien, blowing all her exhaustion and fear to the farthest reaches of her mind. *Oh no you don't.* She seized the snake's consciousness. Then—like she had with the siren—she started to rip at the threads that bound its mind together, tearing and mutilating—

Pain.

Shock rippled through her. She twisted in the water and streaked away from the prey, trying to outrun the agony—

Darien gasped as the connection broke. She opened her eyes to see Sam kneeling in front of her, clutching both her hands in his. She shivered; suddenly, they were the only part of her that was warm.

"Dar?" Sam asked.

"What's its status?" Luke said at almost the same time.

"Lost the connection," Darien stammered. "She ran for it when I tried to kill her."

A wave of tiredness hit, but Darien did her best to push it away. She grasped Sam's hands and leaned forward. "I think I can find her again—"

"Dar." Sam took her by the shoulders. It was only then that she realized how hard she was trembling. "If it's running away, give yourself a little break." He glared up at the others. "Don't you think, guys?"

"Yes," Naomi said emphatically. Jessie—still looking shell-shocked—managed a shrug. But Bill and Luke exchanged a glance.

"How much energy does it take to keep an eye on it?" Bill asked.

Sam's lips turned down in an angry frown, but Darien overrode him before he could speak. "Not much. Honestly," she added when Sam opened his mouth. "It's not that hard. I'm not trying to be a hero."

Bill gave a curt nod. "Do that, then, and warn us if it's coming back."

He grabbed the mic. "Fleet, the sea snake is taking a breather. Full speed ahead to Portlock." He hesitated for a moment, then added, "Stop for nothing. Plan to beach."

The next twenty minutes were the tensest of Oliver's life.

The dread simmering in his belly started to boil when the beach came into view ... and with it, the *Tide Chaser*, which bobbed forlornly, right where they'd left her. Guilt rose in his throat, so sharp he could hardly breathe. He draped an arm around Ellie's shoulders and pulled her close, yet another aftershock of guilt rocking through him at what he'd just done to *her*. She shrank against him, her ribcage rising and falling against his in a tight, controlled rhythm, and he found himself trying to match his own breathing to it.

It worked. Sort of.

"Scannon, heads up."

Oliver's head rose as Bill's voice came over the radio with the fifth warning in the last ten minutes.

"The Snake is circling you. Roger?"

"Roger that," came the reply, and Oliver thought he might have recognized the voice of the lady who owned one of the diners near the harbor. *"We're all crammed in the cabin—"*

The radio went dead. Oliver's jaw tightened, Ellie's hand twitched in his, and Helen and Henry exchanged a scared glance. But then the radio fuzzed again. *"Felt a big bump! I think we're okay, but it might be hitting boats now."*

"Makes sense," Helen grumbled. "We're minutes from beaching. They're probably getting desperate, for better or for worse."

Oliver looked out the windshield, and his stomach jolted like the Snake had rammed it. The beach was so close that he could make out individual branches of the spruce trees wreathing its pale sand. He swallowed. "I'm afraid the fight's only beginning."

Helen twisted in her seat to glare at him. "Listen, you. Slubgob's dead, which means I can be an optimist again. So by damn, I'm going to."

Oliver held up his hands, grinning despite himself. "Fair enough. Don't let me stop you."

Henry patted Helen on the knee, chuckling. "That's my girl. Oliver?"

"Yeah?"

"Grab my binoculars and see if you can see anything waiting for us in the trees."

Oliver rose, grabbed the optics from where they hung from a hook behind Henry's head, and knelt on the hard metal floor between his aunt and uncle. Pressing them to his eyes, he fiddled with the focus until the beach—and everything on it—sharpened. As prepared as he thought he was, his heart still clenched again at the sight of the *Tide Chaser*. The tide had come in and out since he'd last been here, but the boat was still moored fast. An ache rose in Oliver's throat. That was Jordan's doing. He was—had been—the best of them when it came to all things boating.

"Anything, Oliver?"

He panned across the sand, peered into the trees and the bushy, verdant undergrowth, their tips bloodred with fall color. Mist swirled around and through the trees, thickening where the mountain swelled upward. He lowered the binoculars and shook his head. "Nothing on the beach, or just inside the trees. That I can see anyway."

"I don't believe that for a second," Helen muttered.

"What happened to that optimism?" Henry asked dryly.

Helen grunted. "Touche."

Oliver pressed the binoculars to his face again, scanning every clearing and hole in the trees he could find. He pulled back again, shaking his head. "There's a lot of fog higher up. They could be hiding anything in there."

Oliver heard the rustle of clothing behind him as Ellie stood. A second later, her hand grasped his shoulder. He looked up to see her leaning over him, squinting at the beach. Oliver turned forward again, grateful for her comforting touch. "Any thoughts, Ellie?"

She huffed out a humorless laugh—the kind she only used when she was trying to cover up how terrified she was. "Plenty. None of them good, unfortunately."

He squeezed her hand. "You don't have to—"

"We've been over this." She looked down at him, her expression a quintessentially Ellie mix of fear and blazing determination. "Yes, I do."

Love for her swelled so strongly in Oliver's chest that he thought it might crack his heart. He held her gaze for a moment, letting himself float in the depths of those gray-blue eyes, the color of the Alaskan sky but so much warmer. Then, he nodded. "I'm with you."

Helen turned and laid her hand over Ellie's. "We're all with you."

Ellie smiled, but the corners of it trembled. "Thank you." She cleared her throat. "We know we have three sirens left. And we know the Void is somewhere behind us, and that it will catch up fairly quickly once we stop moving."

Oliver narrowed his eyes; was that a flash of movement he'd seen in the bushes to the left? He pressed the binoculars to his face again.

"Oliver?" Henry rumbled. "You see something?"

Oliver examined the undergrowth, but nothing moved again. "No."

"Okay. I'm calling it in, then." Henry raised the mic. "Fleet, *Poor Buoy* speaking. As you're coming in, be aware of the beached boat on the far north end of the beach. We see no sign of anything else, but be on your guard."

Henry lowered the mic, then shrugged. "Not sure what else to tell them."

"I don't think there is much," Helen said.

Something in his aunt's voice made Oliver look more closely at her, and he realized ... she was trembling, too.

Henry glanced over at her. "You all right?"

Helen barked a laugh. "Henry, I don't think *any* of us are feeling all right. The fact that I'm a little extra shivery doesn't let me off the hook."

"Yeah, well ..." Ellie clapped a hand over Helen's shoulder. "We're all with you. We'll shiver together."

Helen looked up at Ellie. Then, she laughed, and Oliver couldn't help it. He chuckled, too.

***

"Updates, Darien?"

Sam gritted his teeth; it was taking all he had not to lash out at Bill, scream at him to leave his wife alone and let her rest. He knew she was pushing herself too hard and trying to hide it. He knew it was necessary—she'd already saved lives. But this prolonged battle with the Snake was visibly taking it out of her.

Not that anyone around her saw it other than him. She was too good at hiding it.

Her eyes snapped open. "*Scannon's* right. The Snake is hitting boats now. She's hit three, though it doesn't look like she's big enough to do any real damage. Her goal is mostly to scare people. Demoralize us."

"Psychological warfare," Luke muttered.

Sam folded his arms. "No one does it better than they do."

270

"She'll still snatch people off boats if she can, though," Darien added. "So tell everyone to stay in their cabins."

"Any idea what she'll do when we're in shallower water?" Luke asked.

"Unfortunately, no."

"Well, getting out's a risk we have to take, obviously," Naomi said. "We can't just beach and then stay in the boats."

"I'll tell everyone to get on dry land as quickly as possible." Bill picked up the mic, but Sam barely heard what he said. He was busy staring down the beach like he could weaponize his hatred of it. Henry's radio message minutes earlier was still correct; there was no sign of anything living there. But he knew better than to believe the evidence of his own eyes at this point.

"Darien," Luke said. "Could you do a scan of the beach for us?"

"Already on it," she murmured, bowing her head again.

Feeling useless, Sam put his arm around her shoulders. She didn't say anything, just leaned into him, relaxing. Just as quickly, though, she tensed again, and her head shot up. "There's a big, nasty demon about halfway up the canyon on the north side—I assume that's the Gatekeeper."

Sam swallowed. "That's where he was yesterday."

"Okay. Then there are several more—four more—scattered across the north side of the canyon. I think they're newly Awakened. They don't feel as sophisticated or, well, *formed* as the others."

"How sure are you about that?" Bill asked.

"Reasonably," Darien said. "Now that I know what to look for, the differences between the older ones who were allowed to form naturally and the ones Death has forced to Awaken are pretty obvious."

Bill nodded. "Okay. What else?"

"There are two hiding just out of sight in the trees by the beach. I can't get a good look at them, but they feel older and more experienced. More like Death, and the Void."

Luke cursed softly. "And that thing's still behind us, right?"

"Yes," Darien said. "He's coming fast, too. I think we'll be lucky to get ten minutes without him."

"Boris is convinced that one's unkillable," Bill said. "But I think we can find a way."

Sam snorted. "You're a bunch of unhinged Alaskan bush people with homemade flamethrowers, Molotov cocktails, and a serious vendetta. If anyone can find a way, it's you."

Luke chuckled, and Jessie and Bill grinned. Even Naomi cracked a smile. Sam felt his heart soften a little toward the captain. They *were* all in this together, and they'd just lost Charlie, and that swirly little demon-cloud switching between the six of them probably wasn't helping anything—

"Darien, can you see if you can find Death?" Bill asked.

Sam's gut clenched again.

But Darien just said, "Yep."

She closed her eyes and leaned against Sam again, more heavily this time. He kissed her hair. *If I can't take your burden, I can at least help you bear it.* For a moment, everything was quiet. Then, Darien's breath hitched. She tipped her head back against his shoulder, gasping in a breath as her eyes flew open. "He's close. I don't know the landmarks around here, but—"

"Describe what you saw," Naomi said.

"Mountains," Darien said. "He's over land now, over mountains high enough that there's snow on the top, and glaciers. But it seemed like he was coming off of those. The land in front of him was green and forested. Still fairly mountainous, though."

Luke and Naomi exchanged a glance.

"Do you think he's in Kachemak Bay State Park?" Naomi asked.

"That would match his trajectory." Luke swept his hat off, rubbing his salt-and-pepper hair. "That doesn't give us much time."

"No, it doesn't," Bill growled. "Luke, any thoughts on our plan of attack now that we know where the enemy is?"

Luke gazed toward the beach, hand still kneading his forehead, the demon wisping around him like a freaky little cloud. Then, he slapped his hat back on his head and turned to them. "I think that doesn't change much. Let's stick to the original plan, provided you're all willing."

"*Willing?*" Naomi's eyes flashed. "I'd tear them apart with my bare hands if I could. So *no one else* has to lose a child to them."

Or a parent. Sam's eyes went to Bill, and Jessie, then to Darien ... and their child. He looked down, nudging his toe against the deck as his eyes grew hot. He was the fastest. He was prepared to die; he had been since their disastrous first attempt to close the gate. So how was it still *this hard?* And more importantly, how was he going to convince Darien not to come with them?

"Dad."

Sam looked up at the sound of Jessie's voice. The teen hesitated; he seemed to be considering his words. "I want to come with you. I won't be much help against the Gatekeeper—I've learned that the hard way. But maybe I can be a distraction, help fight if something else attacks us. Which it sounds like it will."

The cabin went silent, other than the dim roar of the *Redemption's* motor. Then, Bill let out a long sigh.

"Please," Jessie said. "I can fight. I *want* to fight. For ... for Mom. And Jordan. And Charlie." He nodded at Sam. "And your dad."

"Jess," Bill said. "I don't want to lose you."

"If I may, Bill," Naomi said quietly. When Bill nodded, she went on. "Nowhere's safe here. You could hog-tie him to the railing, and something we never saw coming could kill him while we're gone—"

"Snake incoming!" Darien shrilled. "Brace yourselves!"

Sam snatched for the overhead railing. An instant later, a sharp, metallic *BANG* echoed up into the cabin. The *Redemption* jumped and shivered ... then settled right back into its same trajectory.

"That has to hurt," Sam grumbled.

Darien shook her head. "If it does, she hasn't let on. It's like she was designed to be an underwater battering ram."

"I'm just grateful the demons still underestimate modern technology," Sam said.

"You and me both," Bill grunted, then turned back to Jessie. "You can come. But under no circumstances are you to try and sacrifice yourself in any capacity, do you understand?"

"Yes."

Bill nodded. "Let's radio the Call Crew, then."

***

"Come in, *Poor Buoy.* This is *Redemption.*"

Ellie watched as Henry grabbed the mic again, the churn in her stomach so familiar that it was basically her default now.

"Roger, *Redemption*," Henry said.

"You ready to go on the attack?"

Ellie's heart started to pound as Henry looked around at them all. "We game?"

"Yep," Helen and Oliver said at the same time.

"Yep," Ellie heard herself say.

"We're game, Bill. Tell us what we need to do."

"Beach next to us on the far south side. We'll have the *Crab King* and everyone else fight whatever appears on the beach. Then, we'll sneak up the south side of the canyon and hit the Gatekeeper from behind."

"Sounds solid," Henry said.

"We'll have ten of us—" The mic fuzzed for a moment, then Bill's voice came back on. "Nine worst case. Jessie and Sam seem to think that'll be enough for at least one person to get past."

Oliver nodded. "I think that's accurate."

"We agree, or Oliver does, at least," Henry said.

"Roger. Get lined up, then, and be ready to bail and go when we hit shore."

"Roger."

Henry set the mic back in its holder, his expression grim. Ellie felt sick. All the people who were most important to her in the world were marching straight into the mouth of the beast. No matter what, one of them wouldn't make it out alive.

In fact, one death is the best-case scenario.

No one said anything as Henry swung the boat to the left, slowing enough to let the *Redemption* come alongside, then nose ahead of them. Ellie found herself looking for a glimpse of Sam or Darien, then felt a little stupid. They were inside the cabin. With everyone else who had any sense at all.

She turned and made her way to the back of the cabin, checking her weapons as she went. Her pistol—still untouched; she wasn't great with it—was in its holster on her left hip. Knife on the right. Lighter in her pocket. Helen and Oliver had everything she had, and they'd decided Oliver would also carry the bow. Her eyes flicked to the strange contraption that rested beside Henry on the cabin's floor. The best way she could describe it was that he'd taken a small propane torch, retrofitted it to strap across his back, then welded a huge knife blade to its tip so that it could stab and burn at the same time. Ellie knew he'd made several others and distributed them to the Homer and Seldovia boats. It comforted her a little that they were out there, at least.

Movement registered out of the corner of her eye; Oliver had stood and was coming toward her. He stopped and grabbed the railing on the opposite side of the door, his expression difficult to read.

"I have all my weapons," Ellie said. "Anything else I should do to be prepared? Or help prepare? Or—"

He raised his hand, cupping her cheek.

"Oliver." Her vision blurred, and she shut her eyes against the tears.

"Come here."

She let him pull her against him, let him wrap his arms around his waist and press his forehead to hers. A shudder passed through her, as if her body thought that his touch had given it permission to completely unwind.

No, she told it. *Not yet.*

"I'll be here, Ellie," he said. "No matter what happens, I'll be here. I've got you."

Something loosened a little in Ellie's stomach, but it was enough. "Back at you, you heroic idiot."

He let out a tiny laugh, a bare whisper of a sound. And Ellie felt brave again.

***

Darien wasn't aware of much as the *Redemption* streaked toward the beach. People rushed around preparing, grabbing weapons, loading clips, testing torches, and stuffing things into knapsacks. But she sat on the bench, in the same place she'd been since the frantic flight to the cabin, monitoring … everything. Anything. As much as she could.

None of the demons near the beach and in the canyon had moved. The sea snake still harried the fleet, but that was a manageable issue, and she'd already said several grateful prayers that it was new and stupid, as opposed to ancient and brilliant. The sirens tailed them still, the Void wasn't far behind, and Death …

It was terrifying how quickly he was coming.

Someone—Naomi—rushed by, carrying one of the weird torch-bayonet things Henry and Luke had fabricated.

"Any changes, Darien?" Bill asked. They'd listed to the south, and Darien could see the rest of the fleet spread out through the opposite window, including the *Poor Buoy*, which skated gracefully over the water next to them. Though she wished none of them had to be there, she took comfort in the fact that at least she was doing this with family and friends, people she loved.

"Death's still getting closer, and fast," she said. "I think the sirens and the Void are coordinating to hit us at the same time."

"Great," Luke muttered.

Darien shut her eyes. "Before we land, let me make sure they aren't keeping any secrets."

She retreated into her fortress, and Bill's response—and any others—were lost to her. Pushing away her fatigue for the umpteenth time, she drove for one of the consciousnesses just inside the trees. The roar of the *Redemption's* engine became *a many-voiced buzz on the horizon, a drone that grew louder and louder. He curled his hands, his toes, flexed the long sinews in his legs and arms.*

"Tear them apart," Death said. "No quarter."

Somewhere deep inside herself, Darien frowned. *I want to tear them apart.* Could she manage it from this distance? Had she recovered enough from killing the siren? She gripped the railing next to her seat, then started to dig—

Her mind collided with what she could only describe as a wall. Pain shot through her skull, and she doubled over.

"Dar!"

Clutching her still-aching head, she looked up into Sam's worried face. "Something's defending the demons on the shore."

Sam's eyes widened. "Ankle Tickler? Or something else?"

"I don't know." Darien stumbled to her feet. "Death and Ankle Tickler are the only ones I know of who could do something like that. But any one of the ones waiting for us could have the ability to play mind games." She cursed. "And I can't *tell* because—"

"Hey." Sam put his hands on her shoulders. "You are not personally responsible for any of this. You are doing *everything* you can; you are going above and beyond."

Darien looked into his deep gray eyes, emotion swelling within her.

"Stay centered," he said. "Stay focused. When everything devolves into chaos, I bet you'll have plenty of chances to sneak in and do some damage."

"Good pep talk."

Sam smiled faintly. "With how much I'm on the receiving end of them, I'd be ashamed if it wasn't." He stood, eyes fixed on the beach, then glanced back at her. "Dar, I don't know if you should come with—"

"Come with you to the gate?" Darien stood, too, grasping the overhead railing for support. "Sam, I plan to do whatever gets me the greatest chance of protecting you. I want to try going with you first." She put a finger to his lips as he started to protest. "But listen. I do grasp the reality of my situation." She let out a dark, humorless laugh. "Even not pregnant, I'm not known for my speed."

"You're strong, though," Sam protested, "and your endurance—"

This time, Darien's smile was real. "Babe, I'm not insecure about the fact that I'm not a sprinter, don't worry. The *point* is, I'm a weapon right now, and need to act like one." She let her hand fall from his face. "I'll do what I have to do, and go where I have to go, to save as many people as possible."

Sam's eyes grew tender, and the poignancy of the expression was only sharpened by the fear behind his eyes. He pulled her into a hug. "I'm so grateful to be your husband, Darien."

She buried her face in his shoulder, love and terror surging in her belly. "I'm grateful to be your wife."

"Let's end this so our baby can be happy."

"You're on."

Sam released her, but didn't drop her hand. The engine's roar fell, the beach growing closer and closer by the second, the water becoming shallow outside the railing.

"Brace for beaching!" Bill roared.

Chapter Twenty-Eight

Oliver crouched on the deck of the *Poor Buoy*, clutching the gunwale as they sped over the water's surface, its hue lightening now with every yard. The *Redemption* was just ahead and to their right, the rest of the fleet spread out to their left, an army of boats rushing across the glittering water. Ellie shifted beside him, her breathing fast and shallow. He glanced over at Helen, who had adopted a similar posture to his on the other side of the boat. Her face was grim, her eyes fixed on the beach.

Heart thumping, Oliver turned back in time to see several boats beach, people leaping out of them onto the sand. His stomach twisted as he watched them. The Bauers and Richard Lee. Boris and his crew. A schoolteacher Oliver had never talked to, but who looked like she might be able to wrestle a black bear and win. Men. Women. Teens.

How many of them would still be alive after this?

The *Redemption* beached, its huge hull crunching across the sand. They were next.

Ellie took a deep, shaky breath, and Oliver's stomach tightened in sympathy; he couldn't even imagine how difficult this was. He almost reached back to put a hand on her shoulder, but then the engine cut, a deep, mechanical whir taking its place as Henry raised the outboard motor. They drifted at speed, the sand seeming to rise to meet them—

"Look!" Helen shouted.

Adrenaline flooded Oliver's body—along with hope. There, on the beach, stood the Nantinaq.

"Is that ...?" Ellie asked.

"The Nantinaq, yeah." Cautiously, Oliver stood. "He's okay!" he bellowed at the people on shore. "He's a friend!"

Roman glanced back at Oliver, then waved once to show he'd heard. All up and down the beach, people gathered in tense lines, looking up at the stone-still Nantinaq, weapons at the ready. Oliver glanced forward; the sand was close. He crouched again, bracing himself, then watched as Roman and a few others started up the beach toward the Nantinaq, their postures tense and wary, even from this distance.

The Nantinaq just stood there.

Unease seeped through Oliver. "He's always come to me before."

"Maybe he's freaked out by all the people on his beach," Ellie said.

"And the demons in his woods," Helen added.

"Yeah, but ..." Oliver trailed off as Roman and his crew drew closer. The creature on the beach still didn't move. A sudden, sick feeling surged in his stomach. He bolted upright. "ROMAN!"

"Oliver, get down!" Helen said.

"STOP!" Oliver bellowed. "STOP AND WAIT—"

The *Poor Buoy* crashed into the sand, pitching Oliver forward. He careened into the side of the cabin, smacking his head so hard he saw stars. Dimly, he registered both Ellie and Helen yelling his name. Then Ellie shrieked. More adrenaline shot through Oliver; the sound was so reminiscent of the night at the Shack when the Lady had attacked—the sheer helpless terror of it—

He shook himself as reality re-formed around him. The *Poor Buoy's* engine had shut off. Screams and yells echoed from the beach. He lifted his throbbing head.

It was chaos.

Bodies littered the sand where the fake Nantinaq had been, some moving, others morbidly still. The creature itself had already sped down the beach to the boats—and the milling crowd of people there—and was laying into them, punching and kicking.

Henry burst out of the door beside Oliver. "I heard that from inside. You good?"

"I'm good," Oliver gasped.

"Good." Henry slapped him on the back. "Let's go!"

He and Helen scrambled around to the prow, disappearing as they dropped onto the beach. Oliver gave his head one more shake, then followed. He didn't know what was worse: the pain in his scalp or the heart-twisting screams and gunshots coming from the beach.

"Oliver." Ellie appeared at his side, her face ash-pale. "Are you *sure* you're oka—?"

"I'm good. I can see straight." *Mostly.*

"Okay."

Together, they clambered over to the prow and dropped into the soft sand, then pounded up the beach to join the Calls and the crew of the *Redemption*. Oliver's stomach swooped at the noticeable absence of Charlie.

"We ready to—" Bill started, but broke off, his eyes widening in horror. Oliver turned in time to see the fake Nantinaq snatch a woman and throw her, screaming, into the frigid ocean. She went under and didn't resurface. Oliver could hear the howls of rage, hear gunshots as people scrambled to get away from the demon—

Henry grabbed his arm. "No, we gotta go. Stick to the plan, and quick, before they notice we're slipping around."

Bill nodded. "Henry, you lead, you know the area best."

"Yep." Henry shouldered to the front of the line and started to jog, the rest of the crew setting off after him. Oliver adjusted the quiver on his shoulder, glancing back at the fight on the beach as he followed. His heart leaped; they were rallying, pushing the fake Nantinaq back—

Darien cursed. "The other one in the woods is coming. It's coming!"

"Toward us?" Sam asked.

"No, it's going for them."

"That doesn't change our mission," Luke said. "We've got to keep moving no matter what's happening back there."

"Right." Darien started back up the canyon, her face haunted.

Oliver glanced back as they entered the trees. Henry was leading them toward the opposite end of the canyon than they'd climbed yesterday, up an old game trail that twisted and wound its way up the side of the mountain and then disappeared a hundred yards in. If Oliver remembered correctly from his time searching this area for Robert, it would be harder going after that. He looked over at Darien, worried. Her face was flushed, but her breath seemed to be coming easily, and her eyes were alert. On his other side, Ellie was barely breathing hard; her movements were as graceful as a deer's.

"There are quite a few baby demons floating around," Sam said. "Will you be able to feel if one of them is going to Awaken?"

"I hope so," Darien panted. "I'm more worried about Death and the Void than anything else. They're both getting so close."

"How close?" Ellie asked.

Darien's expression grew pained, as if she were straining to hear something. "The Void is closer. I'd guess five minutes, tops. And Death …"

For a moment, there was no sound except for the swish of their passing through the undergrowth and the Alaskans' breathing. Then, Darien's eyes widened, and she pitched herself forward again. "Twenty minutes tops."

"*Hell*," Bill said.

They clambered up a little knoll that afforded them a mostly unobstructed view of the beach. Oliver didn't stop, but he did glance back … and felt sick as he registered what he was seeing. Another demon had joined the fake Nantinaq; it towered over everything else on the beach. Oliver couldn't make out details, but he *could* tell that it was human-shaped, long-limbed, chalk-white, and seemed featureless from head to foot.

The Alaskans had formed two loose half-circles around the demons. As Oliver watched, a gout of flame erupted toward the fake Nantinaq. It jumped back, retreating up the beach, and a ragged cheer echoed toward where they stood. But the other one …

Oliver blinked. It was *in* the other circle.

He hadn't seen it happen, had no idea how it had gotten there. But now it was picking up a wriggling human figure, its huge hands wrapping around its face, twisting its head—

It let go. The person fell to the ground at its feet, limp.

Naomi gasped, Ellie whimpered, and Oliver's chest constricted. They'd gone at least a hundred yards into the bush, and still had another quarter of a mile to go before they could turn toward the gate. Terror spiked through him at the thought of what waited on the other side of the canyon, a cowardly voice within him whispering that a quarter of a mile wasn't long enough.

"Two of the ones on the other side of the canyon are on the move!" Darien said.

"Toward the beach?" Oliver asked.

"One, yes. The other's coming toward us. And the Void's about to land."

"I see him." Naomi pointed at the beach. "Look!"

Oliver shaded his eyes. A … *point* was appearing over the lapping waves, black and roiling—though black still wasn't the right way to describe it. It was a tear, a nothingness, a … well, a *void*. It spread, growing a torso, limbs, a head—

"They're going to get massacred," Helen said.

"We will, too, if one of those is heading our way and we don't *move*," Bill said. "Come on."

"Wait," Darien said. "This is a good vantage point. If I stay here, I might be able to at least slow down the one that's coming toward—"

"Dar, no," Sam said.

She turned her steely gaze on him. "Sam. Yes."

"I'll stay with her," Helen said. "We're the slowest anyway. We can be more useful holding off the demons so you have a clearer shot at the gate."

"She's right, Sam." Darien grabbed him and yanked him down for a quick kiss. "Try not to die if you can help it."

Sam pressed a hand to Darien's belly. "Better me than you two."

Emotion welled in Oliver; he looked away.

"I'll see you soon," Darien said. "I have faith in that."

Henry pulled one of his two-way radios from his pack and handed it to Helen. "Here."

She took it. "Always prepared. Now get out of here."

***

Darien watched Sam pull to the front of the pack with Henry, Ellie, and Oliver as they jogged away. He'd done it so *easily*. Despite her faith that they'd all come through this, she couldn't help the foreboding settling in her gut.

He's the fastest. And because of that, you might never see him alive again.

Shut up, she told the thought, and let a trickle of the baby's consciousness into her own. Its calmness suffused her. She let out a deep breath, then turned away before her presence started to cause it discomfort. *Thank you. Hang in there. We're almost done with this.*

A slick rustling sound made her look up. Helen was pulling the strap of her rifle over her head. "Darien, what if we climb a little higher to those rocks up there? That'll give us a good vantage, make sure nothing can sneak up on us."

Unless that something can move through rock, Darien thought, but quashed the thought immediately. "Let's do it."

"What's their ETA?" Helen asked as they scrambled up the hill.

Still climbing, Darien let her mind expand. Her heart jumped into her throat. "I'd guess less than a minute on the first demon. The other one's just behind it."

Helen glanced up. "That's enough time."

Together, they scrambled over the lip of rock that jutted out over the canyon. Heart pounding—and not just from the climb—Darien pulled out her pistol as Helen surveyed the rocks around them. Wisps of mist dragged long tendrils over the mossy rocks above her head, and did the same to the tallest trees in the forest below. Darien ground her teeth. If they lost visibility ...

Helen laid her rifle against one of the boulders within easy reach and turned to Darien. She jerked her head at the gun. "That's not going to be useful if they're not solid, so here's what I propose. You shoot at close range, and I slash. That keeps you out of the worst of harm's way. You can generally hit what you're aiming at, right?"

"Generally." Darien glanced toward the dark wall of trees below, licking her lips. "If I get the chance, though, I'm also going to slash."

"Fair enough. How long've we got?"

"Twenty seconds or so ... wait ..." She frowned. "It's slowing down. And the other one is ..." She gasped. "It's going up, toward the attack team. It's an older one, too, not an easy takedown."

Helen swore, then tugged the radio out of her jacket pocket. "This is Helen. The second demon has changed course toward you guys, and it's a nasty one, so be alert."

Darien hesitated. She wanted to dive at the demon haring toward Sam and the others, pull it apart thread by thread. But if she did that, she'd be useless when the first one hit herself and Helen—

A third movement twitched through Darien's consciousness. Her stomach bottomed out. "The third one's going after them, too!"

Helen looked sick. "Scratch that, you've got *two* heading toward you. Watch out—"

An impression of speed, of power, roared through Darien's mind. "Helen, number one's coming hard now! He's coming for us!"

Helen dropped the radio and jerked her knife out of its sheath, its blade already glistening with flammable jelly. She bolted to stand by Darien, lighter gripped in her other fist.

"It's almost to the tree line." Darien pointed at a dark gap between the two biggest, mossiest evergreens. "It'll come right through there."

"Okay."

"I get the impression it's new and stupid."

"Oh, good."

Helen set her stance. Darien followed suit. At this point, she was confident in her ability to play the mental game in all of this, even with the potential Ankle Tickler wildcard. But the raw, savage physicality of an actual fight? *That* wasn't getting any easier.

A goblinlike creature burst from between the spruce trees, and Darien barely held in a disgusted shriek. It was crouched, misshapen, with dull, beige skin and facial features that looked like they'd been melted. It locked eyes with them, its lopsided mouth opening to reveal blunt, blocky teeth. Then, it started loping toward them, scrabbling up the hillside. Darien felt its glee from where she stood, *the pleasure it would take in picking up one of the rocks and beating them both, feeding on their pain until the life left their bodies—*

"It's going to charge right into us!" Darien yelled. "It wants to beat us to death!"

"Perfect!" Helen hollered. "Start putting holes in it as soon as it's solid!"

Darien's hands shook so hard that she could barely hold the pistol steady. *Work with it, come on.* She took two steps, then knelt and rested the 9 millimeter's barrel on one of the rocks, breathing a sigh of relief when the gun steadied. The demon's weird, slobbery breathing filled her ears; it sounded like a bulldog on the brink of lung failure. She sighted down the barrel; she could see the whites of its eyes, count every tooth as its melted mouth split—

Darien fired.

The demon squealed and rocked back. A jolt of heady relief rolled over Darien even as the creature's pain seared through her torso. She fired again, shutting out the agony, and again. It roared in pain, then bolted for them again as Darien squeezed the trigger a fourth time—

"MOVE!"

Helen shouldered past her and buried her now-flaming blade in the demon's haunch. For a split second, it looked surprised.

Then a wall of flame erupted out of it.

Darien yelled as she felt it burn, only half aware of Helen's vise grip on her arm as the other woman tugged her back. Then, just as quickly as the pain had begun, it was over. The demon's consciousness disappeared, but this time something ... *heavy* ... lingered.

That's not normal.

She opened her eyes to find herself spread-eagled on the ground, Helen staring at her, eyebrows contracted into a line.

"That went well." Darien coughed. She stood, dusting herself off to try and hide the fact that her hands were *still* shaking. And that she still didn't feel quite ... right.

"You're okay?" Helen asked.

"Yeah."

A faint grin spread across the older woman's face.

"What?"

Helen patted Darien on the shoulder. "You did good. That's all."

Warmth spread through Darien as Helen turned away. Maybe she was better at this than she thought.

"Wait ... Darien ..."

Darien's stomach tightened at Helen's tone. She whirled, feeling for demons, but there were none—at least, none that were close—

"Look at the beach," Helen said.

Darien squinted down at the sand, where the beleaguered Alaskans were now fighting ... Her heart sank. *Four* demons. A new one had joined the first three; it looked like a strange, hairless combination of wolf and whale. It was also large; even on all fours, its back came to the fake Nantinaq's waist.

Her hand fell to her spare clip. "Do you think we need to go—?"

"No, *look*." Helen grabbed her arm, pointing.

Darien studied the beach for a moment. Then her jaw dropped. "Is it ... is the whale thing attacking the other demons?"

"That's what I'm seeing." Helen brought her rifle to her shoulder again, sighting through the scope at the beach, her finger conspicuously off the trigger. She stiffened. "Describe Ankle Tickler to me."

Darien blinked. "He looks like an aye-aye. Small, hairy, and ugly. Something like a cross between a possum and a wolverine, with orange eyes."

Helen lowered her rifle. "Well, I'm not sure about the eyes, but I think he's down there *also* attacking the other demons."

"You're kidding. He's *fighting other demons?*"

"Yeah."

"Why would he do that?"

Helen shrugged. "Don't look at me. I know less than you do."

Darien put her hands on her hips, frowning deeply. "Well, the one thing I *am* sure of is that he's trying to stage a coup."

"Right. That's why he took over Slubgob: so she couldn't give Death reliable information."

"Yep." Darien chewed her lip. Then, her eyes widened as a possibility hit her. "Helen. I bet he's trying to delay the battle until Death gets here. I bet he wants me to help take him down."

Helen's eyebrows shot up. "Interesting."

Darien's heart sank as she realized the implications of that. "Even if we succeed at killing Death—" *which might completely take me out,* "—we'll have to face him and whatever other demons are on his side. And if he can hide the sirens and that whale-wolf from me—"

"Ahklut," Helen interrupted. "It's a Northern Alaskan legend, I believe." She frowned as the Ahklut leaped at the long-limbed white demon, sinking its teeth into its leg. "You really never sensed him at all?"

"No."

"I knew you didn't sense the sirens—"

"Or the Void, or the Snake, until we were right on top of them."

Helen shook her head. "I didn't realize you didn't see them coming at *all*." Her voice lowered. "Makes me wonder what else is out there."

"You and me both."

Helen turned. "Well, either way, we've got to do something other than just stand here. Where're the other demons? The ones that were going after the gate crew?"

"Let me check."

"Okay. I'm going to reload your clip while you—"

Helen shrieked. Darien whirled and found herself looking into a face straight from Hell. Wide, gaping, blood-red mouth. Yellow, needle-like teeth. Eyeless. Long, spiderlike limbs the color of raw chicken skin. A scream tore from her mouth, and she jumped backward—only to find herself teetering on the edge of the precipice.

"Darien!" Helen lunged for her, hand outstretched. The creature let out a weird whistle, then darted for her.

"No!" Darien yelled. She grabbed Helen and yanked, pulling her out of the creature's way. It missed them both by inches. Then it vanished into thin air.

Darien spun, looking in every direction, the heaviness she still felt—Death, she suspected—making it difficult to distinguish where the smaller, closer demons were. Still, she could feel something nearby. A tremor in the air, the bare thread of thoughts, of intents.

"It's not gone, Helen."

That was the last thing Darien said before the ground disintegrated beneath her feet.

Chapter Twenty-Nine

Oliver jogged up the canyon after Henry and Sam, Ellie by his side. Chills chased themselves up and down his back, and he wondered if the others could feel the Gatekeeper's pall as acutely as he did, even from this distance. *Given how little we've talked, probably.*

He glanced into the canyon, looking for flashes of movement, color—anything that could clue them in on the whereabouts of the demons Helen was sure were after them. The timber at the bottom was thick, dark, and ragged with moss, but ended within a hundred yards. He'd guess they would take a sharp left as soon as they were beyond it.

Then the final charge would begin.

Oliver's breath stuttered; it was as if his blood, his *bones* were afraid. He snapped his eyes forward, to where Sam and Henry threw themselves at the mountain, tearing through the undergrowth like a pair of bull moose. They'd been like that ever since leaving Helen and Darien.

"I'm so amazed," Luke puffed suddenly, "that a bunch of ancient Hawaiians with spears defeated these guys."

Sam glanced over his shoulder. "If you'd met them, you wouldn't be."

"Given how ineffective our modern weapons are against them," Ellie said, "I actually think the Hawaiians had an advantage."

Luke grunted. "Sure gives me hope, at any rate."

"Good." Oliver's heart thundered in his chest as the trees started to scatter and peter out. They could pass through easily now. "Hold onto it for dear life."

Henry slowed to a walk. "Let's stop here. Catch our breath before we turn."

They formed into a loose circle, everyone—except the Forths—puffing lightly. The group was wary, fidgety, with darting eyes.

"No sign of Helen's demons?" Henry asked. When no one answered, he grunted. "All right, then. Keep your eyes out."

He gestured toward the reddish-green swath of bushes to their left. "This sidehill's steeper than it looks, so be careful. I don't want anybody breaking a leg, so take it as slow as you need but as fast as you can. Then it's the climb. Once we're on a level with the caves, we'll rest for a few minutes to catch our breath, then do the final run. Everyone good?"

Grim nods greeted his speech.

Henry raised the radio to his mouth. "Come in, Helen. Where's that demon?"

Only silence greeted him.

Henry waited for a moment longer, his jaw tight. Then, he turned down the hill. "Come on. Let's get this gate cl—"

Bill screamed.

Oliver whirled, his hand closing on an arrow shaft, and barely stifled a yell. A red-eyed, bearlike creature had Bill by the ankle and was dragging him down the hill.

"DAD!"

Jessie threw himself after his father. Ellie charged past half a second later, and Oliver ripped his lighter out of his pocket and followed. He could hear the crash of bodies through the undergrowth as his uncle and the rest of the crew followed.

Jessie leaped over a downed log and put on a burst of speed, hands outstretched towards Bill's. "REACH, DAD!"

Bill caught them, and Jessie hauled back for all he was worth. Bill thrashed and bellowed as the monster worried at his leg like a crazed Labrador, but even the two of them weren't enough. It dragged them both down the hill, Jessie's heels leaving dark furrows in the loam. But the extra weight *had* slowed the monster, and Oliver felt a surge of energy; he and Ellie were gaining ground. He leaped the log, slipping and stumbling on the mist-wetted undergrowth as he nocked the arrow. He looked up in time to see Ellie reach the melee. She lunged for Bill's forearm and pulled, her face contorted in a grimace. Bill slid to a stop, caught between his son and Ellie on one side and the monster on the other.

Oliver struck the lighter and brought it up to the arrow's tip as Bill kicked out at the monster with his free leg. "LET GO OF ME, YOU DIRTY CREATURE!"

In response, the bear-thing sank its teeth into Bill's calf and gave a savage twist of its head. An audible *crack* echoed through the forest. Bill bellowed in agony. And Oliver let his arrow fly.

His aim was dead on; the creature erupted into a column of flame. Bill screamed again, and Oliver rushed forward to help Ellie and Jessie haul him away, wrinkling his nose at the smell of singed hair.

"Bill!"

Oliver looked up to see Naomi, Luke, and Henry rushing down the hill. Naomi had her pistol out; Luke and Henry held their propane torch-bayonets in front of him like they were swords. They stumbled to a stop in front of Bill, wincing at the heat of the burning demon. Luke and Naomi knelt by the captain.

"It's broken," Bill said through clenched teeth. "We can ... splint it—"

"We don't have time," Luke said.

"And you can't fight like this," Naomi added.

In Henry's pocket, the radio blipped. He snatched for it. "Helen and Darien, come in." Nothing.

Henry spoke again. "We've killed a demon, but Bill's leg is broken. Anybody copy?" Silence.

"We have to go," Luke said. "We can't wait." He stood, looking down at Bill. "Jess, will you stay with him?"

Oliver thought relief might have flickered across the teen's face before he nodded, and a strange pang of emotion went through him. The Oliver of a month ago might have read Jessie's relief and judged him a coward.

He knew better now.

Bill bit down on a groan as Henry and Luke helped prop him against the trunk of a nearby spruce.

"Good?" Luke asked.

"Good enough. Jess ... hand me my pistol ... just in case. The rest of you, get outta here." His voice quieted. "I'll see you all again, whether in this life, or ... or the next."

Oliver nodded at his captain. Then, he turned away, joining Ellie and the rest of the crew as they started for the other side of the canyon. They'd already crossed half of it during their mad dash. It was, quite literally, all uphill from here.

"This is it," Henry said. "No stopping. Let's go."

***

Darien's feet hit solid ground almost instantly after the knoll collapsed. But it was hillside, so they still slid out from underneath her. She caught herself awkwardly on her elbows, skidding below the canyon's rim before she managed to stop herself.

"Darien!"

She looked up to see Helen half-running, half-sliding toward her. "Are you all right?"

"I think so. I—"

The pale, spiderlike shape fuzzed into view over Helen's shoulder.

"Helen, look out!" Darien yelled.

Helen whirled, pistol in hand, but the demon had already winked away. "Same demon?"

"Yeah!"

Intent drove through Darien—the demon's. She lit her knife, turning in a slow circle. The Death-heaviness in her chest was making it difficult to *breathe*, let alone focus on the creature attacking them. *At least we're not higher, in the mist.*

"He's still here," she hollered, "we just can't see him!"

The air in front of Darien blurred again. She barely had a chance to cry a warning before the spider-thing appeared, its fangs inches from her face. Darien screamed and stumbled backward, slashing at it with her burning knife—

But the demon was already gone.

Helen scrambled toward her. "Put your back to mine."

"Okay." Darien did, and turned back up the canyon—

Yellow fangs in an oblong, eyeless face, inches from her own. Darien screeched and slashed again, careening into Helen, who stumbled forward.

"Sorry," Darien gasped.

"It's okay." Helen staggered to her feet, then limped to put her back to Darien's once more.

The radio crackled. "Helen and Darien, come in."

"We're busy, dammit," Helen muttered.

"We've killed a demon, but Bill's leg is broken. Anybody—"

The thing appeared again—a pale, grinning nightmare. It shoved Darien backward, sending her toppling over Helen in the direction of the beach. She rolled onto her knees and staggered upright, stumbling as the loamy earth slipped and slid underneath her boots.

"—leaving Bill and going for the gate," Henry was saying. "Godspeed—"

"Darien!" Helen caught her elbow, steadying her.

"I'm fine!" Darien raked her hair out of her eyes, trying to ignore the ache in her sides and belly. There was nothing she could do about it right now. "Backs together!"

Helen spun again, her back bumping against Darien's. "*How* are we supposed to fight this thi—?"

Her last word turned into a choked scream. Then, she was gone.

"Helen!" Darien spun in time to see Helen's body crash into the bushes that nestled along the bottom of the canyon and roll out of sight. She took two steps in that direction—

The monster was there, inches from her, spidery limbs waving.

This time, Darien's yell was one of rage. She slashed at it with the knife, cursing as the flames on it guttered and went out. It didn't matter, though; the demon had already disappeared. Closing her eyes, Darien cast her net in a wide arc around her, looking for a thread, a sign, anything ... and frowned. It was ... *blipping*. If she were a radar, the demon would be glitching, cutting in and out, making it difficult to track—

It burst into existence not two feet in front of her, forelimbs raised above its eyeless head, letting out a weird hissy screech. Darien jumped back, stumbling another several yards toward the beach as she fumbled with her newly-loaded gun—

Realization hit her, and she gasped. If the spidery creature had wanted her dead, she would be dead. Tossed into the bushes like it had thrown Helen, just to get her out of the way.

"You're Ankle Tickler's, aren't you?" she asked the air around her. "You're part of the coup."

Silence.

"By choice, or not?"

More silence. Until ...

A piteous moan came from the bushes below. Helen. Darien pitched herself down the side of the mountain. "I'm comi—AARGH!"

The thing appeared again, waving its many pale limbs. Darien still couldn't keep herself from jumping backward—again in the direction of the beach—but this time she managed to keep her wits, more or less. "Tell Ankle Tickler I know what game he's playing."

The thing stopped. Then it came closer, cocking its head. Darien scrambled backward again, revolted. "Death is almost on top of us. I can feel him. And Ankle Tickler wants me to help kill him, doesn't he?"

In answer, the spider-thing dove for her, slashing. The tip of its front leg caught Darien across the arm, opening a slash. Clutching the wound, she stumbled even farther back—

"Darien."

A hazy image swam to the front of her mind, a memory, of ... Sam. It was his voice, and yet, not.

"Darien."

"Give me answers," she snarled.

Memory-Sam dropped to one knee on the beautiful trail where they'd picnicked, where they'd first kissed, where he'd proposed. "Our interests are aligned, Dar."

"That's a jerk move, manipulating our proposal."

Memory-Sam's face shadowed. "If you don't help me destroy him, you condemn everyone you love."

Darien started down the hill. *Helen ...*

Instantly, the spider-creature was in front of her again, rearing, jaws snapping inches from her face. Darien screeched and jumped away. "All right! All right!"

She turned back toward the beach and broke into a slow, painful jog. *"If Helen dies in there, I* promise *I will find a way to kill you."* A twinge went through her belly, hard enough to make her gasp. *"And if my baby dies, I'll* crawl into your world *to do it."*

Memory-Sam—Ankle Tickler—just smiled. "A problem I dearly hope we both have to deal with. I'll see you soon, Dar."

***

Based on Sam's internal map, they still had hundreds of yards of scrambling to do before reaching the gate, maybe a little less. But he could swear he already felt the fear that radiated from its Keeper. He stole a sideways glance at Ellie as they jogged. Her face was pale, her lips pressed in a hard line, her eyes wide. Sam's gut clenched.

"Henry."

Everyone skidded to a stop. The voice on the other side of the radio was Helen's, but a strained, breathless version of it.

"Helen?" Henry said. "What's wrong?"

The radio crackled for a few seconds before Helen answered. "Darien and I ... got separated."

Fear washed over Sam. The same terror entered Henry's eyes.

"Two demons got to us," Helen continued. "We killed the first one, but ... but the second ... It was like a big spider. It threw me. I landed in some bushes, but I don't know where it is, or where Darien is. And I can't—"

"Are you hurt?" Henry asked.

"Yeah. Not ... life-threatening, I don't think. My sides are killing me; I can't breathe well, and I can't put weight on my leg. But don't you dare come after me. I wanted to warn you in case that spider thing was heading for—"

The rest of Helen's sentence drowned in the roar of pistol fire. Sam flinched and swung around to see Oliver in a shooting stance, gun raised, its barrel still smoking. Out of the woods in front of them stepped the Nantinaq.

For a moment, nobody moved. Then, the Nantinaq looked down, the wrinkles on its face deepening as it picked a smashed bullet out of the fur on its chest. He glared at Oliver, holding the twisted piece of metal between its massive fingertips. "Futile."

Relief crossed Oliver's face; he lowered the gun. "Just had to make sure it was actually you."

The Nantinaq stared at him. "I do not understand."

Sam stepped forward. The Nantinaq acknowledged him with a nod. "Angry One." Then, he looked behind him. "Just Ellie. You must all hurry."

"*Yes*, we *should*," Sam said. Darien was down there; if they didn't keep going in the next five seconds, he was going to do ... *something*, even if that something was to charge the gate by himself.

"There's a demon on the beach that looks just like you," Oliver said. "Did you know that?"

The Nantinaq blinked. "It has stolen my form?"

"Yes. And it's killing people. Is there anything you can do about that?"

The Nantinaq shook its head. "I cannot affect them. But ..." It thought for a moment, then turned for the beach. "But I can try something else."

It started to stride away.

"Hey," Henry called after it.

The Nantinaq looked over its matted shoulder.

"There's an injured woman near the bottom of the canyon. Her name's Helen. Will you check on her as you pass by?"

"I can." The Nantinaq turned and melted into the trees.

Sam exchanged a glance with Oliver. "Is that the first time he's ever actually tried to intervene?"

Oliver nodded, grinning slightly. Then, he looked around. "Let's not let it go to waste. Come on."

***

Darien threw up her mental wall and started down the canyon at a jog, ignoring the stinging in her arm. She resisted the urge to look behind her; the spider-thing had left her alone ever since she'd turned in the right direction. Still ... it took so much effort to shut out Ankle Tickler. And since she didn't know what else was out there ...

Reluctantly, Darien lowered her defenses and cast her mind out farther. She winced as she felt the hunger and brutality of the demons on the beach—on *both* sides. A bolt of pain lanced through her, then a deep, awful burning sensation. She gritted her teeth, trying to hold it at bay even as part of her rejoiced because that could mean only one thing: one of the demons had just gone up in a fiery inferno.

The canyon bottomed out, and Darien fought through a thick snarl of undergrowth, tearing through clumps of spiky weeds that clawed at her like angry cats. Scraping thorns out of her skin, she stumbled into a stand of trees, catching flashes of pale sand in between the trunks. Screams, yells, shots, and the low, intermittent *whoosh* of fabricated fire-weapons echoed in her ears, and fear made her stumble. "Sam, Mom, Dad, Ana, Sophie, Ellie, Helen ..."

She was still chanting their names as she burst out onto the sand, and was glad for the extra courage they'd kindled when she took in the scene in front of her. Bodies littered the beach. Rusty stains peppered the sand. People gathered in ragged clumps, surrounding the remaining demons. The Nantinaq-like monster was still swinging, kicking, picking people up and throwing them into trees, out into the ocean, at boats. The whale-wolf combination—the Ahklut—bounded in and out of the water, attacking both people and other demons seemingly at random.

But it's not random, she thought. They were playing both sides, trying to draw the battle out long enough for Death to arrive so she and Ankle Tickler could take him down. Unease stole over Darien. If it weren't for the rogue demons, there were good odds her side would have already lost. For the first time in her life, she thanked God for petty politics. Then, she pulled her pistol and started toward the shore.

Gasping, trying not to think too hard about the pain in her sides, Darien trotted around the corner and skidded to a stop. The Void hovered on the north side of the beach. As she watched, a group of people tried to break around it and head up the canyon, but it moved in their direction, hovering over them as they collapsed, clutching their throats, rolling and kicking in the sand. Darien started toward them, pushing herself as fast as she dared, stumbling in the sand.

"Stop!" she yelled, despite knowing it was a complete waste of breath. She reached toward the Void, feeling its mind, feeling her power build behind her—

"I can't let you do that, Darien."

At the sound of Ankle-Tickler-Sam's voice, the building thread between her and the Void snapped.

"COME ON!" she screamed as the Void's struggling victims weakened.

"You've become a strong little thing," Ankle Tickler said. *"Stronger than I thought you could be. But you are the first of your kind; I guess I shouldn't be surprised."*

One by one, the people in the Void's grasp stopped moving, going limp in the sand. Darien felt sick; she hoped they were just unconscious.

"You have more important things to worry about. Death is here."

Yes. He was. Even without trying, Darien could feel him approaching, could feel that he was about to crest the closest mountain to the east. Her head snapped up. He was on a course straight for the beach.

And he'd hit the beleaguered defenders like a wrecking ball.

"Now you get it," Ankle Tickler purred. *"You don't have a choice but to help me. Not really."*

Darien straightened her spine. *"Fine. Then afterward, it's you and me."*

"I look forward to it."

Everything in her stomach tightened; she didn't know if she could best Ankle Tickler in a mental brawl, but it was the best chance she had of delaying his focus after they killed Death. She couldn't imagine Ankle Tickler would let them waltz right into the cave and shut the gate. *And that's if we manage to kill Death in the first place.*

"I have confidence in us." Ankle Tickler's mind snaked around hers; she felt his power building like a storm outside the walls of her fortress. *"And you should have more in yourself, I think. Are you ready, my student?"*

Darien fixated on that one point, that all-encompassing consciousness coming over the mountain. *He was flying through the mist; he could see the little humans on the sand, running around like ants. His lip curled. They had almost made it to the gate. But it didn't matter now. Not when he was here. He dove,* and Darien saw him coming, a white-shrouded skeleton hurtling out of the misty sky. Adrenaline shot through her; she grasped for the baby.

Its calm was the only thing that held her together when Death hit.

He landed on the beach and threw his skeletal arms wide. The people nearest to him crumpled, and Darien felt a swell of pure *power* flow through him, emanating like a shock wave. Then, he tore up the beach, people dropping on either side as he went, his power growing—

"It's now or never!" Ankle Tickler yelled.

Darien hurtled her mind toward Death like a spear, feeling Ankle Tickler's power spike as he did the same—

Something slammed into Death with enough force to send him tumbling backward.

Darien sank to her knees, realizing she didn't have the strength to keep this up for longer than a couple of minutes.

"Hold him!" Ankle Tickler screamed; even he sounded strained. *"Probe for a weakness or they all die!"*

Chapter Thirty

Dread seeped into Ellie's bones as they climbed, so deep she wondered if she'd ever be able to separate it from her marrow. Maybe it would just metastasize in there and make more of itself until she slowly died of it. She concentrated on the rhythmic pounding of her feet, the burn in her thighs as she climbed the hillside between Oliver and Sam. *Just one more step,* she told herself after every footfall. *You've come too far not to take one more step.*

They crested a little vein of stone that jutted out of the mountain, and then the ground turned flat, rocky.

She knew this ground.

Henry held up a closed fist, looking down toward the pockmarks and depressions that time had worn in the cliffs in front of them. Mist swirled around them; Ellie felt it in her lungs like poison.

"This is it," Henry said. "There's two demons unaccounted for if we count Helen's spider, so watch for them. Luke, any last thoughts on how we approach this?"

The burly fisherman shook his head. "Simple's usually the most effective. I think we just need to charge."

Henry gave a curt nod. "First one in the cave knows what they have to do."

Oliver's fingertips brushed Ellie's jawline. She turned to look at him and saw the same war that had played out on his face a week ago at the wedding: the very human fear of death, and the love and courage that she knew would push it aside. He bent and kissed her, and the contrast between the terror of their situation and the glowing intensity of her love for him brought tears to her eyes.

"I'm here," Oliver whispered. "I love you."

Ellie drank in the planes and angles of his face, the ring of darker blue at the edge of his irises. "I love you."

Henry turned. "Let's—"

Something burst out of the ground and latched onto his calf. Henry yelled and tried to leap away, but the thing clung to him, knocking him off balance. He went down hard, hitting the stone with an audible *oof.*

"RUN!" Luke bellowed.

Sam and Oliver took off almost at the same time. Nerves screaming, Ellie threw herself after them, passing Henry, who was beating at the thing—it looked like a stone *hand*—with his knife. Panic seized her as she remembered her many nightmares of the gate, the unseen monster that had broken her ankles over and over. *Did I accidentally create that thing?*

"Go, Ellie!" Henry bellowed. "Don't stop!"

Ellie bolted. Her feet struck the rocky ground with dull, rhythmic thuds, and she realized with a surge of horror how far ahead of her Sam, Oliver, and Luke had already drawn. *It wasn't supposed to have been them—any of them.* Helpless rage crawled up her throat, and she redoubled her pace. She'd never catch Sam, and probably not even Oliver, but she had to try—

A shout echoed behind her. She glanced over her shoulder to see Henry and Naomi running after them, though the former's was more of a fast limp. There was no sign of the hand. Ellie whipped her gaze forward, toward the gate. Luke was falling behind; he was strong and fit, but Oliver and Sam had both of those things *and* youth on their side. And in any case, very few people could beat Sam in a foot race. He was drawing ahead of them all, widening the gap, and Ellie's throat tightened. It was going to happen again, she was going to lose the last member of her family—

A bulge formed in the rock right in front of Sam.

Ellie yelled her brother's name, but he'd seen it. He dodged, the move graceful, fluid, almost artful. But the hand stretched—an arm, a shoulder, a rocky, misshapen *head* burst out of the stone. Ellie screamed as its fingers closed around Sam's leg. The thing yanked him backward; he went down hard.

"KEEP RUNNING!" she heard Luke yell as Oliver slowed. For a moment, Ellie thought he was stopping to help Sam, but then she felt the fear intensify, enveloping her mind. Oliver brought his hands up to his head, cradling his skull even as he stumbled on.

Luke, on the other hand, bulled forward. He passed Sam, who was getting to his feet, blood pouring from his nose again. He slowed as he passed Oliver, his shoulders starting to tremble. Still, he pressed on. Ellie had made up some ground; she was almost to Sam. He was limping toward the gate again, but she was still going to catch him.

And all the while, the fear grew, just like it had a month ago when the Lady had killed her father, and this nightmare had started.

Sweat broke out across Ellie's forehead, her breath coming harder as terror numbed every part of her mind, her soul. Something shimmered in front of the gate, something tall and humanoid and horrifying, and the fear was a living thing burrowing under her skin, into her lungs, into her gut.

But I've dealt with this, she realized. And not just in the last month. For *years.*

The stone hand burst out of the earth, wrapping around Luke's leg. He crashed to the ground, leaving Sam and Oliver to face the Gatekeeper alone. Then, Sam faltered. Oliver stumbled past him, head up, looking straight at the Gatekeeper. The monster finally shimmered into view, taller than he'd been in Ellie's nightmares and slightly less gaunt, but unmistakable.

Oliver staggered.

Then, he righted himself and kept going.

No! Not you! Ellie forced herself to move faster, keeping her focus on Oliver, not the twisted, sinewy monster in front of him. It was almost a relief when the hand burst out of the ground again, bringing him to his knees less than forty feet from the entrance to the cave.

All of Ellie's world narrowed to that single point.

Focus on the run. On the trickles of sweat dripping down her back and chest, on the uneven pressure points the stone put on the soles of her feet through her shoes. *Focus on the run.* On how the cool, misty air felt on—

Oliver lurched to his feet and started forward again, but a third creature appeared in front of him—tall, spiderlike, pale. It backhanded him with one of its forelegs, sending him crashing to the rocks. He rolled onto his side, chest heaving.

The spider-creature disappeared, then reappeared in front of Sam. He stumbled backward, but not quickly enough. The demon shoved him to the ground, pinning him, one pale, pointed leg raised in the air directly above his heart.

Ellie lunged for him, but her movements were sluggish, her mind molasses, and she realized with horror that she wasn't going to make it.

She wasn't fast enough.

***

Darien gasped for air, beads of sweat dripping down her temples. Even with Ankle Tickler's help, the strain of holding Death back was incredible. The ancient demon was enraged, rampant; *he'd never been bound before. He could see the humans in the canyon, fighting the Hand even as the Gatekeeper crushed their minds—*

Another demon appeared out of nowhere, tall, smooth, and spiderlike. If Death's jaw could have dropped, it would have. Who was *that? Where had it come from? Judging by its behavior, it seemed to be on Death's side. But he had never seen it before; never had an* inkling *that something with powers like Silverskin's existed again—*

Rage exploded through Darien, so strong that it nearly broke the connection. "YOU LIAR!" she screamed.

An annoyed jolt came from Ankle Tickler; apparently, the strain of holding Death back was too much to allow him to speak. Darien hardly cared. *"You sent the Spider after my family!"*

A terrible growl echoed through her brain, followed by a strange, blurred voice—a weird amalgamation of all the voices Ankle Tickler had used to talk to her, she realized. She could hear Sam, Ana, her parents, and even Mr. Kerrige, all overlayed in an overwhelming cacophony. *"If you don't shut up and focus, we'll lose this fight! They'll all die, and we'll be next!"*

Darien's head spun as Ankle Tickler yanked himself free of her mind, and Death lurched forward a few yards. She hurled herself back at him and found herself seeing through his eyes again, *watching as the spiderlike demon materialized in front of one of the humans and hit him with enough force to send him sprawling. Death could feel the creature's delicious pain from here. The man tried to roll, to get up, and a girl—the one who had had the gall to shoot at him back on the Montana prairie—screamed. The spider reappeared, knocking the fastest runner to the ground, spiked limb poised to deal a death blow—*

Darien yanked her mind from Death's and speared toward the Spider. Ankle Tickler's enraged howl clanged through her skull, through every room in her fortress, but it was too late.

She split the mind of the Spider on contact.

It swayed, shaking its head in pain and confusion. The human was still prone on the ground, gasping and white-faced as he looked up at it, but it couldn't make his leg come down, couldn't ... couldn't kill the sad little creature that had been at its mercy just seconds ago. Its fear turned to paralyzing terror as Darien tore at the demon's mind, ripping it apart like so much rotting fabric. The last thing it saw before it dissolved was her husband's shocked face.

And the hope on it.

Darien slammed back to herself and reeled, stumbling to her knees in the sand. But she couldn't rest; not when Death was here. Not when Ankle Tickler alone couldn't hold him. She didn't bother to get up, just dove back toward the ancient demon.

He stumbled to a halt, bound again, a scream of rage stuck in his throat. He was infuriatingly, maddeningly close.

"I'll destroy you!" he screamed at the force holding him. "I'll make you beg for oblivion, I'll take you apart in tiny pieces—"

Ankle Tickler withdrew.

Darien cried out as the full force of Death's mind fell on her. It was crushing, like trying to hold back a bull elephant with her bare hands. "WHAT ARE YOU DOING?"

"It's in my best interests to let Death take care of everyone at the gate," Ankle Tickler said, still in that disturbing fusion of voices.

"You can't do this," Darien whimpered.

"You can't think that I want to go back there, either."

Darien groaned as Death gained a foot, then a yard, then several. "I won't help you."

Ankle Tickler laughed. *"Yes, you will. There are so many lives here on this beach. I know you too well; you couldn't bring yourself to watch them end."*

Death gained another yard. Darien started to shake.

"Besides, then you'll die, too. No one will escape. None of you stands a chance against him."

Darien tried to speak, but all that came out was a wretched moan.

"Your only shot," Ankle Tickler continued, *"is still to help me kill Death, then take your chances against me afterward. Simple as that."*

Darien fell forward onto her elbows, cradling her head in her hands. A little pulse of warmth trickled into her, so at odds with everything else she was feeling that it threatened to cripple her attention. She blinked down at the sand. *The baby.* She reached for it, grasping its simple, perfect little mind. "Help me protect your daddy. I'll spend the ... the rest of my life making this up to you. I'm ... sorry."

Maybe the child understood, but Darien doubted it. She suspected the surge that followed was an adrenaline response, pure and simple, but one reserved for people who *loved*. For people who would stop at *nothing*.

Darien pushed herself up, cradling her baby's mind in her own even as it winced away from her, and sent a desperate prayer winging heavenward. Then, she threw everything she had at Death.

He jolted to a stop.

Darien's triumph—or pain; she couldn't actually tell which—was so strong that she almost screamed again. But as she choked on the sound, Death slipped forward, gaining a few inches. She redoubled her efforts, breath coming in short gasps. Some part of her—the rational part—was aware that she was playing right into Ankle Tickler's plans, exhausting herself so much that his odds of beating her later were all but guaranteed. She didn't care. She believed in the gate crew with all her soul. If she could just give them a *chance* ...

Death slipped forward. Darien pulled back. The demon didn't quite stop, but at least she was holding him to inches now, not feet.

Hurry, she pleaded.

***

It took Oliver a second to realize what a profound advantage being thrown halfway across the mountain had given him. Namely, that no one was paying attention to him anymore.

He propped himself on his arms, blinking away the last of the lingering daze. Maybe it was the Gatekeeper's menace. Maybe he'd just hit his head really hard. Either way, he felt slow and stupid. And now was not a good time for either of those things.

Come on, you idiot. Think like Ellie, or Darien. What's the next logical thing to do?

He dragged himself to his feet, staggered a few yards, then squatted behind a boulder and assessed the situation. Ellie knelt beside Sam, who appeared to be struggling to get off his hands and knees. Oliver felt a detached twinge of sympathy for how terribly the Gatekeeper affected his friend, but there was no time to dwell on it. Behind them, Henry limped toward the gate, but he wasn't going to be fast enough; at best, he'd be a minor distraction. Luke and Naomi, on the other hand, were struggling toward the Gatekeeper, faces screwed up with terror and determination. The monster watched them come on, baring its teeth in a gruesome smile.

Still crouching, heart thumping so hard he thought it might burst from his chest, Oliver crept toward the gate. When the Gatekeeper didn't turn his way, he sped up, half expecting the Hand—or something worse—to appear and drag him away.

But nothing did.

Mouth dry, Oliver glanced back at the Gatekeeper. His blood froze; it was moving toward Luke and Naomi now, walking with the same slow, nonchalant grace as last time. His stomach bubbled as he remembered Jordan's courage, the look on his face as the Gatekeeper's blades had gone through his chest—

Stop. Focus. Oliver stumbled forward; he was less than twenty feet from the cave's entrance and *still* nothing had come to stop him. No one from the gate crew had noticed him, either; the rocks and boulders scattered across this side provided excellent cover. A shudder went through him, and he fought the urge to look at Ellie one last time. He was almost there. He was going to die. Probably for real this time.

Though nothing's certain, a small voice inside him whispered.

Oliver swallowed, his breathing shallow, on the verge of panic. He put his hand against the chilled rock wall next to him, preparing himself for the final sprint—

"JORDAN!"

Naomi's scream was so heart-wrenching that Oliver whirled. His jaw dropped; two shapes were shimmering into view in front of the Gatekeeper, distinctly human and achingly familiar. One was Jordan, who had planted himself between the monster and his parents. The other was Dean.

"OLIVER!" Ellie's yell shattered through him. "LOOK OUT—!"

Something clamped around Oliver's thigh, jerking him off balance. He hit the ground on his back, the air whooshing out of him as he was dragged backward, away from the gate. His stomach bottomed out—it was the Hand. It had found him. Yelling and kicking, he tore his knife free of its sheath and stabbed at the thing, but it was made of *stone*; it couldn't be cut. Its grip was tightening, crushing, bruising; any more force and he thought his femur might snap.

Oliver twisted onto his side, scrabbling until his hand closed on a rock the size of his fist. He swung it at the Hand, beating at it like a madman.

"Dad!" he yelled. "Help!"

***

Ellie screamed as Oliver went down, thrashing and kicking. She started toward him, feeling the Gatekeeper's influence wane with every step she took. "I'm coming, Oliver! I'm—"

Ellie. Look.

The voice was barely more than a whisper, but perhaps its quiet calmness was what arrested her attention. She stopped dead. It sounded like …

"Dean?" she asked.

LOOK, Ellie!

She spun toward the gate. The way was clear.

And she was less than fifteen yards away.

Go now. The voice sounded labored, spent. *Save Oliver. Save … everyone.*

Ellie didn't remember deciding to run, but she was. And not just running, sprinting. She was flying over the ground, past where Oliver fought the stone Hand, dodging around boulders and jumping over smaller rocks. The mouth of the cave yawned in front of her, a jaw open to swallow her whole.

Trust … me … the voice whispered.

"I don't," Ellie gasped, but she realized then that even if she could stop herself, she wouldn't. She hurtled over the cave's threshold and tore down the little incline that led to the pool. It was crystal clear and infinitely deep, its throat descending into the depths of the earth, its color the same unfathomable blue as Oliver's eyes. She took two steps and threw herself into the water.

Cold.

The shock of it was so intense that everything in Ellie seized. She went under, her whole body cramping and curling against horrendous, awful cold. She tried to gasp but couldn't—she couldn't breathe, her chest was on fire, every muscle in her body pulled taut and twisted and frozen, and there was something she needed to do here, but she didn't want to, she just wanted it to end—

A tiny light appeared, and a profound sense of love, security, and familiarity swept over her. It spread, forming into a human shape, vague outlines of features becoming visible. They were confused. In pain.

Dad.

She was almost gone, too, but she had just enough strength to reach out a hand—

***

An awful, keening wail lanced through Darien's skull with so much force it knocked her backward. Something was *sucking Ankle Tickler in, tearing him away from this world that he wanted so badly to possess, ripping him away from the ambition he'd come so close to realizing ... and he'd be trapped in there with Death, the demon-killer—*

Ankle Tickler's thoughts disappeared. The crushing weight of Death's mind lifted.

Darien fell onto her side in the soft, cold sand and knew no more.

Chapter Thirty-One

The Gatekeeper let out a horrible, defeated howl, its edges blackening as it was pulled toward the cave. And Oliver's heart shattered.

She can't be gone. She can't be gone.

But breathing was already easier; moving, too. The Gatekeeper dissolved into a black wisp and was pulled into the cave. Another wisp followed, and another. Tens, hundreds, maybe thousands.

Oliver didn't care.

He broke into a limping run. Covering the last few yards to the cave's mouth, he staggered as he took in the whole scene. Ellie floated facedown in the pool, just like Robert had. Sobbing her name, he stumbled down the incline toward the water, tearing at his jacket, kicking his shoes off, ignoring the endless, silent stream of black swirls that sped past him as they were sucked back into their world.

Oliver hurled his jacket away, then splashed into the pool. He gasped. It was colder than the Pacific, than anything he'd ever felt in his life. The bottom dropped suddenly, and he plunged into the water. His lungs were on fire, his arms and legs already numb. Still, he struck out toward Elllie; she wasn't far … he could make it …

His hand closed on her wrist. He kicked toward shore, towing her body after him, but now his lungs felt like they were full of knives. For a second, he panicked; maybe he'd die here, too. But then peace stole over him. If he did, he'd be with her.

"No, son."

Oliver looked up. His father's ghost stood on the rim of the pool, the only section that was shallow.

"You have a whole life to live." Dean held his hand out to Oliver. Gasping, Oliver kicked out, reached for it … and connected. His father's hand hovered on the edge of being solid, but its gentle pull was enough. Oliver's right foot struck the pool's steep bottom; his left gained a purchase. He staggered into the shallows. Dean backed away and started to fade, but Oliver was already turning to Ellie. Another dry sob erupted from his chest at the sight of her, floating lifeless in the pool, her beautiful hair drifting around her head, eyes open and glassy. He lifted her, cradling her frigid body against him as he stumbled out of the shallows and onto dry ground.

"ELLIE!"

The pain in Sam's voice tore at Oliver.

"She's here!" he tried to yell, but he was so cold and weak that it came out as a whisper.

No time. Act fast.

Oliver lay Ellie down on the ground on her back and knelt beside her, willing his half-frozen limbs to *move.* He brought the heels of his hands together in the center of her chest and pushed hard.

Her whole torso bent under his hands.

Again.

Her bones felt so fragile, like a bird's.

Again.

Her rib splintered.

"I'm so sorry." Tears blazed searing trails down his cheeks. "I'm so sorry." But he didn't stop. He couldn't. *Wouldn't,* not until his own body failed.

"Shift left!"

Oliver glanced up into Sam's tear-streaked face.

"When you give out, I'll take over!" Sam said.

Oliver just nodded. Then ...

He blinked. There were *people* over Sam's shoulder, gathered behind him in a loose group, but none of them were from the gate crew. Dean was one, standing a little off to the side, but the other four ...

Shock rolled through Oliver so hard that he nearly stopped doing chest compressions. They were Ellie's family. He recognized Robert, and the auburn-haired woman next to him must have been Ellie's mother. A young girl flitted around them all, too, excitable as she looked up into the face of—

Oliver's heart nearly stopped. It was Ellie. He could see Ellie's ghost.

Chapter Thirty-Two

The first thing Ellie noticed was that it was warm again. The second was that, even looking straight down into the blue depths of the earth, she could breathe.

Or, rather, she didn't *have* to breathe.

Holy crap, she thought. *I'm dead.*

She looked up. Then *stood* up, since the fact that she was floating in water didn't seem to matter anymore. Black shadows whirled through the air and into the pool all around her, sucked down like a giant drain. And Ellie realized ... if they were being pulled back into their world, that meant ...

"Ellie?"

She turned. Joy flooded her as she saw her father standing next to her, blinking like he was as blindsided as she was. He threw his arms around her—a strange experience, since she didn't really *feel* them. But emotion still welled in her chest, and she still cried, and even though the tears weren't real, she could have sworn she still felt them running down her cheeks.

"My brave Eleanor," Robert said warmly. "I love you so much."

"I love you too, Daddy."

They held each other for a long time, until the tears subsided. Her father released her, but still kept a vestigial grip on her shoulders. He looked down into her face, his expression one of love and deep, deep regret.

"Thank you. Thank you for getting me out of there. That was ..." A shudder went through him. "But also, I'm so sorry that you're here." His eyes flicked up to a point behind Ellie, and his expression turned to one of anguish. "And not there."

Ellie turned in the direction her father was looking, and the stomach she no longer had still managed to clench. Oliver was in the pool, swimming toward her body, which floated facedown at her feet. His face was desperate, desolate. She watched in slow motion as he grabbed her wrist and turned to pull her back toward dry ground.

"We've got to help him!" Ellie said. "He'll die in there!"

She bent and tried to push her body toward the shoreline, but her hands went right through. She cursed.

"El," her father said, his voice gentle. "I don't think you can. We're not corporeal anymore—"

"No, wait, *Dean* could do this. Oliver's dad; he, he said you just needed to be invested enough." Ellie heaved again, keeping her eyes on Oliver as he kicked and struggled. And this time, she *did* feel some resistance. She could swear her body moved a few extra inches. Pitiful, but better than nothing.

Her father crouched beside her and started pushing, too, a strange, morbid look on his face. "This isn't exactly what I imagined the afterlife would be like."

Ellie pushed again, relieved when she definitely felt movement. "Wait, haven't ...?" It dawned on her. "You've been trapped. You don't actually have any more experience with the real afterlife than I do."

"That's probably true. Though I've gotten used to not having a body anymore." He grunted as he pushed again. "As much as one can, anyway."

Ellie let out a strangled grunt, grief over her own death hitting her like a runaway truck. *No. Help Oliver. That's all that matters right now.*

And he *was* close, almost to the shallows. But his shuddering was worsening. He closed his eyes and tipped his head back, his long lashes lying against his bone-pale cheeks, his expression one of a man who was on the verge of giving up.

"No!" Ellie shouted. "Don't you quit, Oliver!"

She shoved at her body again, her heart breaking a little as it moved, as Oliver got even closer to escape, to continued life. Without her.

Movement flashed out of the corner of her eye—controlled movement, *human* movement, not the flailing panic of demons being sucked back into their world. Dean was jogging down the incline toward the pool. He threw them a little salute as he stopped, then held out his hand to Oliver.

"No, son," he said. "You have a whole life to live."

He made eye contact with Ellie. "And you might, too, depending on how the next couple minutes go."

Ellie's jaw dropped. "Are you saying—?"

Dean shushed her, then returned his attention to Oliver, who stared at him through desolate eyes. Then, Oliver reached up and—somehow—took Dean's hand. The ghost pulled his son toward the pool's edge, paling by the second. Still, he didn't let go until Oliver got his feet underneath him and staggered into the ankle-deep shallows, pulling Ellie's body.

Dean staggered toward them, looking drained and exhausted. "I thought that might work." He nodded to Ellie and her father. "Pleasure to finally *actually* meet you both. I don't feel like that business at the gas station in Montana really counted, Ellie."

"Wait, how did you just help Oliver so easily?" Ellie asked. "And where have you been for the last few days? And—"

"Per your second question, I've been saving up for *this*." Dean gestured around them. "I wanted to be in top form for it, because I knew it was coming and you'd need all the help you could get. In answer to your first question, I don't know. But I think helping Oliver is easier because he's been to the In-Between before. There's some ... *thing* about him that's changed. He's slightly more transparent. It's difficult to describe, but it makes him easier to talk to for us spirits—"

But Ellie had stopped listening. Oliver turned; she could see his face fully for the first time, and it was heartbreaking. Tears ran down his cheeks, and his shoulders shook—every part of him shook. His expression was tortured.

Dean's words echoed in her head. *He's easier to talk to for us spirits.*

Her throat constricted. What if she'd read Dean wrong? What if hinting that Ellie could come back had been his way of motivating Oliver not just to give up and drown? Were a few stolen whispers from beyond really all she could hope for now? He'd move on, find someone else, chase his dreams, live a whole life.

And she'd have to watch. From this side.

Alone.

Before she knew it, she was sobbing.

"Ellie." Her father's arms encircled her, and she leaned against him as the tears came again. "I'm so sorry that this is how it's turned out. I wish you hadn't had to—"

"Dean," she sniffed. "Did you mean it when you said I might still have a life?"

Her father's arms went stiff. Dean's eyes flicked up to his face, then back down to Ellie's. "I can't guarantee anything, Ellie, but if I know my son at all, he's not going to let you go so easily. He'll fight for you. And I'll tell you the same thing I told him when he was in your shoes."

Ellie wiped at her eyes out of habit before remembering there was no need to do that anymore. "Which is?"

"You died of shock. You didn't drown. There might be a little water in your lungs, but—"

"Get to the point," Ellie snapped, then immediately felt a wave of guilt; the man was just trying to help. "Sorry."

But Dean just waved it off. "The point is, your body's way less damaged than Oliver's was, and *he* still managed to return. The pain nearly killed him a second time, but he still did it. I think there's a chance you could, too—better than his, in fact. As long as that's what you want." He looked back toward his son. "As long as he can get your body to be habitable again. If he can get your blood moving, keep your brain functioning ..."

Ellie gaped at Dean. Then, she spun back toward Oliver. He was lifting her, splashing out of the pool in slow motion. She stepped toward him; maybe the proximity of her spirit to her body would increase her chances of being able to—

"Wow," her dad grunted, his voice bemused. "Seems like I've missed a lot."

"Oh my goodness, Dad." She spun to face him as she realized what her very clear hopes of coming back to life—*going* back to life?—might be doing to him emotionally. "I'm so sorry—I don't regret saving you, dying, saving the world ..."

She stopped. He was beaming.

"Ellie, I want you to have a life, and to experience all the joys and struggles and beauty of building that life with someone you love, and who loves you." He nodded toward Oliver. "Now, I haven't seen a lot of that boy. Just one card game and then loading up some bags. But given that I just watched him dive into a demon pool to rescue you, I'm feeling cautiously decent about him."

Ellie let out a shaky laugh. "Only cautiously decent? Come on, Dad."

He grinned, then turned to Dean. "I'm gathering that he died and came back? What's the story behind that?"

"He died fighting the Lady," Ellie said, her voice a whisper as she watched Oliver lower her body gently to the earth. "He distracted her so I could kill her."

"I can corroborate that." Dean winked at Ellie's dad. "Eyewitness testimony."

Robert grinned. "Well, I guess the preliminary evidence points to him being a good choice, Ellie. Were you to make it, of course." Her dad raised his eyebrows at her, his grin disappearing. "And as your father, I want to advise you to still take some time. I personally think that committing to someone is the best way to live life in the end. But, you need to make sure he's the right one. And ..."

Her dad broke off, his mouth opening in shock as he focused on something across the cave. Ellie whirled, proverbial heart in her proverbial throat, wondering if they'd accidentally let some other monster loose in the world—

Only to make eye contact with a pair of impish hazel eyes, and a wide, beautiful smile that she hadn't thought she'd ever see again.

"Audrey!" Robert said at the same time Ellie yelled, "Mom!'

They tore across the cave together, her mother laughing and crying as they met in the middle in a weird family scrum.

"Oh my goodness, I missed you," her father said, crying openly now. "Does this mean Lily's—?"

"I'm right here, Dad."

Lily's young voice sent a jolt through Ellie; she hadn't seen her sister appear, but there she suddenly was, looking a little bewildered but mostly overjoyed. Ellie pulled her into a hug, spirit-tears leaking down her cheeks at the sound of Lily's giggle in her ears.

"You didn't bring me any Oreos!" Lily teased. "What's that about, huh?"

"I ..." Ellie laugh-sobbed. "They don't travel well. But if I get to go back, I'll eat a whole package for you, I promise."

Her mother enveloped them both in a hug. "*I* hope you get to go back. If you want to, of course. You're welcome to stay, too. We love you very much, and the Afterlife is wonderful." She pulled away and took Ellie's hands between hers. "Truly, it is."

"Yeah. I ..." Suddenly, Ellie was aware of a *pull* where her heart had been, a sort of tugging to a place that wasn't here, or Earth, but beyond. It was pure peace, and she realized that feeling had a power she'd only ever caught shadowy glimpses of in life.

"What's beyond?" she asked hoarsely.

Her mom shook her head. "That's not for us to tell you. If you come with us, you'll see. If you choose to return—which none of us condemn, by the way—then you'll need to find out the truth on your own." She smiled. "But whatever you decide, know that what's beyond is *good*."

A lump rose in Ellie's throat, and she looked back at Oliver. She loved him so much. But the world suddenly seemed so drab and dull and sorrowful compared to what she could feel on the other side. She turned back to her mom and Lily. "Do *you* want to go back? If you could have a choice, would *any* of you—?"

She stopped. Two more people had entered the cave. One stood a few feet away in low conversation with Dean. She looked like a younger version of Helen, her ice-blue eyes fixed on Oliver's face as he knelt with his hands on Ellie's chest, compressing it in slow motion. The other figure moved with painful slowness down the incline that led to the pool: Sam, his face a mirror of what Oliver's had been earlier. Her brother dropped to his knees beside Oliver with a violence that she knew he'd feel later.

"I can only speak for myself," Ellie's mother said softly, "but no. I wouldn't choose to go back, not at this point. You and Sam are grown. Lily—and you—" She smiled at Robert, an expression that contained so much joy and peace that tears sprang to Ellie's eyes again, "—are here with me. Someday, my parents will be, too." She put a hand on Ellie's shoulder. "I'm at peace. I belong here, and I'm happy, and I look forward to the day when we can all be together."

She let her hand fall, then looked toward where Oliver was still doing chest compressions. "But I don't think that time is now."

Ellie followed her gaze. She could see every minute change in his expression, could watch it play out in slow motion, could study every angle and plane of his face. And *wanted* to. She just wished he were looking back.

As if on cue, he looked up into her eyes, and the *zing* that went through her spirit was the most palpable thing she'd experienced since her death. Ellie stepped forward without realizing it.

Oliver's lips moved. "Please."

Ellie looked back at her family.

"It's your decision to make," her dad said.

"I don't think you have a lot of time, though," Lily said. "I think we're going to be pulled back to the Afterlife soon."

"All of us," Dean added from Oliver's other side.

Autumn raised her eyebrows. "You're not going to try and stay this time?"

Dean looked at their son, then smiled. "I no longer feel the need to."

The tug in Ellie's chest intensified. Her family started to fade around the edges.

"The barriers are all coming back up," her mom said softly.

"And you'll still love me if I choose him?" Ellie asked. Her heart felt like it was tearing in half; she hadn't expected to have a choice. Or for the choice to be so obvious, yet still hurt so much.

"Eleanor." Her mom smiled. "We'll love you across all of time and space and eternity. And we'll have plenty of time to catch up later. If you want to go, and you *can* go, then go. Live."

Ellie turned and ran back to them, gathering them all in a weird, smashed-up hug where she didn't actually feel anything, but still managed to feel *everything*. From somewhere behind her, Dean bellowed. "Chest compressions, Oliver! It's now or never!"

"How long should it take—" Ellie cut off as a jolt of pain lanced across her chest. If she hadn't been supported by the family hug, she would have doubled over.

"Yes!" Dean yelled. "The pain is a good thing, Ellie! Follow it back!"

Another jolt hit her in the center of the chest. Deeper. Worse.

"Thank you," she gasped at her parents. "Thank you so much for understanding, for loving me, for … for everything you gave up for me. I didn't get it before, but now—"

SLAM!

Ellie bit back a scream; she was being sucked away, back into the land of pain and anxiety and uncertainty. But it was where Oliver was. So it was where she wanted to be. "I love you so much!"

"We love you!" her mom cried.

"We're proud of you!" her dad added.

"Mint Oreos!" Lily yelled. "Eat the mint ones!"

Ellie's world turned upside down, she was spinning into blackness, laughing and crying and careening toward the pain that was rising up to engulf her.

***

"Chest compressions, Oliver! It's now or never!"

Oliver redoubled his efforts, feeling Ellie's bones bend and crack under his hands, hating himself a little even as hope surged in him at the sound of Dean's voice. She was still here, she'd seen him, nodded, and he didn't know whether that had meant "yes, I'll come back," or "goodbye," but everything in him begged for the former. He didn't know if he outweighed the love of her family. He dared not hope too hard. But he could at least give her the choice, like she'd given him.

"They're here, Sam! Your family's—" He looked up to see Ellie, and his heart cracked again. She was hugging her family, tears falling down her face. She'd turned her back on him.

"If you're going to stop, then get out of my way!" Sam yelled. He was beside himself, clutching his head in his hands, every muscle in his body tense. Oliver looked down, his tears falling freely now, pattering onto Ellie's jacket like a warm rain. She wasn't coming back.

He begged anyway. "Please. Please, Ellie. I love you."

"Come back," Sam cried.

Ellie gasped.

Her face screwed up in agony, and Oliver snatched his hands back like they'd been burned.

"Ellie!" Sam lunged forward, but stopped at the look on his sister's face. She let out a strained half-scream, half-rolling, trying to double over, her breath coming in short fits.

Oliver leaned down, feeling helpless, shivering so hard he could hardly speak. "It's … it's going to be okay, Ellie. Help is coming. It's going to be okay."

He grasped her hand, crying, and reached down to kiss her cheek as shadows appeared at the mouth of the cave, and voices started to descend on them. The ghosts were all gone and so were the demons, and his vision was starting to blur around the edges …

***

Sam saw Oliver's head tip toward his sister's, his body slumping forward. He came into a half-crouch and caught his friend before he pitched over Ellie, who was still heaving in shallow, painful-sounding breaths and hadn't managed to speak yet. Grunting, he laid Oliver on the ground next to her.

"Is he ok-kay?" Ellie asked weakly.

Sam knelt next to her. "For now, but we have to get you both help. Hang on."

He pressed his palm to her frigid cheek and kissed her forehead. Then he staggered to his feet, shocked at how unsteady he felt. His legs were jelly; his ankle throbbed. He felt generally weak and stupid. And he didn't have *any* idea where Darien was, let alone if she was okay. He stumbled up the slight incline toward the cave's mouth and was just starting to wonder why no one else had made it inside yet when he rounded the bend and smacked into someone huge, bearded, and covered in flannel.

"Henry," Sam said, relieved. "Ellie and Oliver are in there—"

"Which one's ..." Henry's voice quivered. "Which one—"

"Ellie."

Tears welled in Henry's eyes. He pulled Sam into a hug. "I'm so sorry, Sam. She was—"

"No, no!" Sam fought free of Henry's embrace, which wasn't an easy thing to do. "She's alive! They're both alive!"

Henry's jaw dropped. "How?"

"Oliver dove in after her, dragged her out, did CPR, and ..." Sam broke off, remembering the way Oliver had looked up, pleading with someone he couldn't see. He shook his head. "The point is, the water in there is ice-cold, supernaturally cold, and they both were in it for a minute at least. They're in bad shape. We need to get them warmed up, probably to a hospital."

Henry nodded. "Luke! Naomi!"

"Yeah?" came Luke's voice from behind him, and Sam felt another pang of gratitude. They'd made it, too. He turned to see Naomi wrapping Luke's thigh. Bloodstains peeked below the bandage at his knee and down his shins, exposed through the shredded remnants of his pant leg.

"Oliver and Ellie are in the cave, both alive, but they need help," Henry said over the couple's gasps. "You think the three of us can manage to at least assess the situation and start a fire?"

"Yeah." Naomi got to her feet and held out her hand to Luke. Of the four of them, she was easily the most functional—

Sam frowned and turned to Henry. "The *three* of us?"

Henry nodded, his expression turning grave. "Helen's down on the shore with Darien."

Something clenched so hard in Sam's stomach that he thought he might be sick.

"She ..."

Sam barely stopped himself from grabbing Henry's shoulders. "She *what*?"

"Helen thinks she'll be okay, but she's out cold right now. Point is, you might be needed elsewhere. We can take care of your sister for you—"

But Sam had already started down the canyon. "I know you can. Will you radio Helen with updates so I can get them, too?"

"Yep."

Sam flashed a thumbs-up over his shoulder, then broke into a pitifully slow jog. His ankle hurt where the demon had grabbed it, but the pain was already starting to fade—a fact that he could feel with extraordinary acuteness now that he was running on it. It was as if every step was easier than the last. His stomach lurched as he passed the place where he and Oliver had dived into the canyon to get away from the Gatekeeper yesterday.

That happened yesterday.

His head grew light with exhaustion, but he forced it away. He could parse all those emotions later. Or better yet, work them off for the next four months at practice. For now, there was this one last, most crucial run.

***

Darien woke slowly, the noise around her crawling through her ears and rattling around inside her skull. Urgent voices. Cries for help. Sobs.

"She's coming back."

Darien cringed; the voice sounded like Ankle Tickler's. *So we* did *kill Death.* Or ... had they sent the demons back? She'd *thought* that was what had happened. But maybe she'd passed out, and her mind had fabricated a comforting illusion as she was falling, and Death had killed Sam and the others, and now Ankle Tickler was here for her.

"Darien?"

Her eyes snapped open, and she winced as the blinding gray light sent a spike of pain through her head. It wasn't Ankle Tickler—it actually *was* Sam; he was cradling her in his lap. He stroked her cheek with his thumb, a tired smile touching the corner of his mouth. "Not the best time to take a nap."

"I couldn't really control it."

"No, I'm sorry." His palm pressed against her face now, light and soothing, and her eyes fluttered closed again. "Not a great joke."

Darien waved a weak hand. "Nah. I'm just grumpy when I wake up. You know that."

Sam chuckled, and Darien managed a smile. From somewhere nearby, she heard Helen's voice. "Update on our end: Darien's awake and being sassy, so that's a good sign."

Luke's voice answered. "Roger that. We've revived Oliver and need to get him walking so he doesn't freeze, but he won't leave Ellie. Could you send the Nantinaq to carry her? That frees up Luke and Naomi to go after Bill and Jess."

"Sure thing," Helen said.

Darien let her head flop to the side. Helen was propped against a nearby tree. She flashed her a thumbs-up. "Glad you're back with us."

Darien took a deep breath, then sat, fighting a wave of nausea as she did. "I didn't even see you get here."

Helen chuckled. "No, you were a little busy when the Nantinaq and I arrived."

"The Nantinaq?" Darien swallowed again, resting her head between her knees.

"You were having a serious fight of your own when we showed up. You weren't aware of much." Helen hesitated. "Death, I assume?"

Darien didn't dare open her mouth. She just nodded.

Helen's voice gentled. "I think you saved a lot of people today. Not to mention the world itself."

But I couldn't save everyone. Darien raised her head, averting her eyes from the beach where all the bodies lay, a bolt of grief hitting her straight in the heart. "Who went into the cave?"

"Ellie," Sam said gently.

Darien's head started to spin; she leaned forward again. Of all the people, Ellie made the *least* sense—

"Wait, Dar." Sam placed a hand on her shoulder. "She's not dead, though. She came back."

"What? How?"

She listened with rapt attention as Sam described what he'd seen in the cave, from the CPR to Oliver appearing to talk with people Sam couldn't see, to Ellie's first, gasping breath. About halfway through the story, the Nantinaq appeared, plunking himself down on the sand in a curiously human pose. By the end of Sam's story, Darien could swear he looked smug.

"I knew Just Ellie was enough," he rumbled.

"Great," Sam said. "Will you go get her? Please?" he added, when the Nantinaq continued to loom.

"I will." The Nantinaq stood, then disappeared into the bushes without a sound.

"Boy, I'm so grateful for him." Helen turned back to them. "He carried me down the mountain, too. He …" She chuckled. "You should've seen him when we got here. He marched right up to the demon who was impersonating him—didn't even notice the bullets hitting him—and started telling him off like a mom scolding a toddler. The demon was so confused that Boris's crew was able to light it up."

Darien smiled weakly, letting her head drop to Sam's shoulder. Today—no, the last *week*—had been terrible, an ordeal more difficult than she'd ever imagined. But it was over. The weight wasn't gone; maybe it wouldn't ever be … but maybe that wasn't the point. Perhaps the point was to get strong enough to bear it.

Not sure what she was going to find, she reached for her baby's mind. Relief swept over her as its familiar glow blossomed up to meet her. It was safe. It was over. And even though shouts and cries and sounds of mourning drifted from the beach, Darien had a little, whispering impression that it was all going to be okay.

She opened her eyes and found herself looking into Sam's. This time, her small, trembling smile was more heartfelt than it had been in a long time. "Hey. Let's go home."

Epilogue

The weeks after the battle at the gate were a blur to Ellie. She only remembered flashes of the aftermath: being carried down the mountain by the Nantinaq, crying when she saw how many bodies littered the beach, the long, painful boat ride back. Despite the stabbing pain in her ribs, she'd passed out before they reached Nanwalek. Hours later, she'd come to in Homer's hospital to see Oliver slumped over the foot of her bed, fast asleep underneath a heated blanket.

Ellie still smiled when she remembered the look on his face when he'd finally woken. His open joy, his sorrow at her condition and the people they'd lost, his whispered apology for breaking her ribs, and the blissful minutes of gentle kisses that followed. There was no better painkiller than that, she'd thought.

Then there was the dawning realization that—even with three broken ribs and two cracked ones—a weight had lifted. Life was *better*, and not just for her, but for everyone. The nurses. The ferrymen. The Alaskan teenager that Sam sold his beat-up, heroic white pickup to for five hundred dollars and a case of salmon.

"For Darien and the baby," he'd said when Ellie had started snickering (that was all she *could* do without her ribs feeling like they were going to stab her to death from the inside). "Omega-3s are crucial for eye and brain development."

She grinned. "I'm just glad they're both okay."

"You and me both, El," Sam said fervently. "You and me both."

It was a relief when Ellie's professors provided her with generous makeup options for missing the first week of her sophomore year. After all, recovering from an "accident" in the Alaskan backcountry was no picnic. But recover she did. Slowly at first, then quickly. By mid-October, she was taking brisk walks around her neighborhood; by late November, she was jogging again. There were days when her heart ached for her parents and Lily, and for that all-consuming peace she'd glimpsed on the other side. But overall, she felt ... *better*. More secure in herself, more confident.

Still, her friends noticed a difference; even their biggest smiles didn't quite succeed at covering the sideways glances they'd shoot at her when they thought she wasn't looking. She didn't blame them. Turning around and running right back to the place where her dad had died only weeks before? Then breaking ribs in her own traumatic accident? And not trusting them—not trusting *anyone* (except the mysterious "Alaska Man" that none of them had ever actually met)—with details?

No, Ellie decided. She didn't blame them for looking at her a little differently. Not when she *was* a different person now.

When it was quiet, her mind sometimes drifted to those precious moments she'd spent in the In-Between with her parents and Lily, and the joy—and agony—of re-awakening in her own broken, wonderful body. Sometimes she cried when she played in the symphony now, partially because of the sheer beauty of the music, but also because she was *here*. *Playing* it. All of life was a gift; her talents, her challenges, her friendships, her family both blood and chosen—everything.

But one relationship—one person—eclipsed them all.

Ellie lay on the couch one evening in March after the sun had gone down, munching on Mint Oreos and having her nightly conversation with Oliver. She'd spent all of Christmas break at the Shack with him, where they'd entertained some of Ellie's friends (who were relieved to learn that Alaska Man wasn't just a figment of her imagination), half of Sam's football team, and sometimes just Sam and Darien, who somehow made maternity clothes look like high-end luxury fashion. They'd spent hours—whole nights—entwined in each other's arms, but it hadn't been enough. And as she'd kissed him goodbye at the Denver airport and watched him walk away, she felt like her ribs were cracking all over again.

"How's Darien doing?" Oliver asked.

Ellie blinked the mist out of her eyes and made her voice steady. "As good as she can be." She grinned. "Sara's getting so big that you can see Darien's whole belly move when she kicks."

"No kidding!"

Ellie nodded. "It's pretty wild. I can't wait until she's here."

"And she still looks ... like a normal baby? Sorry, I don't know how to ask that."

Ellie smiled. "Yeah. The doctors are happy with how everything's going. They don't know what really happened up there, of course, but she doesn't have any abnormalities that they can see. She's a healthy, happy baby. With a much healthier, happier mom now that Darien isn't a demon radar anymore."

Oliver chuckled. "That's great. And what about Sam? Has he stopped seeing shadows yet?"

"I think so, for the most part." Ellie frowned as she thought about her brother. Given that he had both finals week and a baby happening within the next month, she was glad all symptoms of his … *ability* … had finally disappeared.

"I'm surprised it took that long," Oliver said.

"I think we all were, especially him. Though, I guess since the Nantinaq said the demons' world borders ours, it sort of makes sense." Ellie lowered her voice. "Do you still see spirits?"

"Sometimes. You?"

"Also sometimes. I'm …" She swallowed. "I'm glad they don't seem to want to stay in the In-Between, because if I were taking a quiz and looked up and saw a ghost staring at me again, I think I'd—"

The front door burst open, Ellie's roommate Tiffany and their mutual friend Alanna piling through. Annoyance flashed through Ellie; she covered it by sitting up.

"Oh, sorry," Tiffany said.

Ellie waved her off. "It's fine. I'll go in my room."

"Alaska Man?" Alanna said knowingly as Ellie passed.

Ellie grinned. "I love him. What can I say?"

Her friends giggled and "aaw'ed," but it was Oliver's quiet laugh that filled her to the brim as she closed the bedroom door and sat on the edge of her bed.

"Ellie …" He chuckled some more.

"What?" she asked.

"You have no idea how happy you make me."

Tingling warmth spread from her chest through every cell in her body. She lay back on the bed, unable to stop smiling. "Likewise."

They lapsed into comfortable silence, and Ellie's smile faded as she stared up at the recently de-popcorned ceiling. "I'm done with this."

Oliver's voice took on a note of caution. "With … what?"

"Not being with you."

Silence greeted her words. Then he sighed. "I'm pretty done with it, too."

"What do you propose we do about it?" she asked.

"Well …" He seemed to hesitate. "I have one big proposition I could make."

Ellie's heart started thumping, sending a strange, wonderful ache through her veins. "Are we ready for that? We're still so … young."

It sounded lame even as she said it. They'd been successfully long-distance for almost seven months now, their only time together that blissful week at Christmas. Yet her need for him had only grown. It was fierce now. She wasn't sure she'd ever recover if they went their separate ways.

"I'm sorry," she stammered. "I'm absolutely, fully committed to us. Don't take how awkwardly I said that as—"

"Ellie."

Oliver's voice was low and husky, and a wave of goosebumps washed over her. She sank back onto her pillow, turning her face into the phone like she could almost fool herself into thinking it was his callused, gentle hand.

"I don't care that we're young," he said. "I care that we love each other and want to build a life together."

Emotion welled in Ellie, and her vision blurred. "Me, too. Life's so short and fragile. I don't want to miss another day of … of *us*. It's killing me."

"Would you say yes, if I asked?"

The tenderness in his voice pierced Ellie to her core. "Oliver. Yes."

He let out a breathless laugh. Elile rolled over onto her side, hugging her pillow. "I can't imagine sharing life with anyone but you. After all we've been through—we *died*! We've literally both *died*, Oliver! Who else could we possibly talk to about *that*? Who else would know how to comfort me when I wake up from a cave dream? The fact that you're the greatest man on earth aside, how would I even *explain* that to anyone else?"

"'Greatest' might be a little far—"

"Shut up and own it, Oliver."

"Okay, okay," he laughed. "I'll own *at least* fifty percent of it."

"Awesome." Ellie's smile faded, and she buried her face in the pillow. "I just …"

"Ellie." His voice was so warm.

"I just want you," she blurted.

"Done."

"In every possible interpretation of the phrase."

"Also done."

"To grow old with you—"

"Let's do it."

"Have a couple kids—"

"Two or three, like we talked about."

Ellie laugh-cried at the thought, then snorted straight into the phone. Oliver burst out laughing. "And whatever that was. I'm game for it. Forever."

They giggled for a few seconds more, then Ellie sobered. "Are you sure you're okay with moving down here?"

She could practically feel him shrug. "Yeah. And are you sure you're okay with trying out Anchorage and its symphony if I can't stomach the lower 48?"

"Of course."

Ellie smiled. Those *mountains*, their savage beauty, the promise they held for people who weren't afraid. *Or maybe who are the right amount of afraid,* she thought. Because she wanted a long life. A happy life.

And, because of that, fear was sometimes her ally.

"Maybe we could start in Alaska, actually," she mused.

"After you get your doctorate. I can study business from anywhere. Location matters a lot more for you."

They lapsed into comfortable silence for a moment. Then ...

"Your semester ends on May 13th, right?"

She grinned. "Not that you're counting or anything. But yes."

"I ... I'd like you to come visit the day after. If you can."

Ellie's smile widened. "Done."

***

Almost two months later, Ellie landed at Ted Stevens International Airport in Anchorage and fell into Oliver's arms. Together, they boarded a little commuter plane—the smallest Ellie had ever been on—and flew to Homer's airport, landing gracefully on the long stretch of tarmac that scored its way across the snow-spotted green landscape. They walked hand-in-hand to the docks, catching up, confirming summer plans, chucking snowballs at each other whenever they passed a drift. But when they got to the dock, Oliver turned away from the ferry, instead leading them down into the harbor proper.

"Where are we going?" Ellie asked.

Oliver smiled. "To the *Poor Buoy*."

"Ooo, a private boat ride to Seldovia. How bourgeois."

Oliver's grin widened as he started the motor. "Not to Seldovia, actually."

Ellie's heart started to flutter; she thought she knew where this was going—even if she didn't know where they were *actually* going. "Okay. Where to, then?"

"You'll see," he said as they motored out of the harbor.

Ellie hadn't paid enough attention to any of her ferry rides to Seldovia to know immediately that it *wasn't* where Oliver was going. But after about half an hour, even she got the gist. They glided down Alaska's stunning coastline, past endless ranks of frowning Sitka Spruce and bushes that were just starting to show hints of green, past wisps of mist that rose off the tops of the glacier-capped mountains.

"This is so beautiful, Oliver."

"Wait 'til we get there."

"How close are we?"

Oliver didn't answer. Instead, he turned the wheel, arcing the *Poor Buoy* around a small jut of rock and into a little bay. And at its mouth ...

Ellie gasped. A beautiful cabin was tucked into the trees, all knotty wood and blue siding that blended perfectly into the forest around it. She grabbed Oliver's shoulder. "Don't tell me that's it."

His face split in a huge grin. "That's it."

"Seriously?!"

"Seriously. Welcome to Bear Cove Retreat, Ellie."

She gaped at it for a moment longer. "How did you even know about this place? Do we have it all to ourselves?"

"We do have it all to ourselves. For the next five days. You want to kayak to a glacier? We can kayak to a glacier. Want to make amazing, decadent desserts? We pretty much have a chef's kitchen. Want to hike? We can hike. We can do anything you want."

"*How?*"

Oliver's smile turned soft. "I know the people who own it. They fought on the beach, actually. They're really great, gave me a discount."

Ellie gaped at him, drinking in his smile, his happiness, as he maneuvered the *Poor Buoy* next to the dock. She helped him moor it, then minutes later, they were climbing the steep gangplank up to the deck that overlooked the cove. When they got to the deck, Ellie pulled him around to face her and kissed him. Hard. His arms twined around her waist, and Ellie's head grew a little light. As always, their lips, their hands, their bodies fit together perfectly.

Oliver kissed her again, softer and sweeter this time. She let the kiss's afterglow linger after he'd pulled away, and opened her eyes to find him looking down at her, love and something else—nerves, she realized—in his expressive eyes. Without letting go of her hands, without breaking eye contact, he knelt.

Tears welled in her eyes.

"Eleanor Forth," he said softly, and Ellie was glad he was holding her hands, because if he hadn't been, she might have just floated away.

"Oliver Cole," she whispered.

One corner of Oliver's mouth lifted in a helpless smile. "Will you do me the immense honor of marrying me?"

Ellie smiled, two tears falling down her cheeks. "Yes. Oh, yes, Oliver."

Joy broke across his face like a sunrise. He bounded to his feet and crushed her against him in a bear hug, his quiet laugh in her ear, his heart pounding next to hers, right where it belonged. "I want to share my whole life with you."

She nuzzled into his neck. "Everything." Slowly, she pulled back, tilting her face up toward his. "Now kiss me, Oliver."

Oliver smiled. Then, he did.

The End

Afterword

While artistic liberty was taken with the various settings in *The Portlock Trilogy*, Bear Cove Retreat, where Oliver takes Ellie to propose, is both very real and very amazing. If you want to experience an authentic Alaskan adventure in the areas where the trilogy takes place, there's no better way to do so! For more information, visit their website at https://www.bearcoveretreat.com/.

Get Your Free Demon Fighting Playlist!

Sign up for Caitee's email list and get instant access to the Demon Fighting Playlist – over three hours of doubt-killing, fear-smashing music that's there to lift you up whenever you need it. Fun fact: it's also a *living* playlist, meaning music is being added all the time at the request of readers all over the world. (If you have a suggestion, send it to caiteecooper@gmail.com)

Go to caiteecooper.com to sign up!

If you enjoyed *Portlock*, please consider leaving a review (or rating) on Amazon or Goodreads. Reviews help both authors and other readers, so you'd be doing everyone a huge favor. Thanks so much for your support!